# My Lord
## by
## L. B. Shimaira

My Lord
By L. B. Shimaira

Published by Gurt Dog Press

Edited by Nem Rowan
Cover design by Jesse Snowdon
Zenda font by Paul Lloyd

Digital ISBN 978-91-986187-4-7
Soft cover ISBN 978-91-986187-5-4
Hard cover ISBN 978-91-986434-1-1

# My Lord

## L. B. Shimaira

### The Transcended
### Book 1

To all who have suffered.
Be kind to yourself—you are worthy of love.

**Content Warning**

The story you are about to read contains sexual abuse (rape is condemned), explicit sexual content (consent is emphasised), some kink play, violence, vampirism, and cannibalism.

It deals with PTSD and features a queer, polyamorous relationship.

# Prologue
## Spring, 1232 AD

The soldiers stood in a circle around the crackling campfire, living shadows dancing on their focused faces. It was still dark, though the first light was just an hour away.

"Dawn will be upon us soon," a tall, broad man said. His heavy leather and chain-mail armour glinted orange with the reflected flames. "They have decided to invade our lands. To plunder our villages. To destroy our farms. To kill our people!" His heavy voice boomed and his grey eyes burned with determination. "We will drive them back and slaughter those stupid enough not to run in fear. We will show them that our fertile lands are not theirs to take. We will show our people that we will protect them." He unsheathed his sword and raised it high. "For the honour and victory of Tristanja!"

The other soldiers followed his lead. "For the honour and victory of Tristanja!"

He placed his sword back in its scabbard. "Andreas has spoken to me about an ancient pre-war ritual." He looked at the dark-haired man to his right before returning his gaze to the circle. "He has kindly offered to share it with you, my generals, my best men." He turned to look at Andreas again and gestured to the group. "You may go ahead."

Andreas gave a courtly nod. "Thank you, Lord Marius." He turned around and retrieved a stone bowl and a silver knife from a tree stump, a small, mischievous smile tugging at the corners of his lips as he took his place in the circle again. "This is a blood sacrifice. A ritual that will grant you increased strength, heightened senses, and additional stamina. You will become stronger, faster..." His gaze went over every man's face. "*Deadlier*." He turned to the lord. "Lord Marius, if you would have the honour of making the first sacrifice..." Andreas held out the bowl in his left hand, while the silver blade lay in the palm of his right.

Lord Marius took the weapon. The strong scent of herbs and garlic wafted up to his nose from the bowl as he held his left hand over it and cut the side of his palm with the knife. Dark droplets slid off his skin and into the liquid already present in the bowl. His face didn't betray any pain, and he passed the blade to the man on his left.

1

Every man contributed some of his blood to the bowl. When the last one had made his sacrifice, Andreas took both items back to the tree stump. He placed the stone bowl down and held his own hand over it. Instead of cutting the side as the rest had done, the silver blade sank into the delicate, light olive-coloured flesh of his lower arm. Blood gushed out into the bowl, yet the stream quickly reduced to a mere trickle, then drops, before it completely stopped. He licked the knife clean before sheathing it into a small scabbard on his hip, then he took the bowl and swirled the contents carefully but thoroughly, mixing the blood with the herb- and garlic-infused water. Once satisfied, he returned to the circle.

Andreas held the bowl up to Lord Marius, who took it from him. "For victory and honour!" And he drank. His expression did not reveal anything regarding the taste of the fluid. He returned the bowl to Andreas, who repeated the same words, swirled the contents and drank.

As the mixture was passed around the circle, several soldiers' faces betrayed that the liquid tasted foul—yet every single one repeated the four words and drank without hesitation.

When the bowl finally reached the last person, there was enough left for at least six people. The young man looked at the lord, silently requesting permission.

"Deminas, my son, go ahead—empty it."

His brown eyes shimmered with excitement. "For the honour and victory of Tristanja!" Deminas bellowed and he drank it all.

# Part One
## Autumn, 1239 AD

*The wheel turns and seasons shift.*
*Autumn leaves fall, portending the end.*
*But seeds carry the promise of new life.*

# One

Meya rose from sleep covered in sweat, her heart beating in her throat. Panting, she looked around the small, dark room.

*Relax*, she told herself. *It's the middle of the night. You're in a village, safe, far away from the wars.* Still, her gut was telling her something was off.

She took a deep breath and exhaled slowly. She didn't recall waking from a nightmare, but she figured that that was what was troubling her.

Memories of events that had transpired a year ago flooded her mind, and she shook her head in an attempt to erase them. *There are no raiders, and there is no fire.* She groaned and dropped back onto the mattress, the straw inside rustling. *You are safe here. Stop worrying.*

The more she tried to comfort herself, the stronger the gut feeling became. Wide awake, she stared into the dark. She thought back to what had happened at her family's inn.

*I woke up in the middle of the night then, too. If I hadn't gone out to the latrine...* She closed her eyes as she remembered the fire, the screams of her loved ones, the raiders. Her eyes snapped open. *No. I will not think about that.* She sat up straight and combed her fingers through her red locks.

The sound of a door creaking followed by several sets of footsteps made her freeze. She held her breath as she listened intently.

There were whispering voices of men down the hall.

Meya stepped out of bed, grabbed her robe off the floor and put it on. She sat on the edge for a moment, but then rushed to the door to ensure it was locked, only to scold herself soon after. *They are probably just travellers arriving late at the inn. Stop worrying already!*

Yet her instincts were telling her something different. Her slippers were right next to the door and she slid them on, hoping to calm the anxiety bubbling up in the pit of her stomach—but it didn't help. Despite the darkness surrounding her, she felt her way towards a small table. Her fingers found a heavy jug still half-filled with water and she grabbed it, holding it close to her chest. *Better safe than sorry.* She felt silly for standing in the dark in just her robe, holding the piece of pottery, but her head was thumping from the anxiety. The footsteps halted at her door and her breath hitched. A loud slam echoed through the room. Meya yelped and dropped the jug, the contents splashing all over her legs and feet. A second slam and the door gave in.

She stumbled away from the blinding lamplight that flooded into the room until her back was against the wall. Four men blocked the only way out. One of them held the lamp up, a sinister grin spread across his face. "Yes, that's her."

The other three men walked towards her, and Meya scanned her surroundings for a possible weapon. Not seeing anything in range to help her fight, her body prepared to flee instead. She ducked for the bed, but the room was too small to allow for much manoeuvring. One of the men grabbed her arm and pushed her down, the other approaching with a length of rope. With her heart pounding in her throat, she kicked and screamed, but the men easily overpowered her.

"No! Let me go!" She tried to struggle, but it was futile. "I've done nothing wrong, please!"She continued to plead as they bound her hands and feet. "Let me go!" A dirty cloth was forced into her mouth to silence her screams.

"She's a feisty one," one of the men stated.

The man holding the lamp stepped into the room. "Don't worry." He grabbed her roughly by the hair. "The market isn't until a few days from now. I'm certain I'll have her docile by then."

*Docile? Clay-brained sard!* Fire burned in her green eyes as she stared into her captor's malicious ones. *I'm not some animal for you to tame.*

"She'll fetch us some good coin, that's certain." He tugged at her hair, causing her to wince. "Docile or not."

They dragged Meya outside to a large, barred carriage, drawn by two horses. One of the men unlocked and opened the door and she was practically thrown inside, where she landed roughly with a grunt, bumping her head against the leg of a boy dressed in rags. There were a total of seven other people in the cart, all bound and some gagged. Judging from their appearance, most had been homeless. Without a second glance, one of the men closed and locked the door.

*There must have been some mistake.* Her rage quickly transformed into confusion and fear. *Why did they take me? I haven't stolen anything. I paid the inn-keep. They wouldn't know about the raider, right?* A cold shiver went up her spine. *That was far away from here and almost a year ago! But then, why?*

Shuddering, she curled up and the carriage started to move.

~*~

The morning sun stood low on the horizon when the carriage finally halted, though there was no town to be seen. The man who had carried the lantern earlier unlocked the door, a sack in hand. The three other men stood close behind him, one of them bearing a large jug.

"Alright, time for some breakfast." He removed the gag from the people who had one. When he got to Meya, he had to quickly pull his hand away as she attempted to bite him. He growled and slapped her across the face. "It seems you still need to learn your place, *slave*."

Meya spat at his feet. "I'm no slave! Nor am I some thief! I don't know why you—"

Another slap. "Silence!" He crouched down in front of her. "You're a slave now because I say so. You've got no friends or kin in these lands to claim otherwise."

Rage and sorrow washed over her. She breathed heavily but held her tongue.

"It'll do you best to learn to behave if you wish to please your new owner."

"And who might that be?" Meya fumed. "You?"

The man grinned. "For the next few days; longer if no one buys you at the market."

Blood drained from her face, except for where the slaver's hand had collided with her skin. "Buy me? I'm not for sale! Unhand me already! I told you, I—"

A third slap. "Better start listening soon. I can do this all day."

Meya bit her lip as she tried to remain calm. *I need to get out of here!*

The man stared down at her for a bit before he was pleased with her lingering silence. He turned to un-gag the last person. "I have some bread here." He motioned for the man with the jug to enter. "And some water. I will untie

6

two of you, and you must help your fellow to some food and drink. Am I clear?"

Everyone aside from Meya nodded. The slaver noticed and grabbed her roughly by the hair.

"You really are a tough—"

Meya spat in his face.

He released her hair and slowly wiped himself clean, a malicious glint in his eyes. "Oh, you've done it now." He yanked her up by the hem of her robe. The moment she was on her feet, he punched her in the gut.

Meya buckled over, gasping for breath.

"Let this be clear to every last one of you. I am your master now until you are sold to your new one. You will obey and respect your master. Understood?"

Everyone nodded again, though Meya was still on her knees, gagging.

"Good." He untied a boy and a young woman and handed them the sack of bread. The other man placed the jug on the floor and they both left the cart.

~*~

"Sir," the boy asked through the bars.

One of the slaver's henchmen turned around. "What?"

"I need to pee."

The man snorted.

"I... I need to go too," a woman said, followed by others stating the same.

"Fine, give me a moment." He disappeared from sight, only to come back with the other men and the slaver.

"We'll let two of you out at a time. Don't try anything funny," the slaver said, his eyes lingering on Meya.

*Oh, I'm not going to* try *anything—I'm going to escape.* She gritted her teeth, another surge of anger washing over her.

When it was finally her turn, she was escorted out by two of the men. She walked behind a bush and glared at them. "Do you mind giving a lady some privacy?"

The men just smirked and kept staring at her.

*Ruttish louts.* She grunted, turned her back to them, and did her business. When she was done and decent again, she didn't even bother to look at the men standing behind her—she sprinted away.

Angry voices were close behind her, but she kept running. Adrenaline fuelled her body as she shot through the forest and she tried to discern how close her captors were, but they had stopped screaming. The only things she could hear were the wind, her frantic heartbeat, and her laboured breath. Her feet hurt from all the rocks and twigs poking through the thin leather of her sandals. She realised her speed was dropping as exhaustion started to claim her. She wanted to look behind her but was too afraid it would cause her to trip and fall.

Her side stung and her throat burned. Unable to keep her speed up any longer, she slowed down a bit but continued at a jog. Not five seconds later, something tugged at her robe. The sudden loss of momentum caused her to lose her balance and she plummeted to the earth. She groaned from the fall, the rough terrain having caused cuts and chafes to her palms and knees. Suddenly, strong hands wrapped around her upper arms and her heart skipped a beat. Panting, she looked up to see the two men. Their faces were red, their chests rising and falling just as fast as hers.

*Oh, God, no!* Fear paralysed her as the men dragged her back to the cart. *Damn, damn, damn! I need to get away!* Her body hurt more with each passing second and she feared a beating on top of it all.

She allowed the men to lug her for a while, remaining limp in their grasp. With a sudden outburst, she tried to struggle free from their grip—but it was pointless. Their hold on her intensified, and she whimpered from the pain it caused.

*I can't escape. I need to escape. I can't let them take me back and sell me. I've done nothing wrong!* Yet terror struck her. *But what if they know?* She was still panting, but her face had paled.

*No,* she tried to reason with herself, *if they knew, they wouldn't be selling me into slavery—they'd be hanging me.* The thought wasn't as comforting as she had hoped.

The slaver had awaited their return to the cart. His expression was one of anger, though his eyes betrayed that he was going to enjoy what was coming next. "Still tried to run, eh?"

Meya wanted to struggle, but the men's tight grip on her arms hurt too much. "Why don't you just let me go? Please?" she begged.

He shook his head. "Oh no, no, no." He stepped towards her. "Someone as pretty as you will do good at the market." His hands lowered to his belt where he unsheathed a knife.

Fear flooded her system and she froze, not knowing what to do at the sight of the sharp weapon.

"Still, you'd be worth more if you'd learn to behave." He turned his gaze to his men. "Hold her tight."

Meya whimpered as they restrained her without mercy, to the point they would certainly leave big bruises all around.

*Please, no. Please, no. Please, no…*

"Don't move too much now. I'm going to teach you some manners."

Her eyes followed the knife. *No, no, no… Please, no…*

"First lesson. When I tell you to do something, or when I ask you something, you will answer with: yes, sir."

Her vocal cords refused to produce any sound. She kept her eyes locked on the blade in utter terror.

"Do you understand?"

She remained silent, so he punched her in the stomach with his free hand—though not as hard as he had done previously. She buckled slightly and gasped for breath, but the men firmly kept their hold on her arms.

"It's almost a shame to cut such beautiful skin." He lifted her robe and this caused a fresh dose of adrenaline to flood her bloodstream.

She yelped and lashed out with her right leg. The slaver noticed just in time, causing her foot to collide with his shin rather than his crotch. He retaliated with another punch to her gut. As Meya gagged, saliva dripping to the ground, the slaver gestured for his third man to join them. He pointed to her legs and the man crouched down between the others, gripping her ankles tightly.

"It's really not hard. I will explain it to you again…" He lifted her robe once more, but this time Meya was unable to stop him. With her stomach and chest now bare, he brought the knife closer to her skin.

*Don't hurt me. Don't hurt me…*

Her muscles tried to get all flesh as far away from the cold metal as possible, but being restrained, it was of no use. Meya's breath hitched the moment it touched her and her muscles remained tense—relaxing now would surely cause him to cut into her.

"When spoken to, you will always reply with: yes, sir. Do you understand?"

She didn't answer, her head thumping from anxiety.

The slaver put some pressure on the blade, causing a small, superficial cut on her abdomen. A constricted yelp freed itself from her throat.

"Again. Do you understand?"

She drew a sharp breath. *Churlish, unmuzzled dog!* Despite the pain and her desire to not get hurt again, her determination to not give in to the slaver was greater. *I will not call you sir!* She wanted to say it aloud, but she feared what would happen if she did.

9

Another shallow cut. "Answer me."

She gritted her teeth, refusing to speak. *I can take a few cuts. I can do this. I'll—*

A third cut, followed by another punch.

The world spun. If not for the men holding her, she would have fallen to the ground.

"I told you, I can do this all day. Now answer me: do you understand?"

*Scite...* Realising he would indeed not stop, she yielded. "Y-yes, s-sir."

"That's better." He took a step back so that he could have a better look at her. "Are you going to behave now?"

*Now...* She swallowed. "Y-yes, s-sir." She kept her eyes on the ground, not wanting to see the smug grin on the slaver's face.

"No more escape attempts?"

"N-no, sir," she lied.

"Very well." He stepped aside. "Throw her back in the cart and tie her up."

They dragged her to the cart, bound her limbs, and closed the door. Miserable and aching all over, Meya slid to the floor and cried in silence.

# Two

The slaver stopped at two towns that day, picking up several more people to throw into the cart. Meya stared at the others as the carriage moved over a rocky path, the sun low on the horizon.

"You know... If we helped one another, we could get out of these bonds and try and break free," she suggested softly. "We outnumber them. It would work."

Most of them didn't respond, and the ones who did only shook their heads.

Meya frowned. "You're all fine with this then? You don't care that you're going to be sold like cattle?"

"Don't get yourself worked up," a man said. "It's not that bad. I was a slave before."

*Worked up?* She was about ready to rage at the man, but she suppressed the desire and instead turned to face him. "If you were a slave before, how did you end up here?"

He sighed. "The wars. My mistress and master got killed, along with the other servants. I only survived because I knew a good hiding place. I've been on the road for a month now, looking for a new home."

Meya huffed. "Well, I suppose you will get one soon."

He shrugged. "I'm hungry and weary. I wouldn't mind having to serve again if that means a bed and a meal every day."

Several of the others murmured in agreement.

*These people are crazy! If I had known that customs here were so different, I would have stayed far away.*

She licked her lips. "Well, I was *not* a slave before. I worked for my bed and meal and I enjoyed them in freedom."

"Don't worry, miss," a young boy said. "Really, it won't be so bad. My parents told me so."

"Your parents *sold* you?" Meya couldn't believe what she was hearing.

The boy nodded. "We were starving. This way, my parents will be able to survive, and I will too."

*Well, if you look at it that way...* She mentally shook her head, still disagreeing.

"It's not always good though," a young woman said. "I fled from my mistress a few weeks ago. She used to beat me, even if I was doing my chores right." She sighed. "I just hope my new owner will be nicer."

A cold chill ran up Meya's spine. "And you still don't want to escape from here?"

"Where would I go? I have no friends, no family—I'd be hunted down. I'd rather be a slave under someone's protection than face the world alone." Her voice trembled and she cast her eyes down. "The whole reason why I became a slave in the first place was because I was left all alone. I willingly went to that mean woman and offered her my servitude in exchange for a place to call home."

Meya didn't know what to say. *These people all sound so desperate.* After a moment of silence, she decided to ask again. "Then maybe, if no one else here wants to escape, someone can help untie me so *I* can try, at least?"

"Don't. You won't get out of the cart, and even if you do, they'd just catch you again and beat you up," the woman said.

"That is my problem then. Please, anyone?"

No one offered.

Disheartened, Meya hung her head and sighed deeply.

~*~

The next day was spent on the road. The slaver seemed satisfied with the number of captives as they passed a village without stopping. They made a few stops to allow people to relieve themselves, but aside from that, they appeared to be making haste to reach their final destination. The sun had already disappeared below the horizon when the cart came to a halt. Meya looked

12

outside, but clouds darkened the sky, making it hard to see the surroundings. Nevertheless, she was able to discern that they were still on the forest path. *Maybe this is my chance.*

She lay down on her back and brought her ankles as close to her rear as she could, then she lifted herself, allowing her tied hands to reach the ropes that bound her feet.

"What are you doing?" someone hissed. "You're going to get in trouble!"

"Shhh, that'll be my problem, not yours." She closed her eyes as she focused on moving the rope. The knot was on the front but after a lot of tugging, it was within reach of her fingers.

*Thank God for people who don't know how to tie someone up properly!*

She bit her lip as she worked frantically on undoing the knot. The moment the ropes loosened, she grinned. She plucked them off and tried to get her still-bound hands to her front, but she was unable to. She sighed.

*Well, at least I can try to make a run for it. It will have to do.*

After a few minutes, the cart door opened. Meya's heart rate increased and a cold sweat covered her skin. She swallowed as she tried to decide when the best opportunity would be to run.

Two men entered the cart and to her shock, they came to get her. They pulled her up by the arms and dragged her out, not noticing the lack of rope around her ankles.

*This can work to my advantage.*

She allowed the men to carry her into the woods, her mind set on escaping so much that she didn't take the time to wonder where she was being taken, or why. A small clearing came into view, illuminated by a lantern hanging from a tree branch. The slaver stood in the light, a sinister grin on his face. Her stomach turned and it took her a lot of effort not to try and run already. The men threw her to the ground, and she groaned as she landed on her knees in the damp soil.

"Thank you. Now, leave us."

Meya shuddered. She turned her head to watch the men go. The slaver grabbed her by the hair and made her face him instead.

"The village is just below the hill. You're going to be sold there in the morning." His fingers traced her jawline and she gritted her teeth. "But for now, you're still mine."

The moment he released her hair, she shot up and her head collided with his chin, knocking him backwards. Quickly, she found her balance and made a run for it.

13

The darkness was thick, making moving through it with her hands tied behind her back even harder, and unable to feel her way, overhanging branches smacked in her face. She could discern most of the trees and managed to avoid them, but she missed a protruding rock, which caught the toe of her sandal. With a yelp, she tripped and fell to the ground.

The world spun and she moaned from the impact. Dazed, it took her a moment to recollect herself, and when she started to rise again, a foot pressed against her back, pushing her into the damp soil.

"I expected that you would have learned from your first attempt."

Meya froze, fear seeping through every pore.

The slaver turned her over and punched her in the face, then he placed the lantern he was holding on the ground and sat down on her upper legs. Stars clouded her vision and she needed to blink a few times to see clearly again. The moment the knife in the slaver's hand came into view, her chest tightened.

"Now, you're going to start behaving, or I am going to have to make some more cuts in that pretty skin of yours. Do I make myself clear?"

Unable to think properly, she just nodded in the hopes of refraining from getting hurt more.

"Good." His hands went down to loosen his trousers.

Meya's breath caught in her throat. Panicking, she tried to get out from underneath the man, but he pressed the knife against her neck. Whimpering, she closed her eyes and stopped her struggles. Her entire being was focused solely on survival now, and with her hands still tied behind her back and the slaver holding the weapon, this meant she remained deathly still, praying it would all be over soon.

The market opened not long after sunrise. Meya sat in the carriage, hands and feet bound, eyes cast down. She could hear the people in the distance, the auctioneer's voice booming above all of them. Finally, it was her turn. One of the slaver's henchmen came in, removed the rope from her ankles, and escorted her to the auction area.

She looked up and saw the boy standing on the stage. It didn't take long before he was sold to a rather fat merchant.

*Good for him. I'm sure he won't have to be hungry anymore.*

The woman who had fled her former abusive master was next. It didn't take long before she got claimed by a madam.

Meya swallowed. *What if I get forced to work at a bordello?*

14

A cold sweat broke out as she was shoved onto the stage. The slaver stood next to the auctioneer and she quickly averted her eyes. *Lumpish canker.* With trembling legs, she moved to the centre and anxiously scanned the crowd. She felt terrible standing there, her face dirty, her hair in tangles, and her robe tattered and covered with mud stains.

*What must they think of me?* She was all too conscious of the many scrapes covering her, not to mention her black eye. *Would they think I got a beating? And if so, would that be a good or a bad thing?* She swallowed and bit her lip. *Please, let someone pick me who will treat me with decency.*

She looked at the faces of the bidders. To her great dismay, she realised it was now between two people: the bordello madam, and some fancy-dressed man with a predatory look in his eyes. As the price went up and up, her heart sank.

*My life is over.* She trembled and it took all of her willpower to refrain from crying.

"Going once, going twi—"

"I'll pay double that offer," a lightly tanned man on the front row suddenly said loudly. He looked up at Meya and their gazes connected.

*Who is he?* A cold chill ran up her spine. *And why would he pay so much for me?*

"Sold!" the auctioneer yelled with a smirk.

The man walked to the side of the stage to pay the slaver the hefty sum he owed him.

The slaver grinned. "I hope you know what you're getting yourself into. This one is quite feisty."

"I doubt there will be any trouble," he said as he glanced at her.

Meya tried to discern who the man was and what her fate was going to be. Shoulder-length brown hair framed his face, his dark eyes warm. She guessed him to be in his mid-twenties, only slightly older than herself, and his muscular upper arms suggested that he was a worker. The clothes he wore didn't look fancy at all. *If he has that much money, why doesn't he dress better? Could he be some kind of thief? But what would a thief want with a slave?*

The slaver nudged for her to come over and she reluctantly obeyed, her body still quivering slightly, and she refused to look at him.

"Do you wish to keep the ropes on or off?" he asked.

The man looked at her. "Off."

The slaver sighed. "As you wish."

Meya trembled from having the slaver so close to her as he cut the ropes binding her hands. The moment she was free, she struggled with the urge to either run or to break the guy's nose—and then run.

"Come," the man who had bought her said and he offered his hand.

She looked from the slaver to the man and finally decided not to risk another beating—or a public lynching. *It would have felt good to break his nose, though*, she thought. Deciding to give the strange man a shot, she took his hand. *I could always try and escape later like that woman did. I need to get away from this crowd at any rate.*

The man gave her hand a reassuring squeeze, before shifting his grip to her arm to keep a better hold on her should she try to flee.

~*~

They had both been silent the entire walk through the town. Now, finally outside the city walls, the man decided to speak first.

"My name is Juris. I'm head of the housekeeping at Castle Tristanja, home of Lord Deminas. He will be your new master."

The blood drained from her face. *He's a servant? I got sold to a lord?* A chill went up her spine. *Not just some lord... Lord Deminas.* She thought of all the things she had heard about him and shuddered.

"I apologise, I don't know your name. Would you mind telling me?"

"Meya." Her voice trembled a bit.

Juris remained quiet, clearly debating on what to say to her.

Meya didn't mind the silence; her mind was too jumbled to think clearly.

They walked for several minutes along a path between two pastures before Juris finally attempted conversation again. "Are you from around here?"

Meya shook her head.

"Lord Deminas is the ruler of these lands. I'm not sure if you're familiar with him…" He glanced at her.

She swallowed, hesitant to speak. "I saw the corpses of invaders—or, what was left of them—when I crossed the border." She took a deep breath. "And I've heard some gossip, both here and when I was in the neighbouring lands."

Juris visibly cringed.

*He must know the rumours of which I speak. Does that mean they are true, or not?*

"Well, Lord Deminas came into power seven years ago. His father died defending Tristanja from invaders. Lord Deminas took revenge in a rather… bloody way. This seemed to be quite effective though, and the territory's size has increased since then. The current neighbouring lords ceased their attacks three years ago. Lord Deminas is not someone to underestimate, nor someone to disrespect. As a servant of his, you are to remember that very well."

Meya nodded. *I just hope he keeps his hands to himself.*

"If you want to know more or if you have any questions, please speak up."

"Maybe later." She sighed. *At least this guy seems nice. Would he chase me if I ran?* Her body still ached all over. *I don't want to find out if this niceness is just a façade... What if I run and he—* She tensed up inside and suppressed the urge to cry. Gritting her teeth, she focused on walking. *Left, right, left, right...*

The journey continued in silence for several hours. The fields had changed into forest some time ago, and the sun had already passed its zenith, yet they still hadn't reached the castle.

"Why haven't you tried to escape?" Juris suddenly blurted out.

A surge of panic went through Meya and she looked at him, wary. "Is that a serious question?"

"Yes, it is actually." His eyes were kind but questioning, a very faint smile on his lips. There was nothing threatening about him and Meya relaxed a little.

*Maybe I should just tell him...* She sighed. "I already tried escaping— several times. It seems I'm not too good at it." She pointed at her eye. "I know you noticed."

"I've noticed more than just that," Juris admitted.

Meya looked away, her heart rate increasing. "I... I'd rather not talk about it." She tensed up and struggled to keep her emotions in check, not wanting to cry in front of him.

Juris moved his hand down again to meet with hers and gave it a little squeeze, just like he had before. "I can't promise anything, but I can tell you that, for me, life as a servant to Lord Deminas has been good. You'll be alright."

# Three

They arrived at the castle just as the sun started to disappear below the tree line. Meya's gaze was fixed on the ground, her thoughts elsewhere. The guards at the gate let them in with a mere nod as a greeting, though they made sure to take a good look at the new servant. The sudden presence of other people brought her back to reality, and she tensed up when she noticed the guards were staring at her as she walked through the courtyard. Juris gave her arm a little comforting squeeze. She relaxed a bit but remained wary, and turned her attention to the castle before her.

The magnificent structure of pale stone with grey rooftops was built against the mountain. There were two small, rounded towers at the front and two similar ones near the precipice, while a big, rectangular tower that disappeared partly into the cliff-side rose high above them. The sudden realisation that this would now be her home made her shudder. Uncertainty was tearing away at her mind and she fought to not give in and break down on the steps leading to the castle's entrance. Juris let go of Meya's arm and opened the heavy, wooden doors. The great hallway that loomed in front of them was illuminated by lamplight. A black and scarlet carpet lay in the centre of the path, whilst paintings and statues decorated the sides.

Meya stopped at the top of the steps to take it all in—she had never seen anything like this in her entire life.

*It's beautiful!*

Juris grabbed her hand and she almost yelped in surprise. "Come," he said softly as he led her forward into the castle.

Meya couldn't help but look around in awe as they progressed. *Maybe this place won't be too bad...*

They halted in front of big, wooden doors decorated with curly carvings. They waited, and after a few minutes, the doors opened and a tall, muscular man walked out. He was clad in heavy leather and chain-mail armour and his dark hair hung sleek around his face.

"General," Juris said as he bowed.

Meya blinked before realising the situation and quickly curtsied.

The general merely grunted an acknowledgement, looked at Meya, and paced away.

Juris straightened himself and watched the man disappear around the corner. He turned to Meya, who still had her head low.

"Come," he said and walked into the room. Meya followed him and suppressed a gasp.

The room had a very high ceiling with a fresco depicting various scenes of battle and conquest. The walls bore paintings in golden frames that illustrated similar scenes, together with portraits of former Lords and Ladies.

Meya was so busy looking at the works of art that she bumped into Juris, who had come to a halt.

"I'm sorry," she said hastily as she cast her eyes down.

"Juris, is this the new servant you bring me?" a deep, dark voice asked.

Juris stepped aside so that he was next to Meya. He bowed. "Yes, my Lord."

Meya was unsure of what to do. *Is it insulting to look him in the eyes, or is it insulting not to?* She chose to keep her eyes on the ground and swallowed.

The sound of heavy boots walking down stone steps echoed through the large room. It didn't take long before the boots appeared within Meya's vision of the floor. Fear crept upon her and her heartbeat increased. She swallowed again.

"This was the best you could find?" Lord Deminas asked harshly.

"Yes, my Lord. She was by far the most healthy-looking of the lot; all she needs is a good bath. The entire walk here, she did not complain even once. I haven't experienced that with any of the previous ones, my Lord."

Warm fingers wrapped around her chin, startling her. She looked up at the Lord and for a moment, she forgot how to breathe.

19

Lord Deminas had long, black hair that cascaded onto his armoured shoulders. A well-trimmed goatee and moustache adorned his face, whilst a scar interrupted his left eyebrow. He was younger than Meya had expected; she guessed him to be around the same age as Juris. Still, she understood what he had meant about not wanting to underestimate or disrespect the lord.

Her green eyes locked with his cold, grey ones and immediately she regretted it. *It's as if he's trying to look straight into my soul.* She wanted to avert herself from the lord's prying gaze but realised that could be seen as disrespectful. *If he didn't want me to look at him, he wouldn't have made me look in the first place,* she reasoned. Despite her growing unease, she kept her eyes connected with his.

After a while, he let go of her chin. "Very well, I will give her a chance."

*I can do this.* She curtsied. "Thank you, my Lord." She looked up and saw a small smile grace his otherwise emotionless face.

"What's your name?" he asked, the smile no longer visible.

"Meya, my Lord."

Lord Deminas walked around her, observing her. "Were you a servant before?"

"N-no, my Lord."*Why is he asking this?*

"Did Juris instruct you on how to address me?"

She cringed inside, her thoughts going back to the slaver. She quickly pushed the memories away, not wanting to break down because of them. "He—" Her voice broke. She swallowed and tried again. "He did not, my Lord. He only told me about the history of these lands and the current situation." She wetted her lips. "I… I'm sorry you lost your father in battle, and I want to thank you for taking care of the people of these lands."

"I don't need your sympathy, but your kindness is noted." He stood in front of her again. "As is your intellect. Know your position well and keep addressing me as you have and I will have no reason to discipline you." He walked back to his chair, a massive, wooden one with carvings and scarlet padding. "Unless," he added as he turned back around, "you fail at doing your duties." The slight hint of a grin tugged at the corners of his lips. "But I doubt that will be a problem."

A shiver went up her spine, but she managed to curtsy. "Thank you, my Lord. I promise to do everything in my power to please you." The moment she had finished speaking, she realised just what she had said and her cheeks flushed.

The grin on Lord Deminas' face that had been a mere ghost before was now clearly visible. "You're both dismissed," Lord Deminas said as he turned back to his seat.

Juris took Meya by her arm and directed her towards the big doors.

"You've done well," Juris said as they walked through the halls. "It's not often that such an introduction goes so smoothly."

Meya frowned. "What do you mean?"

Juris halted and looked around, making sure they were alone. "A lot of first-time servants don't know their place. They make a lot of mistakes. Some don't know how to behave themselves, forget to show respect, forget they are a servant now. And some are just plain rude or rebellious. The latter often don't last long here, sadly."

Meya's eyes widened in shock. "What do you mean by that?"

Juris scanned the hallway again before he whispered, "Lord Deminas does not tolerate disrespect and misbehaviour. A servant that does not know their place is no servant and thus of no use."

*I doubt he lets them go free*, she thought. "What does he do with them?"

Juris sighed. "That's something you'd rather not find out. Now come." He started walking again. "I'm going to show you the parts of the castle that are of importance to you."

~*~

Juris took Meya to the kitchen and the servant dining area. The mere smell of food made her stomach growl.

"There are three meals a day. The first meal is at early morning before you start your duties, the second is at noon, and the third is at the end of the day. They will start serving soon so let's not dawdle."

They made their way to a different wing of the castle.

"The servants sleep in these chambers." Juris pointed at the several doors down the hallway. "I think there was a bed free in here." He opened one of the doors and looked inside. "Yes, in here." He motioned for Meya to follow him.

The room had a window opposite the door, which gave a view over the forest. There was a large wardrobe next to the entrance and a hearth at the far end; it was burning low and emitted a pleasant warmth. The six beds each had their own small table.

Juris pointed at the middle one on the left. "That one will be yours."

Meya walked up to the bed; it was the only one that was bare. She sat down, the straw inside the mattress rustling, and looked around. *So far, it's not too bad. I guess I could give this a try for a while… Maybe escape once it's spring.*

"There are clean linens in the wardrobe." Juris motioned for her to come along. "I will get you some clothes after supper."

"Thank you," Meya said as she followed Juris to their next destination.

"This is the laundry room. You won't be working here, but this is where you will deliver all your dirty clothes and linens."

Meya looked into the large room. There was a slight fog inside from all the hot water and she saw several women at work. Two of them were hauling sheets around whilst another two were busy scrubbing clothing clean on a washboard.

The sound of a bell echoed through the castle.

Meya looked around in confusion. The women hurriedly finished what they were doing, and Juris tapped Meya on the shoulder.

"Come—that bell means supper is going to be served."

The prospect of food made her saliva flow and she quickly followed Juris out of the laundry room.

~*~

Supper was surprisingly good. There were vegetables, a chunk of bread, and a small piece of meat for every servant. Meya couldn't remember when she had last had such a decent meal.

"Is this really how we eat every night?" she asked Juris, who sat next to her.

Juris nodded. "Though the meat is not an everyday thing. Every few days we get either meat, fish, or fowl." He emptied his cup of ale. "Oh, and in the mornings we all get a cup of cider."

"Such luxury." Meya smiled as she took a bite from her bread. *Maybe being a slave won't be so bad—at least to help me get through the winter.*

Juris grinned. "Yes, we're lucky. Lord Deminas believes we must all stay strong and healthy, for a weak servant is a useless servant."

"Lord Deminas is a wise man," Meya said contentedly before stuffing her mouth with more food and washing it down with ale.

"Wise, yes," a female servant next to her suddenly spoke, "but be warned: stay on his good side."

Meya turned her head to look at her neighbour. To her horror, she saw that she was missing an eye.

22

The older woman grinned when she noticed Meya's reaction. "Yes dear, that's just one of the things the Lord can and will do as a punishment. When he tells you to do something, you do it. No questions asked, aside from details on how to perform the task the best you can." The woman drank from her cup. "Learn fast, listen, and obey. That way you won't have to suffer like I," the woman paused to look around at the other servants sitting at the table, "and a lot of others have."

Meya swallowed and the delight she had felt a mere minute ago faded away. "What happened?" she whispered.

The woman gave her a sour smile. "I failed to listen. Multiple times." She sighed. "I was a rebellious youngster, let's keep it at that." She crammed the last piece of bread into her mouth, stood up, and walked away.

A bit shocked, Meya turned to look at Juris. He was still eating, seemingly ignoring what had just been said. Silently, Meya emptied her plate. Whilst she did, she looked at the others who were still eating.

There were two more servants, as far as she could see, who were missing an eye. With great dismay, she also noticed a few were missing an ear.

She refilled her cup and emptied it in one go. Looking around, she spotted servants who were missing parts of or an entire finger. There were two servants with bandaged digits; she couldn't really tell what was wrong with them, though the fact that their fingers didn't appear shorter suggested enough.

*All those rumours… If the mutilations are true, then what else is true?* Meya shuddered.

An elderly man sitting across of Meya placed his hand on hers. "Don't worry, child. Such drastic physical punishments aren't given without reason. You will need to misbehave several times or very badly to get yourself in such trouble."

This eased her mind a little. "Thanks."

The man smiled and left the table.

Meya sighed deeply and looked over at Juris. He had finished his meal and seemed to be waiting for her.

"Come," he said as he stood up. "I'll take you to the bathing area so you can finally get cleaned up."

Meya simply nodded and followed him in silence, the food in her stomach weighing heavy.

~*~

There were separate bathing areas for men and women, and Juris left Meya there as he went to get her some clean clothes. He had told her that there were towels inside and had asked if she knew the way back to her quarters. Meya had nodded, for it was only a few hallways further.

She walked into the room; moist air and the sounds of excited chatter surrounded her. There were a dozen other women bathing, and Meya felt rather uncomfortable.

*Everyone is too busy to notice me or how I look. Just don't dawdle and get into the water.*

Feeling a bit reluctant, she undressed and deposited her dirty clothes in a basket that was already filled to the brim, then turned towards the baths. She wanted to pick one that was free, but there were none. Most of the baths had two or three women in them, but she spotted one in the back that had only a single occupant. She hurried over and quickly sank into the tepid water.

"Hey, you're the new girl, aren't you?" the person across from her asked curiously.

Meya nodded, not really in the mood to socialise.

"My name is Abi," she said and Meya looked up.

The rather pale woman seemed to still be in her teens. She had long, dark brown hair and matching eyes. She looked nice enough and Meya tried to relax a bit.

"Sorry," she excused herself. "I'm Meya."

Abi smiled. "First days are rough." She pointed at Meya's eye. "Lord Deminas didn't do that, I hope?"

Meya hurriedly shook her head. "Oh no, it seems he was actually quite nice to me."

It was silent for a moment before Abi realised Meya was not going to tell more. "Then, eh, who did give you that black eye?"

Meya sighed—she knew this question had been pending. Acknowledging that it would be of no use to keep hiding it, she reluctantly told Abi half of the story. "I tried to escape from the slave trader. I failed."

Abi cringed. "I'm sorry to hear that. But rest assured, it's not too bad here." She smiled again. "I've been here for several years. As long as you obey and behave, there is nothing to fear." She moved closer to Meya. "And if I have to be honest, my parents could have never provided me with the meals I get here. Especially not three times a day."

Meya hesitated a bit before asking, "So, you're happy here? You don't miss your freedom?"

24

Abi shrugged. "I am, I guess. I'm happier than when I still lived with my parents."

"What happened to your parents?"

She shrugged again. "I don't know actually. I hope they're alright. They had a farm, but after two failed harvests, times were getting rough. I had two older sisters, an older brother, and a younger brother. We had long and short talks about our options and eventually, they decided that they were to sell me to Lord Deminas directly. They didn't want to do it via the local slave traders—they can't be trusted—and also because they couldn't bear seeing me grow up in a bordello. They taught me well on how to behave in the presence of a Lord and I got accepted."

There was silence for a bit, before Meya hesitantly asked, "Do you hate your parents for having done that?"

"Oh, no!" Abi exclaimed. "I'm happy that I could take care of them by sacrificing my freedom like this. That, and like I said: this place isn't bad if you behave."

Meya thought about this for a while. "Did you ever get punished?"

"I got disciplined with the whip a few times at first, but I'm a fast learner. To be honest..." She crept closer to Meya and whispered in her ear, "I don't understand how some people keep messing things up, so often or so badly, that they get mutilated."

"Do you know what some of them did to get a certain punishment?" Meya asked softly.

Abi nodded. "I know a few. Some of the younger boys loved the taste of meat so much they wanted more, so they started to steal it from the storeroom. That cost them a finger on each hand. Taking food from other servants is also not allowed and could cost you a part of your finger."

Meya swallowed. It was not uncommon for a hand to be taken from a thief, so a finger from a food thief was understandable.

"Some of the servants found it interesting to listen to things they were not supposed to and so they had to part ways with an ear. Also, there have been a few that were not able to keep their tongue to themselves, so it was taken from them."

"What about an eye?" Meya questioned.

"Lord Deminas hasn't done this as far as I know, but his father did. Lord Deminas believes a servant functions better with both eyes intact."

Meya sighed in relief. *It sounds like Lord Deminas is not unreasonably cruel, at least.*

Thinking about the numerous rumours she had heard about him in the villages she had passed, she mustered some courage to ask Abi about them. "Are you aware of what is being said about Lord Deminas by the townsfolk?"

Abi seemed to stiffen a little. "I heard some of the rumours surrounding Lord Marius. I suppose similar stories are being told about Lord Deminas."

"How many of them are true?" Meya asked with a hushed voice, her heart rate quickening. "I've seen the remains of enemy soldiers. Is it true? Does he—"

"Shhh!" Abi looked frightened. "It's best if you do not talk about such things. Gossip isn't appreciated."

Meya lowered her eyes. "Sorry."

Abi fully submerged herself for a few seconds before rising and getting out of the bath. "I'm heading back to my quarters. I advise that you don't take too long to do so yourself. There is no real curfew but walking around the castle late at night without a good reason can be… dangerous."

Before Meya could ask for clarification, Abi had gone.

# Four

Meya waited for the other women to get out of the baths and dry themselves off. With the remaining crowd now at the other side of the room, Meya finally dared to thoroughly clean herself. She started with her face and hair. Her black eye still stung a bit, so she was careful not to rub her face too hard. Once she was certain that all of the filth was gone, she continued with the rest of her body. Most of the mud and dirt had already soaked off, but she made sure to check and clean all of the various injuries scattered over her body. She sighed heavily. The cuts on her legs and torso weren't deep and had already closed up, but she still needed to wash away all the dried blood without reopening anything.

Then came the part she had been dreading: she had to wash her privates. She bit her lip, swallowed, and brought her fingers between her legs.

She winced.

*Yep, the swine hurt me good*, she thought as she cleaned herself as gently as she could. Her vagina stung as her fingers touched the several little wounds on the in- and outside.

Tears rolled silently over her face. She tried her best not to cry—she didn't want to give him the satisfaction—but it just hurt too much. She took a deep breath and submerged herself. She finished cleaning herself underwater, ensuring that she wouldn't make a sound that the other servants might hear.

When she could no longer hold her breath, she resurfaced. It took her a minute to find her centre and become calm again.

*All will be fine,* she told herself. *Just consider yourself lucky the churlish boar had enough brains to not finish inside.* She shuddered. *You'll heal and forget, in time.* The lie didn't work and she gritted her teeth. *I wish I did break his nose—or worse.* She took a few deep breaths as she tried to drive the dark thoughts away. *It's alright... What happened, happened and can't be changed. You're safe now, that's what matters.*

When her heart rate had finally slowed down to a normal rhythm again, she splashed some water on her face, took a deep breath, and got out of the bath. As she walked over to where the towels were, she realised she was the last person there. Surprised, she quickly dried off, wrapped herself in the towel and walked out.

"Ah, there you are!" Juris exclaimed the moment Meya stepped out.

Meya stifled a scream—she hadn't expected anyone to be standing in the hallway. "J-Juris... You startled me," she said, breathing heavily.

He smiled and raised the lantern he was holding. "Now, I'm not *that* scary I hope?"

Meya didn't reply and avoided his gaze.

Juris noticed and looked away, clearly uncomfortable with the situation he had created. "I apologise if my presence disturbs you; I just wanted to make sure you didn't get lost."

"It... it's fine," Meya managed to utter. "Thank you." She started to walk towards her quarters; Juris tagged along in silence.

They stopped in front of the door to Meya's room and before she could open it, Juris placed his hand on her shoulder, causing her to stiffen.

"If there is anything upsetting you, feel free to tell me. You won't get into any trouble—I'll do my best to ensure that."

*There's a lot upsetting me—but nothing I'd want to tell you.* Meya looked at him and managed to produce a little smile despite the darkness in her head. "Thanks, Juris, I'll keep it in mind."

"I'll see you at breakfast then. I've placed clean clothes for you in the wardrobe. I'll help you get started on your chores, but I'm afraid I can't be by your side the entire day."

Meya nodded. "I didn't expect you to be." She bowed her head. "Goodnight Juris, thank you for your kindness."

Juris bowed his head too. "Thank you, too. I wish you sweet dreams."

As Juris turned to walk away, Meya finally entered her quarters. *I hope to have a dreamless sleep, actually.* She suppressed another surge of dark emotions as she closed the door behind her. *No. Not now. Not ever.* She swallowed and took in her surroundings.

The room was pleasantly warm as the hearth was now well lit. In front of the fire sat five women, talking and giggling—they hadn't even noticed Meya walk in.

As she moved closer, an older woman with short, auburn hair looked up and waved. "Hello there, you must be Meya?"

Meya walked up to the group and nodded. The hand that clasped her towel gripped it a little bit tighter.

"Juris informed us when he came to deliver your clothing," a small woman said, her long, brown hair flowing over her exposed breasts. She pointed to Meya's left. "I hope you don't mind; we already took care of your bed."

Meya turned her head and saw that it was no longer bare. *That's so kind of them.* She faced the group and smiled. "Thank you."

"Come, sit with us," a young, raven-haired woman said. She patted the place on the carpet next to her; all five of them were sitting in front of the fire with their towels draped around their waists.

"There's no need to be ashamed," said another woman with long, dirty blonde hair. The person who had been sitting next to her had scooted over and smiled at Meya; they looked alike. Meya sat down between the two blondes but kept her towel in place.

"This here is Gail," the older woman said, pointing at the smallest of the group. "And this here is Nina," she said, pointing at the raven-haired woman. Nina's hazel eyes seemed to twinkle as she smiled at Meya. "The ones sitting next to you are sisters. The oldest on your left is Brittany—or Brit—and the youngest on your right is Winnifred—or Winnie." The sisters smiled sweetly. "And my name is Lea," she concluded.

"Nice to meet you all," Meya said, looking from left to right.

"You're not from around here, are you?" Gail asked, her excitement barely contained.

Meya hesitated a bit before answering, "No, I'm not. Is it that obvious?"

Gail shrugged. "You just look a bit outlandish, I guess. I've only ever seen one other person with red hair and such fair skin before—though, he had twice the amount of freckles you have."

Meya looked at her arm and compared her skin tone to that of her roommates. She knew she was quite pale—it had always given her issues with working in the sun—but it was all the more noticeable because their arms and faces were tanned, whereas hers were not. Nina's arms were darkest of them all; even her untanned chest was clearly a shade darker than that of the others.

Brit suddenly entwined her fingers in Meya's hair, startling her. "It's pretty," she said. "Is it straight when it's dry?"

"It…it curls," Meya stammered as she tried to free her locks from Brit's fingers in the friendliest way she could manage.

"I love how pale your skin is and how many freckles you have! Do they cover your entire body?" Nina asked as she crawled towards Meya on hands and knees, her breasts dangling from the motion.

"I…I'd rather—" Meya started, but she was unable to finish her sentence as Nina reached for her towel. Brit was still combing her fingers through Meya's hair. "P-please, don't—" Meya stammered as she tried to move away.

Lea coughed. "Girls, give her some distance. Can't you see you're making her uncomfortable?"

Brit removed her fingers from Meya's damp curls and Nina sat back down with a slight pout.

"I'm sorry," Lea said. "You'd think they were still children at times."

"It…it's alright," Meya said softly.

"If you wish to not be touched, we will respect that. Right, girls?" Lea looked sternly at Brit and Nina, though Winnie's face was also quite flushed.

"Hopefully once you get to know us a bit better, you'll feel more comfortable around us," Gail said.

"Perhaps," Meya responded meekly.

"Who gave you that black eye?" Nina asked and quickly added, "If you don't mind me asking."

Meya was even more embarrassed now, but she knew there was no use in trying to lie or avoid the women. She sighed deeply. "I tried to escape from the slave trader, and as you can clearly see, I failed."

Their faces contorted in pain for a moment.

"Well, it doesn't look too bad. It should be gone in a few days, I'd reckon," Lea said.

"Can I make you feel more at ease by offering you a cup of water?" Nina asked.

Meya blushed. "Yes please, thank you."

With a broad smile, Nina jumped up to get it. In front of the window stood a table with a large jug and an unused cup.

"So, where are you from?" Gail asked.

"I'm originally from the western lands, though we moved more to the east because of the wars." Meya fell silent and gladly took the cup of water from Nina. "My father was a soldier and he died when I was six years old. My mother and I moved east to where our only living family remained and,

30

eventually, all of us went even further east to flee the wars." She took a sip of water. "We had our own inn and it flourished due to the many travellers." Meya fell silent again, unsure if she wanted to tell more.

The silence was broken by Lea. "But if your family had a well-running inn, how did you end up here?"

Meya looked at the cup in her hands. She hesitated, then finally said, "Pillagers, soldiers, I don't even know who they were. They came and killed everyone. I...I barely managed to escape, I—" She swallowed.

*Am I really going to tell them this?* she asked herself. *It would be nice to finally tell someone what happened.*

She took a deep breath. "One of them found me hiding in the woods. He...he tried to..." Her voice trailed off. The silence seemed to linger for a very long time as Meya gathered the strength to continue. "He tried to rape me," she finally managed to whisper. "My hand found a rock and before I realised what I had done, he... He..." She shivered and tears escaped her eyes.

Comforting hands seem to appear from every angle.

*Great move, Meya,* she chided herself. *And here you thought you could finally talk about what happened.*

"Did you get away before he...?" Gail asked cautiously.

Meya nodded. "He just lay there next to me. Blood everywhere." She sighed deeply as she prepared herself to confess her biggest sin, her soul yearning for the loss of its weight. "I...I killed him with the rock." As soon as the words had left her mouth, she regretted it. *I just told them I'm a murderer. They must—*

Nina took Meya's head in her hands and gently pressed it against her chest, comforting her. "It's alright. He would have killed you instead after whatever he had planned. It was either you or him."

The other women muttered in agreement.

Surprised by their support instead of their condemnation, Meya broke down. Her body shook as she sobbed, and she clung to Nina. The others closed in around her, rubbing her arms and back to try and offer some comfort too.

When Meya started to gather herself back together a bit, Lea gently took her hand off Nina's back and placed a kerchief in it. "Here," she said, her voice warm and kind.

Meya released Nina, and the others moved away to give her some space. She dried her face and blew her nose. With her voice a little raw, she continued her story.

"I ran away, further east... The inn was set ablaze, and even hours later, I could still see the glow of fire against the sky."

"When did this all happen?" Gail asked.

"About a year ago. The end of the harvest season was nearing and the nights were getting colder."

The women looked at each other in horror.

"How did you survive?" Lea asked.

"I went from farm to inn, working for a bed and a meal. When the nights became warmer again, I dared to travel further east, hoping to find a safe haven... A town I could perhaps call home." She sniffed and wiped the tears from her eyes, trying to compose herself again. "I guess I went *too* far east. Single women without family were frowned upon." Meya straightened herself, corrected her towel, and emptied her cup. "I was a few towns up north when a slave trader caught air of me. He lifted me from my bed in the middle of the night with three other men—I stood no chance. I was stuffed into a cart with seven other people, and during the night, we rode to another town where even more people were picked up. The day after, we entered the town where the auctions were going to be held. And, lo and behold, today I was sold and now I am here."

Nina looked at her with a puzzled look. "That black eye looks rather fresh to be from several nights ago when you were captured. When did you try to escape?"

Meya was startled; she had not expected someone to notice that. She sighed deeply and bit her lip. *I doubt I can hide it from them. The moment I get into bed, someone is bound to see,* she thought gloomily. *I've already told this much... Might as well spill it all and hope it makes me feel better.* She swallowed and gathered all her courage. "I got the black eye last night, as I tried to get away from the slave trader. He... He—" Meya was about to break down into tears again and Nina hugged her tightly.

"It's alright, you're safe now," she whispered.

"Men are such pigs," Lea said angrily. "How bad did he hurt you?"

*If I say it out loud, I'll cry again—I don't want to cry again. Hell, I doubt I can even say it.* She bit her lip to help keep her emotions under control. *I'll just show them.*

Meya loosened the towel and Nina let go so the towel could drop. The women looked at the cuts and bruises in silence. Finally, Nina picked up the towel and draped it around Meya's shoulders.

"I'm sorry you had to experience that."

Everyone whispered apologies and sympathies, and this caused Meya to cry again despite her initial desire not to. *They're all being so nice.*

After several minutes, Meya finally calmed down a bit. She lay in front of the warm fire with her head in Nina's lap, her red curls stroked gently by Nina's hand. It had been nearly a year, yet she had kept it a secret all that time, that she had killed a man in self-defence, out of fear of what people might have thought of her. On top of that, she still needed to process what the slaver had done. Having talked about it felt good and she sighed in relief, snuggling up to Nina.

*At least now I no longer have to worry about wars, shelter, food, or pigs disguised as men.* She relaxed a bit. *Perhaps I might even end up having friends again. People who care about me.* Feeling a bit better and a lot more at ease, she drifted off to sleep in Nina's lap, the warmth of the fire consoling her.

# Five

Meya woke up in the middle of the night. To her surprise, she was still in front of the—now glowing—hearth with Nina wrapped around her. As she sat up, Nina stirred and opened her eyes.

"I'm sorry I woke you," Meya whispered.

Nina rubbed the sleep out of her eyes. "It's fine. We should probably get off the floor anyway."

"I have to use the latrine," Meya whispered. "Where—"

"It's alright. Just walk out and go right; it's at the end of the hallway."

"Thanks," Meya said as she grabbed the towel and wrapped it around herself.

Nina yawned and crawled into her bed.

~*~

Meya quickly went to the latrine and relieved herself. The hallway was dark, but at least the several windows in the room allowed for some moonlight to enter. She couldn't help but feel frightened, her heart pounding loudly in her throat.

After washing up, she walked out and noticed there was a light at the far end of the hallway to her left. Her heart skipped a beat and she rushed back to

34

her room, fighting the urge to run instead. She was not in the mood to encounter a guard—if the light indeed belonged to a guard. She crawled into her bed, her breathing still heavy and her heart thumping. Just as she was starting to relax, she heard footsteps outside the wooden door. She held her breath, her ears straining to catch every little sound.

The steps halted.

Just as she was barely able to keep her breath any longer, whoever had stood on the other side of the wood started to walk away. Panting, she finally relaxed.

*Great, spooked by a guard.* Meya sighed and made herself comfortable. Despite the adrenaline present in her veins, she fell asleep rather quickly.

~*~

Meya woke up to the sound of bells. Confused, she looked around. It was gloomy outside—the sun hadn't risen yet.

Everyone else in the room was also stirring and Brit yawned loudly. "Good morning all," she added as she stretched herself.

The other women also mumbled good mornings and Meya chimed in. She got up and opened the wardrobe to see what she was going to wear. A tap on her shoulder made her jump.

"Sorry," Nina said. "I just wanted to tell you that if you need to use the latrine, it's best if you use it now. There will be a line soon."

Still half-asleep, Meya simply nodded and Nina practically dragged her outside—Meya had just enough time to grab a towel and pull it around herself.

To Meya's surprise, there already was a small line leading up to the latrine door. There were a dozen seats inside though, so they didn't have to wait long. When they walked out, the line had tripled, and the people standing at the end were already dressed.

Back in the room, Meya quickly got dressed too. Her outfit was rather simple: undergarments, a brown dress, and a white apron. She was about to slip into her old sandals when Lea pointed at a pair of new shoes. Pleasantly surprised, she stepped into wooden-soled, leather clogs and met Nina and Lea at the door; the other women had already left.

The three of them went down to have breakfast. The meal was a simple one, consisting of just a chunk of bread, half an apple, and a single cup of cider, but Meya enjoyed it nonetheless.

After breakfast, Nina and Lea went off to do their chores. Lea worked in the laundry room and Nina in the soldiers' quarters. Meya remained seated, waiting for Juris.

*I have no clue what my chores even are...* She played with the empty cup, anxious.

~*~

The breakfast hall was almost empty when Juris finally came to pick Meya up. He seemed to be slightly startled upon seeing her. Unlike her shabby appearance the day before, she was now well-dressed, clean, and her red hair curled over her shoulders without muddy chunks and strands of hay entangled in them. The lamplight he had seen her in the previous night had done her no justice.

"Good morning," Juris said, recovering his composure. "Did you sleep well?"

"Good morning, Juris," Meya replied. "Yes, I did, thank you." She didn't feel like telling him of her near encounter with a guard in the middle of the night.

"I apologise, but I have a very busy day so we must hurry a bit with explaining your chores." He led Meya out of the servant dining hall.

"What exactly will I be doing?" Meya asked as they walked with a fast tread to the nearest stairwell.

"You will be cleaning Lord Deminas' chambers."

Meya almost stopped dead in her tracks at hearing this. "I...I did not expect the Lord to be accepting a new servant to clean his chambers," Meya said, shocked.

"Lord Deminas is very picky about who he lets into his chambers. Only a few servants are allowed in, and he demanded a new servant instead of changing a current servant's tasks."

As they climbed the stairs, Meya asked the question that was burning on her tongue. "What happened to the previous servant?"

Juris walked slower and eventually halted. He turned around and looked at Meya, his expression grim. "Let's just say that the woman was very foolish. She disobeyed and kept disobeying. When she made one final, thoughtless mistake towards Lord Deminas, he..." Juris fell silent.

"He... what?" Meya asked cautiously.

Juris sighed heavily. "He dropped her from the balcony." He turned away from her and continued to climb the stairs.

36

Meya's mouth was dry, her tongue useless. She had seen the castle's location and they were still climbing the stairs. She had a vague idea of from how high the woman would have plummeted to her death. A shiver ran up her spine and she wrapped her arms around herself for a moment. *I'll be fine*, she thought. *How hard can it be to obey Lord Deminas?*

~*~

After a long walk, Juris halted in front of a big wooden door, the wood carved in the same manner as those of the room where Lord Deminas had been seated the previous day, and knocked.

There was no answer, so he knocked again.

Silence.

"Always knock," he said. "If there is no reply after knocking twice, you are allowed to enter and when you do, announce yourself."

Meya nodded and Juris opened the door.

"Juris, my Lord," he called loudly.

"And Meya, my Lord." She feared her voice had sounded awkward.

"I suppose the Lord is still having breakfast. Afterwards, he often visits the military quarters and has a meeting with the generals."

Juris walked over to a big desk at the rear end of the room, facing the door. Behind the desk was a broad bookcase filled with tomes and scrolls. The grand wooden chair accompanying the desk was padded, the leather looking slightly worn. Meya admired the several paintings adorning the walls until she noticed the large window and balcony that provided an astounding view over the forest below.

"You will be performing standard household duties. Dusting, cleaning the floors and windows. The desk will need to be polished every now and then, same for the chair. The hearth is maintained by the castle's fire-keepers."

Meya frowned and Juris realised he hadn't mentioned this to her yet.

"There's a group of servants we call the fire-keepers. They are in charge of the firewood, keeping the stocks filled next to the hearths, cleaning the hearths, and lighting them when night comes. They also ensure that all the oil lamps are filled; and in case of Lord Deminas' chambers, replace candles when required."

Juris walked to a door that was on the right side of the room and Meya followed. He knocked on the door, but there was no answer. He knocked again. When there was still no answer, they entered and announced themselves.

It was the master bedroom.

37

The room was quite spacious, decorated in black and scarlet just like the entrance hall had been. The ornate four-poster bed dominated the room, with a large hearth on one side and a lavish wardrobe on the other. Several oil lamps were placed along the wall to provide light; there were no windows in this room, for it rested against the mountain. On a low but broad wooden cabinet across the bed stood two candelabra and a candlestick.

Meya looked at the door that was opposite the bed in the left corner of the room. A large wooden plank barricaded it. Juris noticed Meya staring at it.

"It's a precaution against raiders," he said. "Also, the Lord doesn't wish to be disturbed in his bedroom, ever, from out of the hallway directly. It's an emergency door at best."

Meya nodded.

"Your tasks here are also simple: keep the floors and carpets clean, make the bed, and refresh the sheets when the Lord wishes so. If the sheets are up, only make the bed. If the sheets are down like this,"—he nudged towards the bed—"you will need to replace them. You can take the dirty linens to the laundry room, together with the dirty clothing. The servants at the laundry room will handle the rest; they will also ensure that all the Lord's clean clothes and linens are ready for you to take back up."

"All's clear so far, anything else?" Her eyes scanned the room. *So far nothing strange or hard to do,* Meya thought.

Juris walked over to the door opposite the one to the sitting room. The knocking ritual was performed once more, and they entered again without having heard an answer.

Before she could announce herself, Meya gasped.

They stood in a very large bathroom. The bath itself was slightly larger than the servant ones. In the corner of the room, next to another large window and balcony, stood a lavish latrine. There was another similarly barricaded door like the one in the bedroom that provided an emergency exit.

Meya licked her lips. "I suppose I have to clean the floors, the windows, the latrine, and the bath. Ensure there are clean towels and bring the dirty ones to the laundry room. Did I miss anything?"

Juris thought for a moment. "No, I think you just about summed it up. The bath is filled around suppertime by another servant. Just be sure to have it cleaned beforehand; that is all I can add."

"I know where to find the laundry room, but where can I get cleaning supplies?"

"The closet in the hallway, I'll show you on my way out. I will have to leave you to your chores afterwards. When the bells ring, it's lunchtime and you can finish up your current chores and come down. I would like to talk during lunch about how it's going, so if you don't mind, please come sit with me."

Meya smiled. "Sounds good."

He showed her where the closet was that contained all of the necessary cleaning materials and left her to her chores.

Meya managed to finish cleaning the bathroom before lunch. When the bells chimed, she left the dirty towels in the bedroom as she planned on doing that room next and wanted to take all the dirty laundry down in one big haul.

Before she walked down, she opened the bathroom and sitting room windows and left the bedroom doors wide open, ensuring some fresh air could come in.

~*~

Meya ate her lunch without Juris, as she was unable to spot him. Just as she had finished, he tapped her on the shoulder.

"I'm so sorry, I got held up. Today truly is a very busy day."

"It's alright. Everything's going just fine so far." Meya smiled. "I have to get back to my chores now though."

"But of course." Juris stepped aside. "Meet me at supper then?"

She nodded as she rose. "Sure."

Meya returned to the Lord's chambers where the windows and doors were still open and began cleaning the bedroom.

*So far, so good,* she thought. *Nice people, good meals, and the work I have to do isn't that much different from what I used to do at the inn.* She smiled a little. *I can live with this—for now.*

# Six

Meya finished up removing the old linen from the bed, then placed all the laundry in the centre of the sheet and gathered the corners, turning the sheet into a bag. Just as she dumped the bundle of laundry by the door, she noticed a small piece of cloth lying underneath the bed, which she hadn't spotted earlier as the scarlet sheets had obstructed it from view. She had to get down on her knees to pick up the handkerchief and once in her grasp, she noticed the linen was rather damp. As she stood up again and turned to the laundry bundle, she couldn't help but wonder what the cloth had been used for. Her fingers played with the fabric, her face becoming slightly red as she did.

*He probably just used it to blow his nose.* She bit her lip as she was about to unfold the thing, curiosity getting the better of her. *Am I really going to open this and look at lordly boogers?*

She peeled two layers of linen from each other. A very vague scent drifted up from the cloth, a sticky, white substance residing in the centre.

*Not boogers!* She quickly folded it back up and stuffed it deep into the laundry bundle. With a face as red as her hair, she turned to the large wardrobe to get clean linens. Meya finished dressing the bed and looked into the wardrobe once more to see if she had forgotten anything. The earlier blush had left her face when she had continued her work, but as her eyes fell upon a stack of linen handkerchiefs, her cheeks flushed bright red again. She bit her lip, deciding what to do. Not wanting to be scolded for forgetting something, she took one of the handkerchiefs, folded it neatly, and placed it on the centre pillow. Still blushing, she took a step back to admire her work.

The four-poster bed looked good, though the velvet curtains were a bit messy. She neatly rearranged all the curtains and smiled at the result, the blush slowly receding from her face.

The sound of a shoe scraping the floor made Meya jump, and when she turned around, she found Lord Deminas standing in the doorway, leaning against the frame.

*How long has he been standing there?* Meya wondered fearfully. "M-my Lord," she stammered, and she cursed herself for her inability to utter those two words without stuttering. She curtsied in the hope that it would please him enough to not berate her. When she looked up again, Lord Deminas had walked up to the bed and was examining it.

"Is this how you used to make your own bed?" he asked without a hint of emotion.

Meya swallowed. "No, my Lord."

"Then where did you learn this, if you weren't a servant before?"

*Damn, he thinks I lied to him!* She wetted her lips, her mind racing. "I used to work at my family's inn, my Lord," she said slowly.

Lord Deminas walked up to her and lifted her chin, forcing Meya to look into his eyes. "Not a servant perhaps, but a servant's tasks nonetheless."

Keeping her eyes locked on his, Meya swallowed. Her heart seemed to have relocated to her throat. "I...I apologise if I misunderstood my Lord's question yesterday."

Lord Deminas released her chin with a grunt. "Good to know your memory is functional." He turned to observe the bed again. "I find it quite amazing," he said slowly. "I've had several chambermaids, and you're the first to have done this." His eyes lingered on the neatly folded handkerchief.

Blood rushed to her cheeks, though the words lingering in her mind caused it to run cold. *Several chambermaids... Did he drop them all from the balcony?*

The lord turned and sat down on the bed, placing one leg over the other as he observed Meya's face reddening more and more by the second. "Judging from the colour of your cheeks, I'm certain you realise I will not be using it to blow my nose." A small grin seemed to play at the edge of his lips.

Meya bowed her head in shame. "I...I'm sorry, my Lord, if my actions have—"

"Silence!" Lord Deminas bellowed and he uncrossed his legs.

In a mere instant, the blood drained from her cheeks, leaving them pale, her eyes wide in fear. She couldn't help twiddling her fingers as anxiety swept through her body.

"Come here," Lord Deminas ordered, and he pointed to the spot in front of him.

Meya obeyed instantly, afraid to do anything else.

"Kneel."

She obliged. Once on her knees, she averted her eyes to the ground to avoid looking straight at the lord's crotch.

"Look at me."

Meya swallowed and looked up into the cold, grey eyes of Lord Deminas. She kept her eyes locked, only interrupting her gaze by blinking every now and then.

After what seemed like a very long time, Lord Deminas finally spoke again. "I expect you to be a better chambermaid than the previous one, though from what I've seen so far, that won't be much of a challenge for you." His gaze still bored into hers. "Have you heard of what happened to your predecessor?"

Meya hesitated, but it was clear the Lord was awaiting an answer. "Only that certain actions led to a certain fate," Meya uttered softly, and quickly added, "My Lord."

"Do you know what actions and what fate?" he asked coldly.

"Only that she disobeyed multiple times, my Lord. And eventually..." Meya swallowed, unsure of how to phrase her next words.

"You can say it," Lord Deminas said, a hint of amusement in his voice.

"That...that you dropped her down the mountainside."

There was a glint in his eyes and, for a moment, a vague grin flashed over his face. "Indeed, I did. Are you afraid of suffering the same fate?" His eyes seemed to pierce her soul and Meya had to fight the urge to look away.

"I...I can only say that I will do my very best to serve you, my Lord. But I admit that I am afraid of making mistakes and the consequences they might bring."

The grin finally took shape and an icy shiver went up Meya's spine. "You want to know what she did, or didn't do, don't you? What made her deserve such punishment..."

Hesitantly, Meya nodded. "Yes, my Lord." And she quickly added, "But only if my curiosity doesn't displease you."

Lord Deminas laughed and patted Meya on the head, breaking their eye contact. "The other servants must have told you quite some tales for you to be so docile and obedient, especially considering your history as a free woman."

He looked down at her again and lifted her chin up so their eyes locked once more. "Or was it the recent beating you received that made you this submissive?"

The comment felt like a slap in the face. It took Meya all her willpower to not look away, but she was unable to stop her eyes from tearing up or her jaw from clenching.

Lord Deminas released her chin and placed his hand on her head again, making her face the ground. "Your predecessor never succeeded in finishing her chores, sometimes it seemed even deliberately, testing me. She appeared to take pure delight in my punishments. When I caught her with another servant in my personal bath, I was simply done with her. The other servant didn't know how fast and how many times to apologise and thus still lives today, though without his manhood."

Meya trembled underneath his fingers.

"The girl, on the other hand, seemed to lack the intellect to perceive the situation for what it was. She tried to fight me, and when that failed, she made the fatal mistake of spitting in my face."

Lord Deminas grinned slightly as he noticed how Meya stiffened under his touch.

"It's good to know you're not as dumb as she was. Her face though, as I held her over the edge of the balcony by her throat..." He sighed. "She remained defiant, perhaps even until her skull cracked upon the mountainside below."

Another shiver went up Meya's spine.

"Ah, but I'm certain you'll behave a lot better than she did." The lord's fingers entwined themselves in Meya's red curls and with a firm grip, lifted her head towards his face again. "Right?"

*Please, don't hurt me!* Meya had to fight the tears that threatened to spill, and she suppressed the memories of the slaver that bubbled up with them. Lord Deminas wasn't pulling her hair painfully hard, but, combined with the recent events that weren't even his doing, it was hard enough to make her feel powerless under his grasp.

He raised a brow, still waiting for an answer.

Her mind almost derailing, it took her a lot of effort to utter, barely audible, "I...I'll do my best, m-my Lord."

He grinned at this and released her. "Good."

He stood up whilst Meya was still on the ground, his crotch very close to her face. For a moment, a paralysing fear spread through her limbs, but then the lord stepped away.

"Continue with your chores," he said.

Meya had to close her eyes to try and calm herself. Finally, she managed to reply, "Y-yes, my Lord."

As he walked out of the room, he suddenly spun back around. "After supper, you're to return here."

Meya's eyes widened as a new wave of terror washed over her. Knowing she needed to answer, her lips moved on their own accord and she croaked, "A-as you wish, my Lord."

Before he walked out of the room, Meya spotted the small grin playing at the corners of his mouth again, but his cold eyes revealed nothing of his intentions. Staggered by what had just happened, she hugged herself and closed her eyes. The fear of what could have happened still clung to her, and it took her awhile before she managed to get rid of it and return to work. Any thoughts about what the Lord wanted with her after supper were pushed away as she refused to think about it.

~*~

The dinner bell echoed through the castle. Meya stuffed the cloth she had been using to scrub the bath into the bucket. She was about to walk out of the room when she noticed that the window was still open, so she quickly turned to shut it and made her way to the sitting room. The window there was open too, but as she closed it, she couldn't help but gaze outside.

*Would the body of that girl still be there?*

Meya bit her lip. Curiosity got the better of her and she opened the balcony door before stepping out onto the stone terrace, the cold autumn wind whipping up her hair. Slowly, she moved towards the edge.

The view of the forest and the mountainside was astonishing. She could see a big river cascading through the rocks and meandering down into the land below. She placed one hand on the balustrade, the other still holding the bucket, and gazed down into the depths.

Suddenly, the bucket clattered to the floor, water spilling over her shoes. She stared at the rocky cliff, her eyes wide in horror. "Oh, dear lord," she whispered as she covered her mouth in disgust.

Far down below, on the jagged rocks, lay the mangled remains of a human being. The woman had been naked when she had been dropped, but there was still a lot of flesh clinging to her bones.

Meya turned away, bile rising in the back of her throat. *How long has she been dead? A week, maybe two?* She closed her eyes, but she still saw the woman's face in her mind. Her eyes had been pecked out by the crows—or so she hoped—and it seemed something else had feasted on her guts.

She looked down at her feet and stepped out of the puddle. With trembling fingers, she used the cloth to dry herself. She dreaded what would happen if Lord Deminas caught her. When she was certain her shoes were dry enough to not leave any footprints, she put them back on. She then left the balcony and the lord's chambers in a hurry and stashed away the bucket in the hallway closet. Despite having lost her appetite, she made her way towards the servant dining hall.

*"After supper, you're to return here."*

Meya shuddered as the lord's words finally managed to push themselves into her consciousness, and the image of the woman on the rocks flashed through her mind.

*I'll be fine,* she told herself. *As long as I listen and do my work well, I'll be fine.* And she pushed the thoughts away again.

# Seven

During supper, Juris found that Meya was rather quiet.

"How was your day?" he asked in an attempt to get her to speak.

"Fine," Meya answered curtly.

Juris wanted to know more but he realised that Meya was not in the mood to talk. Instead of pestering her, he decided to let her be—though he did sigh deeply in an attempt to let her know of his displeasure.

Meya continued to eat her meal in complete silence, ignoring everyone around her. She thought back to what had happened with Lord Deminas earlier, and why he wanted to see her after supper. The image of the mangled corpse on the rocky cliffs still haunted her, reducing her appetite and increasing her anxiety. It didn't take long before her thoughts started to wander. Memories of the events at the family inn returned to her and she tried to dismiss them, yet they were only replaced by visions of bothersome men that had tried to persuade her into acts she had had no interest in. Most of them had left her alone after a repeated refusal, though some left mean words lingering in the air as they went. A few had actually got physical, but there was only the slaver that had successfully ignored her protests.

Meya bit her lip as she thought back to what the slaver had done. She shivered at the memory of the knife he had threatened her with, had cut her with… Swallowing the bile that had risen in the back of her throat again, she pushed the remnants of her meal into the centre of the table—she had just lost her appetite. Paying no attention to Juris' questioning look, she left the dining hall.

~*~

Meya stood frozen in front of the big wooden door leading to Lord Deminas' private chambers. Her heart was racing, the pounding clearly audible in her ears. She swallowed.

Still, she just stood there.

After a while, Meya shook her head, took a few deep breaths and took the plunge.

She knocked.

There was no answer.

She knocked again.

Silence.

Although her body felt heavy, she managed to lift her hand to the handle and open the door. She stepped inside cautiously and noticed that the oil lamps were burning, as was the large hearth. There was no sign, however, of the lord.

With a slight squeak, Meya managed to announce her presence.

Unsure of what to do, she walked to the door leading to the master bedroom.

It was closed.

Meya started to sweat, her breathing heavy and her heart still thumping loudly in her throat. She knocked, once, twice, but no answer came. With a deep breath, she opened the door and announced herself once more.

The bedroom was empty, the bed in the same state she had left it in. She eyed the last closed door with dread.

*Perhaps he's still having supper*, she thought.

Nervously fidgeting with her apron, she walked up to the door leading to the bathroom. She was just about to knock when she heard water splashing on the other side. Her heart skipped a beat and she froze, her fist inches away from the wood.

*Would he really...?* Her face burned up. Biting her lip, she knocked.

"Who's there?" the low voice of Lord Deminas demanded from the other side of the door.

"It's Meya, my Lord, as you requested." She congratulated herself internally for speaking without stammering.

47

It remained silent for a moment and Meya swallowed nervously. Doubt started to set in and she wondered if the lord disliked the last bit she had said.

"You may enter."

Meya breathed in deeply in an attempt to calm herself a bit, then entered.

To her surprise, Lord Deminas was still in the bath—facing her. From where she was standing, she could only see his bare chest, but it was enough to set fire to her already glowing cheeks. Lord Deminas was a warrior and this was clearly visible in his physique. His arms and torso were muscular, and a scar across his left bicep clearly stood out against his tanned skin.

"Is my appearance to your liking?" he spoke with a hint of amusement.

Meya quickly averted her eyes. "I'm sorry, my Lord." She bowed her head. "That was very indecent of me."

"I did not ask for an apology, nor did I tell you to stop looking. I asked if my appearance is to your liking." His eyes seemed to gleam as he gazed at her, the corners of his mouth slightly curled into a grin.

"I...I—" Meya stammered.

Lord Deminas leaned towards her, his face stern. "Answer me, now."

"It is, my Lord," she squeaked.

The slight grin returned to his face, and he relaxed back into the bath. He motioned for Meya to come closer. "And shut the door behind you."

Meya's heart pounded in her chest and her stomach felt heavy, but she did as she was told. As she walked closer to the bath, more of the lord's body revealed itself. Just as his lower abdomen would come into view, she averted her eyes back up to his face. His long, dark hair clung to his cheeks and cascaded over his shoulders. His eyes seemed to pierce hers and Meya had a hard time keeping her anxiety under control; she was afraid he might do—or ask *her* to do—something unpleasant.

Lord Deminas' gaze slid over Meya's body. "Strip," he said coldly.

Meya's mouth opened a little in shock. She stood still, unmoving.

Lord Deminas leaned towards her again. "Do not make me tell you twice," he said. "Unless you'd rather have me cut the clothes from your form."

She gulped and slowly moved her trembling fingers along her apron, searching for the bow-tie on her back. Her mind was hazy, numb. She complied out of pure fear—she knew there was nowhere to run to. There was no point in trying to disobey or fight either, for she didn't want to get hurt or worse: killed.

The grin on Lord Deminas' face showed just how much he was enjoying the scene.

Meya closed her eyes as she removed her robe and kept them closed as she freed herself from her undergarments.

"Open your eyes."

She complied.

"Look at me." Lord Deminas' voice sounded stern, slightly angry even.

Meya swallowed, bit her lip, and tried her best to not let any tears slip from her wet eyes as she moved her gaze to the lord's face.

"Good. Was that hard to do?"

"N-no, my Lord."

The sudden splash of water surprised her, but not as much as the Lord's fingers suddenly clasping her chin. His face was but a mere inch from her own, his nose almost touching hers.

"Don't lie to me," he said dangerously, his eyes boring into hers.

Meya was unable to speak, yet the tears rolling down her cheeks seemingly said enough.

"Gah," the lord exclaimed as he let go of her and sat back down in the hot water.

"I...I'm sor—"

"Silence!"

Meya winced. She wanted nothing more than to run away, to find herself a nice, secluded, quiet spot where she could break down and cry.

Lord Deminas motioned for her to turn around. "Slowly, so I can take a good look."

Sniffling, Meya did as she was told. Once she was back facing him, she was slightly confused by his expression. She had expected lust, perhaps still some anger—disgust even—yet the almost hidden expression on his face seemed to be one of concern.

The lord shifted to the right side of the bath and gestured to the now free space. "Get in."

Meya was utterly confused. "B-but, my Lord," she started.

"If my bath is not good enough for you then neither is the servants' bath."

Shocked, she realised that he was threatening to take away her right to bathe and she quickly stepped into the hot water.

*Oh God, this is so warm*, Meya thought. Despite all the adrenaline in her veins, and the stress, she relaxed slightly upon sinking into the water. She closed her eyes for a moment, and when she opened them again, she spotted the smirk on Lord Deminas' face.

"Nice, isn't it?"

Meya blushed. "Yes, my Lord. Thank you, my Lord."

"Now how about you explain to me why you almost broke down simply because you had to undress in front of me." The smirk had left his face and there actually seemed to be genuine interest.

Meya opened her mouth, but no sound came forth. Even her mind seemed to have ground to a halt, unable to grasp what was happening.

"Then perhaps you can explain the history of those cuts and bruises first."

Meya repeated her former response, only this time Lord Deminas kept silent, waiting for her to regain speech.

It was difficult for Meya to start talking, but once she did, she managed to tell Lord Deminas the same story she had told her room-mates. After some prodding, he also made her tell the rest of her history, including that she had killed one of the men that had raided her family's inn when he'd tried to rape her.

After a moment of silence, Lord Deminas simply said, "You're an unlucky one, aren't you?"

Meya shrugged as she stared at her hands. "I think it could have been worse, my Lord. I could have died with the rest of my family, I could have been raped and killed, and I could have been sold to a bordello... Just to name a few options."

To her surprise, Lord Deminas shot forward, pressing her body by the shoulders against the bath wall. Shocked, her heart pounded painfully in her chest, a new dose of adrenaline coursing through her veins.

The lord's eyes were cold, his face stern. "You try to comfort yourself with visions of events that didn't happen, but that doesn't mean that what did happen left no scars."

Meya looked away, not wanting to face the truth of his words.

"Look at me," he growled.

Slowly, Meya shifted her head back to face the lord.

"Do you feel pity for the man you killed?"

It was silent for a few seconds. "N-no, my Lord," Meya whimpered.

"Would you have done the same to the slaver, if you had had the chance?"

Her eyes widened in shock. "My...my Lord!"

"Would you?"

"I... I think so," she whispered, though every fibre in her body screamed *yes*.

Lord Deminas moved away from her and stepped out of the bath. "Finish washing yourself, take one of the towels and head back to your room. You can leave your clothing here and simply take it along with tomorrow's laundry."

"Y-yes, my Lord," she uttered, and overwhelmed by his gesture, she quickly added, "Th-thank you, my Lord."

As Lord Deminas dried his hair with a towel, his back faced towards Meya. Despite everything, she couldn't help but peek at his toned body. Without turning to look at her or even saying another word, he left the bathroom.

Utterly confused by what had just transpired, Meya submerged herself in the warm water. *Was he being mean, or nice?* She didn't know. She swallowed as she relived the events in her mind. The sensation of his fingers gripping her chin, the feeling of his hands pressing against her shoulders… She hugged herself. *He made me undress in front of him, yet he didn't do anything indecent to me. He could have, but he didn't.* She bit her lip. *The former chambermaid got thrown off the balcony for being in his bath, but he as good as forced me to get in. Not to mention that he actually seemed concerned for a moment.* She closed her eyes in frustration, unable to understand the lord's intentions.

Giving up on trying to figure it all out, she quickly finished washing up—though she regretted having to leave the still warm water. She dried herself and wrapped the towel around her torso. She nearly opened the door leading to the bedroom without knocking but corrected herself just in time.

"Yes, you may enter."

Meya hurried inside, curtsied, and wished the Lord a good night. She quickly made her way out of his chambers with her breath held, afraid that he would ask her to stay. The moment she closed the bedroom door, relief washed over her.

*I made it*, she thought and left for her own room.

# Light

After using the latrine, Meya silently opened the door to her room. The other women didn't notice her at first, but Winnie looked up the moment Meya closed the door. She poked her sister, who then turned around to look too, followed by the rest.

"Where were you?" Lea exclaimed. "Juris said you left supper in a hurry without saying a word and he couldn't find you anywhere. We didn't see you either at the baths…" She fell silent as she realised Meya was only clad in a towel and her hair was still wet.

"I…I," Meya started, but she didn't know what to say. She swallowed and tried again, as the silence of the women told her they weren't going to let it go. "Lord Deminas had asked for my presence after supper, so I complied."

Everyone's eyes widened in shock and some mouths stood agape.

Nina gasped loudly. "Don't tell me he—"

"Did he really—" Gail started.

"—used his bath?" chimed Brit.

Winnie muttered something inaudible.

"Shush!" Lea said and she gave them all a stern look before turning back to Meya. "Please dear, sit down."

Meya shuffled towards the group and sat down next to her.

"Now, first things first: were you punished?"

Meya wanted to say no, but that wasn't completely true. Her silence caused the women to glance at one another with fear in their eyes.

"Did he—" Nina started, but her voice faltered. "Did he... hurt you?"

Again, Meya wanted to say no, but doubt set in. He hadn't physically hurt her, but in a way, perhaps, emotionally? Meya was still quite confused about what had happened. "I...I'm not sure," she eventually managed to whisper.

Nina grabbed Meya's hand and squeezed it. "You can tell us."

Meya wriggled her hand free from her grasp. "It's fine. He didn't hit me or anything like that—if that's what you all fear."

Winnie pointed to her crotch and Meya's eyes widened in shock.

"No, no! He did not force himself on me if that's what you're trying to say." Meya frowned. "Why don't you just say it? I've never heard you speak before, come to think of it..."

Winnie pointed at her mouth and opened it. She stuck out her tongue—or at least what remained of it. The little stump of flesh was just able to touch her lips.

Meya looked horrified at the display, the colour draining from her face. "What...what happened?"

Brit spoke for her sister, "As kids, Winnie was able to taunt Lord Deminas without much consequence, be it the occasional beating with a whip or exclusion from supper. When Lord Marius died in battle and his son became Lord, Winnie couldn't comprehend that her rebellious actions were now no longer directed at the son of a Lord, but at the Lord himself. Her behaviour didn't improve, in fact, it only got worse. She told the Lord, multiple times, that she refused to call him by his title. After several warnings and mild punishments, she stated, in front of everyone, that she refused to ever call him Lord. That's when Lord Deminas decided that if she wasn't going to use her tongue to speak nicely, she wasn't to speak at all."

Winnie looked at the floor as she played with her long hair.

Meya couldn't believe what she had just heard. The punishment was cruel to say the least, but she just couldn't comprehend how stubborn someone must be to keep acting in such a way.

"But why?" Meya asked. "Why didn't she just behave?"

Brit smiled wryly. "Winnie craved attention from Lord Deminas, and any form was good enough for her. He knew this when his father was still Lord, and we think he actually liked it. When he became Lord himself, his attitude changed. He no longer desired to play games, but Winnie never understood the signals. The removal of her tongue made it clear enough though, right?" Brit looked at her sister.

Winnie looked up, smiled, and shrugged. She whispered something, though Meya was unable to understand it.

Brit translated, "She said: I merely wanted his love and wouldn't see the rejections."

Meya shivered.

It was silent for a while until Gail broke it. "But Meya, why did you have to go back to Lord Deminas?"

Meya sighed and closed her eyes. *Switching subjects doesn't help, it seems.* "I'd rather not talk about it, alright?" She opened her eyes again.

"Fine," Gail stated—it was clear she wasn't pleased.

Meya already felt uncomfortable, but the awkward silence that hung in the room made it even worse. In an attempt to escape the situation, she excused herself and went to bed. With her back towards the women, it didn't take long before they started to talk again—albeit in hushed whispers. Meya listened to their gossip about relationships amongst the servants, but it didn't catch her interest and her mind quickly trailed off. She thought about what had happened back in the lord's chambers. Eventually, she surrendered to sleep, unable to figure out if the lord had been kind to her or not.

~*~

The next day Meya did her chores without seeing the lord even once. At supper, Juris was nowhere to be seen, and Meya made sure to eat quickly to lower the odds of running into him. She was in no mood to speak to him, afraid that he was going to ask her about the previous night, too. When she was done, she hurried back to her quarters.

She opened the door and to her relief, no one was there. The hearth had already been lit, warming the cold room. Meya walked over to the window and stared out into the night. Lost in her own thoughts, she didn't notice someone entering the room.

"Hey," a soft voice said.

Startled, Meya jumped a little. She turned and realised it was Nina.

"Sorry, I didn't mean to scare you," Nina said, walking over to stand beside her. She stared up at the dark sky. "No stars tonight, huh?"

Meya returned her gaze to the darkness outside. "No, but I find it soothing to look anyways."

It was silent for a bit, until Nina finally spoke, "So, how was your day?"

Meya didn't reply immediately, and Nina turned to face her.

"If you want to tell me, that is. No pressure!"

Meya couldn't help but smile a little. "Today was fine, thanks. I didn't see the Lord all day, so no need to worry about that."

Nina relaxed a bit. "I'm sorry about yesterday." She looked back outside. "We were just worried, is all."

Meya sighed. "I thought so, and it's alright. It was just a very confusing day for me, and I needed some time to think."

"Just... eh..." Nina took Meya's hands in her own. "If anything bad happens, please do tell me. If you want, I'll keep it a secret. Winnie can be rather... jealous, so it might be better not to tell too much regarding Lord Deminas. Not to mention, Gail loves to gossip. Tell anything to her and the next day, half the castle will know."

Meya smiled and gave Nina's hands a little squeeze before letting them go. "Thank you, but I think it'll be fine."

Nina bit her lip. "You did hear what happened to your predecessors, right?"

"The stupid girl that got herself thrown off the balcony?" Meya suppressed a shiver as the image of the corpse on the cliffs flashed through her mind.

Nina fumbled with her apron. "Well, she was the last one. And she had it coming, if you ask me. But the ones before her..."

Meya frowned. "What about the ones before her?" There was a heavy, sinking feeling in her gut. *There was only one body on those rocks.*

"Sorry, forget I said anything." Nina turned around, but Meya clutched her arm, stopping her.

"Oh, no you don't!" Meya stared intensely into Nina's hazel eyes. "You don't get to start such a thing and then decide not to tell me."

Nina turned to look at the door, seemingly afraid that someone might barge in anytime soon. "There were eight girls before you. Two of them had stayed in this room. They were happy, vibrant... But as time went on, they became silent. They both appeared to always be tired, and their bodies had these little cuts all over. We used to ask what had happened, but they never told. None of the previous chambermaids did—except Jaimy, the one before you. She was a feisty one, one of a dozen slaves gifted to the Lord by one of the neighbouring lands little over a month ago. Though, from what I heard, her markings weren't like those of the other girls. They didn't get beaten or whipped—Jaimy did."

"But what happened to all those girls before Jaimy?" Meya asked, her voice trembling slightly.

"They disappeared. All of them did, within a year. They had left their beds in the middle of the night, and by morning, their beds were still empty. No one knows what happened to them. All we know is that a few days after each disappearance, the Lord sends out for a new slave."

It was silent for a bit. "So... Did they escape? Did they get killed?" Meya asked hesitantly.

Nina shook her head. "We don't know." She grasped Meya's hands again. "That's why I want you to promise me. Please, if anything weird happens, tell me." Her eyes shimmered with held back tears. "I don't want you to disappear too."

Meya swallowed. "I... I don't know if I can promise that. But I'll remember this, alright?"

Nina pulled her into a tight hug. "The others will be here soon, I'm sure. Do you want to come with me to the baths tomorrow after supper? The water will be old, so not a lot of people will be there. We'll be able to talk more."

"That sounds like a good idea," Meya said.

~*~

The next day started rather uneventful, though it was halfway through the afternoon, when Meya was cleaning the sitting room floor, that she noticed a presence behind her. She looked up and saw Lord Deminas standing in the doorway, just staring at her.

A shiver ran up her spine. "Good afternoon, my Lord," she said, and continued her work.

She heard the door close, followed by his nearing footsteps. As he loomed over her, she doubted for a moment if she should continue her work or stop to look up at him. She decided to continue, and it was only after a while that he finally spoke.

"Stop what you're doing and stand up."

Meya did as she was told, though her hands trembled slightly as she draped the cleaning cloth over the bucket. She stood up and faced the lord; his countenance did not betray his emotions and this scared her.

"Strip," he said unsympathetically.

A shiver went up her spine. She didn't want to do it—not again—but she knew she had no real choice. Hesitantly, her hands moved back to loosen her apron, and in doing so, her eyes slipped away from his.

"Look at me," he growled and Meya's eyes shot back to meet his.

Her mind was consumed by a whirlwind of emotions, her bottom lip quivering slightly. Despite the paralysing fear, she undressed. Her fingers trembled as she removed the layers of fabric from her skin. As she stood naked in front of her lord, she managed to keep the tears from falling, but she knew he could see that her eyes were wet.

The lord took a step back. "Turn around, slowly."

Meya swallowed and did as she was told. *Why is he doing this?*

As she came back to face him again, he grinned slightly. "Good. Was that hard to do?"

Meya was inclined to say no, but she had learned from the last time. "Y-yes, my Lord."

His grin broadened. "You're a quick learner, I like that."

He stepped behind her and goosebumps rose on her skin. She shivered as his breath touched the back of her shoulder.

"Are you afraid of me, of what I might do?"

"I...I am, my Lord," Meya managed to utter. Her heart pounded so hard, it was almost painful.

"What are you afraid of, precisely?"

She hadn't expected this question, and she had no answer at the ready.

"Answer me." He had spoken so closely to her ear that Meya was unsure if his lips had touched her or if it had been only his breath.

"I...I'm not sure, my...my Lord. I fear pain... P-punishment... That you...you might..." She swallowed. "That you might a-assault me, my Lord." Cold pearls of sweat ran down her body, a slight tremble accompanying them.

The lord huffed. "You don't know me very well it seems, but that will come with time." He walked towards his seat and sat down. "Continue your work."

Meya picked up her undergarments and wanted to pull them back on, but Lord Deminas intervened.

"I did not give you permission to get dressed again."

She bit her lip and swallowed. She picked up all her clothes and placed them on a nearby counter before continuing with what she had been doing, only now in the nude.

Meya blushed feverishly during the entire ordeal. Every now and then, her eyes shot up to see what the lord was doing, and every time he was doing the same thing: looking at her.

When she was finished, she stood in front of the lord's desk. "I've finished my chores, my Lord." She wanted to ask if she could get dressed now but decided not to.

"Very well, you may get dressed then."

Meya curtsied. "Thank you, my Lord." She had difficulty not to run towards her clothes. Despite her quivering hands, she got dressed as fast as she could, though she made sure her outfit looked decent. Once done, she turned to Lord Deminas and curtsied again. "Good day, my Lord." She picked up the cleaning items and left the lord's chambers as calmly as she could.

# Nine

After supper, Meya followed Nina to the servant baths. To her surprise Nina had been right: the place was abandoned.

Nina started to strip, causing Meya to feel slightly awkward. Seemingly oblivious to Meya's flustered expression, Nina neatly folded her clothes and placed them on a shelf. "The day they refresh the water and the day after is when most people bathe. The water might be a bit on the dirty side now, but at least it's not crowded." Nina turned to look at Meya and frowned. "You're not coming with me?"

Meya fumbled with her apron. *How could I not have realised that she wanted to actually take a bath when she asked me to come here?*

"Meya, are you alright?" Nina placed her hand on Meya's shoulder.

Shocked, she looked up. "Huh? Eh, yeah. I'm…" She trailed off. *Oh, who am I kidding?* She looked into Nina's eyes, the scarce lamplight still providing enough illumination to show the concern in them.

"You can tell me," Nina said softly.

Meya trembled and she closed her eyes. She let out a deep sigh, swallowed, and pulled Nina into a tight hug, surprising her. "I…I guess I'm just not comfortable undressing in front of others."

Nina placed her hand on Meya's head, her fingers entangling slightly in her curls. "Well, you've been through a lot. First the raiders, then the slaver…"

Tears welled up in Meya's eyes, a heavy, constricting sensation in her chest. *Should I tell her...?* She swallowed. "He... He made me strip." Her voice was weak, not much more than a whisper.

Nina had been rubbing Meya's back, but at hearing that, her hand froze. "Lord Deminas?"

"He made me clean the floor... in the nude." She shivered. "While he watched me."

"Ugh..." She released Meya and looked at her. "Come on, chin up." Nina wiped away the tears that were rolling down Meya's freckled cheeks. "It may sound harsh, but we're servants. Sadly, if he wants to see you scrubbing the floor with your naked arse up in the air, he can. Just be grateful he doesn't ask for more."

Nina's attempt to make her feel better had the opposite effect: Meya sank to her knees, weeping.

"I...I'm sorry!" Nina said, quickly squatting next to Meya. "I didn't mean—"

"Not... your fault," Meya said between sobs. "You're right. It's just..." She sniffed. "I...I guess... I'm just not used to it... yet."

Nina held Meya to her chest, the closeness of her bare breasts causing Meya to flush. "It takes a while to get used to being a slave. And some people never get used to it."

When Meya had stopped sobbing, Nina rose to her feet and pulled Meya up with her. "Come, before it gets too late." She helped Meya undress, ignoring her initial objections. "You will have to get wet, otherwise Gail will start to interrogate us on our whereabouts."

Meya submitted with a sigh. When her clothes also lay neatly folded on the shelf, Nina dragged her to one of the baths. They slipped into the semi-cold water, and Meya instantly longed for the hot water of the lord's bath.

"So... What else has Lord Deminas been making you do?" Nina asked.

Meya shook her head. "Let's not talk about that. I want to hear about you. What's your story?"

Nina looked startled. "You want to know how I got here?"

Meya nodded. "Where are you from, how did you end up here?"

"Well... I'm a long way from home. I used to live in a seaport town in the southwest. My father and older brothers used to fish in the Mediterranean Sea." She entangled her fingers in her black locks, avoiding Meya's gaze. "I was seven when a large part of the town burned down. I was the only one of our household to survive, as I had sneaked out to play with a friend of mine." She sighed deeply. "His family died that night, too. Homeless and hungry, we lived on the streets and ate whatever we could get our hands on—my friend was a good thief." Her voice trembled slightly.

Meya placed her hand on Nina's wrist. "It's alright. You don't need to—"

Nina shook her head. "No, you told your story. It's only fair that I tell mine." She smiled, but the sorrow underneath was still visible. "We were good for several months… But then he got caught. They cut off his hands, and he died not long after that from infection." She rubbed her eyes and swallowed.

Meya felt bad for causing Nina to relive her past. She moved closer to her and opened her arms to hug her, but before she could pull Nina in, Nina hugged her instead.

"I roamed the streets alone for a month or so. Then a bunch of travellers came through, and they took me along with them. Turned out they were all a bunch of thieves." She laughed. "They wanted me to help them out. I was good at distracting people and even better at nicking stuff. In exchange, I finally had a family again, a bed, and enough to eat."

Meya stroked Nina's hair. "I never expected you to have been a thief."

"Desperate times…" Nina nuzzled her face into Meya's neck. "I spent four years with the travelling thieves. We would go from south to north, from west to east, and back again. I think you can guess what happened."

"You came here, and got kidnapped?"

"Close. We got caught in the act. I think a few managed to get away, but most of my newfound family were imprisoned. I was taken to a slave market because I was only eleven. I was quite lucky to have ended up here though—I was nearly sold to a bordello!"

Meya shivered, goosebumps rising all over her body. The mere thought of being forced to have sex with strange men froze her to her very core.

Nina noticed her reaction but thought it was due to the cold water. "How about we get out and join the others at the nice, warm fire?"

"Good idea," Meya replied with a sincere smile.

~*~

The mood was a lot better that evening in the women's chamber. Gail still seemed to be slightly offended at being denied the details of Meya's night-time visit to Lord Deminas, and Winnie was a little distant. Still, Meya didn't feel awkward in their presence like she had the night before. The women chatted about all kinds of things; the current hot gossip around the castle seemed to be about a new prisoner.

"They dragged him in this morning, took him straight to the dungeons!" Gail said.

"Do they know who he is, or what he did?" Lea wanted to know.

Gail shook her head. "Only a few people saw it happen. As far as I heard, even the man's name is a mystery."

"Is it a spy from one of the neighbouring lands?" Brit asked.

Nina paled a bit. "I have heard some of the soldiers mention there was some tension again. It seems something is stirring in the southeast."

"I don't think so," Gail said, seemingly ignoring Nina's comment. "According to the people that saw the man, he was wearing normal clothes; though, they did say they looked rather fancy."

"Fancy? So it *could* be a spy..." Brit mused.

The women went on and on about it, but Meya's attention was elsewhere. She stared into the hearth, watching the flames devour the wood. *What if war does find its way here?* She remembered the multiple burned down villages she had seen when she had travelled with her family further east. Despite her mother's attempts to shield her, Meya had still seen several mutilated and burned corpses. They had eventually settled far away from such areas, but still... She closed her eyes as images of the raid on the inn filled her mind, causing her to shake slightly. *I don't want anymore destruction and slaughter in my life.*

Meya stood up, said goodnight to her room-mates, and slipped into bed. Trying to think of anything else, her mind went back to her earlier conversation with Nina.

*"If he wants to see you scrubbing the floor with your naked arse up in the air, he can."* Nina's words haunted her. *"Just be grateful he doesn't ask for more."*

*But what if he decides he wants more?* Meya clutched her sheets and curled up into a little ball. *What would I do? What* could *I do?*

~*~

The next day, Meya did her chores whilst her mind wandered elsewhere. The entire morning, there was no sign of the lord. During lunch, Juris sat down next to her.

"Hey, Meya. How are you holding up?"

She looked up, not expecting him. "Oh, hey Juris. Just fine, thanks." She didn't feel like discussing anything in detail with him—especially not the things Lord Deminas had made her do.

"How are your chores coming along?"

"Just fine," she said again. "I plan to give the bathroom a good scrubbing after I finish my meal. I cleaned the bedroom this morning."

Juris nodded contently. "I spoke to Lord Deminas earlier; he seems rather pleased with you so far. Told me you were doing your work properly, and you listened well."

Meya's cheeks burned up. "That's... That's pretty nice of him to say."

Juris smiled. "I'm glad he seems to like you. I was afraid that after the previous maid, he'd be rather harsh."

"Jaimy?" Meya asked.

Juris looked slightly taken aback. "Yes, Jaimy. Did someone tell you about her?"

Meya's face reddened further. *I forgot he never told me her name. Will we get in trouble for gossiping? Then again, he did tell me the Lord dropped her from the balcony.* Trying to retake her composure, she replied, "Yeah, we talked a bit about her. Seems she wasn't here that long."

"She lasted about three weeks," Juris stated and he shook his head. He took a bite from his piece of bread and Meya also continued her meal. After a few mouthfuls, Juris turned his attention back to Meya. "How do you find your room-mates?"

Meya swallowed the contents of her mouth. "Oh, they are alright. Lea seems quite caring, and Nina is especially sweet. Winnie seems a bit distant though, but that might be because of her..." She stuck out the tip of her tongue.

Juris cringed a little. "Yeah, I still remember when that happened. Poor girl..." He shook his head. "She had quite the crush on the Lord. No matter what he did, she would twist it in her head, one way or another, until she believed it was a sign of affection. That day, when he cut out her tongue... I think it was then that she finally realised that he did not love her." He emptied his cup. "She started to behave after that, became quite docile too." He shook his head again. "If only she had acted like that sooner, then she would still be able to speak."

Meya played with the last bit of her meal. "Well, she can still talk a little. Though, it seems only her sister is able to make any sense of it."

"Yeah, though I sometimes wonder how much she actually understands and how much she just guesses."

Their conversation fell silent and they both finished the remainder of their meals. "I better get back to work," Meya said as she stood up.

Juris rose too. "Same here. Take care, Meya."

~*~

Meya had retrieved some cleaning supplies from the hallway closet before she headed to the door leading to the lord's chambers and knocked. To her surprise, Lord Deminas' voice boomed from the other side.

"You may enter."

Meya bit her lip and took a deep breath through her nose. *Come on, don't fear him.* She opened the door and walked in. Lord Deminas stood by the window, looking over the mountain valley below. *Was he waiting for me?* Dread washed over her and she felt weak at the knees.

"Is there anything I can do for my Lord?" she asked. As the words left her lips, she already regretted trying to please him.

He turned around, the slightest hint of a smile gracing his face.

Meya swallowed, her heart rate increasing rapidly. The lord's eyes seemed to glimmer, and she was unsure of what it meant.

"As a matter of fact, yes, you can." He walked over to her, but instead of stopping in front of her, he stepped behind her.

Meya turned her head in an attempt to see what he was doing, but he remained out of sight, even as she spun around a bit. The moment his hands touched her shoulders, Meya jumped slightly and her entire body stiffened.

"Shhh," the Lord whispered in her ear. "What is it that you're so afraid of?"

His hands gently slid off her shoulders, down her arms, to her sides. Goosebumps rose all over her body and a cold shiver ran up her spine.

"Answer me," he said softly, yet stern.

Meya gulped. She tried to form words, but her mind was hazed by the fact that the lord's hands were still slowly moving over her body—they had now reached her hips.

"One..." He started to count slowly. "Two..."

Panic washed over Meya. *What is he going to do? When is he going to do it? On ten? On five? Three?* "I...I—" she started but couldn't find any other words. Her vision blurred and she felt unsteady on her feet. "I...I think I'm going to—" Her knees buckled, but Lord Deminas caught her.

He sighed deeply as he gently positioned her down on the floor, her back against his front. "Calm down; my touch doesn't hurt, does it?" His hands were holding her upright by her sides.

"N-no, my Lord," she uttered softly, still dizzy.

"Are you afraid of my touch?"

Meya swallowed and closed her eyes in an attempt to rid herself of the dizziness. "I am, my Lord. Sorry, m—" She didn't finish her sentence as his grip tightened and a low growl entered her ear.

"Why do you keep apologising?"

Confused, a few tears slipped from her eyes. "I...I'm afraid of being p-punished, if I... if I—" She swallowed. "If I don't please you, my Lord."

"What do you think I would do to you?"

His voice was so close to her ear that it made her shudder, and for a moment, Meya was unable to breathe. After taking a second to focus on her breathing, she calmed down a bit and answered, "The other servants, they... They talk of punishments ranging from being denied food, being whipped, beaten, or...or—" She closed her eyes and took a few deep breaths. "Or having their tongues cut out."*Or eyes gouged out, or fingers removed*, her mind added.

The lord let out a chuckle.

The short sound paralysed her. She sat there, rigid, on the floor with her back against a sadist, his firm hands holding her in place.

"Do you think you deserve to be punished in any of the ways you just mentioned?" he whispered into her ear.

"I...I'd hope not, my Lord," Meya replied in an undertone.

"I didn't ask what you are hoping for; I asked what you are thinking."

*Is this a trick question*? she wondered, thinking back to him asking if it was hard to strip and show her body to him. She closed her eyes tightly, cleared her mind and thought of what would just have to be the correct answer. "No, my Lord."*Please be the correct answer, please, please, please*, she cried inside.

"Why not?" he asked softly, his hands moving up to her shoulders and resting there.

Meya slowly breathed in and out a few times before answering, "I do as I am told, I perform my chores to the best of my abilities, and I try to always be respectful towards you, my Lord."

"That is very true, so perhaps you don't deserve punishment."

Meya frowned. *Deserve?*

"You're just forgetting one thing though..." He sounded so close now that she was very sure she could feel his lips gently caress her ear. "What if I just enjoy punishing people...?"

Meya closed her eyes, her stomach was in a knot and she was unsure if she was going to pass out or not.

"Are you scared?" he whispered in her other ear now, a slight hint of amusement in his voice.

"I...I am, my Lord," she uttered. She had to fight to keep steady as the world spun around her.

"Good." With that said, he moved away from her and stood up.

Meya had to place her hands on the ground to support herself from not falling over. With his presence gone behind her, the dizziness started to fade. She opened her eyes and saw the lord standing in front of her, observing her.

"Get up, we're going for a walk."

"Y-yes, my Lord," Meya squeaked. She got back on her feet, though she was still a bit wobbly. *Am I in trouble?* she asked herself. She was terrified of where this walk was going to lead her.

Lord Deminas stepped out of the room. "Follow me."

# Ten

After a long walk that also went several stairs down, they stopped in front of a large, iron door.

The dungeons.

Meya trembled, her mind in complete chaos.

"I find it amusing… I have yet to do anything to you, yet you're so afraid, I can smell it." Lord Deminas turned to look at Meya, who was staring at the door. He grabbed her chin and she went stiff. Her fear-filled eyes met his cold ones, though there was a slight shimmer of amusement in them. "We're going to have some fun, you can trust me on that."

Meya felt her heart beat in her throat, her lips and mouth dry, yet her eyes were wet. "Please, my Lord, don't hurt me," she pleaded.

Lord Deminas grinned maliciously. "I can't promise anything." He let go of her chin and reached for the heavy key-chain hanging from his belt.

~*~

They walked past several cells; almost all of them were empty, save for a few holding dirty, battle-worn men.

*Prisoners of war*, Meya thought and as she did so, images of the bodies she had seen on her way east flashed through her mind. The bodies of invaders—or at least what had been left of them. She shivered. Part of her pitied the captives for what their future would hold, but another part of her did not, as the men that had killed her family and destroyed her happy home had most likely been invaders too.

They walked to the back of the dungeon where there was a large room used for interrogations—also known as the torture chamber.

To Meya's surprise, there was a man hanging in chains in the middle of the room. She could not see who it was, for his head hung low, and the lamplight caused shadows to shroud his face. She could, however, see that he was in a bad shape.

His entire body was covered with cuts and bruises, some still oozing blood. The large bloodstain on the front of his drawers made Meya's stomach lurch and it took her all her focus to not throw up. Whatever was underneath those drawers—or what was left of them—had to be one hell of hurt.

Meya turned away from the man. "My Lord…"

"Does this sight really trouble you?" he said, amused.

"What happened to him, my Lord?" Meya uttered, still trying to keep her lunch down.

"I had some fun punishing this man for his… misbehaviour."

Meya looked up at Lord Deminas and was surprised to see his face filled with emotions, though they seemed to be mostly that of delight.

*Is he going to torture me too?* Meya wondered, fearfully. She turned around to look at the man again; his face was still hidden in shadows. The number of cuts and the blood on his drawers made her wonder, and she dared to speak out loud, "Is-is he going to live, my Lord?"

The Lord's malicious grin broadened. "Do you care for this man, then?"

Meya looked from the man to the Lord, and back at the man again. She thought of how best to reply. "Should I, my Lord? I fear I do not recognise him and as I do not know of his wrongdoings, I can't judge over his fate."

Lord Deminas laughed loudly, sending waves of anxiety down Meya's spine. "You give such perfect answers." He walked over to Meya and grabbed her chin. "Let's see if you're able to become my little pet." His eyes bored into hers, and for a moment, Meya feared that he saw into her very soul, but then he let go and walked away.

*I'm doomed*, Meya's mind echoed. Adrenaline rushed through her body as it prepared to flee. She was unsure of where to, or even how, but her body seemed very set on that particular action.

Lord Deminas went up behind the man with an oil lamp in his left hand. He lifted the man's head up and held the lamp in front of his face so that Meya could take a good look.

She did.

As she realised who was hanging there, in that particular state, Meya broke down and fell to her knees. She was very confused and as tears started to roll down her cheeks, her mind only repeated two words. "How...? Why...?" She uttered the words so softly, the lord almost didn't hear them—almost.

He let go of the man's head and walked over to Meya. "You didn't expect this, did you? Tell me your thoughts." He licked his lips as his eager eyes stared into her wide-open ones.

Meya's gaze shifted back and forth from the lord to the man, as the lord's expression scared her. Still, she was busy trying to comprehend the situation. "My...my Lord, why is he here?" she managed to ask.

"Take a guess."

Meya swallowed and she looked back at the man. Though his face was shrouded in darkness again, she now knew who he was, and thus her mind filled in the shadows with his features.

*Because he beat me up, because he raped me*, she thought as her gaze shifted to the bloodstain on the slaver's drawers. *Did he cut his prick off for that?* she wondered, and she looked back at Lord Deminas.

"Well?" he said, still waiting for an answer.

"I...I don't think I can believe my Lord would find a crime against a mere servant enough to... to..." She swallowed. "To capture and torture her ra—" Meya closed up, unable to speak the word. She looked away from the lord, feeling more shame now than those two times stripping in front of him combined.

"Say it."

Meya closed her eyes tightly, tears running down her face. She breathed in deeply several times and then said, very slowly, "Rapist."

"Consider yourself lucky that I do not condone acts of such a barbaric nature. Also, know that you weren't the only one—and had I not brought this man here, the last one." He grabbed Meya's chin and made her look up, facing him in all her sobbing glory. "Consider this man a thief if you will. He can also be accused of selling me damaged goods. As I am not impertinent, I shall attempt to fix them instead of replacing them. Just be warned though: if something that is broken can't be fixed, I *will* eventually replace it."

Meya cringed inside at being viewed that way, but part of her realised this was perhaps a nice gesture. "Th-thank you, my Lord," she whispered.

A pleased grunt left his lips and he placed a comforting hand on her head.

"May… may I ask something, my Lord?"

He seemed to think this over for a moment before answering, "Yes, you may."

"What happened to his… his…" She hesitated. "His crotch?"

Lord Deminas let out a chuckle. "I gave the man some room in his trousers. He lost a lot of blood; I doubt he will be amongst us much longer if left this way."

Meya bit her lip. "What will be done with him now, my Lord?"

He grinned. "He will die, of course."

The hairs all over her skin rose up.

"Seeing as you were able to kill the man that had *tried* to rape you, do you wish to do the same to the one that succeeded?" The amusement in his eyes was hard not to see.

Meya's mind was in pieces; she had never expected that question. She had had some issues dealing with the fact that she had killed a man, and it had taken her several months to find peace in her actions. If she hadn't done it, he would have killed her instead at the end of whatever else he could have imagined doing to her. So where did that leave the slaver? Sure, he had hurt her on several levels, but she was still alive. At this moment in time, her life was in no danger, so was it right to take his now?

"I…I don't think I can, my Lord," Meya said softly. She wanted to apologise but was afraid of being scolded for it.

"Very well," Lord Deminas stated emotionlessly. He turned away and walked over to the back of the chamber where he picked up a bucket filled with water. He dumped the contents over the slaver, who regained consciousness with a scream. The lord took a large knife from the table beside him and grabbed the slaver by his hair. "Meya, please stand in front of him, in the light where he can clearly see you."

Though wobbly on her feet, Meya got up and did as she was told. Her heart raced in her chest, her mouth dry. Beads of sweat dripped down her back, causing her to shiver.

"H-hey, y-you," the slaver muttered, a little stream of saliva mixed with blood leaking from the side of his mouth.

"Do you have anything to say to this young woman?" Lord Deminas asked the slaver as he pressed the blade against the man's throat.

"I…I'm sorry!" he squealed like a pig. "I'm sorry f-for hurting you, for t-touching you! P-please, I—" He didn't get to finish his pleading for Lord

Deminas pulled his head back and slit his throat in one smooth move. Blood gushed out of the wound and some of it splattered onto Meya's apron and face.

Lord Deminas cleaned the blade and placed it back onto the table. "Come, we're done here. I'll have someone clean up this mess later."

Meya felt like she was dreaming; everything seemed unreal. *What just happened?* she asked herself.

The lord waited for her in the hallway. He was about to call for her again when Meya finally moved towards him, albeit slowly.

~*~

Meya followed Lord Deminas back to his chambers in a trance-like state. She was barely aware of the lord approaching a servant on their way back and giving him several instructions. The young man bowed and hurried away.

As Lord Deminas started to walk again, Meya followed automatically. Her mind was filled with questions regarding the lord's intentions and how she should feel about what had just happened. Even though her head was so crowded with thoughts, somewhere in the back of her mind, she was still able to wonder what the lord had just asked that servant. Although Meya followed the lord with her head low, she still noticed the fearful looks of the servants they passed. She pondered why but discarded the question after spotting the bloodstains that covered her white apron.

*But it's not my blood*, she comforted herself.

Meya nearly collided with the lord's back when he stopped in front of the door leading to his chambers. She moved to follow him inside and, to her surprise, the Lord held the door for her.

A chill shook her. *Why...?*

Confused, she turned to face Lord Deminas. He observed her, his right arm in front of his stomach while his elbow rested on his wrist and his fingers stroked his goatee.

For some reason, this made blood rush to Meya's face. Before her cheeks matched her hair, she managed to utter, "M-my Lord..." She wanted to ask, *What now?* but was afraid that would sound inappropriate.

To her relief, Lord Deminas spoke. "You're covered in blood; go to the bathroom and clean yourself. Get rid of those filthy clothes, too." With that said, he walked over to his desk and sat down, seemingly no longer interested in her.

Baffled, Meya started to walk towards the hallway.

"Where are you going?" the lord's voice bellowed through the room.

71

Meya cringed. "I…I was going to the servants' ba—"

"You're not going anywhere looking like that. Use my bathroom."

Meya curtsied, uttered a thanks, and hurried away in utter confusion.

~*~

After cleaning her face and neck, Meya looked at herself in the mirror. She was only wearing her undergarments. *There's no blood on them, would it be alright if I kept them on?*

She bit her lip. Considering the lord had made her strip two times in front of him already, she was almost certain that he would prefer seeing her naked. Still, she didn't dare walk back into the sitting room naked without being specifically ordered to do so.

*I don't want him to get the wrong idea about me... I've still got* some *decency left*, she thought with determination.

She turned around, took a deep breath, and walked back. Before she even knocked on the bedroom door, her heart had almost doubled its pace. When she got an answer to her knocking, it skipped a beat. *Why is he in there?* her mind screamed as it filled with panic.

She opened the door and entered cautiously. The room was lit only with lamplight, and Meya was unsure if this made it look cosy or ominous. The lord was but a mere shade sitting on edge of the bed.

"My Lord," she spoke.

"Why are you still dressed?" The lord's voice was low and dark.

Meya hesitated a moment before answering, "I…I… There was no blood on them, my Lord. I…I thought—"

"Remove them."

Meya opened her mouth to answer, but no sound passed. She swallowed and finally uttered, "As you wish, my Lord." Fear almost paralysed her, but she managed to remove the remaining pieces of clothing. The moment the last piece fell to the floor, the lord spoke again.

"Come here."

Meya trembled and her stomach was in knots. She feared that she was going to pass out, but she still walked up to the lord and stood in front of him.

"Turn around."

She complied.

"It seems your cuts are healing quite well. Good." He stood up and his body briefly brushed against hers, making her head whirl. "Come, I was just

72

informed that the water is ready. I want to wash away the stench of that filthy animal, and you will join me."

Meya's eyes widened in shock. *He wants to take a bath with me, again?*

"Do you have any experience in giving massages?" Lord Deminas asked as he headed into the bathroom, leaving Meya frozen to the floor in the bedroom.

It took her a moment to snap out of it.

"A…a little, my Lord," she stammered as she slowly made her way into the bathroom.

He huffed in reply but gave no further response. He plugged the large bath and started to fill it up using the pump standing beside it. After a few gushes of cold water, hot water poured out. It didn't take long before the room started to steam up.

Meya just stood awkwardly next to the bath, feeling out of place. *I'm the servant, shouldn't filling up the bath be my job?* she wondered.

Lord Deminas seemed to notice her discomfort. "Why don't you make yourself useful and light all the lamps in here."

"Yes, my Lord," she said, and got to work. It was already starting to get gloomy outside so a little light was welcome.

Lord Deminas was still pumping the water when Meya finished illuminating the room. The bath was almost full and Meya couldn't help voice her thoughts.

"My Lord, would you like me to finish filling the bath so that you can—" She didn't finish her sentence, for the lord had turned around.

He glared at her, a slight hint of lust in his eyes and beads of sweat on his brow.

Meya swallowed and wondered if she was in trouble. To her relief, the lord let go of the pump and moved away. Meya kept looking at him, but when he started to undress, she quickly averted her eyes and started to pump. *Damn, no wonder he normally has a servant doing this for him*, she thought. After only a few pumps, she was panting heavily. She didn't want to show Lord Deminas how hard this was for her, so she kept going. The effort soon brought her into a trance-like state and she didn't even notice when the lord slipped into the bath.

"That will be enough," he said.

Meya didn't process his words until two pumps later. Winded, she leaned on the metal to relax and regain her breath. When she looked up at the lord, she saw him grin slyly.

"You can consider yourself lucky that filling my bath isn't your daily duty."

"Thank… you… my Lord," she panted.

73

Lord Deminas moved to the right side of the bath. "Come."

With a little effort, Meya released herself from the pump's embrace and stepped into the hot water. She couldn't help but relax from the warmth that spread through her body as she sat down opposite Lord Deminas. As she leaned backwards, she closed her eyes; the water washed over her face, removing the droplets of sweat that had covered it. Relieved, she surfaced again, and when she opened her eyes, her heart skipped a beat.

Lord Deminas was looking at her very intently—or rather, at her breasts.

Meya wiped her face with her hands and removed a lock of hair that was in front of her left eye. Lord Deminas was still ogling her body, his eyes now focused on her abdomen.

*What is he doing?* Her face was red from embarrassment. *Has he no shame?* She bit her lip. *How do I make him stop?*

She was afraid of getting in trouble for even coughing to get his attention. Not knowing what to do, she just waited and felt very, very uncomfortable as she saw his eyes go further down, before going back up again.

*I don't like this.* Fear was nibbling away at her mind, stiffening her body as it suppressed the urge to jump out of the bath and run away. *He's just looking now, but what if that's not enough?*

Lord Deminas finally locked his eyes onto Meya's and his grin widened before he continued what he had been doing, his next stop being her breasts again.

Meya's mouth opened slightly in a silent gasp. *Does he think this is a game?*

He looked at her again, raised a brow—though the smirk didn't leave his face—and lowered his eyes again to gaze at her body.

*He does!* The fear that had held her in its grip moments before was replaced with anger. *How rude!* Before she even realised it, words started to tumble out of her mouth. "Oh, come—" The lord's grip on her throat was tight and came so suddenly that even Meya's thoughts were silenced for a moment.

"Is there a problem?" he hissed into her ear.

*Why yes, there is!* her brain screamed. The pressure on her throat increased. *Oh God, why couldn't I just keep silent?* she wondered as her initial fear came back tenfold.

"Answer me," the lord's voice was low and threatening.

"Can't… breathe," Meya uttered as stars started to cloud her vision.

The lord let go of her and she sank into the water.

She could still feel his fingers around her throat, and she wanted to massage it, but she was afraid this would only trigger another reaction out of

74

him. Instead, she just sat there, catching her breath, looking down into the water to avoid having to look at him. *Oh God, what do I do now?*

"You still haven't answered my question," he said darkly.

*He's playing with me*, Meya thought. *That look before, he* wanted *me to react.* Anger returned slightly, but the nagging of her sore throat ensured that fear remained supreme. She bit her lip. *Will I reply like a good little slave or do I dare stand my ground?*

The water splashed as he moved closer to her. His fingers gripped her chin and made her look him in the eyes. The single raised brow said enough.

Deciding she was in trouble either way, she gathered all her courage and spoke slowly, "You...you were looking at me like...like a boy who...who..." She swallowed and hesitated for a moment, wondering if she really wanted to say the next bit. "Who sees a woman naked for the first time." She closed her eyes, fearing a slap in the face. "I...I just thought... I...I don't think that... It's not very Lord-like."

As his fingers left her chin, she braced herself for some form of pain. Instead, she heard a deep laugh. Lord Deminas was *laughing*. Loudly. Carefully, she opened her eyes and looked up at him. He was still going at it, one hand even on his stomach.

*What the hell*? She was utterly confused.

The laughter finally died down and the lord glared down at Meya.

Her blood seemed to freeze and goosebumps rose all over her skin despite the hot water. *That's it, now I'm dead.*

"You've got more guts than I thought." He gripped her chin again. "I do love playing games; however, if I wish to simply stare at you like I've never seen a woman before, I will do so. Do you understand?"

"Y-yes, my Lord," Meya croaked, her heart pounding heavily in her chest.

"I don't want you to get the wrong idea about your role here after today. You are still my slave, my property. I can and *will* do with you whatever I please. You will respect me and my decisions. I only want your opinion when I ask for it. Do you understand?"

Hurt, Meya's voice broke as she replied, "Y-yes, my Lord."

"Good." He let go of her. "Now, let's see how good your massaging skills are." He turned around, presenting his back to her.

Meya straightened herself and mentally slapped her cheeks. *It's alright, you're alright. It could have been worse.* She took a few deeps breaths and warmed up her hands, loosening the joints. "Which part does my Lord want massaged?" she asked meekly.

"You can start with the neck and shoulders."

Trembling slightly, she positioned herself behind Lord Deminas and started to massage his shoulders.

# Eleven

The task itself wasn't too demanding; Lord Deminas' neck and shoulders weren't very tense and his skin was quite supple. However, Meya was sitting on her knees in hot water that reached to just below her breasts—it only took a minute or two before little droplets of sweat started to slide down her face. As she massaged the lord's shoulders and neck, she couldn't help but wonder how he could be so void of tension. She had expected him to have some stress knots, some rigidity in the muscles, but there was nothing.

Lord Deminas simply fully relaxed under her kneading and rubbing hands.

"Lower," was the first thing he said after a while.

Meya complied and shifted her hands to his mid-back. Despite his supple skin, she had some difficulty performing the massage techniques she knew—she was used to having oil to make it easier for the skin and underlying muscle to glide through her hands.

"My Lord…," she started, hesitating for a moment. "This would probably work better with some oil." She wanted to ask if there was any and if he wanted that, but her lips failed to continue.

"This will do," he stated. "However, I will keep it in mind for another time."

Meya couldn't see it, but she was quite certain that Lord Deminas was grinning.

Several minutes later, the lord spoke again. "Lower."

Meya moved her hands further down, submerging them in the hot water, which had already given her a very flushed face, but having her hands so close to the lord's buttocks made it even worse.

*Is the skin on his chest also like this?* she wondered as she massaged his lower back.

Her eyes moved over his strong arms and she licked her lips. She had gotten a good look at his front once and she couldn't deny that his physique was highly attractive. She had to suppress the urge to simply cling to his back, wrap her arms around him and explore his chest with her hands.

*Oh God, bad Meya!* She mentally shook her head in an attempt to rid herself of the improper desires. Still, the memories of the lord's front plagued her mind. The fact that her hands were still kneading his skin didn't help much in quenching the thoughts in her head, either. *I guess there's only one place I didn't get a good look at...* Her cheeks burned up even more and she bit her lip. There had been a few opportunities, but she had been raised a decent girl, and so she had looked away.

Lost in her own thoughts, Meya's hands were no longer just on Lord Deminas' lower back. They went up to his neck and shoulders, returned to his back, and then made a detour to his sides and upper arms. She didn't even notice that her breathing was becoming heavier in the process.

Lord Deminas *did* notice.

"Meya," he said slowly.

"Yes, my Lord?" she purred, massaging his shoulders.

"Are you enjoying this?"

Her hands slowed down and finally came to a halt. "I...I suppose I am, my Lord," she admitted, not daring to lie to him. He turned around and Meya moved backwards slightly. *Oh God, what now?* Her heart pounded heavily in her chest as anxiety swept over her.

"In what way are you enjoying it?" the lord asked, a grin appearing ever so slightly, accompanied by a glimmer of amusement in his eyes.

Meya blinked, not fully understanding the question. "I...I guess I just find it an enjoyable task, my Lord."

"Are you cold?"

Not expecting such a question, Meya frowned. She could clearly feel droplets of sweat sliding down her face, so she was quite certain the lord must be able to see them. "Not at all, my Lord," she answered.

"I thought so. Your flushed complexion and perspiration tell me that you're hot, however..." His eyes went down her body and lingered on her breasts for a moment before returning to her face. "Your nipples are erect."

Blood rushed to her face and she bit the inside of her lip.

The lord moved closer, placing his head next to hers, and whispered in her ear, "Are you aroused?"

Meya was frozen in place by pure shame. She didn't dare to admit that she was, for she didn't want to voice the desires she had felt only moments ago when her hands had slid over his masculine form. *How could I have even felt that way after what the slaver did?*

*Maybe because he tortured the swine and killed him in front of you.*

Her cheeks heated up further. *Such things shouldn't be arousing.*

*It is when they're done because someone cares about you and wants to protect you. And, let's be honest: the Lord is highly attractive. If it weren't for—*
The sound of a single chuckle interrupted her internal discussion.

"You do realise that your silence says more than words..."

She opened her mouth to speak, but not a single sound came out.

Lord Deminas moved back so that he could observe her better. He grinned deviously as his left hand moved forward and gently landed on the skin just above her hip.

Meya drew in a sharp breath and her heart rate increased a bit—even though it was already quite high.

He moved his right hand in front of her face, droplets of water dripping from it, and caressed her lips. She parted them slightly, unable to stop herself. The fingers of his left hand slowly went up her side, his nails scraping her skin, sending shivers up her spine and leaving goosebumps in its wake.

"You can be honest with me," he said, looking into her eyes intently.

She sank back into the water in a miserable attempt to get away from his prying gaze. Lord Deminas moved closer, parted her legs with his knee, and smoothly took up the space that was formed between them. She gasped as his fingers entwined themselves in her hair and gripped it tightly—enough to ensure she wouldn't fully submerge, but not enough to actually hurt.

Fearing her lust could be seen written all over her face, she looked away and closed her eyes. Two fingers of his left hand circled her breasts, the nails prickling her senses even more than if he had used only his fingertips.

*What am I doing? Why am I allowing him to do this?*

*Because you like it*, her mind answered, and at the same time, the lord's fingers found their way to her erect left nipple and gently squeezed it.

Meya half gasped, half moaned in response.

"Are you aroused?" Lord Deminas asked again in a low voice.

*Yes, I am,* she thought, *but I'm not going to say it.*

He squeezed her nipple again, just a little harder this time. Her response was the same—though louder.

"If you won't tell me yes or no..." He pulled her head up, next to his own. "I will simply have to check it." His breath on her ear made her shiver, but when his tongue slowly trailed the outer ridge of her ear and at the same time his fingers shifted to her right nipple and pinched it, she couldn't stop a loud moan from escaping her throat.

He lowered her again so that he could get a good look at his servant: Meya's cheeks were bright red, her eyes closed, her breathing heavy. He let out a few low chuckles.

Meya's mind was in disarray. She couldn't think clearly anymore.

Lord Deminas' hand slowly slid down from her breast, his nails trailing over her chest, her stomach.

Meya's eyes popped open as his hand went down to her nether regions. Yet, he skipped it and instead stopped about halfway down her inner thigh.

"Shhh," the lord shushed as he noticed her tense up. "I'm not going to hurt you."

Meya was still breathing heavily, but part of her arousal was now replaced with fear. *What is he going to do? Do I want that?* she asked herself. *Sure, I'm turned on—a lot—but am I ready to actually have sex? Do I even want to give in to my lust to that degree? And to him?*

"If you want me to stop, all you need to do is say so." His fingers crept back up until they rested against her warmth. He placed one finger on her left outer-labia, and another on the right. Slowly, he started to move them back and forth, his thumb resting on her Venus mound. A part of her wanted to stop him but didn't dare. Another part of her couldn't help but admit that it felt good. *Damn it*, she thought. No longer wanting to resist, she surrendered and relaxed. Lord Deminas was still holding her by her hair, and this was the only thing now that kept her from submerging completely in the warm water.

"Do you want this?" he asked softly as he kept moving his fingers up and down. "Be honest."

Meya swallowed. It took her a moment, but she managed to answer, "I...I do..."

His fingers stopped moving. They were still resting on her outer labia, but his middle finger was now hovering enticingly between them. Slowly, his thumb started to caress the hood of her clitoris.

Meya took a deep breath and held it in as she bit her lip. The lord's middle finger touched down and slipped between the folds of her inner labia. Meya arched her back in response. His finger kept moving back and forth whilst his thumb continued to stimulate her, drawing soft moans from her lips.

"You're very slippery down there," he said in a low voice. "So let me ask you one more time..." He pulled her up by her hair until her face was level with his. "Are you aroused?"

"Y-yes... my Lord," Meya answered between pants.

"Are you enjoying this?"

"I...I am... my Lord."

He grinned broadly. "Do you want more?" He increased the pressure and speed of his thumb, and the sudden wave of pleasure made Meya moan loudly. Not receiving an answer, Lord Deminas stopped. "Well?"

"Y-yes, my Lord. P-please," Meya begged.

"Look at me and answer me again."

Ashamed, she wanted to avoid his gaze, but she managed to look him straight in the eyes. "Yes, please," she panted, "my Lord."

"Very well." With a devilish smile, he stimulated her clitoris for about ten seconds before pulling his hand back and letting go of her hair.

Not expecting the sudden release, Meya fully submerged. She came back up, spitting out water and taking a gasp of air as she removed the many locks of hair out of her face. To her surprise, she saw the lord stepping out of the bath, his back towards her. Utterly confused, she simply stared at him.

"Wash up and get out, the food is probably getting cold." He wrapped a towel around his waist, barely concealing his erection, and walked out of the bathroom.

Meya watched him leave. Even after the door had closed behind him, she didn't move. It took a while before she realised what had happened. She was still very much aroused, a little angry, quite disappointed, and ashamed beyond words. Flustered, she started to clean herself thoroughly. The slickness between her legs made her bite her lip in utmost embarrassment, and she tried to ensure that not a trace of it remained before stepping out of the water.

As she dried her hair, she heard the supper bell in the distance. *He sure has a good sense of timing*, she thought grimly. Having nothing to wear, she wrapped the towel around her torso. She walked up to the bedroom door but stopped there. *What now?* She bit her lip as she imagined the lord ravishing her as soon as she stepped over the threshold.

She mentally shook her head. It troubled her that the thought both aroused and frightened her. She took a few deep breaths, lightly slapped her cheeks, and straightened her back.

*Stop worrying over things that are beyond your control,* she lectured herself. *Nina is right, he is right: you're a slave now.* A chill went up her spine. *If he wishes to have sex with you, you don't really have much of a choice.* The previous arousal faded away and the lord's words echoed in her mind.

*"I can and will do with you whatever I please."*

She wrapped her arms around herself. *Still, he actually went and captured the slaver. Tortured and killed him even. He seems rather against rape...* She thought back to what he had said about the slaver's actions, and his reply when she had told him of her fear of him assaulting her. *No... I shouldn't be afraid of him doing that.* She swallowed as her mind returned to what had just transpired in the bath. *I think he takes way too much pleasure in making me want him, making me beg for him.* She huffed. *And to think I actually gave in, too!*

She took another deep breath and checked if the towel was covering her properly.

*Alright...* She swallowed. *Let's go.*

She knocked on the bedroom door. After three times, there was still no answer, so she went inside. The door leading to the sitting room was slightly ajar, the flickering of the hearth visible on the stone floor. Meya hesitated to walk straight in, so she held the knob as she knocked on the wood.

"You may come in, Meya," the lord said.

She pushed the door open, blushing slightly as she noticed him staring at her from his seat. It was bad enough to be only clad in a towel, but the memory of what had just transpired in the bath was still quite fresh, too.

"What took you so long?" he asked.

Meya searched for words. "I...I..." She lowered her eyes. "You told me to wash, my Lord... So I did."

Lord Deminas stood up and walked over to her. He cupped her chin, making her look up at him. "I didn't realise you were so dirty that washing yourself would take that long."

Blood rushed to Meya's cheeks, shame setting her face on fire. "I...I," she stammered, but she gave up on saying anything as the lord started to chuckle.

He released her and walked back to his seat. There were several covered dishes on the desk, along with two cups and a jug. He filled the cups, the burgundy liquid clearly wine.

"Come here." He gestured for Meya to come closer and she did.

*Two cups?* Meya wondered. *He wants me to dine with him?*

"I have arranged enough food for two," Lord Deminas stated. He picked up one of the cups, swirling the contents gently. "And good wine." He stared into Meya's eyes intensely as he sipped. "However…" There was an ominous shimmer in his eyes. "I know of a way to make this wine even better."

Meya swallowed. *Why do I feel like he's not referring to my company?* She wetted her lips. "What do you mean, my Lord?"

A sly smile tugged at his lips and he placed the cup back on the desk before turning and opening one of the drawers.

Meya tilted her head slightly, both curious and anxious as to what he was retrieving. The moment she saw the glint of metal, her heart skipped a beat. Without realising it, she took a step back.

In the lord's hand rested a small, silver blade.

*That's no eating utensil!* Meya's mind screamed, and she took another step back. *He's going to kill me!* Her mind was no longer thinking rationally, her instincts kicking in instead. As Lord Deminas approached her, her eyes scanned the room for possible exits. When he was just an arm's length away, she turned around and dashed towards the door.

After merely two steps, she fell roughly to her knees, the lord's grip firm on the towel wrapped around her body.

"My, my," he said amusedly. "Where were you going?"

Frightened, she turned her head to look at the lord. The silver blade was in his right hand, his left holding her towel tightly. Her heart raced in her chest, adrenaline coursing through her veins. *He's close enough to stab me.*

He raised a brow, still awaiting an answer. "Well?" He pulled her up by the towel until she stood on her feet again. Not releasing the fabric, he stepped in front of her, his face mere inches from Meya's. "Answer me."

Meya struggled internally. She could easily kick him in the crotch and make a run for it, but then what? If, on the other hand, she remained still, would he kill her? Her eyes darted left and right, mirroring the thoughts in her mind. The lord's free hand moved to her face, the silver reflecting the flames from the hearth. Sheer terror paralysed her, her eyes fixed on the weapon.

He traced a finger over her lips, the cool silver tantalizingly close to her skin. "Last chance. Speak."

Meya opened her mouth, but it took a few seconds before any sound managed to escape her throat. "Don't kill me," she squeaked. Having found her voice, she swallowed and pleaded, "Please, don't kill me, my Lord!"

Lord Deminas chuckled. "You're amusing. What makes you think I would want to kill you?"

Her gaze shifted from the blade to his face, and back to the blade again. Her lower lip trembled, but she didn't need to speak.

"This is what frightened you so?" Lord Deminas released Meya, took a step back, and observed the blade. He looked up from the weapon to glance at her.

She shook, her arms wrapped tightly around herself. Realising he wanted an answer, she nodded meekly.

He smiled roguishly. "So just because I have a blade, you assume I'd want to kill you with it?"

Meya nodded again, repressing the urge to take a step away from him, or to even run out of the room entirely.

"You do realise that if I wanted to kill you, I could do so with my bare hands."

She swallowed and her feet acted on their own accord, taking a step back.

"Such a well-behaved, hard-working servant... Now, why would I want to kill you?" He took two steps in her direction.

"I...I don't know... m-my Lord," Meya stammered. Unable to stop herself, she took several more steps away from his threatening form.

Lord Deminas moved towards her, shaking his head. His eyes gleamed with mischief, the grin tugging at his lips slowly becoming bigger. Just before Meya's back met the stone wall, he placed his hands upon it either side of her, locking her in. Her eyes widened with fright, panic clearly visible in them. She contemplated ducking below his arm and making a run for it, but the lord pressed his body against hers, pinning her against the wall.

She whimpered and closed her eyes, turning her face away from his. "Please, I don't want to die..."

The lord's fingers enclosed her chin and turned her face back towards his. Meya opened her eyes, her curiosity of what he was going to do stronger than her fear—or heightened because of it. To her surprise, she saw him lean in a fraction of a second before his hot lips touched hers.

Her already chaotic mind seemed to shatter. Every thought of the impending doom that had plagued it mere moments ago was now silent. His lips moved against hers hungrily, and without knowing why, her lips answered just as passionately. She closed her eyes, lost in ecstasy. When his tongue asked for entrance, she opened her mouth, allowing it, but to her surprise, he pulled away. Her eyes fluttered open, confused by his actions.

Lord Deminas smirked. "Nice to see you're enjoying yourself."

Meya flushed red, her mind unable to form any coherent thoughts.

84

"Now come here, and don't think about running off." He walked back to his desk.

She licked her lips and swallowed. The feeling of his mouth against hers haunted her, clouding her mind. *What does he want from me?* She stood beside the desk, her knees a little weak from all the conflicting emotions. Gazing at nothing in particular, she didn't even notice Lord Deminas taking her left hand.

"Now don't move," he said. He held her hand above one of the wine cups, his fingers wrapped tightly around her wrist. With his free hand, he lowered the silver blade to her delicate flesh.

Meya was suddenly brought back to reality as the cool metal pressed against the side of her palm. She shrieked in pain, but the lord held her firmly. The silver sliced through her skin with ease, blood flowing from the cut. She whimpered, tears streaming down her cheeks. He held her hand above the cup so that the crimson droplets mixed with the burgundy wine. It was silent for a while, aside from the constant dripping of blood and the occasional crackle coming from the fireplace.

Seemingly satisfied with the amount of blood, Lord Deminas lifted Meya's hand away from the cup. To her shock, he brought it to his lips, and she stared at him with wide-open eyes as he licked at her cut, his saliva stinging the wound. With most of the blood gone, he turned his attention to the silver blade. A little bit of blood stained the metal, and he licked it clean. He locked his gaze with Meya's as he turned the blade, his tongue now sliding over the sharp edge.

Meya winced, her heart constricting in her chest. A small droplet of his blood slipped down the silver edge, and he placed the blade on the desk. He raised Meya's hand back to his face and placed his mouth over the cut. Her breathing hitched. The wound stung, and in a reflex, she tried to pull her hand away, but the lord held it firmly.

*What is he doing? He's mad!*

His tongue flicked over her skin, and when he finally released her, Meya was surprised to see no trace of blood remained. She brought her hand closer to her face in order to inspect it, and she paled. The cut was still there, but it had closed up. She gently touched the thin crust that had formed on it, not believing her eyes.

Lord Deminas lightly placed his hand on her arm, pushing it down. "Don't touch it, let it heal. We wouldn't want it to scar, now would we?" He smiled wolfishly, sending shivers up her spine.

"N-no, my Lord," Meya said softly. *What just happened?* She glanced at her hand, but the lord took hold of her chin, making her face him instead.

"Does it still hurt?"

Meya frowned slightly. "No, my Lord."

"Good." He released her once more and turned to the desk. He picked up his cup and the silver blade; using the latter, he stirred the contents of the cup.

Meya's stomach turned as she envisioned her blood mixing with the wine. She watched, enthralled, as the lord licked the blade clean once more, this time without cutting himself, and he dried it off using the towel that was still wrapped around his waist.

He placed the blade back into the desk's drawer and then sat down in his chair. He motioned for Meya to sit on the floor beside him. "Let's eat."

He lifted the cover from the biggest dish, revealing a roasted chicken. A smaller platter contained herb fritters, with a small bowl of honey to dip them in. The last dish was a mix of various fruits and berries.

The delicious smell of the chicken reached Meya's nose. Despite everything, she couldn't help but regain some of her appetite. Swallowing her pride, she sat down on the ground next to the lord and waited for him to pass her something to eat.

*I'll think about all that has transpired later, with a full stomach.*

# Twelve

"Thank you, my Lord." Meya bowed her head, turned around, and walked towards the door as calmly as she could manage. "Goodnight."

She clutched the towel wrapped around her body and stepped out into the hallway. The moment the door was closed, she sighed in relief. *Today was a messed-up day.*

Her mind flooded with images: the blade slitting the slaver's throat, the blood gushing out; the knife cutting her hand, red drops dripping into the wine; the lord's skin under her touch, her hands roaming his back; his fingers stimulating her, waves of pleasure coursing through her body...

She shook her head and closed her eyes in the hopes of ridding herself of the conflicting emotions. *Get yourself together, Meya!* She sighed deeply and started to make her way back to her quarters. *It hasn't even been a week.* She looked at her hand. The scarce lamplight made it hard to see, but the faint line from where Lord Deminas had cut her was still visible. She shuddered and started to walk faster. *Don't think too much about it. There's probably a logical explanation.* She clutched the towel closer. *Why would he drink my blood? He's not a demon, right?* Lost in thought, she nearly bumped into someone.

"There you are!"

Meya looked up and was surprised to see Nina. "Oh, hey..."

Nina observed her room-mate, raising the lamp she was holding a bit higher. "Are you alright? We were worried when you didn't show for supper." She leaned forward to whisper in Meya's ear. "And people were saying they saw you coming out of the dungeons with the Lord, covered in blood."

Meya swallowed. She wanted to say she was fine, but the lie refused to leave her lips.

"Come." Nina wrapped her arm around Meya. "Let's go somewhere private."

"The baths?" Meya asked.

Nina shook her head. "Winnie got dirty in the stables today, along with some others. They're all taking a bath."

Nina led her through several hallways and Meya looked around; this part of the castle was unknown to her.

"Where are we going?"

A coy smile appeared on Nina's face. "My secret place, if you will."

At the end of the hallway, Nina stopped in front of a large door. She gave the lamp to Meya. "Please, hold this for me." She reached into her apron, retrieved two metal pins, and knelt down in front of the door. "This will only take a few seconds." The metal pins slipped into the lock and Nina moved them around until a click was heard. She placed the pins back into her apron and took the lamp from Meya. With her free hand, she pushed open the door. "Enter."

Meya hesitated for a moment, but Nina's hand pushing against the small of her back made her step into the dark room. "If it's locked, doesn't that mean it's off-limits?"

Nina closed the door. "I suppose, but no one ever told me explicitly that we're forbidden to enter this room." She grinned cheekily.

Meya swallowed, nervous. "What if the Lord finds out?"

Nina shrugged. "Like I said, I've never been told not to come here. At any rate, I've been coming here for years now without getting into any trouble. Relax." She walked further into the room. The lamplight illuminated the area and revealed a large bed. Nina placed the lamp on a shelf and sat down.

"Whose room is this?" Meya asked as she walked over to Nina.

"This used to be Lord Deminas' room before he moved to his father's quarters."

Meya paled. "W-what?"

"Relax, sit down." Nina grabbed Meya's arm and tugged, pulling her onto the bed. "It's a bit stuffy in here, but I actually clean the floor and change the sheets every now and then. The soldiers' quarters are also in this wing, so no one notices." She smiled.

Meya anxiously looked around the poorly illuminated room, adrenaline coursing through her veins. "And the Lord doesn't come here anymore?"

Nina shook her head. "I first broke into this room after I noticed it had been unused for a whole year, and I have come in here ever since. It's only used rarely for special guests—and those always come announced to ensure the room is cleaned and aired."

Albeit reluctantly, Meya relaxed a little. "So… What now?"

"Well, from now on: keep your voice down. The men will go back to their quarters soon and we wouldn't want them to hear us. We will sneak back later when the halls are clear." She reclined and turned to face Meya. "Until then, we have some time to talk."

Meya sighed deeply and lay down next to Nina. "I guess you want to hear what happened today…"

Nina nodded. "If you want to share, of course."

Meya bit her lip as she thought about telling or not, and just how much she would tell. After a while, she finally opened her mouth and told Nina all about what had happened in the dungeons. As she recounted more and more, her body started to tremble, and Nina pulled her close into a hug. By the time Meya whispered about how Lord Deminas had slashed the slaver's throat, she was sobbing softly into Nina's dress.

When Meya had finally fallen silent, stopping her story at the point where she had left the dungeons with the lord, Nina spoke quietly, "I can't believe Lord Deminas actually went through all the trouble of capturing that pig. I never would have expected him to care for us servants like that."

"It's weird, right?" Meya's voice cracked slightly.

"Perhaps…" She shrugged. "Then again, he's a cruel man. The things he does to invaders…"

Meya shivered. "I know, I've seen bodies on my way here."

"Perhaps he just needed an excuse? You know, to capture and torture someone?" Nina mused.

"He's the Lord, does he really need an excuse?" Meya asked in a murmur.

Nina thought about that for a bit. "I'm inclined to say no, but he still needs his men to follow him. And I doubt he would want the people of Tristanja to hate him. Fear him, yes. But hate? That leads to trouble."

Meya sighed. "I guess you've got a point there. Randomly torturing and killing people without a good reason would be a bad idea."*Unless they are slaves,* she thought grimly.

Nina stroked Meya's back. "But let's not think too much about it. He killed the man who hurt you. That's a good thing. Besides, you're his slave, so it's not like he did that to impress you." She giggled.

*Maybe not to impress, but what* does *he want from me?* Meya sighed again. "I suppose you're right."

It was silent for a little bit.

"So… What happened after you left the dungeon? Some saw you covered in blood—the slaver's—but eh…" She tugged softly on the towel that was wrapped around Meya's body.

Meya flushed red. "I…I—" Her mind raced. *Ah fuck it, I've told her everything up to now. And I want to tell someone everything that happened. I don't want to keep this all to myself!* The blade cutting into her hand flashed before her eyes. She licked her lips and swallowed. "Promise this is just between us? That you won't tell anyone else?"

Nina moved back a bit so that she could look Meya straight in the eyes. "I promise that whatever happens in this room, stays in this room. The Lord himself will have to torture me to make me spill the secrets you entrust to me."

Meya wanted to ask if she really meant that, but Nina's eyes already told her she did.

"Thank you," she whispered and pulled her back into a hug. Holding her close, the words started to roll off her tongue. The bath, massaging the lord, him massaging her… Despite the shame she felt, she told it all. Supper, the knife, the kiss, the cutting, the wine… Coming to the part about him licking her wound and healing it, she hesitated. *Can I really tell her this?*

Having fallen silent, Nina gently took Meya's hand in her own and moved it into the light. Observing the faint line, she frowned. "Is this where he cut you?"

Meya sighed deeply, gathered her courage, and finished her story. She ignored Nina's baffled look as she continued to stare at the mark on Meya's hand.

"That sounds like some form of dark magic." Nina shivered. "I never thought Lord Deminas could become more scary, but he just did." She turned her gaze to Meya, but she didn't let go of her hand. "Did he actually drink the wine?"

Meya nodded. "He drank it during supper. When he refilled the cup, I feared he was going to cut me again, but he didn't. He simply asked me things about my life at the inn. What kind of chores I would do, what kind of travellers would come through…"

90

Nina swallowed. "You know... I have heard stories about demons who drink blood. Do you think the Lord's a demon?"

"I...I don't know." She bit her lip. "But humans don't just turn into demons, right? And we can be quite certain he's human because so many of you have known him since he was young."

Nina thought about that. "I guess... But it would explain why his demeanour changed after his father died. He returned from that battle a different man."

"Wouldn't everyone return from war a different person? Killing people can't be good for one's soul..." Meya added softly.

"True... But still... I doubt many men return from battle and suddenly want to drink blood, let alone have the capability to heal wounds by licking them."

"Well, it's not really healed," Meya said. "The cut closed faster, is all... It's still there. If it had been healed, there wouldn't be a trace of it anymore."

Nina sighed. "Again, true. But it's still not normal."

Meya lowered her eyes. "No, it most definitely isn't normal... But what can I do?"

Nina thought for a moment before answering, "I fear you can't do anything, really. However, I think we might have discovered what happened to all the chambermaids before you..."

"With the exception of Jaimy, that is..." Before Meya realised it, she told Nina about the body on the jagged rocks.

Even in the poor lamplight, it was clear that Nina's face had paled a bit.

As the silence lingered, Nina finally decided to speak, "Well, what can I say... We knew he had thrown her off the balcony. It's to be expected that her body was still there."

"I guess I just didn't expect it, for some reason." Meya sighed and held Nina close. "What do you think will become of me? Will he kill me? Will he drink my blood until I turn lifeless like my predecessors?" Her voice quivered. "Will I eventually vanish like them?" Tears formed in the corners of her eyes.

Nina shushed her. "Don't worry too much, alright? Those before you, they never told anyone what happened. We cannot be sure he did the same to them as he did to you. We cannot be sure that he will do what he did tonight again in the future." She cupped Meya's face, wiping away the tears that slid down her cheeks. "For all we know, the other maids just got sick from worry, from stress, more than whatever the Lord did to them. You've got me, though. You can confide in me. Whatever happens, I will be here to help you remain strong. You just do your job, be a good servant. You do what he wants, and you don't complain. Try to make sure he never has a reason to punish you. And whenever you need to talk, you just tell me. We will sneak in here so we have some privacy. No need to worry about people like Gail, then." She smiled.

Feeling better, a slight smile appeared on Meya's face. "Thanks, Nina, this really means a lot."

~*~

Nina extinguished the lamp before opening the door to their quarters. Meya entered the room right after her, preparing herself for the prying eyes and questions of her other room-mates. *Just let Nina do the talking,* she thought as she turned her gaze down.

"Nina!" Lea exclaimed. "Meya! Where have you two been?" She rose up and hurried towards them, placing her hands on Meya's shoulders, but she removed them when she saw Nina shake her head.

"She's had a rough day, please," Nina said as she walked past Lea, Meya following her.

"Are you alright?" Brit asked, who still sat in front of the fireplace with the others.

Gail scrutinized Meya. "Don't tell me the Lord had you stay for another bath!"

Nina shot her a deathly look. "I said: she's had a rough day. Leave her be."

Trying to ignore the questioning gazes of the women, Meya sat down in front of the fire. Nina poured a cup of water and handed it to her.

"Thank you," Meya mumbled.

"We heard you came out of the dungeons covered in blood," Gail continued to push.

Nina huffed. "It wasn't her blood. Now leave her be."

Gail muttered something and rose. "Fine." She walked away but made sure her leg brushed against Meya as she did.

Nina sat down next to Meya, sighing deeply. There was an awkward silence for a while, until Lea started talking to Brit about what had happened to her sister in the stables earlier that day. Meya didn't listen to their conversation, her attention fixed on the crackling fire instead. She jerked up slightly when Nina's hand found hers and gently squeezed it. She smiled faintly at her attempt to try and cheer her up.

After a few minutes, Nina rose and said she was going to bed. Lea agreed and both Brit and Winnie also stood up.

Meya emptied her cup and followed suit. *I hope I can get some decent sleep—without nightmares.* She folded up the towel and placed it on the bedside table.

"Goodnight," Nina said to everyone, and Lea, Brit, and Meya echoed back.

Meya noticed Gail's silence and peered at her, but she appeared to be sleeping. *Great, Gail seems to hate me... Or us... She probably realises Nina knows more.* She looked over at Winnie. *I wonder what she would say if she could actually speak.* With a sigh, Meya crawled into bed. *Please, let me have a dreamless sleep.*

~*~

The next morning started like most mornings did, though Gail seemed to ignore Meya to the best of her ability—she didn't even look at her. Nina noticed this and made sure to bump into Gail several times. Lea simply observed it all, sometimes shaking her head disapprovingly. Brit and Winnie were too busy with each other and seemed oblivious to the negative vibes in the room.

Nina almost dragged Meya along with her to the dining hall, not wanting to wait for the others. They sat down at a table, next to a middle-aged man with olive-brown skin, long, dark hair tied back, and umber eyes.

"Good morning, Kadeem," Nina greeted him.

"Morning," he said back, glancing at Meya.

"This here is Meya. Meya, this is Kadeem." Nina drank from her cider. "We work together in the soldiers' quarters."

"Nice to meet you, Kadeem," Meya said, and the man simply nodded back with a smile, before returning his focus to his meal instead.

"So..." Nina turned to Meya. "Did you manage to get some decent sleep?"

Meya swallowed the piece of bread she had just bitten off. "Decent enough... No actual nightmares." She lowered her voice a bit and moved closer to Nina. "Tell me, does Gail hate me?"

Nina huffed and took a bite from her bread. With her mouth half-full, she answered, "Gail loves a good gossip. She really can't handle the fact that you seemingly told me stuff she doesn't know. It will pass the moment another good story catches her attention." She smiled. "Don't worry about it."

Meya raised her cup to her lips but hesitated before drinking. She placed the cup back on the table and looked at her hand. The faint line where the blade had cut her was still there. *I guess I can't say it was a nightmare then.*

Nina noticed and placed her hand gently on Meya's wrist. "Don't worry, alright?" She smiled sweetly, and, after a few seconds, Meya smiled back.

"Remember what I told you yesterday." She squeezed her reassuringly. "I'll be here. You can do this."

Meya nodded and took another bite from her meal. "Thanks, Nina. I'll try."

~*~

Meya stood before the door leading to the lord's chambers. It felt like there were stones in her stomach instead of her breakfast. The levels of adrenaline in her system were slowly increasing and she could feel her heart pounding in her throat. She swallowed and wetted her lips. *Come on, you can do this. Just knock,* she tried to urge herself.

After another minute of just standing there, frozen to the ground from sheer anxiety, she finally managed to raise her hand and knock on the heavy wood. For a moment, she feared she wouldn't hear the Lord answer, her heart was beating so loudly in her ears. When she was certain there had been no reply, she knocked again, and again.

She sighed in relief. *He's not here!* She opened the door, stepped inside, and announced herself. *I hope he will stay away all day.*

She walked to the bedroom and knocked. Her heart skipped a beat when there was an answer this time.

"Yes?" Lord Deminas' voice boomed from the other side.

It took Meya a few seconds to remember how to speak. "M-Meya, my Lord."

"You may enter."

The blood rushed to her face as she pushed open the door. *Oh God, oh God...*

"I was just on my way out. Replace the sheets and be sure to scrub the bath," the lord said as he walked past Meya, not even waiting for her response.

"Y-yes, my Lord," she uttered as she watched him leave. The moment she heard the door close, she sat down on the bed, placed her head in her hands, and sighed deeply. She trembled slightly, and the moment she realised this, a nervous giggle escaped her throat. *Great, just great...* She lightly slapped her cheeks and rose again. *Come on, Meya. You can do this.* She took a few deep breaths, straightened her back, and got to work.

# Thirteen

Flustered, Meya hurried through the halls, carrying a big pile of laundry. *How could he?* she thought in both anger and confusion. *Why would he do that? Does he enjoy making me feel uncomfortable? What kind of a sadist is he?* She sighed deeply as she neared the laundry room. *I hope Lea is there, perhaps I can explain it to her.*

To her great relief, she spotted Lea when she walked in. She dumped the pile of laundry on the ground next to the already existing heap, and was about to go to her when she noticed Lea was coming her way instead.

"Meya, can I talk to you for a moment?"

Meya nodded and followed Lea to a quiet corner. "I actually wanted to talk to you, too."

"Well, you go first," Lea said as she dried her hands with her apron.

Meya bit her lip and thought for a moment of where to start. "Well, first off... My clothes from yesterday are in that bundle and well... They are covered with blood."

Lea nodded. "I already expected that from what I heard. No worries about that." She smiled sweetly.

Meya fidgeted with her apron, avoiding Lea's gaze. "That's not all though..."

The smile on Lea's face faded. "What is it?"

Meya closed her eyes and sighed deeply. *Damn you, damn you, damn you!* Gathering her courage, she opened her mouth and started to speak slowly, weighing every word. "Well... You know how the Lord uses these special kerchiefs?" She looked up at Lea, and her expression told her enough.

"Yes..."

"Well... Ehm..." She averted her eyes again. "I...I don't know why... But..." She sighed again and clutched her apron. "For some reason, Lord Deminas decided to use something else."

Lea frowned. "What?"

Meya could feel her cheeks burning with shame. "He... He used my undergarments."

Lea's eyes filled with shock. "Oh my..." She placed her hand on Meya's shoulder, comforting her. "Well, don't worry. I'll be sure to wash your bundle so no one else will have to find out, alright?"

Relieved, Meya looked up and hugged Lea. "Thank you! I...I don't want anyone getting the wrong ideas, you know..."

Lea patted Meya on the back. "It's fine, don't worry."

Feeling a lot better, Meya let go of Lea. "What did you want to talk about?"

"About yesterday and this morning, really. I'm not sure if you've noticed, but Gail is pretty upset."

Meya huffed. "It's kind of hard *not* to notice."

"I understand that you might not want to talk about certain things. Especially things like..." She looked at the pile of laundry for a second before looking back at Meya.

"Well, I'm glad you understand. I just wish Gail did too. Some things I would just rather keep private."

Lea nodded. "When you're a slave, you don't have much to call your own. For some, all they cherish is their privacy. Though, on the other side, all some other people cherish are the stories of others."

"Can't Gail entertain herself with the stories of all the other people here? Why is she so interested in what happens to me?" Meya was starting to feel frustrated.

"Gail just wants to be friends with you. Yesterday, it was quite clear that you did tell Nina some things. The fact that you told her, but refused to share with us—with her... Well..." Lea sighed. "She feels left out I suppose."

"And what do you want me to do about it?" Meya crossed her arms. "I've been here for almost a week now. I'm still getting used to living here, to the Lord's... actions... I do hope you didn't expect me to be best friends with everyone. I can be *friendly* to everyone, but being *good* friends? That takes time with me. If Gail acts the way she has been doing just because I want some privacy, then I don't know if I can be good friends with her."

Lea looked hurt. "I understand, but please, do give her a chance. Like I said, we don't have much here. We only have each other, really."

Meya's frustration dwindled a bit. "I guess you're right. I'll try to be nicer to her." She thought for a moment. "I suppose I could always tell some more of my life's story before I came here. Though it hurts to think about the raid, I do have a lot of great memories about the inn." She smiled, though it was bittersweet. "Perhaps it will even help me feel better, to talk more about the good things. It might help take my mind off the bad stuff."

Lea smiled. "Thank you. I'm sure she will appreciate that."

~*~

Feeling a lot better, Meya made her way to the dining hall for lunch. After getting her food, she looked around for Nina. She spotted her in a quiet corner and hurried over. "Hey Nina," she said as she sat down. The smile on her face faded when she looked at her room-mate and noticed reddish-brown smears on her white apron. "Is… Is that…?"

Nina looked around, making sure no one was within earshot. "Yes, it's blood. The Lord asked me to clean up the dungeons."

Meya's eyes widened. "Why did he ask *you*?"

"It's either Kadeem or me who does the dungeons. Consider it a part of the soldiers' quarters, I suppose." She smiled sourly. "I've seen messes before, don't worry." She bent forward to whisper into Meya's ear. "He hurt that slaver *bad*. I actually took a look in his drawers…"

The blood drained from Meya's face. "You…you did?"

Nina sniggered softly. "Lord Deminas must like you. He really tortured that pig. But damn, there was so much blood! Took me a while to clean it up."

Meya swallowed as she remembered the lord cutting the slaver's throat, the blood gushing out and some of it spraying onto her. A shiver ran through her body.

"The damn guy was heavy too, a lot more so than the other man. Why didn't you tell me about him?"

Meya frowned. "What other man?"

"Well, considering his looks, my best bet is he was an invader."

Meya remembered seeing the battle-worn men in the cells. "There were some other prisoners, but they were locked up and seemed to be alive."

97

"Well, this man most certainly wasn't. He was hung upside-down next to that pig, his throat slit too." Nina lowered her voice again. "He was drained of all his blood. However, for some reason, the floor underneath him was clean... I'm pretty sure that all the blood that was on the floor belonged to that pig."

Meya shuddered. "What—" Her voice faltered.

"You told me the Lord drank some of your blood during supper..." Nina was whispering, cautious of anyone picking up on their conversation. "What if he wanted more? If you didn't see him hanging there when the slaver got killed, that means the Lord went back later to kill that man."

Meya swallowed, fear flooding through her like ice. "Do you really think..."

"I don't know. I'll have a chat with Kadeem, ask if he's seen anything like that before. Maybe he knows more." Nina turned to her food.

Meya eyed her own plate. Despite her initial hunger, she didn't feel much like eating now. *What if the Lord did drink that blood?* She thought back to all the corpses of enemy soldiers she had seen near the borders of Tristanja. *A lot of them had been drained of blood too... But according to the rumours, the blood was used to mark the borders.* She shivered. *What if they don't use all the blood for that?*

~*~

Meya returned to the dining hall for supper after a hard day's work. She was glad the lord didn't come to his chambers in the afternoon, but she knew she would eventually have to face him again. She was just about to sit down in a quiet corner when someone familiar appeared beside her.

"Hey Meya," Abi said.

She looked at the young woman and smiled. "Hey Abi, haven't seen you around."

The girl sat down next to Meya. "Well, I work in the kitchen. I normally eat later than the rest, but I wanted to speak to you so they allowed me to eat now." She smiled.

Meya smiled back, though she had a gut feeling that something was off.

Abi leaned towards Meya. "You remember what I said about gossip?"

"That it's not appreciated?"

Abi nodded. "Well, thing is... I've heard some people whispering things today and I wanted to know if it's true."

Meya frowned. "What did you hear?"

Abi stirred her stew. "That you killed someone."

98

Meya froze. *Who told her that? Why would anyone mention that?* She thought of Gail and clenched her jaw. *What else did she tell?* Gathering her composure, she looked at Abi. "Sorry, what?"

"Yesterday, people saw you coming out of the dungeons with the Lord. They said you were covered in blood." She lowered her voice. "And that the Lord made you kill that new prisoner."

At first, Meya was relieved. *They're not talking about the raider!* But then she started to get angry. *How can people think I killed someone just because I had blood on my clothes?* She swallowed. "What makes people think *I* killed that prisoner?"

"Because you said the blood wasn't yours... And why else would the Lord take a murderer with him down to the dungeons?"

Meya's head spun. *What did she just call me?* It took her a few seconds to calm down before she could ask, "*Murderer?*"

Abi flushed red. "I'm sorry. Several people were telling the same story, so I figured it was true."

Meya closed her eyes for a moment. "What story?"

Abi whispered, "That... That you killed your keeper, set the brothel on fire, and ran away."

Meya couldn't believe what she was hearing.

"They said you got caught and you had the choice of death or enslavement for your crimes, and that you chose enslavement instead," Abi continued softly. "You...you told me you tried to escape from the slaver, and it kind of made sense to me." The girl looked up at Meya and was startled by her expression. "I'm so sorry! I told you gossip was bad."

Meya was fuming. *So people think I'm a murdering harlot?* She bit her lip in an attempt to keep her emotions in check. *Why would anyone tell such lies? Butcher my real history to this abomination?* Tears threatened to spill from her eyes. *Turning the raider into a keeper, the inn into a brothel...* She stood up and rushed out of the dining hall, leaving her untouched stew and a very upset Abi behind.

~*~

Lea and Nina were the first to enter their quarters and they spotted Meya in her bed, underneath her covers, crying softly. Nina rushed over.

"Meya? Meya what happened?" She gently peeled away the sheets and pulled Meya close to her. "What's wrong dear? You can tell me."

It took Meya a bit to collect herself and explain to her what had happened. When she finally finished her story, Lea and Nina were both upset.

"If you'll please excuse me, I'm going to find Gail," Lea stated.

"Where is she?" Nina asked.

"I don't know why, but she decided to go to the baths today instead of tomorrow," Lea said, the anger clearly audible in her voice.

Nina huffed. "I can think of a reason why she'd go today…"

Lea didn't answer. She turned around and exited the room.

Nina sighed. "I'm so sorry Meya. I don't know what came over Gail. She loves to gossip, but I've never caught her spreading such nasty lies before."

"How am I ever going to walk around this place without feeling ashamed?" Meya asked, her voice quivering.

"Lea and I will make sure everyone knows it's not true. Don't worry." She smiled sweetly.

"But I don't want them to know the truth, either," Meya whispered, her tears close to spilling again.

Nina shushed her. "It's fine. They don't need to know everything. Your family's inn got raided and burned down, you fled, got captured and sold. No details. No need to tell about killing that raider, and no need at all to tell anything more about that slaver. Alright?"

Sniffing, Meya nodded.

"Good. Now stop worrying." She wiped the tears from Meya's cheeks. "We will fix this."

~*~

Everyone was sitting in front of the hearth when Lea came in with Gail. Neither of them looked very pleased.

"Tell them what you told me." Lea as good as shoved Gail towards the group.

Gail fixed the towel around her torso. Avoiding everyone's gazes, she sat down. "I did not tell anyone that Meya used to work in a brothel, nor did I claim that she killed her keeper."

Lea stood behind Gail, her arms crossed. "What *did* you tell?"

Gail grunted. "I gave no details! I just said Meya did once kill someone— but I added that it was in self-defence!"

Meya bit her lip as she suppressed the urge to either slap Gail right across the face or start crying again—she wanted to do both, actually. Nina, who sat next to her, took her hand in her own and squeezed it slightly for support.

"What about the harlot story? Where did that come from?" Lea continued.

"I don't know! I never said anything about her working in a brothel!" Gail huffed and crossed her arms in defiance. "I never told such lies."

"Well, what *did* you tell?" Lea asked angrily.

It took a moment before Gail replied, "I... I did mention that she's stayed with the Lord a few times... Bathed with him... Had supper with him..."

"So basically you were implying she might have—" Lea started, but Gail interrupted her.

"I was not implying anything! I was just telling people what happened. She *did* stay with the Lord after supper, and she *did* bathe with him! I have no influence on the conclusions people draw from that."

"Well, you might want to stop and think about possible conclusions people might draw and shut your mouth accordingly!" Lea snapped.

Gail winced.

"Thanks to you, people now think the poor girl's a harlot!"

"I'm sorry," Gail murmured.

"Tell that to Meya." Lea finally sat down.

Gail bit her lip and turned to face Meya. "Meya, I know you probably don't believe me... But truly, I *am* sorry. I never meant for people to think those things."

Meya looked up. "Then stop talking about me behind my back."

Gail seemed to be at a loss for words.

Gathering her courage, Meya added, "You know what? Until people stop believing those vile rumours about me, I will no longer be talking to you."

This really seemed to hit Gail where it hurt most. "What? Why? I already said I am sorry!"

Meya looked at her intently. "Then prove it. Make those rumours go away and don't talk about me anymore."

Gail's face reddened. After a few seconds, she stated, through clenched teeth, "Fine."

~*~

The next day, Meya's thoughts were still occupied with the rumours, and this made her forget about the lord's actions. She was cleaning the windows when he entered. "Good morning, my Lord," she said as she continued her task.

Lord Deminas remained silent as he walked over to her. When he stood right behind her, Meya turned around. "It seems a very peculiar rumour is going around the castle..."

Meya's stomach lurched and she swallowed. *How does he know?* Cold sweat started to trickle down her back. "I...I'm certain, my Lord, that—"

"It seems that some of my men believe I have a former harlot, who murdered her keeper, working as my chambermaid."

Meya paled. "That...that's not true!"

"Do you know where this rumour originated?" Lord Deminas took a step closer to her, his face mere inches from Meya's.

Meya opened her mouth to speak, but it took a few seconds before the words found their way out. Though reluctant, she explained everything to the lord.

Pleased with the confession, Lord Deminas took a step back. "I'm glad the rumour is false and that you have not been lying to me."

"I...I can honestly say, my Lord, that I wouldn't dare lie to you," Meya said softly.

Lord Deminas chuckled. His fingers curled around Meya's chin and he looked deep into her eyes. "*I know.*"

A chill went up Meya's spine, but at the same time, her knees felt weak and her heart leapt.

The lord released her. "Continue your work." With that said, he turned around and left his chambers.

Meya sighed deeply. She replayed her conversation with the lord in her head and the blood drained from her face. *What have I done?* She thought about Gail. *Will she be in trouble?* Abi had told her the lord disliked gossip, and it seemed the vile rumours that had been spread had even made it to the soldiers' ears. *And the Lord didn't seem pleased about that at all.* She swallowed. *I'm sure Gail's going to get punished... And she'll probably dislike me even more for it, too.* She closed her eyes and sighed. *Damn it.*

# Fourteen

At lunch, Meya was relieved to see that Gail was seemingly unharmed. Not in the mood to talk to her, she sat down somewhere else and Nina joined her not much later.

"Well, I talked to Kadeem despite him not being very talkative. He said he has disposed of bodies before that had been drained of blood, without any trace of the blood on the ground. I tried asking what he thinks happened to it, but he just shrugged, stating it wasn't of his—of *our*—concern." Nina sighed. "And that was the end of the conversation, really."

Meya took a sip from her cup. "Well, at least we know it has happened before." She thought for a moment before continuing in a hushed tone, "I heard several rumours on my way to Tristanja. People said that Lord Deminas uses the blood of his enemies to mark the borders. Maybe he drains the captives, collects the blood, and uses it for that?"

Nina swallowed the contents of her mouth. "Well, I often hear the soldiers talking. I know they do that on the battlefield. They take the corpses and line them along the border, with their throats cut so they bleed out."

Meya bit her lip. "I have seen some of those corpses, but that's not the thing I saw the most."

Nina raised a brow. "Oh? What then?"

"Mangled and beheaded bodies would be lined up… And the heads…" She closed her eyes as memories of the horrific sight flooded her mind. She remembered the stench and her stomach turned. "The heads would be on pikes, facing away from Tristanja, their eyelids cut off."

Nina remained silent for a while, playing a bit with her food. "I always thought they were exaggerating… You know, like boys would always do to impress one another." She sighed. "I guess we should just be happy we're living inside the castle, away from all that violence."

Meya stared at the cup she was holding. "Are you sure we are safe from that violence though?"

Nina looked up at Meya and blinked a few times in confusion. "I'd hope so! Alright, so the Lord can be cruel if we misbehave, but you can't compare that to the slaughter that happens on the battlefield." She lowered her voice. "Or the raids that happen to villages in the dead of night."

Meya's heart ached. "You're right." A surge of sadness washed over her, and she could feel tears prickling her eyes.

Nina noticed and placed her hand on Meya's. "Hey, look at me."

Meya moved her focus from the cup in her hands to Nina. The sweet smile on Nina's face soothed her a bit.

"Trust me: you're safe here. What happened to you before won't happen again. The Lord even went as far as to punish that pig." She squeezed Meya's hand. "Don't worry. Just be a good servant, make sure the Lord never has a reason to discipline you, and you will be fine."

"I hope you're right." Meya sighed, thinking of what Lord Deminas might do to Gail.

~*~

Meya was busy dusting off the cabinets when Lord Deminas entered the room. "Good day, my Lord," she said as she continued her work.

"Come here for a moment, Meya."

Anxiety instantly took hold of her, but she did as she was told. Standing in front of the Lord, she felt small, fragile, weak. *If I wanted to kill you, I could do so with my bare hands,* his words echoed in her head. It took her a moment to get her tongue to function. "Y-yes, my Lord?"

There was a glint in his eyes, accompanied by the corners of his mouth inching up ever so slightly. "As you are room-mates with Gail, I want you to tell her to come down to the dungeons tomorrow after breakfast."

A sinking sensation washed over Meya and the world spun slightly. *He's going to punish her!* She opened her mouth to speak, but the words were stuck in her throat.

Lord Deminas raised a brow. "Is there something wrong? Don't tell me you're unable to pass a simple message like that along."

That comment seemed to ground her again. "Is...is she in trouble, my Lord?"

A sly smirk appeared on his face. "You already know the answer to that question."

Meya thought of Winnie and what remained of her tongue. "Please, my Lord, don't cut off Gail's tongue." Meya's voice trembled, unsure if her asking such a thing would get her in trouble.

The lord's eyes shimmered with delight. "She has spread such nasty rumours, yet you would still ask me to not perform a certain punishment?"

Ashamed, Meya lowered her eyes.

"Look at me," the lord growled.

Meya's heart jumped and she quickly looked back up at him. *He's enjoying this,* she thought, biting her lip. "She already said sorry to me, my Lord," Meya said softly. "I told her to fix this, to tell people those stories aren't true."

"Well, she can tell me sorry before I punish her accordingly." Lord Deminas cupped Meya's chin. "This isn't the first time Gail has spun tales, and it seems denial of food or getting a few lashes is not punishment enough to stop her from repeating her mistakes."

Meya quivered slightly. "P-please, my Lord, just don't cut off her tongue."

Lord Deminas whispered in her ear, "Don't worry, that's not the punishment I had in mind for her." He let go of Meya and walked towards the door. "Now, be a good servant and tell Gail I will be expecting her at the dungeons tomorrow morning."

Frozen in fear, Meya watched the lord leave his chambers.

~*~

Meya was silent all throughout supper, and again when she was waiting in the servants' quarters for Gail to show. Nina and the others were at the baths, but Meya hoped Gail wouldn't be there as she had gone the previous day.

Finally, the door opened and Gail walked in. Her expression went from neutral to grave. "Hey Meya," she said softly, her eyes lowering. "I remember what you said, so don't worry: I don't expect you to answer. However, I did my best today to tell everyone that those rumours about you were wrong. I just wanted you to know that."

Hearing this made Meya feel even worse. She gathered her courage. "Please, could you come sit here for a moment?"

Wary, Gail sat down next to Meya. "What is it?"

Meya sighed deeply. "Lord Deminas asked me something…"

Gail's eyes enlarged. "Oh please, don't tell me he knows!"

Meya nodded and Gail's face paled. "He heard the rumours and asked me if they were true." Meya swallowed as she noticed Gail stressing out. "He… He asked me to tell you that tomorrow, after breakfast… you need to come down to the dungeons."

Gail jumped up and started to pace through the room. "Shit, shit, shit…" She ran her hands through her hair.

"I-I'm sorry," Meya said.

Gail sat back down, though she still kept her hands intertwined in her brown locks. "Don't be; this is not your fault." She sighed and rocked back and forth slightly. "I have been warned and punished for gossiping before, but…" She groaned. "I don't know, it just happens!" She jumped up again. "It's just… It's boring here! Life has no meaning when there's nothing to look forward to, to live up to! I can't get married, raise kids… Basically, I have no future here but to work my ass off every single day until I become too weak to work and get killed, or I simply die." She sat down on the edge of her bed, burying her face in her hands. "I like to talk about the lives of others, as then it feels like I am living those lives a little bit, too. The stories of others are the only things that keep living interesting for me."

Meya's heart ached for Gail and she stood up. She sat down next to her and Gail flung herself around her neck. Meya wanted to comfort her, but her mind failed to form any sentences for her to say.

"I'm sorry that I hurt you by altering your story. I wanted to make you sound brave and rebellious. The young woman who wanted to take control of her life, but ended up here, with us."

Meya felt both flattered and angry by Gail's confession. Swallowing her anger, she said, "If you like altering stories that much, why not make up stories entirely? Stories don't need to be about people who live here in the castle to be interesting. You can create your own stories, with your own characters, and they can be as brave and rebellious as you'd want them to be."

"You mean like fables and legends?" Gail murmured.

106

"I suppose, yes. Just weave your own tales, your own stories. They don't even need to take place around the castle, they can take place in faraway lands. That way, you can tell exciting tales, without harming anyone."

Gail was silent for a bit. "I... I never thought about it like that. I always loved hearing fables and legends from others—especially if they came from far away, as they'd often have tales I had never heard of before. I never thought about making my own." She giggled nervously. "God, you must think I'm stupid." She released Meya and looked at her, a slight smile tugging at the corners of her mouth. "If the Lord lets me keep my tongue, I will start doing that." The smile faded and she cast her eyes downwards. "God, I hope he won't take my tongue." Her voice trembled slightly.

Meya wanted to comfort her and tell her that he wasn't going to do that, but her lips refused to part. *I don't want to get her hopes up. What if he plans to do something even worse?* A shiver ran up her spine. Deciding it was best to not say anything on the matter, she remained silent.

"Thanks for trying to make me feel slightly better, it means a lot to me. Especially considering what happened." Gail hugged Meya. "I truly am sorry though, and I will continue to try and make sure everyone knows those rumours are false."

"Thanks," Meya said softly, but deep inside, she was still a bit angry with her room-mate.

~*~

The next morning, the women all went to breakfast together—an attempt to provide Gail with some moral support. Despite her trepidation, Gail still managed to eat most of her breakfast. With a sigh, she pushed the remainder of her meal to the centre of the table. She refilled her cup and downed the ale before standing up.

Everyone just looked at her in silence; no one knew what to say, so they just nodded in respect.

Gail took a deep breath, straightened her back, turned around, and made her way out of the dining hall to the dungeons.

They all watched her go. When she had disappeared from view, Lea sighed. "Poor girl... She brought this onto herself, but that doesn't make this any easier."

"I wonder what the Lord will do to her," Brit said wistfully, and she looked at her sister.

Winnie cast her eyes down, the remnant of her tongue wetting her lips.

107

Meya sighed and stood up herself. "I'm going to work. See you all at lunch."

The others also rose and went their ways. Nina tagged along with Meya, but neither of them said anything. Gail's pending punishment was weighing down on them all.

~*~

For the entire morning, Meya had a knot in her stomach. She did her chores and made sure she had collected all the laundry before lunch. Going down to the laundry room, she wondered if Lea had heard anything from Gail—she hadn't seen Lord Deminas yet and this worried her.

The moment she walked into the steamy room, the bells sounded through the castle. Meya quickly dumped the pile of laundry next to the others and looked around for Lea. Spotting her, she hurried over.

Lea looked up the moment she realised someone was standing behind her. "Oh, Meya…" She immediately clung to her, her face as grave as her voice.

Dread filled Meya and she swallowed. *How bad is it?* She took a deep breath. "How's Gail?"

Lea shook her head. "It's… hard to say."

"What did he do?"

Lea released Meya so she could look at her. "Well… He didn't take her tongue, at least." Her eyes glistened with unshed tears.

*I'm glad to hear the Lord spoke the truth on that part.* "Will Gail be at lunch?"

Lea shook her head and walked away, the tears freeing themselves from her eyes.

Meya watched her go, fear gripping her heart and nailing her to the floor. *What did he do to her?* She bit her lip. She didn't feel much like eating, so she decided to go see Gail instead.

~*~

As Gail wasn't in their quarters, Meya went to her workplace next—Gail worked as a seamstress. Meya entered the room and immediately saw Gail sitting at a desk, working on an apron. The fact that she was sitting there, working, relieved Meya a bit.

"Hey Gail," she said in a hushed tone as she walked over to her. "Lea told me you weren't joining us for—"

Gail turned around and the mere sight of her froze Meya to the core. She gasped loudly and instantly understood why Lea had been so upset.

The poor woman's lips had been sewn shut.

Meya quivered in both fear and anger. *Lord Deminas is mad! How can he do something so cruel? How is she supposed to eat? To drink? Is she to starve?* Slowly, she moved closer to Gail. "Does… Does it hurt?"

Gail turned her gaze down and shrugged.

Meya knelt down before her. "Did the Lord say for how long you must suffer this?"

Gail shook her head.

Meya shivered in horror. "Can you still drink?"

Gail shook her head again, the gloom surrounding her deepening. Gently, she touched the stitches that held her lips together. They were pretty tight.

*This can't be happening... She'll die!* Trembling, Meya grasped Gail's hand. "It'll be alright. You'll get through this." She eyed the sharp scissors and knives that lay on the desk. *I could easily free her... But Lord Deminas would surely find out and then what will happen?* She closed her eyes. *Damn it!*

Gail placed her hand on Meya's and stroked it. She breathed in deeply through her nose and exhaled loudly—a sigh.

Not able to handle the emotions, Meya excused herself and stood up. "I… Ehm… I'll see you tonight." Meya hurried out of the room, back to the lord's chambers. Despite the anger she felt towards Gail, she didn't think she deserved this. *Those rumours were vile, but not vile enough to suffer like that! And no way near bad enough to die for!* She bit her lip anxiously. *I need to know when the Lord is going to free her.*

~*~

It was nearing suppertime when Lord Deminas finally entered his chambers—Meya had started to fear that he wasn't going to appear. She greeted the lord and continued her work. It took her a lot of effort to control herself, for she actually wanted to rush straight towards him and ask him about Gail's punishment.

The lord sat down at his desk and started to read some letters, seemingly ignoring Meya.

With a racing heart, she continued to polish the shelves behind him. *When should I ask him? How should I ask him?* Her mind went over dozens of possible approaches, and they also came with possible responses. Some good

109

for Gail, some bad, and some ended with her getting punished too, just for being rude enough to question the lord's judgement.

Tormented by her own mind, Meya forgot the time. The supper bells rang through the castle and shocked, she looked up from her work. She put away the polishing rag and turned to the lord.

*It's now or never...* She took a deep breath. "M-my lord...?"

He put down the letter he had been reading and looked up at Meya. The glint in his eyes suggested that he already knew what was coming. "Yes?"

"I...I don't want to be rude, but..." She swallowed. "I wanted to know for how long Gail's lips are going to be sealed." She fumbled with the fabric of her apron as she tried her best to not look away from the lord's prying gaze.

A mischievous, little grin tugged at the corners of his mouth and he reclined in his chair. "I haven't decided yet. A day or three at least, perhaps until she collapses." His eyes shimmered maliciously.

Meya stood frozen, the hairs all over her body on end. *He can't be serious, right?* She opened her mouth to speak, but her voice failed her.

Lord Deminas raised a brow. "Is there a problem?"

*You. Your attitude*, Meya thought angrily, but she controlled herself—she still remembered the last time she had had the guts to speak her mind to him, and her throat still ached at the memory.

"Well?"

Meya gathered her courage and carefully weighed her words. "I don't think Gail deserves such suffering, my Lord."

He laughed. "Well, I do." He looked at Meya, his face stern and eyes cold. "And your opinion doesn't matter."

Meya swallowed, a nervous sweat coating her skin. "I...I know, my Lord."

"Good." He stared at her intensely. "Then you are free to go. I will see you in the morning."

Meya clutched her apron. *But...*

Lord Deminas noticed and his eyes gleamed. "Anything else on your mind? Better say it now."

Thoughts of Lea and of how the others would react when they heard Gail was to suffer at least three whole days with her lips sealed, unable to eat or even drink, made her heart tense up in her chest. *Or until she collapses... What if she dies?* Tears stung her eyes. *Damn you, Gail.* Meya pushed aside her self-worth and dropped to her knees in front of the lord, her head low. "Please, my Lord," she started. "Don't make Gail suffer like that, please."

A low chuckle rang through the room. "And why would I listen to your pleas, *servant*?"

110

The last word stung hard, and it was the final push required for the tears to finally escape Meya's eyes. "I...I know that I'm but a servant, my Lord. I know my position, yet I still wish to implore you: please, don't make Gail suffer for three or more days."

The lord placed his booted foot on Meya's head, pressing her further down. "You haven't answered my question: why would I listen to your pleas?"

Meya gritted her teeth and swallowed her pride. "I'd do anything, my Lord. Just ask me what to do to lessen Gail's punishment, and I will."

More laughter. "You're my servant. Anything I ask of you, you must do already." Lord Deminas removed his foot and grabbed Meya by her chin, lifting her up so their eyes could meet. "You have nothing to offer me that I can't already take from you, if I so desire."

More tears rolled down Meya's cheeks as she realised he was right. "Please, my Lord... Isn't there a way for me to reduce her punishment?"

Lord Deminas scoffed and released her. "Why do you even care?"

Meya lowered her eyes. "Because she's not a bad person. What she did was bad, and I'm still a bit upset about that, but we talked about it and she understands that what she did was wrong." She looked up at the lord. "She won't spread rumours or gossip any more, my Lord. We agreed that she would create her own tales from now on—her own fables and stories. Those won't harm anyone."

The lord seemed to think about this. The stern look on his face slowly morphed into something more sinister. "I suppose I *could* cut Gail's punishment short... I'd free her tomorrow, however..." He smiled with malicious joy. "You'd have to be willing to suffer in her stead."

Meya's eyes enlarged and her heart clenched in her chest. *I should have expected this.* Her lower lip trembled as she tried to speak, but it took a few seconds before she managed to utter the words, "How much?"

Lord Deminas bent forward so that his face was next to Meya's. "Don't worry..." His fingers wrapped around her chin. "Unlike with Gail, I'll make sure to not leave any permanent marks on your body."

Meya's mind raced. *What does that mean? A beating? A whipping? At least I won't have to fear my lips being sewn shut...* She swallowed. "What will you do then, my Lord?"

He moved back a bit so that their eyes could meet. "There's no fun in telling you." He grinned slyly. "So, what will it be?"

Meya bit her lip. *No permanent marks... What could he do that's so bad without leaving permanent marks?* She thought about being beaten or whipped and concluded that she could handle such pain if that meant saving Gail. She was about to speak when a coldness spread through her veins. *What if he means to have sex with me?*

Nina's words echoed in the back of her mind and she almost laughed, especially after what the lord himself had stated earlier: *You have nothing to offer me that I can't already take from you, if I so desire.*

She straightened her back. *If he's after my body, he'll claim it eventually at any rate—Gail or no Gail.* She nodded. "I'll suffer in her stead."

Lord Deminas' eyes gleamed with wicked joy, a devilish smile curling the corners of his lips. "Good, then go downstairs and enjoy your supper. Afterwards, you're to come back here."

Meya swallowed. "As you wish, my Lord."

# Fifteen

Meya sat down next to Nina, who was already halfway through her supper. "Hey, where have you been?" Nina asked. "I didn't see you at lunch."

Meya stirred her potage. "I went to see Gail during lunch."

Nina looked up. "How bad is it? I tried asking Lea, but she didn't say much."

It was silent for a few moments, as Meya had just taken a spoonful of potage. "The Lord sewed her lips shut."

Nina gasped. "Are you serious?"

Meya nodded. "Gail can't talk, eat, or drink."

"How long is this supposed to last if she can't even drink?" Nina was visibly upset.

Meya hesitated for a moment. *Should I tell her?* Some people were already leaving, and their table was rather quiet. Not wanting anyone to hear what she was about to say, she moved closer to Nina and whispered in her ear, "The Lord told me she was to suffer for at least three days, or even until she collapses."

The colour drained from Nina's face. "What if she dies?" she asked in a hushed voice.

"That was my concern too. Which is why I am to return to the Lord after supper. He will shorten her punishment if I suffer in her stead."

Shocked, Nina pulled away so she could look Meya in the eyes. "No," she hissed. "I don't want you to get hurt just because Gail is unable to keep her lips shut." A chuckle bubbled up from her throat. "I must say, the punishment is quite fitting in that regard."

Meya looked at her angrily. "Gail might have been at fault, but I think we can both agree that a whole day of having your lips stitched, unable to eat or drink, is punishment enough."

Nina huffed. "No doubt, but still…" She pouted a little. "I don't want you to suffer for her mistakes."

Meya's expression softened. "Thanks for your concern, but I think I should be fine… The Lord didn't state what my punishment will be, but he did say that he wouldn't leave any permanent marks on my body."

"Well, that's a relief, I suppose…" Nina stirred the last bit of her potage, avoiding Meya's gaze. "I hope you won't be too bruised then, in that case. Bruises might not be permanent, but they can still hurt a lot and for a long time, too."

"But at least bruises won't kill you. Not drinking for several days is a different thing." Meya sighed and turned her attention to her supper too.

Nina swallowed the contents of her mouth. "Just one thing though, if you indeed shorten Gail's suffering by doing this, she will owe you. Heavily! And I will make sure that she knows it."

Meya smiled at this. "Thanks, Nina." Her hand found hers and squeezed it. "I'm glad I have you to talk to."

Nina blushed a little. "Well, I'm glad you want to talk to me."

~*~

Meya stood in front of the lord's chambers. Her stomach felt heavy and she was having second thoughts. *What if he beats me really badly? It would leave no permanent marks, but still...* She remembered the black eye the slaver had given her all too well, not to mention the other punches and slaps she had received whilst in his possession.

She bit her lip, struggling internally. *Gail's a strong woman. I'm sure she can handle this.*

*But what if she doesn't even last three days? What if the damage can't be undone? Could you live with yourself knowing you could have prevented it?*

Meya closed her eyes and groaned softly. *Damn it, Gail!*

*Don't be afraid of a little bit of pain. You're a strong woman too! Go in there with your head high! Show Lord Deminas that you're willing to suffer for your friend!*

*A friend I've only known for a week and who ain't even much of a friend.*

*Well, after this, I'm pretty sure she will be. Like Nina said: she'll owe you!*

*But is that worth it?*

*Then think of Lea. Think of every one of them.*

The memory of Lea's pained expression made her heart ache.

*Come on, you can do this. Walk in there, and show Lord Deminas that you're a strong woman and a great friend.*

Meya took a deep breath and knocked on the door.

~*~

To Meya's surprise, the lord was in the bathroom. After receiving permission to enter, Meya opened the door and saw that the lord was just taking off his shirt. She immediately wanted to excuse herself but caught herself before doing so. *If I was intruding, he wouldn't have told me to come in.*

Lord Deminas caught her glimpsing him, and the vague hint of a grin appeared on his face. "Undress," he stated as he continued to do so himself.

Meya swallowed, her heart pounding in her chest. *What is he up to?* Still, she did as she was told. Trembling slightly, she stood naked before the lord.

Lord Deminas stepped into the bath. "Come, join me."

Meya's mind was slipping into chaos. *What is he planning to do? How is he planning to make me suffer?* Despite the hot water, Meya shivered. *Please, don't touch me.* She wanted to wrap her arms around herself protectively, but she managed to restrain herself, fearing the lord's response.

Lord Deminas smirked slightly as Meya sank into the water. "Are you afraid?"

Meya nodded. "Y-yes, my Lord."

"Good." He turned around, presenting his back to Meya. "You know what to do."

Perplexed, Meya simply stared at him for a few seconds. *A massage? That's it?* She moved closer to him and loosened her wrists and fingers for the task to come. *This can't be it,* she thought as she started to massage his neck and shoulders.

Just like the previous time, it didn't take long before the lord demanded Meya to go lower. Still quite confused at how this was supposed to make her suffer, she simply did as she was told.

*If this is indeed it, I'm not going to complain.* Her initial fear was slowly ebbing away and she was starting to enjoy the task. *A nice, hot bath and massaging a man with his build... No, not going to complain.* Meya mentally slapped herself for that thought. *He might be attractive, but he's still a sadist!*

As if to remind herself of that fact, her brain showed her images of Gail with her lips stitched and of the various servants she had seen with missing body parts.

*Alright, so he's cruel. But, so far I haven't heard anyone being hurt without having done something to be punished for.* She thought about Jaimy and her corpse on the rocks below the balcony, and an involuntary shiver went through her body. *Well, from what I've been told, she wasn't very smart in regard to doing her work properly. Let alone behaving...*

Images of the lord cutting the slaver's throat went through her mind and her hands fell still for a moment before continuing a little lower, at the lord's request.

*I still wonder why he did that...* Her mind wandered a bit until it lingered on what had happened after the last time they had bathed. Her hands fell still and adrenaline filled her.

"Meya, is there a problem?" Lord Deminas asked.

With a shock, she realised she had stopped massaging him. "I...I'm sorry, my Lord." She immediately wanted to continue her task, but the lord turned around.

Lord Deminas scrutinised her closely, a sly grin tugging at his lips. "You're still afraid."

Meya blinked a few times. She opened her mouth to speak, but it took a few seconds for the words to find their way out. "I...I am, my Lord."

He leaned closer to her, their noses almost touching. "What are you afraid of?"

Meya's mind was having trouble forming coherent thoughts. One part of her wanted to run away from this sadist before he decided to hurt her, another part of her desired him and wanted him, while yet another part of her feared any form of intimacy.

The lord's fingers folded around her chin, his fingers digging slightly into her skin. "Answer me."

The world spun a little. "I...I..." The lord's hold on her chin intensified for a moment, and this seemed to bring a little order back to her mind. "I'm afraid that you will cut my hand again."

He released her, a low chuckle echoing through the bathroom. "That's not what I had in mind."

Meya stared at him, fear putting all the hairs on her body on end. *What's that supposed to mean? Did I just give him an idea? What does he have in mind?*

Lord Deminas submerged, ran his hands through his hair a few times, and surfaced again. He stood up and got out of the bath. "Wash yourself and get out—faster this time than last. I'll be waiting for you."

The water was still quite hot, but Meya felt frozen. Not wanting to incur additional punishment, she managed to force herself back to life. She quickly washed herself, got out of the bath, dried off, and wrapped the towel around her torso.

Lord Deminas had disappeared into his bedroom, leaving the door slightly ajar.

Meya stared at the thin gap, the flickering of light visible beyond. *Whatever he plans to do, you will have to face it.* She swallowed. *Come on, you can do this.*

She took a deep breath and walked towards the door, her legs feeling a bit wobbly despite trying to be strong. She raised her chin, straightened her back, and knocked on the door.

"Enter."

She stepped into the room illuminated by candle and lamplight, and the hearth next to the bed emitted a pleasant warmth. Lord Deminas stood next to the four-poster bed, the towel wrapped around his waist. Meya's mind was torn between two extremes. Seeing the lord standing there, his toned chest still gleaming from the bath, she couldn't help but desire him. At the same time, she wanted to run—and if he tried to catch her, she would use hands, feet, and even teeth to get away.

"Take off that towel and lie down on the floor, on your back."

Meya's heart pounded loudly in her ears, the levels of adrenaline in her blood increasing. *The floor? Why the floor?* Trembling, she removed the towel. The lord turned his head ever so slightly to the corner of the room, and that's where Meya dropped it. *Oh God, what is he going to do to me?*

Suppressing the desire to storm out, she sat down on the stone floor. Shivers ran through her body as she lowered herself. Goosebumps covered her skin, intensified by the cold stones touching her back. Once she was down, she stared at the ceiling, petrified of what was going to happen next.

Lord Deminas knelt next to her on one knee. "You're so scared, I can smell it."

Meya bit her lip. *And you're loving it, aren't you? Please, just get it over with, whatever you're planning!*

**117**

The lord ran his finger over her skin, starting at her neck, going down to her side, then towards her belly button, and up between her breasts. A sharp intake of breath caused Lord Deminas to grin with amusement. He stood up and walked towards the cabinet. "We're going to play a little game. The rules are simple: keep your eyes closed and don't move."

The blood drained from Meya's face. Her mind was foggy from the fear and tension. *What's he going to do?* She lifted her head so that she could see the Lord and her heart skipped a beat.

Lord Deminas returned from the cabinet holding a candelabrum in his hand. The flames created a wicked glint in his eyes. He placed it down on the ground, right above Meya's head. "Do you understand?"

Meya's lips parted, but no sound passed. *Is he going to burn me?*

The lord raised a brow. "Answer me."

"Eyes closed... D-don't move... I...I'll try," Meya managed to utter.

His eyes shone with a devilish joy. "Then close them."

Her lower lip quivered and she swallowed back a sob. *Oh God, please...* Slowly, she shut her eyes. Her world reduced itself to the cold stones against her back, the sound of her heart racing and the occasional crackle coming from the hearth, and the presence of the lord next to her. She braced herself for intense pain, for—

A screech left her lips as something touched her leg, but it was just the lord's finger.

Lord Deminas chuckled. "You truly are frightened. Try to relax." He lowered himself and whispered into her ear, his unexpected closeness shocking her, "Relax, or this will be worse than it actually is."

Meya tried to focus on her breathing. It took a minute or so, but finally the chaos in her mind lessened and her heart rate slowed down a bit. The lord trailed a finger along her arm, and this time, she only responded with a sharp intake of air.

"That's better."

Despite having her eyes closed, the world spun. *Dear God, this is torture already and I'm sure he hasn't even begun yet.* She swallowed and continued to focus on her breathing, the anxiety of what was going to happen eating away at the edges of her mind. She wanted to open her eyes so she could at least see what he was up to, but she trusted her hearing and she knew he hadn't moved.

Suddenly, something hot and liquid touched her stomach. Shocked, a short scream left her lips, her eyes opened wide, and she rose slightly from the floor. A firm hand against her chest pressed her back down.

"Don't forget the rules now. Close your eyes and don't move," Lord Deminas growled, though he sounded more entertained than angry.

Panting, Meya closed her eyes, but at least she now knew what was going on. *It's just hot wax... It's just hot wax...* It took her a few moments to calm her breathing down. *It's just hot wax.* Despite telling herself that, when the next drop fell, another screech left her lips. This time, she did manage to keep her eyes closed, though her body twitched.

"Good, you're getting there."

She focused on her breathing and tried to relax her body. *It's not even that hot, so why do I scream?*

A drop landed just below her rib cage and this time she squeaked instead, causing Lord Deminas to chuckle sadistically.

*Oh, come on Meya!* She reprimanded herself. *This is nothing compared to having your lips stitched!* Another drop fell, and she squeaked yet again, her body twitching slightly against her will. She felt the wax cool to a pleasant temperature until she barely noticed it was there at all.

More drops fell, and Meya managed to reduce her responses to mere gasps, yet her body kept twitching involuntarily. Every time she spasmed, she could feel the solidified drops that were already on her skin. She was able to remain calm, but after every drop, the wait for the next one was excruciating. Her entire body would tense up in anticipation and she had to force herself to relax.

Lord Deminas noticed how Meya adapted, and with a mischievous smile, he let the next drop fall onto her right breast.

Meya squealed and nearly opened her eyes as the hot wax landed on the soft flesh and continued to glide down to her sternum, cooling on the way. *Evil! Evil, sadistic—*

Another drop landed on her breast, quickly followed by another straight on the nipple.

Meya gasped loudly, the hot wax cooling on her sensitive flesh sending shivers down her spine. More drops fell, one by one on her breasts. The world spun and her mind blurred. *This is wrong,* she thought. She was afraid, anxious, yet there was something about it that aroused her.

"Do you like this?" Lord Deminas whispered into her ear, his voice breaking the silence and causing Meya to gasp.

*Yes. No!* She groaned. "I...I'm not sure, my Lord."*Does he expect me to like this? This is supposed to be torture, right?*

More drops fell. On her chest, her stomach, even her upper legs. She twitched and squirmed slightly, gasping, and even moaning, with some of the drops. Her mind went silent, occupied only with the hot wax cooling, and the anticipation of the next drop.

She lost all track of time.

The patches of solidified wax tugged at her skin, though some lay loosely, freed from her flesh by her twitching and squirming. Her nipples were covered by little caps of wax, and every now and then, the lord dripped a new, hot droplet on top of it, the heat radiating through.

"Do you like this?" Lord Deminas asked again.

Breathing heavily, Meya answered, "Yes, my Lord."

His fingers trailed her jawline, and she opened her mouth in a silent moan. "You've been a good servant. Keep your eyes closed and remain where you are—it's time to remove the wax." He placed the remainder of the candle back in the candelabrum, stood up, and set it back on the cabinet.

Meya listened to his footsteps distancing themselves from her, and then coming closer again. The sudden warmth of the lord's hand on her leg sent a shiver through her body. He pushed her legs apart, and the fog in Meya's mind instantly cleared. *What's he going to do?*

His fingers tugged at the solidified wax, plucking all the drops and patches from her legs one by one, and she relaxed slightly. The lord moved up, cleaning her stomach next. Meya tensed up as she realised the next area was going to be her chest—more importantly: her nipples.

The lord took his time removing all of it, and when he finally started on her breasts, he saved the wax covering her nipples for last.

Meya panted slightly, both from anxiety and arousal.

Slowly, Lord Deminas loosened the patch of wax from the skin beneath until he could lift it off the nipple. He lowered himself and trailed his lips along Meya's neck, causing her to moan softly. "Such pretty imprints," he whispered into her ear. "I'm going to save these." His words caused her to blush feverishly. He freed her other nipple, then he got up and walked away.

Meya waited with her eyes still closed on the stone floor. She swallowed and focused on her breathing—she was panting from arousal. It didn't take long before she regained control over her body and her breathing returned to normal. She realised the floor was cold, something she had seemingly forgotten during the entire ordeal. Goosebumps started to cover her body and she had to resist the urge to hug her legs close, to warm herself.

Lord Deminas returned. "Open your eyes."

Meya complied, and she was surprised to see the lord standing over her, a towel in one hand. He stretched out his free hand.

"Get up."

Slowly, Meya rose into a sitting position. When she was sure that there was enough blood going into her head, she took the lord's hand and let him pull her onto her feet. She closed her eyes as the room spun, but it lasted only a moment.

The lord took the towel and used it to wipe Meya's body off, removing the final remnants of wax. Meya simply let it all happen, holding onto the lord's shoulders to keep herself from falling over. *Why's he doing this?*

He deposited the towel on top of the pile of wax. "You can clean that up in the morning."

"Yes, my Lord," Meya answered, slightly confused by everything that had happened. She shivered, the cold getting to her despite the fire in the corner of the room.

Lord Deminas noticed, a cruel grin tugging at his lips. "If you're cold, you have my permission to crawl underneath the covers."

Meya turned to look at the bed. It looked mighty inviting, warm and comfortable. Still, she hesitated. *If I get into that bed, what will happen?*

Noticing her doubt, Lord Deminas stepped behind her and placed his hands on her shoulders. "Stop being afraid," he whispered into her ear. "If I want your body, I will take it."

Meya's heart clenched in her chest. *I know, but that doesn't mean I don't fear it.* Still, the desire for warmth and comfort won. On wobbly legs, she walked over to the bed and climbed under the thick covers. She curled into a little ball, preserving her body heat.

Not a minute later, Lord Deminas took a seat on the edge of the bed. "Sit up."

Reluctant to leave the warmth, she clung to the covers as she complied.

The lord presented her a cup. "Here, drink."

Confused, she took the cup from him. Water. Perplexed by the rather kind gesture, she almost forgot to thank him and she quickly did, causing him to smile coyly. Grateful, she emptied the cup.

The lord stood up again. "I'll be right back."

Meya watched him leave for the sitting room. She placed the empty cup on the bedside table and crawled back under the covers. Despite no longer being cold, she still shivered. *Oh God, I'm in the Lord's bed. What's going to happen next?* She dreaded the possibilities that ran through her mind, her arousal from before replaced with fear.

Peering at the door leading to the sitting room, she apprehensively waited for the lord to return.

# Sixteen

Lord Deminas appeared in the doorway, holding the silver blade in his right hand.

Meya stiffened. *What's he going to do?*

The lord walked over to the bed and pulled down the covers slightly, exposing Meya's chest, then he climbed on top of her and sat down on her legs. "Now for the next bit, I want you to remain still." He lowered himself so that he could whisper into her ear, "I told you I wasn't going to leave any permanent marks, but if you move, I might cut you deeper than intended."

Meya whimpered at the thought of what was coming next. *Why did I agree to suffer in Gail's place again?*

Lord Deminas rose and he placed the tip of the silver blade against her lips. "Shhh…" His eyes shimmered with sadistic delight. He lowered the blade to her collarbone, and slowly traced it over her skin down to her solar plexus. The blade left a white path, which very slowly reddened into welts.

Meya lay frozen, even forgetting how to breathe. The lord's fingers on her chin triggered her lungs into functioning again.

"Such delicate flesh…" He pulled the blade over her breast, ensuring a red line would appear there after several seconds.

Meya suppressed a shiver. *He's evil.*

With his free hand, he cupped her right breast, massaging it, while the blade created several more welts on her chest.

Meya bit her lip as her cheeks heated up. *Sadistic, evil—*

Lord Deminas lowered himself and flicked his tongue against her nipple, causing Meya to gasp. His hand gently squeezed her breast as his teeth grazed her nipple, before lightly sucking it.

Meya's mind shattered into pieces as waves of pleasure rolled through her body. She arched her back and moaned softly as the lord stimulated her.

With a grin, he straightened himself again. He placed his left hand firmly on Meya's chest and brought the knife closer to her right breast. "Now, remain still."

Flustered, Meya didn't quite understand what was happening. Suddenly a sharp, burning pain rushed through her breast, clearing the fog that had settled in her head. She nearly shot up in a reflex, but the lord's hand kept her in place.

"I told you to keep still."

Meya whimpered as the wound on her breast throbbed painfully. She could feel the blood seeping down, the tickling sensation contrasting with the burning of the cut.

Lord Deminas put the blade down on the bed and used his now free hand to cup Meya's left breast, while his other hand held the side of her right breast—away from the cut. He bent down and started to slowly lick up the blood, sending shivers through Meya's body.

*He's insane.* Meya trembled slightly, wincing every time the lord's tongue connected with her skin. *Drinking blood...*

It didn't take long before the lord had lapped up all of the blood and had his mouth directly over the cut. His tongue flicked against the wound, setting Meya's already screaming nerves on fire.

She groaned and whimpered, tears escaping her eyes. The fact that the lord was simultaneously massaging her breast caused great conflict in her mind—pleasure and agony weren't two things she was used to experiencing at the same time. Her head whirled. Despite herself, she realised she was becoming aroused.

Lord Deminas noticed Meya's breathing was becoming heavier and responded by flicking his tongue against her nipple a few times.

A gasp escaped Meya's lips, and she quickly shut her mouth. *Damn him.* The lord continued to lick the wound, the hot pain contrasting greatly with the pleasure she had just felt. She bit her lip in an attempt to silence the agonised whimpers that wanted out, but she only succeeded in muffling them instead.

Lord Deminas rose and looked Meya straight in her eyes, his gaze filled with sinister delight. "Are you enjoying this?" His right hand gently pinched her nipple.

Meya bit her lip, but she couldn't stop herself from arching her back slightly. Despite the arousal, the cut on her breast stung like hell. *What do I answer?*

"Well?" The lord pinched her nipple a bit harder.

Meya squirmed. "Y-yes and no, m-my Lord."

The corners of his lips rose a little. "Explain."

*Oh, damn it... Really?* Meya swallowed, unsure of how to continue. "The cut... It hurts."

Lord Deminas lowered himself and licked the wound a few times, his eyes fixed on Meya's, taking in her suffering.

Meya's nerves screamed from the sensory overload. *Fucking sadist!* Tears slipped from her eyes as she clutched the sheets in anguish.

The lord rose a bit and licked her neck. "Don't forget that this is *meant* to hurt." His hot breath against her ear made her feel weak.

He flicked his tongue against her earlobe, while at the same time pinching her nipple, causing her to moan softly. Meya's mind had trouble forming coherent thoughts.

"You agreed to suffer in Gail's stead." He moved down again to lick the wound.

Meya winced. "I...I did, my Lord."

He looked up, blood glistening on his lips. "If you can't take it anymore, you may tell me so." He licked his lips clean. "I'll stop, however..." A devilish joy was visible in his eyes. "Gail's punishment won't end tomorrow morning."

Meya swallowed. *Is he seriously offering me a way out?* She was quiet for a few seconds. "If... If we stop now... When will Gail's punishment end, my Lord?"

Lord Deminas thought this over. "Tomorrow, after supper." He lowered himself so his nose almost touched Meya's. "Does that mean you wish for the pain to stop? Is it too much?"

Meya bit her lip. *He's enjoying this... But I'm no weakling!* She kept her eyes locked on his and gathered her courage. "I don't enjoy pain, my Lord," she said calmly. "Yes, I want it to end, but no, it's not too much." She felt stronger having said that. *And I've suffered this much already; I'm not going to quit now.*

Something changed in the lord's eyes, and he smiled slyly. "Is that so?"

Meya nodded. "Please, my Lord, continue so that Gail's punishment will end in the morning." She hesitated for a moment, then added, "I can handle it."

His grip on her breast increased, squeezing it rather roughly. Meya groaned and turned her head away from him, her eyes closed. He grazed his teeth over her exposed neck and whispered into her ear, "You amaze me..." Then he straightened himself, that same sinister delight burning in his eyes.

Meya looked at the man sitting on top of her, though he looked more like a demon now. *I'm going to regret this, aren't I?*

Lord Deminas placed his left hand on her chest again and picked up the blade. "Then let's continue."

Meya took a deep breath and braced herself for the pain. The moment the silver bit into the already sensitive flesh just below the existing cut, she whimpered loudly. *Yes, regretting this already!* Tears streamed down her face as her chest felt like it was on fire.

Greedily, Lord Deminas relished the fresh blood.

Meya cried as silently as she could, but every time the lord's tongue touched one of the cuts, she squealed softly. Lord Deminas kept massaging her breasts and stimulating her nipples every now and then, and Meya was unsure if this was making it easier or harder for her to suffer through the pain.

~*~

Time blurred as Meya lost herself in the chaos of sensations. Floating, she was simply aware of the fresh, sharp pain of two new cuts on her other breast. She was too far gone though, to recall when the lord had made them.

The burning sensation on her left breast started to lessen, despite Lord Deminas' tongue flicking over the wounds. Slowly, Meya came back to her senses, and just as the lord started to lick the cuts on her other breast, she realised the left one was no longer hurting. The remaining pain lessened rapidly, and then it was gone. Confused, Meya looked at the lord. He rose up and licked his lips clean, though his goatee was smeared with blood—some fresh, some coagulated.

Meya swallowed. *What happened to the pain?* She wanted to voice her questions, but her head felt heavy and talking seemed like something that simply cost too much energy—energy she didn't have.

Lord Deminas stood up. "We're done." He smiled. "I'll end Gail's punishment in the morning."

Still confused, Meya watched him leave for the bathroom. *I... made it?* She wanted to look at her chest, to see the damage, but she was too tired to raise her head from the pillow. *What happened?* Her head was still rather hazy, and her eyes slipped closed. *Why's the pain gone?*

125

Meya awoke from her half-slumber when she felt something cold and wet against her chest. She slowly opened her eyes and realised Lord Deminas was cleaning her with a cloth. He had cleaned himself too—his goatee was devoid of blood.

When he was done, he helped Meya sit upright a bit and presented her a cup of water. "Drink."

Slowly, she emptied the cup. The fog seemed to clear a bit in her head, but the tiredness in her limbs remained. "Thank... you... my Lord," she whispered.

"Lie back down, you need to rest," Lord Deminas said, and he took the cup from her.

Meya gratefully sank back onto the bed, and to her surprise, the lord pulled the blankets up to her neck. Baffled, she watched him blow out the candles and leave the room again. *Why is he allowing me to stay here? Hell, why is he even mindful of me?* Her mind was full of questions, but the weariness claimed her and she drifted off to sleep.

~*~

It was the middle of the night when Meya woke up with a full bladder. Reluctant to leave the comforting warmth of her bed, she turned onto her other side. With a shock, she noticed there was someone lying next to her, and she gasped when she realised just who that person was.

*Oh, God... Did we...?* Meya's brain was suddenly fully awake as it tried to remember what had happened earlier. *He left me alone in the bed... Did he seriously just crawl in beside me later? Why didn't he kick me out?* Her head whirled. *This is crazy.*

Carefully, so as to not wake the lord, she slipped out of bed and tiptoed to the bathroom. Sitting on the latrine, she placed her head in her hands and stared out into the darkness.

*I don't understand... Why? Why would he condone my presence in his bed?*

Her fingers entwined themselves in her hair and she pulled at her locks in frustration.

*He makes me strip in front of him, makes me bathe with him. He killed the slaver after he made him apologise to me. He punishes Gail extremely for spreading a nasty rumour about me. Yet, he allows me to suffer in her stead and then halfway in, he offers me a way out.*

She groaned.

*What does he want? If he wanted sex, why not just order me?*

Sighing, she threw her head back and stared at the ceiling.

126

*I don't get this man. He's cold, cruel, yet he seems to care. Why?*

She muffled a frustrated yelp and tugged her hair roughly.

*Damn it! I'm sure he's just playing with me! I doubt someone like him actually cares about his servants. He's a fucking sadist—I saw that much in his eyes when he hurt me.*

She took a deep breath and relaxed a bit, untangling her fingers from her hair.

*Yes, that's it... This is just a sadistic game to him. Confusing me, messing with my head. It's all probably just a huge turn on for him.*

Shivering from the cold, she stood up and made her way back to the bedroom.

*Well, I won't let him get to me! If he wants to play, I'll play along.* She smiled slightly. *I have Nina. With her help, I'm sure I can stay grounded.*

She stepped into the warmer bedroom and closed the bathroom door silently. Abruptly, all the strength and confidence she had had a mere moment ago slipped away.

*Oh God, what do I do now? Do I crawl back into bed with him?* She bit her lip. *Well, what other choice do I have?*

She contemplated getting her clothes and sneaking out to her own quarters but dreaded encountering a guard—let alone the lord's reaction. Reluctant, she slipped back under the covers. She made sure to stay as close to the edge of the bed as was possible without falling out. Still shivering, she relished the warmth that started to surround her.

"Cold?"

Meya stiffened at the sound of the lord's voice and her heart skipped a beat. *Oh dear God, he's awake!*

"I asked if you're cold…"

Noticing the hint of impatience in his voice, Meya tried her best to get her vocal cords functioning again. "A…a bit, my Lord."

"Then why don't you move away from the edge, or are you afraid I might bite?"

*Not bite...* The silver blade flashed before her mind's eye.

"Well?"

Meya groaned internally. *I don't have a choice, do I?* Reluctant, she shifted closer to the lord, but she didn't dare turn around. Thinking she was far enough from the edge, she stopped moving.

Suddenly, Lord Deminas' hot body pressed against her back and her breathing hitched. His lips caressed her ear as he whispered, "You haven't answered my question."

Meya couldn't think straight. The lord's body heat ensured she was no longer cold, but it didn't stop her from trembling. She could feel his groin against her backside and her mind was spinning out of control.

"P-please," she managed to utter. "D-don't..." She was terrified that the lord would force himself on her. Tears stung her eyes and she closed them. She wanted to plead again, but her voice refused to cooperate.

Lord Deminas wrapped an arm around Meya's chest, pulling her tightly against him. "I have the feeling that that wasn't the answer to my question." His fingers brushed Meya's cheek, spreading her tears. "As much as I enjoy being feared, I want to be feared for what I actually do or *might* do."

His hot breath against her ear sent shivers up her spine and her head reeled. *Oh God, please...* Her heart was beating frantically in her chest. She wanted to jump out of bed and run out of the room, but she was too petrified to even open her eyes.

"Shhh..." The lord moved his hand over her face, the tips of his fingers sliding gently over her eyes, nose, and mouth. "Relax." He rested his hand on her chest, just below her neck.

Meya tried her best to do as she was told, but it was already taking all of her effort to not simply break down into a quivering, sobbing mess. Seconds turned into minutes, and the lack of anything happening caused her to relax— she was simply too exhausted to remain in an agitated state. Her breathing became regular again and her heart slowed down. The fact that Lord Deminas didn't do anything aside from hold her close, his hand not even on one of her breasts, put her mind somewhat at ease.

*If he wants me, he could just take me. Nina's right about that, and it doesn't matter if I like it or not. I'm his servant, his slave, his property... But that doesn't mean I can just accept it.* Her breathing was slow and deep. *Why does he even mind if I am cold or not? Or bother to try to calm my nerves?* The warm body pressing against her was soothing, the desire to snuggle up against him rising above her fear—but she was too tired to move. *Is he really just playing games, or does he actually care?* Sleep claimed her pondering mind and she drifted away.

~*~

The sound of bells woke Meya from a deep sleep. Disorientated, she searched for the window that would show a gloomy sky, but it was pitch black in the room. She stumbled out of bed, and the size of it made her realise it wasn't hers.

128

Shocked, she sat on the edge. *Oh my God, I spent the night with Lord Deminas!* Memories flooded her mind and they left her utterly confused. *Why? Why did he allow me to stay here until morning?* She thought of her room-mates, of Nina. *How the hell am I going to explain this?* The door to the bathroom opened, startling her.

Lord Deminas walked in, holding the candelabrum. The multiple flames illuminated the room, and the lord grinned playfully upon seeing Meya. "Did you sleep well?"

Meya flushed red. "Y-yes, my Lord." She swallowed, gathering her courage. "Thank you for allowing me to—"

"Oh, shush." He walked into the room and placed the candelabrum back on the cabinet. "Don't get the wrong idea now." He moved towards her and cupped her chin, making her look up at him. "You're mine to use as I please, and I simply enjoyed your company." The light flickering on his face created eerie, dancing shadows.

Meya froze at hearing his words, but something felt off to her. *If he really just did it for himself, then why did he let me rest alone after he was done torturing me?*

"You did well last night. As agreed, I will end Gail's punishment." He let go of Meya's chin. "Get dressed and tell Gail to come to the dungeons after breakfast."

"Yes, my Lord," Meya said meekly.

A sly smirk crept upon the lord's face, but he turned around and left the room without another word.

Meya took a moment to arrange her thoughts, but she quickly gave up. *That man is simply too confusing.* With a deep sigh, she rose and started to look for her clothes. The floor was littered with little pieces of wax and Meya cringed at the memory. *Great, I get to clean that up later.*

Thinking about what she had suffered through the previous night, she examined her chest. The multiple cuts were still visible on her breasts, but the wounds had closed up neatly. A shiver ran through her, and she hurried into the bathroom to gather her clothes and get dressed.

~*~

Meya rushed through the castle in search of Gail. She hadn't been in their quarters, so she instead made her way to Gail's workplace. As expected, Gail was sitting at her desk, her shoulders slumped as she worked on a pair of trousers.

129

"Gail?"

She jumped slightly and turned around. Her dull eyes lit up for a moment when she saw that it was Meya. She placed her needle down but didn't stand up.

"I've got some good news," Meya started. "You're to go to the dungeons. Lord Deminas will end your punishment after breakfast."

Gail's eyes widened in shock, and now she *did* stand up. She flung herself around Meya's neck and murmured something unintelligible, though it seemed to resemble a thank you.

Meya gently pushed her room-mate away so she could look her in the eyes. "Just realise though, that I had to suffer in your stead to convince the Lord to end your punishment prematurely. So you owe me for this, heavily!"

Gail nodded, her eyes tearing up, and she took Meya's hands in her own. She bowed her head in gratitude multiple times, murmuring the same thing over and over—despite the fact that Meya couldn't understand what she was saying.

"Just go, you can thank me properly with words later."

Gail smiled for as far as the stitches would allow, gave Meya another hug, and left.

Feeling weak and slightly light-headed, Meya made her way to the dining hall. *She's going to miss breakfast, but if I hurry, I should still be able to get some. And God, do I need some.*

# Seventeen

With a plate of food, Meya sat down at an empty table. Most of the servants had already finished their meals and were leaving to commence their daily chores. Famished, Meya started to devour her chunk of bread. She wasn't even halfway when she noticed a presence behind her. She turned around and was surprised to see not only Juris but also Nina and Lea standing there.

Juris and Lea looked at Meya worriedly, while Nina avoided her gaze, fumbling with her apron.

"Where were you?" Lea asked. "You were gone all night! We were scared you—" Her voice broke.

Juris placed a hand on Lea's shoulder to comfort her. He looked at Meya. "You probably don't know this, but there have been a few disappearances in the past. We didn't know where you were, and I think you can imagine what we thought..."

Meya's gaze went from Juris to Nina. Her cheeks had reddened and she was looking at the floor. *She didn't tell them what I was doing?* For a moment she wondered why, but then she realised she probably didn't want to tell anyone anything without her permission. *Oh, Nina...*

Lea suddenly hugged Meya. "We were so worried! We hoped Juris would know, but he was just as surprised by your absence as we were."

"It's fine." Meya sighed. "To keep it short... I made a deal with Lord Deminas. He would shorten Gail's punishment if I was to suffer in her stead."

Lea gasped. "You what? Are you alright?" She held Meya at an arm's length and looked her over. "You look pale—paler than usual. What did he do?"

Meya shook her head. "That doesn't matter. At any rate, I was away all night because of that. However, Gail's stitches are to be removed after breakfast." She smiled.

Juris looked quite shocked. "That's... extremely brave of you to do. I'll go get some food for Gail and drop it off at her desk, so she can eat when she returns—I bet she's hungry."

"That's very sweet of you. Thanks, Juris. Just eh..." Meya hesitated. "Try not to let too many people know about this, please? I don't want anyone getting the wrong idea."

Juris nodded and walked away.

Lea looked a bit uncomfortable. "I'm not so sure if we can keep this from the other servants, though. We sort of asked around." She noticed Meya's expression and quickly added, "We were worried! We thought you had been taken, or..." She trailed off.

Nina sighed. "I'm sorry. I tried telling them not to worry, but they wouldn't listen to me."

Lea turned to Nina, her eyes large. "So you knew? You *knew* she was with the Lord?"

Nina nodded, clearly ashamed. "I didn't want to tell... It wasn't my place. I also didn't want to raise any false hopes on account of Gail... If Meya hadn't succeeded, it would have been so shameful for her if we had all been expecting—"

Lea slapped her—though not hard—and then hugged her tight. "You're a terrible room-mate, but an amazing friend. You left us worried, but all because you were trying to protect Meya." She let go of her and smiled. "At least I can be certain that the Lord won't ever have to sew *your* lips shut."

They giggled. When the laughter died down, Lea excused herself and dragged Nina along with her, leaving Meya to finish her meal.

~*~

That evening, Meya and Nina sneaked into the lord's old chambers again. They sat on the bed while Nina braided Meya's hair.

132

"I have to say, I never expected you to not tell anyone about what I was doing yesterday for Gail. Thank you for that."

"No worries. It was well worth that one slap." Nina chuckled. "Lea didn't even hit me that hard. And considering how worried they were..." She sighed. "They really feared you were gone, like the previous maids."

"It must have been hard for you to keep your mouth shut."

"Not really, to be honest." Nina's fingers brushed through Meya's red locks, parting them to create another braid. "I did tell them not to worry, that you'd show up soon enough. But, to be fair, I was worried too... I was afraid of what he was doing to you."

There was a moment of silence.

"What... What *did* he do?"

Meya bit her lip. She had expected Nina to ask this, and she had already decided to tell her everything. She *needed* to tell someone everything, for she feared she'd go insane if she kept it all to herself.

Despite finding it very difficult to voice what had transpired, she managed to tell it all. When she was done, she turned around to face Nina. She had completed the braiding about halfway through but she hadn't moved. "What do you think? Is the Lord a demon of sorts?"

Nina wetted her lips, but it took her a moment to reply. "I don't know... His obsession with blood is rather... unusual, that's for sure. But a demon?" She shook her head. "I truly don't know."

Meya touched her hair that was now tied in a waterfall braid. "Where did you get a string to tie the end with?"

Nina seemed to welcome the change of subject. "Gail. I went to her this afternoon and asked her for some pieces." She smirked. "I told her I wanted to braid your hair, so she couldn't really refuse, considering what you did for her."

Meya giggled. "Already abusing the fact that she owes me, huh?"

"Yup." She grinned broadly. "Considering what the Lord did, I think a few strands of string aren't a lot to ask for." Her expression turned serious.

"What's wrong?"

Nina avoided Meya's gaze. "I... Ehm..." She looked up. "Can I see what he did to you?"

Meya frowned. "What do you mean?"

She pointed at her chest. "Where he cut..."

Meya flushed red. "Why?"

Now it was Nina's turn to blush. "I...I just..." She looked away again. "You have a very pretty body and I wanted to make sure he didn't ruin it."

Meya giggled nervously. "Are you serious?"

Flustered, Nina played with her apron. "You don't have to if it makes you feel uncomfortable."

*She* is *serious.* Meya's heart rate quickened and she considered Nina's request. *Well, it's not like she hasn't seen me naked before... And we're both girls...*

Nina took Meya's silence for a no. "I'm sorry I asked! I should've realised you're not comfortable doing such a thing, especially after everything that happened."

Meya shook her head, smiling softly. Nina's caring words made her feel more at ease. "I think I can show you." She undressed, though she still felt tense while doing so. *Come on, it's just Nina. She's kind and won't hurt you. Stop being afraid already and relax,* she berated herself.

Nina took the lamp from the shelf and used it to illuminate Meya's chest. Her fingers reached out to touch the lines running along the pale skin of Meya's breast, but she hesitated and looked up. "May I?"

Meya considered this, then nodded. "It's alright, it doesn't hurt."*Not anymore...*

Nina carefully touched the healing cuts, amazed at the state of the wounds. "This is truly mind-boggling. He cuts you, drinks your blood, and then uses his own blood to make your wounds close up?" She shook her head. "I don't think he's a demon, but maybe he's some sort of warlock? I mean, how does one heal wounds with blood? That has to be magic."

Meya shivered. "I don't know which I'd find more disturbing... Him being a demon or a warlock."

"Both would explain his success out on the battlefield." Nina froze, eyes widening in shock. "I just remembered something. The generals, I once overheard them talking about some ritual..."

Goosebumps covered Meya's skin. Her mind flooded with visions of satanic rituals and she pushed them away, frightened.

"It seems the generals drink this special brew before going into battle. One of them said it tasted rancid, but that it was worth it. Some others also commented on the foul taste, said the herbs didn't do a good job at masking the blood." Nina swallowed. "Then one of them told them to shush about it and to never talk about it outside the circle." She shifted on the bed, her eyes low. "I thought they were talking about animal blood. I've heard stories of people from the north drinking animal blood before going to battle, as a means to bolster themselves. I never even considered they might have been talking about human blood."

"Well, we still don't know if they were talking about human blood or not."

Nina looked up. "True. But, considering the Lord's obsession, wouldn't it be logical?"

"Not really. What if they did do this animal blood ritual and Lord Deminas just wanted to take it further? Go from animal to human blood? It wouldn't necessarily mean the generals drink human blood too."

Nina sighed. "I suppose you're right." She placed the lamp back on the shelf and sat down on the bed. "Still, I'll keep my ears open. I find this rather disturbing and I wish I knew what was going on."

"Same here. Considering this strange interest the Lord seems to have... I don't want to end up dead." Cold, Meya collected her clothes and got dressed again. She noticed the disappointed look in Nina's eyes and asked, "What's wrong?"

Nina shook her head. "Nothing..." She patted the spot beside her and Meya sat down. The moment she did, Nina hugged her close. "Please don't worry too much."

"I try... But still, I fear I might end up like the previous maids."

"You won't. Just obey the Lord and ensure he has no valid reason to dispose of you." She cupped Meya's cheek. "I will be here for you. I'll make sure you won't go crazy from his mind games. I'll help keep you grounded. I may not be able to take away any pain he inflicts on your body, but maybe..." She briefly bit her lower lip. "Maybe I can ease your mind?"

Meya smiled at Nina's kind words. "I hope—" She wanted to say more, but Nina had pressed her lips against hers. The kiss took her by surprise, silencing her thoughts, freezing her in place.

Nina pulled away the moment she realised Meya didn't answer her kiss. "I...I'm sorry."

*What just happened?* Meya's heart raced in her chest, tension rising in her stomach. *Did she just kiss me?* Her face heated up as her mind tried to come up with a reply. "No... It's fine."

Nina's expression went grave. She wanted to turn away, but Meya placed her hand on her shoulder.

"You... You took me by surprise."

Nina shook her head. "It's alright, you don't need to apologise. I understand if you don't feel—" Nina's eyes widened as Meya silenced her with a kiss.

They kissed passionately and Meya's head whirled from ecstasy. *Oh God, what am I doing?* Her lips kept moving against Nina's, her arms tightly wrapped around her frame. She felt light-headed, her breathing heavy. The sexual tension that had been building up wanted out, and she had trouble controlling herself. She thought back to when Lord Deminas had kissed her and quickly pushed the memory away. *No, let's not spoil this.* She opened her mouth and Nina followed her lead, their tongues entwining. *This can't be compared. This I want.*

Panting slightly, Nina was the one to pull away after a while. She smiled upon seeing Meya pout. "As much as I love this, we must get going soon. I... kind of lost track of time there."

Meya sniggered. "I wonder why."

Nina planted a fierce kiss on her lips, playfully nibbling Meya's lower lip before she withdrew. "I'm serious though. I doubt Gail would start any gossip after what happened, but others still might."

Moping, Meya sat up. "You're right. I... I just rather enjoyed what we were doing just now." She sighed. "Lord Deminas messes too much with my head." She looked into Nina's eyes and caressed her cheek. "But you know what? You *did* manage to ease my mind."

Nina smiled and hugged her. "Well, we can come here at night as often as you'd like. We just need to make sure we avoid running into anyone on our way here, or back."

Meya bit her lip. "What about rumours though? What do we tell the others when we return to our quarters so late?"

Nina shrugged. "To mind their own business. Seriously, they can pry all they want, but you don't need to tell them anything you don't want to." She grinned slyly. "The fact that you got Gail indebted to you is quite... convenient."

"You've got a point there." Meya leaned towards Nina, hoping to steal another kiss, but Nina placed a finger on Meya's lips.

"Ah-ah... Come on, we need to go." With a coy smile, she stood up and retrieved the lamp from the shelf.

Meya sighed and got off the bed, straightening her clothes. She looked at Nina and the butterflies in her stomach fluttered. "Just one little kiss, before we go?"

Nina considered this for a second. "Just *one*."

She kissed her hungrily, their tongues circling each other for a brief moment before parting. Flushed, Meya licked her lips, already missing the sensation of Nina's against hers.

"Now let's go."

~*~

They reached the door to their chambers and Meya couldn't help feeling anxious. She swallowed and mentally slapped her cheeks. *They won't be able to tell what happened, relax. If you think too much about it, you're just going to look suspicious, so stop it!* But her mind refused to be controlled and continued to rerun what had happened earlier with Nina. *Her lips were so soft...* She unknowingly licked her own.

"Meya?"

Startled, Meya looked at Nina. "Sorry, what?"

Nina smiled mischievously. "Nothing." She leaned towards her, their mouths almost touching.

Meya closed her eyes, awaiting the kiss, but instead she suddenly heard Nina whispering into her ear.

"You're cute." She playfully flicked her tongue against her earlobe, causing Meya to tremble. "But you need to snap out of it."

Meya moaned internally. *But I don't want to...* She hated to admit it, but she wanted her. *Even if it's just holding one another. I want to feel safe and warm and—*

Nina planted a quick kiss on her lips. "Come on." She opened the door and stepped inside.

Flustered, Meya followed her inside. She tried her best to avoid the curious eyes of her other room-mates, while nervously biting on her lip. *Great, just great. It feels like what we just did is written on my forehead. Let's just hope they can't see how red my face is with this light.*

The way Gail furrowed her brows made it quite clear that she was trying to figure out where they had been, and what they had been up to. The several dark crusts on her upper and lower lip seemed to keep her from asking though.

Nina shot Gail a glare as if telepathically telling her to indeed keep her mouth shut.

Lea was the first to speak. "I don't know where you two have been, but I doubt I need to tell you not to wander the castle so late."

Nina sat down in front of the fire, warming her hands. "Sorry, we lost track of time." She smiled at Lea. "I doubt I need to tell you I'm careful, so don't worry."

Lea sighed deeply. "I will always worry, about every one of you."

Meya joined them by the fire, glad to get rid of the goosebumps despite the fact that the desire burning within had kept her from even noticing she was cold. She listened to Lea and Nina bickering and smiled a bit. *Well, this went better than expected.* She jumped when someone touched her hair: Brit.

"Lovely braiding. I take it this is Nina's work?"

Meya nodded. She didn't know why, but her touch was unsettling her and she had to resist the urge to slap her hand away. *Go play with Winnie's hair or something.*

Winnie scooted over and mumbled something. Brit moved closer to her and Winnie seemingly repeated what she had said.

Brit giggled. "Winnie said she tried the same braid with my hair once. If I recall correctly, that was the time I ended up with a head full of tangles instead of braids." She stopped laughing and grimaced. "It hurt a lot to get them all out again."

Now it was Winnie's turn to laugh, but she quickly stopped when Brit gave her an angry glare.

Feeling rather displeased that the sisters were ruining her happy buzz, Meya excused herself and rose up. She got a cup of water, emptied it, and went to bed.

Lying comfortably under her covers, she let her mind wander. She thought back to Nina kissing her and her cheeks instantly heated up. *God, get a hold of yourself!* She sighed. *But it felt so good... I enjoyed her embrace.*

She remembered being held by the lord, frozen against his hot body, the both of them naked, and she groaned internally.

*I shouldn't be comparing the two of them. The Lord does whatever he pleases. It's not like I can tell him no. Nina on the other hand...* A warmth spread through her body and she bit her lip again. *She's so kind and supportive. I like her.* She relaxed as she thought of their earlier moment together. *I actually felt safe in her arms. There was no fear. It felt good.* She drifted off to sleep.

# Eighteen

"Just go ahead, we'll join you shortly," Nina said to Lea and Gail.

Gail turned to follow the sisters to the dining hall, but Lea remained to look at Meya for a moment. There was a glint in her eyes and she smiled before exiting the room.

Blood rushed to Meya's face. "I think she knows!"

Nina walked over to Meya and wrapped her arms around her waist. "Knows what? About us?" She nuzzled her neck. "Even if she does, don't worry about it. Lea's a good person."

Meya bit her lip as Nina trailed kisses down her neck. Her heart raced in her chest and she wanted to pull her close, but she fought the urge. "Nina," she whispered. "Come on, we have to get going…"

Nina backed away slightly but kept her hands on Meya's hips. There was a hint of disappointment on her face. "Don't you like this?"

"I…I do. It's just…" She swallowed, her eyes shooting back and forth between Nina and the door. "What if someone sees us?"

An impish smile graced Nina's light brown face. "I'd say let's give them something to look at." She gave Meya a hard push.

With a yelp, Meya toppled onto the bed behind her. "Nina! What are y—" Nina's soft lips pressed against hers, silencing her protests. *Oh, damn you…* She closed her eyes and gave in, her fingers entangling themselves in Nina's raven locks.

Finally, Nina pulled away, smirking. "Come now, or we'll be late."

Flustered, Meya sat up. She licked her lips. "You do realise just how evil you are, I hope."

Nina's hazel eyes gleamed. "Of course." She bent forward so their noses almost touched. "But you're just so cute when you're all hot and bothered." She flicked her tongue against the tip of Meya's nose and sprinted to the door, giggling loudly.

Meya wiped her nose dry, her cheeks on fire. She stood up and followed Nina to the dining hall. *And now I have to pretend like nothing happened. Great.* She took a few deep breaths, hoping her face would return to its usual tint soon.

~*~

Meya was busy with the lord's bed, happily humming to herself. She picked up the dirty kerchief from the floor, her nostrils flaring for a moment, and dumped it on the laundry pile. Turning to the bed again, her heart skipped a beat and she stopped humming.

Lord Deminas stood in the door opening, a sly grin tugging at his lips. "You're rather cheerful today." He walked into the room, his eyes shifting to the pile of laundry before settling on Meya. "What happened?"

His grey eyes bore into her green ones and Meya swallowed, a cold sweat covering her skin. *What do I say? I'm sure he will notice if I lie.* Her pulse quickened. *What would he do to liars?*

The lord clutched Meya's chin. "Well? Tell me."

Meya parted her lips, but it took a moment before she was able to speak. "I...I suppose I'm just happy, my Lord."

There was a mischievous glint in his eyes. "Is that so? And why is that?"

Blood rushed to Meya's cheeks. *Because Nina kissed me.* She swallowed. "I...I guess I'm happy to have nice room-mates, my Lord. People who care about me."

Lord Deminas raised a brow, indicating he didn't quite believe her.

Meya's thoughts raced to come up with things to say without actually lying. "It's safe here in the castle. I don't have to fear war anymore."

A single chuckle left his lips. "So you're happy because you're delusional." He let go of her chin. "You let me hurt you just so your gossiping room-mate wouldn't have to suffer, and you claim you have nice room-mates that care

140

about you?" He shook his head. "You disappoint me. As for no longer fearing war... You seem to forget where you are and whom you serve."

Anger rose in the pit of her stomach, but she suppressed it. "Are you saying I shouldn't be happy, my Lord?"

A devilish smile appeared on his face. "I'm saying you shouldn't lie to yourself." He moved behind her and whispered into her ear, "Nor should you lie to me."

Meya's blood ran cold and she froze. *He noticed? But I didn't lie! Not really...*

"You're too easy to read."

His hot breath made her squirm inside and she wanted to run away, but her body was petrified.

"If you're so happy here in this castle as my chambermaid, then you won't mind keeping me company tonight after supper again."

Meya's heart constricted in her chest for a moment and her breath hitched.

"Well?"

"Of...of course, my Lord," Meya stammered, the world spinning slightly. *What's he going to do?* She shivered involuntarily as she remembered the blade cutting into her flesh.

"Good." He moved away. "Then get back to your chores."

Meya watched him leave. The moment she heard the door to the hallway close, she exhaled loudly in relief. She sat down on the bed and rubbed her temples. *It's alright. You'll be alright. Just don't worry about it, because worrying is not going to change whatever he's got planned.* She groaned. *He ruined my good mood though!*

~*~

Later that evening, Meya approached the lord's chambers with her supper still heavy in her stomach. *He better not be in the bath again!* She took a deep breath and knocked on the door. To her relief, his voice boomed from the other side, allowing her in. Biting the inside of her lip, she stepped inside, and she gasped when she saw Lord Deminas enter the bedroom, completely naked.

"You're just in time. I was about to take a bath."

*Just in time? Don't make me laugh! I can all too well imagine him waiting for me in the nude just to pester me!*

With a face bright red, she followed the lord to the bathroom, and silently, she watched him sink into the steamy water.

141

*What does he want me to do?* She swallowed. *If I ask, he might use that opportunity to make me do something I don't want.* Her blood chilled at the thought of him requesting sex.

"Meya."

She looked up from her thoughts and faced the lord.

He raised a brow. "Did you hear what I just said?"

Her face heated up even more. "I…I'm sorry, my Lord. I did not."

He scoffed. "I thought so. I told you to strip."

A shiver went up her spine. *Great, just great. This again.*"As you wish, my Lord." She started to undress, her fingers trembling. *I wonder if I will ever get used to this…*

The sly smile on the lord's lips made her feel even more uncomfortable as his eyes glided over her now naked form. She placed her clothing on a nearby shelf and returned to stand in front of the bath, her hands folded in front of her crotch—a meagre attempt at trying to keep some of her dignity intact.

Lord Deminas gestured for her to come closer, and she reluctantly took a few steps forward. He rose from the water and cupped her right breast, causing Meya to inhale sharply. His thumb ran over the remnants of the cuts he had made two nights ago.

"Good, it's healing nicely." He looked up at her, a mischievous glint in his eyes. "It seems I will keep my word then, on not leaving any permanent marks on your body."

Meya trembled slightly, eagerly waiting for the lord to remove his hand from her skin. *I wonder why he even cares about leaving marks.*

Lord Deminas sank back into the water. "Get in."

She obliged, the hot water instantly reducing the tension in her body. *Come on, Meya. Relax…Enjoy the warmth.* She wanted to follow her own advice, but her mind kept playing possible scenarios of what would happen next—and they all frightened her.

The lord kept his gaze fixed on her as she settled into the water. "You are still afraid of me," he stated instead of asked.

Meya averted her eyes, her heart throbbing in her throat. *Can you blame me?*

"Look at—" He paused for a moment as her eyes instantly locked back onto his. "Me." The hardness in his expression faded as the corners of his lips moved up slightly. "Good." His fingers curled around her chin, gently. "As obedient as you are, why do you fear me?"

It took Meya a moment to organise her thoughts and decide on her answer. She wetted her lips before she spoke, "Y-you enjoy punishing people. You said so yourself, my Lord. And I—"

"You fear that I will hurt you just because it gives me pleasure?"

Meya closed her eyes for a moment and swallowed back a sob as she nodded.

He chuckled. "Then tell me. What have I done so far that has hurt you? And your suffering in Gail's stead does not count, as you willingly submitted to that." He bent forward to whisper in her ear, "And I even gave you the privilege of reconsidering during the punishment, yet you wanted to continue."

She trembled as his hot breath tickled her skin. *He's right about that, but...* Her mind raced as it went over all her moments with him. "Y-you cut my hand, my Lord."

His fingers left her chin and grabbed her wrist instead. "And just how much did that hurt?" He turned her hand so the side faced up and traced a finger over the cut, which was barely visible anymore.

Meya gazed at her own flesh, still not quite understanding how his blood could heal wounds like that. *It hurt, but... how much? What a silly question! How do I answer that?*

"Well?"

"It... It just hurt, my Lord. I...I don't know how to explain it further."

"Compared to these cuts..." His index finger traced the marks on her right breast, then her left.

Meya's breath got caught in her throat for a moment. *Of course more cuts hurt more! Not to mention a hand is not as delicate...* She bit her lip in an attempt to keep her tears from spilling. *And he healed my hand not long after, which made the pain stop. These cuts...* She swallowed the lump in her throat as she remembered the lingering pain.

"Meya, look at me."

Lord Deminas' voice lifted her from her memories and she locked eyes with him. There was something in them that she couldn't quite place. *Is he... concerned?* Her cheeks heated up. *Why would he—* Her mind ground to a halt when the lord closed in, his lips almost touching hers.

"Just don't forget why I do the things I have done."

Her heart thumped painfully in her chest, and her lungs felt constricted. The lord's hand slid up her body, his fingers trailing her collarbone, neck, jaw, cheekbones, and ending up entwining themselves in her red locks. His face moved alongside hers, his lips momentarily brushing against her ear.

*Oh God...* Meya gasped as his hot breath covered her in goosebumps.

143

"And don't forget that you are still my slave, my servant." He backed away, a sly grin plastered on his face, his grey eyes gleaming mischievously.

Meya's world spun. *What...?* She looked at the man in front of her, her mind clouded, confused.

Lord Deminas turned around so his back was facing Meya. "Enough talk. Massage me."

*You've got to be kidding me. Really?* She shook her head in an attempt to help clear it. *This guy is unbelievable!* She loosened her joints and started on his neck. *Why did he do all of that just now? What was that all about?* She closed her eyes and suppressed a grunt while her hands kept working. *"Just don't forget why I do the things I have done." I don't even know why he does most things! Why does he make me strip? Why does he look me over when I am naked? Why does he cut my hand?* She swallowed. *Why did he torture and kill the slaver? Why did he want to punish Gail so heavily over a stupid rumour?*

Meya let out a surprised yelp as the lord placed his hand on hers. "Focus on what you're doing, or I'll ask you to massage something else."

Meya's eyes widened in shock—not only from what he said but also because the tone with which he had said it betrayed his amusement. "I...I'm sorry, my Lord."

His hand slid off hers, and she continued massaging his neck. *Sadistic, evil bastard.* She tried to focus on her job, but in the back of her mind lingered a new question she had no answer to.

*Why doesn't he make me do anything sexual?*

~*~

Mentally exhausted, Meya returned to her quarters. To her relief, Lord Deminas had dismissed her after the massage.

*That guy has some serious issues. What does he want from me?* She ran her hand through her hair in frustration as she walked through the castle halls. *One moment he just seems to be playing around with me, the next he seems to care, and then he simply reminds me I am but a mere slave!* She grunted. *And then there's the blood thing.* She shuddered.

She halted in front of the door leading to her quarters, the voices of her room-mates audible through the wood. A heavy sigh passed her lips. *I suppose I need to get used to this.* She straightened her back. *At least Nina will have my back.* A slight smile played on her lips, and she opened the door.

144

Gail had been in the middle of a story. She paused as she looked up to see Meya, but continued right after. "So the princess went back into the gardens to meet with the faun."

Relief washed over her. She looked over at Lea. Their gazes met and Lea gave her a small nod before turning her attention back to Gail.

Nina smiled sheepishly and patted the space next to her. Meya's heart rate increased and her cheeks heated up slightly as she walked over to sit next to her. Nina's hand brushed against hers for a moment—a sign of comfort without having the others notice.

Just as she thought no one would pester her about what had transpired, Winnie tugged on her towel, nearly dislodging it from her frame. Meya quickly grabbed it, still not feeling all too comfortable being fully exposed in the presence of others—especially now with the cuts still visible on her breasts. "What?" she snapped, and she instantly regretted her tone of voice.

Winnie's gaze had been questioning, but now it hardened. She said something, but Meya couldn't understand.

*I have a bad feeling about this...* She turned to look at Brit.

Brit sighed and tapped her sister on the shoulder. "Go on, tell me and I'll tell her."

Winnie whispered into Brit's ear, and Brit bit her lip. Her eyes shifted from Winnie to Meya, and back to Winnie again. When Winnie was done, Brit turned to Meya, her eyes cast downwards.

"I'm not sure if I should repeat what she just told me."

Everyone else remained silent, the crackling of the fire the only sound in the room. *Great, just great.* Meya swallowed. "What is it?"

Nina's fingers entwined themselves with Meya's and gave a reassuring squeeze.

Brit sighed. "Winnie wants to know how it feels to be the Lord's..." She shook her head and Winnie elbowed her angrily. She grunted and continued, "The Lord's concubine."

Blood rushed to Meya's face as her mind flooded with anger, confusion, and denial. Before she could think of anything to say, a loud slap echoed through the room.

"You should learn from what happened to Gail!" Nina spat. "Don't you start any vile rumours now, too!"

Winnie held her cheek, a red handprint slowly emerging on her skin. Brit wisely kept her mouth shut and her eyes down.

"Meya is the Lord's chambermaid. If he asks for her presence at night, that's his right. Hell, he even has the right to request *your* presence! What he wants of Meya is none of our business and you most definitely do not simply assume such a thing!" Nina fumed.

Meya looked over at Gail and Lea, but even they seemed to not want to interfere as they had looked elsewhere.

Winnie mumbled something incomprehensible, her eyes burning with just as much anger as Nina's.

Nina turned to Brit. "You either translate that, or I will just assume the worst and slap her again."

Brit raised her hands. "Fine."

Winnie spoke to Brit a whole lot longer than what she had initially tried to say to Nina. When she was done, she sat back across from Nina, her arms folded and back straight.

Brit sighed. "Just don't slap me, alright?"

"Just spill it."

"Basically, there are two things… First off, she wants to know why you even care. Secondly, she wants to know what else the Lord could be doing with Meya that would have her return here with wet hair and clad in a towel."

Nina's arm moved back for another go at Winnie, but Lea grabbed her wrist. "Come on, Nina. You know better than to pick a fight with her."

With a grunt, Nina pulled herself free from Lea's grasp. "And *she* knows better than to start vile rumours!"

"Just answer her then," Brit said.

Before Nina could retort, Meya finally found the courage to speak. "I don't know why this would concern any of you, but if it pleases you to know: the last man to have *touched* me was that accursed slaver and I would appreciate it if you would not look at me like I am some damned harlot!" Her heart pounded heavily in her chest from all the tension, and tears prickled her eyes. "Nina has been a good friend to me and I have confided certain things to her and *only* her. She knows more about me than you and *that's* why she cares! As for the towel—" She was about to tell them, but reconsidered. "That's none of your business." Meya trembled slightly from the adrenaline, her hands clenched into fists.

"I…I'm sorry," Brit muttered with a face red with shame.

Without warning, Winnie launched forward and tugged hard on Meya's towel, pulling it to the ground.

Meya cried out and quickly tried to grab it, but missed. She crossed her arms in front of her chest and turned around. Another loud slap resounded, but this time it was not Nina who had dealt it.

"You are despicable!" Lea hollered. "How dare you do that to her when you know how she has suffered? She even reminded you just now what that slaver did to her and still you go ahead and strip her against her will!"

Tears trailed down Meya's cheeks as she found herself frozen to the ground. She wanted to run, to hide, to simply vanish into thin air. As Lea berated Winnie, someone else draped the towel back around her shoulders.

"Here," Nina whispered. "I'm so sorry." She moved in front of her and closed the towel so that it covered her chest, even though Meya still had her arms crossed over it. "Winnie is—"

Meya hugged Nina close, the towel falling to the ground. "I don't care about her," she whispered, her words barely audible as she fought against the sobs that wanted to free themselves from her throat.

Nina wrapped her arms around Meya's quivering form. "Come then." She guided Meya to her bed and pulled the sheets over her.

"Please, stay with me." Meya looked at Nina pleadingly.

Nina glanced at the others still sitting by the fire. Lea continued to scold Winnie, while Gail and Brit just stared at the ground, Gail fumbling with her apron and Brit twirling her hair. "Ah, what the hell," she mumbled. She undressed and crawled into bed with Meya, holding her close.

"Thank you," Meya whispered as she relished Nina's embrace.

"Just know, even if the Lord does ever make you his concubine, I would not think any less of you."

Meya sniffed and squeezed Nina's arm reassuringly. "I know."

# Part Two
## Winter, 1240 AD

*The wheel of time keeps on turning.*
*Escape winter's deadly grasp*
*to awaken in spring's warm embrace.*

# Nineteen

Meya sat down on the bed in the lord's old chamber as Nina stacked some wood in the fireplace. "When did you get wood in here?"

Nina grinned. "The soldiers have been so busy lately, they are barely around in their quarters. I've been sneaking some logs in here every day." She used the flame of the oil lamp they had brought with them to kindle the fire. "You've been complaining about the cold for weeks now, so I figured I should fix it."

"Aren't you afraid the soldiers will notice?"

"Don't worry. Like I said, I took only a few logs each day, so they won't notice."

"No, I mean…" She nudged towards the door. "Don't you think they will see the glow of the fire?"

Nina stood up, grabbed a slightly dusty towel from a shelf, and placed it in on the floor against the door. "There, all covered." She smiled triumphantly. "Now stop worrying and enjoy the warmth."

Meya coughed a few times as she got off the bed and sat down on an old hide in front of the growing fire. "You always take such good care of me, thanks for that."

Nina sat down next to her and wrapped her arm around Meya's shoulders, pulling her close and planting a kiss on her temple. "Who else is going to do that? Lord Deminas?"

A giggle escaped Meya's lips before her hand pressed tightly against it. "Oh, shush you!" She playfully shoved Nina. "Seriously, what that man wants is beyond me."

"You had to stay for supper again yesterday..." Nina gently took Meya's left hand by the wrist. "Did he cut you again?"

Meya didn't need to answer as the healing cut was clearly visible in the light of the flames. "It bothers me that he does this every other week." She shook her head. "Still, I'd rather have him cutting my hand than my breasts." A shiver ran up her spine as she recalled the torture.

"Just look at it from the bright side: you get a very good meal out of it."

Meya smiled. "You've got a point there. Yesterday it was a lovely stewed rabbit." She licked her lips at the memory. "To be honest, I can handle a bit of pain just fine. I mean, he cuts me with this really sharp knife, drains some blood, then does his little magic to close the wound. The pain stops straight away."

Nina huffed. "I'd let him cut my hand and drain some blood for such a meal. Especially when the wound heals like that and the pain lasts only a few moments."

"You're such a scrounger!"

"I prefer to consider myself an opportunist." Nina grinned. "Don't forget how I grew up."

"Thieving in the castle will cost you your fingers, or worse," Meya said teasingly.

"There's only one thing I've been thieving the past few months..."

The smile faded from Meya's face. "I do hope you're not serious! Just because I was able to reduce Gail's punishment doesn't mean I could save you from—"

Nina suppressed a giggle. "You're so cute when you get all heated up like that." She nuzzled Meya's neck. "I meant *you*, silly! I feel like I've been stealing you from the Lord."

Meya's cheeks flushed red. "You haven't been stealing me any more than I have been stealing you. We're both his servants."

"Yeah, but you're his chambermaid—or his *concubine* if you were to ask Winnie."

A grunt escaped Meya's lips. "That girl has some serious issues. Fine, he touched me sexually *once*. Aside from that, it's mostly just being naked in front of him and giving him massages." She sighed. "He frightened me so in the beginning. I really thought he would force me to actually be his concubine."

"Well, I'm glad he's man enough not to force himself on you." Nina's fingers found Meya's hand and squeezed it reassuringly. "He might be a sadist, maybe even a warlock or a demon, but at least he's not a pig."

Meya chuckled and looked at her left hand. "It's so strange…"

Nina's fingers folded her hand shut and moved it out of sight. "Just… Don't worry about it, you hear me?"

"I know… You're right. You're always right." She kissed her. "I suppose I'm just glad that Gail no longer gossips and that Winnie has no tongue to do it in her stead."

"And luckily, Brit is smart enough not to do it for her." Nina shook her head. "I truly don't get Winnie. Brit claims that she learned her place after the Lord removed her tongue, but, if you ask me, she still has a thing for him."

Meya scoffed. "Well, I wouldn't mind skipping being nude in front of him. He might not touch me sexually, but his eyes… The way he looks at me?" She shook her head. "I'm pretty sure he wants me… There's always so much lust, so much *longing* in those grey eyes of his. If Winnie wants to swap places, I'd be happy to. Hell, I'm pretty sure she'd *love* to be his concubine!"

Nina laughed. "I'm quite certain! Though I doubt the Lord would want to drink *her* blood. I'm sure it tastes as dirty as her attitude."

Meya giggled. "Not to mention she doesn't deserve even one bite of his meals."

"Oh, feisty, aren't you? Not a moment ago you didn't even seem to realise that your blood for food deal is a good deal." She teasingly stuck out her tongue and Meya gave her a playful shove.

"Well *excuse* me for not wanting to sound like a scrounger like you!"

Nina laughed as Meya tickled her. Snorting, she tried to wriggle away. "Stop," she managed to say. "We're being too loud." Meya immediately ceased her attack. Nina took her chance and threw herself on top of her, pinning her arms above her head.

"Cheater," Meya whispered, though she was unable to suppress the grin tugging at her lips.

"Couldn't resist." Nina kissed her passionately.

~*~

Meya stared out over the grey and white landscape that stretched beyond the castle. Huge snowflakes drifted lazily from the sky, covering what little was left untouched. *Such a magnificent view...* She leaned on the stone balcony, a bucket by her side filled with murky water. Her gaze shifted from the blanketed trees to the mountainside below.

She picked up the bucket and heaved it onto the balustrade. She tried to remember where on the rocky slope the remains of the previous chambermaid rested. With clenched teeth—to keep them from chattering—she threw the contents of the bucket down the mountainside. The water slammed onto a snowy mound and revealed a ghastly skull.

Meya grinned. "Found you!"

Snowflakes landed on the wet skull and melted, but it was clear that it wouldn't take long before the remains would be hidden from view again. Meya placed the bucket on the ground and leaned on the balustrade so that she could get a good look at Jaimy. The grisly remains intrigued her instead of appalled her, as they had before.

"You were a stupid girl." She shook her head. "It's really not that hard to be his servant." A sly smile crept upon her face. "But I guess I must thank you... If it weren't for your rebellious ways, I would have been sold to someone else. I could have been a harlot!" She shivered from both the idea and the frigid cold. "So yeah, thank you, Jaimy." She chuckled. "Thank you for spitting in the Lord's face and getting your sorry ass thrown off the balcony! Thank you for ensuring my life isn't *that* miserable." She blew a kiss to the wind.

The snowflakes landing on the skull were no longer melting and started to form a thin layer of white upon the ochre surface. Meya coughed a few times and wrapped her arms tightly around herself, rubbing her torso.

*Enough fooling around.* She grabbed the bucket and hurried back inside, where a low fire in the hearth kept the cold at bay.

~*~

Meya closed her eyes in both pain and delight as Nina massaged her back. "Thanks for doing this."

"Any idea what you did that caused your back to hurt?"

"I don't know. It doesn't even really feel like I strained anything. It just hurts."

"Hey, Nina," Brit called from over at the fireplace. "Winnie wants to know if you can do her back too."

Nina scoffed. "Winnie, just ask your sister."

Meya rolled her eyes. She was about to make a remark when Lea intervened.

"Now don't you start another quarrel." She gave Winnie a stern look.

Winnie innocently raised her hands and turned to whisper something to her sister, who didn't look too pleased with what she was being told. Brit sighed, but she had seemingly yielded: Winnie bared her back to her and Brit started to massage it.

"Little copycat," Meya grumbled softly so that only Nina would hear.

The door to their quarters opened and Gail entered the room, a towel wrapped around her torso. "Girls!" She rushed over to the fire and sat down. "You won't believe what I've just heard!"

Lea groaned. "Gail, please... You've managed not to gossip for months now; don't go back to your old ways!"

Gail stared at her intensely. "This is not *gossip*." She cleared her throat and licked her lips, the small scars from her punishment still visible. "One of the soldiers confided this to me."

"One of the soldiers?" Brit raised a brow. "And what did you do to have him tell you this?"

If looks could kill, Brit would have died then and there. "None. Of. Your. Business."

Brit raised her hands defensively. "Sorry."

"Anyway, he told me that scouts had come across signs of the Golden Horde closing in. Lord Deminas is probably going to send men down the eastern mountain pass soon to deal with them before they attack Tristanja first." Gail looked over at Nina. "Have you picked up any hints of this?"

Nina swallowed. "Well... The soldiers' quarters have been rather quiet lately. I thought they were in another training routine or something— considering all the muddy tracks and dirty garments. Normally, I pick up talk about impending battles, but, to be fair, there haven't been many soldiers around to eavesdrop on."

Meya stiffened at the thought of impending war. "So you're telling me Tristanja is going to be under attack?"

"Well, that's the thing... From what I've been told, the Lord wants to attack *them* first."

"Let's keep this to ourselves, alright girls?" Lea asked. "We don't want to cause any restlessness in the castle." She looked over at Gail. "Or get Gail into trouble."

Gail's mouth dropped. "This is not gossip!"

"Still, best to keep this between us," Lea stated. "If you had to pry it from a soldier, I doubt we were meant to know any of this."

Gail's face flushed red and she looked away. "Fine."

*Why is there so much war in the world?* Meya sighed, but the sigh ended in several violent coughs.

"Meya?" Nina sounded concerned. "Are you alright?"

"I'll be fine." She coughed again, the contractions causing a jolt of pain to shoot through her chest.

Lea presented her a cup of water and Meya gladly took it. "You don't sound fine to me." She placed the back of her hand against Meya's forehead. "It doesn't feel like you have a fever, but still..." Her expression turned grave. "Don't get sick."

"Yeah, the Lord doesn't like sick servants," Brit said.

Meya cast her a deathly glare, but it was Winnie whom she ended up staring at. The blonde was covering her mouth, but her eyes still betrayed the smile she was trying to hide. *She truly hates me, doesn't she?*

~*~

*Dear God, what did he do? Train in a pool of mud?* Meya wiped the sweat from her brow. She was cleaning the lord's bath; the sides were covered with a grimy, brown film. It was still morning, but Meya felt as exhausted as she would have after an entire day of scrubbing the floors. She coughed a few times and winced at the pain this sent through her chest.

*Damn it...* She stretched her back, but it didn't lessen the pain. *Maybe Lea is right and I am getting sick.* A wave of sadness washed over her. *What happens here when a servant gets sick? Lea sounded really grim when she mentioned it, and the way Winnie looked at me...*

She grunted, and this caused her to cough a few more times as well.

Tears stung her eyes as she swallowed the phlegm in the back of her throat. *This is not good.*

Despite the fatigue plaguing her limbs, she continued her work.

~*~

"What do you think the odds are of the Golden Horde reaching Tristanja, or worse: the castle?" Meya asked as she sat huddled in a blanket in front of a raging fire.

Nina and Gail exchanged glances. They were the only ones in the room—the others were still at the baths.

"I don't think we should worry too much. Tristanja has been involved in wars for as long as I can remember, and none have ever reached the castle.

And, as far as I know, not long after Deminas became Lord, there have been no big armies crossing the borders, either," Gail stated.

"That's true." Nina smiled at Meya. "Don't worry. Behind these walls is probably the safest place to be."

"And hey," Gail added. "If they *do* ever raid the castle, I know some secret passages out."

Meya stared at her. "Are you sure?"

Nina smirked. "Oh, yeah. I know them too."

*Well, Nina I believe.* Meya pulled the blanket tighter around herself, hoping its warmth would ease the pain deep in her chest. "Let's just hope we will never need to use them."

"I hope so, too. They probably haven't been used since they were built." Gail shivered. "It must be crawling with vermin and spiders!"

Nina raised a brow. "Are you telling me you never hid anywhere filthy just to get a juicy story?"

Gail elbowed her playfully. "Look who's talking."

They laughed, but Meya only smiled—she knew laughter would trigger another coughing attack.

~*~

*What's Lord Deminas doing?* Meya scrubbed away at the muddy floor. *I haven't seen him in days now!* She dipped the cloth in the murky water beside her and wrung it out. *He should be ashamed of himself for walking in here with half of Tristanja on the soles of his boots!*

Her arms were tired and her chest and back hurt. Still, she kept scrubbing the floor.

*Rinse and repeat. Rinse and repeat.*

Meya blinked a few times as she looked at the spot she had been cleaning. *It's not really getting much cleaner with this dirty water.*

She rose and pressed a hand against her head as the room spun.

*Damn it.*

Her chest burned, but she tried to ignore it. She picked up the heavy bucket and walked towards the balcony. *Jaimy, time for a shower!*

The frigid wind hit her face and for a moment she couldn't breathe. She coughed a few times and spat the phlegm over the balustrade. *Yuck.*

Squinting, she looked down the mountainside, searching for the remains of the previous chambermaid. The cold air had felt good against her heated skin at first, but now she was starting to shiver. She couldn't spot Jaimy anywhere under the thick layers of snow, so she emptied the bucket on the spot where she thought she would be.

Rocks.

*Oh well, better luck next time.* Breathing was becoming hard to do, and small, black pinpricks were appearing in her vision. *Let's go back inside.*

She as good as stumbled in and made her way to the bathroom to refill the bucket. The black spots were increasing in number and becoming bigger. She meandered through the bedroom, nearly colliding with the wall next to the doorway.

*The Lord doesn't like sick servants*, she reminded herself. *You can do this.*

Her stomach turned and light-headedness claimed her. The world spun. Black dominated her sight before she collapsed to the ground, unconscious.

# Twenty

Meya slowly regained consciousness. Feeling utterly horrible, she groaned and gripped the blankets that covered her. When she opened her eyes, it took her a moment before she realised she was in her own bed. The room was empty, but there was a low fire in the hearth. Confused, she tried to remember what had happened. *I was about to get new water to clean the floors and...* She coughed and her chest burned. She felt like crying. *Did I really faint? How did I get here?*

She imagined the lord entering his chambers and finding her sprawled on the floor. The already present blush on her cheeks worsened.

*Did he carry me here?*

Then she realised something: she was naked underneath the sheets.

*Oh, God, did he...?*

The anxiety triggered another few coughs, and scowling, she swallowed the phlegm in the back of her throat.

*Oh, what the hell.* She sighed. *It's not like he hasn't seen me naked before.* She hoped thinking that would make her feel better, but it didn't.

Her body ached and her extremities felt heavy. She turned left, then right, but neither position seemed to bring her any relief. Miserably, she sat up a bit and pulled the blanket to her chin.

*I hate this. I hate this so much.* Tears prickled her eyes and she fought to keep them at bay. *I need to get better, and soon!* Images of how Lord Deminas would be displeased with her absence—with her inability to do her duties—crossed her mind. *I don't want him to be upset with me, or worse: punish me!* She swallowed the lump in her throat and suppressed another cough. *This is punishment already.*

~*~

"Hey Meya," a soft voice said.

Meya opened her eyes slowly, tired still. *Nina?*

"How are you feeling? You gave me quite the shock!"

"I—" she started, but a cough forced its way out of her chest. *Damn it!* She swallowed and tried again. "Terrible."

Nina took her hand and rubbed it. "Just rest, alright? You need to get well."

"What about… my duties?"

Nina smiled. "That's really the first thing on your mind?" She shook her head, but the smile didn't leave her lips. "Don't worry about that. Juris has asked me to take over for you. As I normally do the soldiers' quarters, Lord Deminas agreed to this. Someone else will help Kadeem in the meantime."

Meya's eyes enlarged. "Aren't you… afraid?"

"Ha!" Nina sat down on the edge of the bed. "You've told me plenty of stories to know what I can expect. Don't worry: I'll behave." She winked.

*You're braver than I am. I still stress every time he's near.* She wanted to tell Nina this, but she was too tired to waste her precious breath on that many words. Instead, she voiced the question that was burning for an answer. "How did I… get here?"

"Juris carried you in."

Meya stiffened. *Did he strip me?*

"He came looking for me after, and I tucked you in." She planted a kiss on her forehead. "Wow, you're burning up!" She rose and went over to the nearby cabinet. "I'll be right back." Grabbing a piece of cloth from a shelf and the large jug from the table by the window, she rushed out of the room.

A feeling of despair washed over Meya. *No, don't feel sad now. Nina is taking care of you!* But there was still a painful emptiness in her chest.

Her mind's eye showed her how Lord Deminas would have found her, a scowl on his face. She even imagined him poking her side with his mud-coated boot before storming out of the room to get Juris.

She shook her head to rid herself of the negative thought. *No, he wouldn't have done that. He was probably worried. He must have been worried... He cares...*

Her chest clenched and a sob escaped her throat. She hid her face in her hands as tears slid down her heated cheeks.

*Why do I even care? It's Lord Deminas!*

She ran her fingers through her hair, tugging at the strands. She wanted to scream but knew that was not an option.

*Stupid, stupid Meya! If he cared, it would only be because he wouldn't want to miss out on your blood. That, and massages.* Her mood darkened further. *Will he ask Nina to do those things?*

She started to really cry now, her chest burning with each heavy breath she took.

Nina came back and nearly dropped the jug upon seeing Meya. "My dear, what's wrong?" She hurried over and placed the items on the floor. She held Meya's red head in her cool hands. "Shhh, don't cry," she cooed as she wiped away a tear with her thumb and smiled slightly.

Meya swallowed as the tears slowed down. She locked eyes with Nina and seeing her made her heart feel a little lighter. She raised her arms and Nina took the hint, pulling her into a gentle hug.

"Come on, tell me what's wrong," she whispered into her ear.

"I just... feel terrible," Meya panted. She sniffed and wiped her eyes dry.

"You already felt terrible. What made you cry?"

*Her memory is good.* She sighed, a slight rattle in her breath. "I don't even... know why. But it just... saddened me that... Lord Deminas..."*Damn, I need air!* "I thought... he cared..." Her chest constricted again from despair.

Nina held Meya at an arm's length, a knowing smile on her face. "You're starting to like him, aren't you?"

Meya would have blushed if it wasn't for the fact that her face was already glowing from the fever. "I didn't—"

"It's fine." She grinned, her eyes shimmering playfully. "I understand—he's growing on you." Her expression went neutral. "Be careful though. Winnie fell in love with him and look where that ended."

Meya's jaw dropped. "But I don't—" She started to cough again and Nina patted her back.

"Sorry, I didn't mean to upset you. I know you love *me*." Her attempt to lighten the mood was futile as Meya only had eyes for the gunk that rested in her palm. "Here." Nina handed her the kerchief from her apron.

"Thanks." Meya wiped her hand clean of the yellow lumps.

"What I meant was... He's a Lord and you're a servant. You shouldn't have any expectations. That way, you can't be disappointed." She sighed. "I know he has been rather kind to you, and I do think he likes you in a way... But I don't want you to hurt over him, do you understand?"

Meya nodded, but she didn't feel any better being told all that.

"Now lie down." Nina grabbed the cloth, wetted it, and draped it over Meya's forehead. "As much as I wish I could stay and take care of you, I have to return to scrubbing a rather dirty floor."

Meya turned to look out the window. It was gloomy outside, so she guessed it to be late in the afternoon. "Won't he be... upset that you left?"

A coy smile appeared on Nina's face. "I actually have permission to come and check on you a few times a day." She noticed Meya's eyes lighting up. "I asked him for that permission, though! Well, *begged*, really..."

Meya sighed. *Nina's right, I shouldn't get any weird ideas. I am but a servant after all.* She suppressed the need to cry.

Nina filled a cup with water and placed it on the small bedside table. "I'll see you tonight, alright?" She planted a kiss on her crown. "Get some rest and stop worrying." She caressed her cheek. "There's a bedpan under the bed if you need to relieve yourself. I don't want you walking down the hallway and blacking out again."

Meya smiled. "Thanks, Nina."

She stroked Meya's hair. "Anything for you." She walked away, hesitating slightly at the door before disappearing.

The cold cloth on Meya's head was soothing and she closed her eyes. *Just do as Nina says. Stop worrying. Rest.* She took a deep, rattling breath and almost had to cough again. *I can't believe the Lord still manages to have such influence on my mind after all this time!* She shifted a bit in an attempt to get comfortable. *Just don't think about him.* The fatigue quickly caught up to her and her thoughts stilled as she drifted off to sleep.

~*~

A knock on the door roused Meya from her slumber. She turned her weary head to see Juris coming in, carrying a big bowl.

"Hey Meya, how are you feeling?" He placed the bowl on the bedside table.

Meya swallowed before carefully answering, "Not too well."

The corners of his mouth drooped. "I figured." He sighed. "I arranged some broth for you. Also, Nina will be taking over your duties while you're sick."

"Thank you," Meya said slowly, conserving her breath. "She told me."

Juris nodded. "Good."

Meya rose carefully to an upright position. *It smells good!* She wanted to take the bowl, but her chest contracted and she coughed a few times. Using Nina's kerchief, she cleaned the yellow lumps of slime from the palm of her hand. With sadness she noticed Juris had taken a few steps away from her, the unease clearly visible in his eyes.

"I'll, eh… I'll make sure you're brought breakfast in the morning, too. Make sure you eat that so you get well soon." His gaze kept shifting from Meya to the door.

"Thanks, Juris." The words felt hollow to her, as seeing the muscular man standing there, eager to get away from her, made her heart heavy with sorrow.

"Take care." He gave her a curt nod and exited the room.

Tears stung Meya's eyes. *Don't cry—he brought you soup! He cares! He's just afraid to get sick too.* A quivering sigh escaped her lips. *I hope this is not contagious.*

Images of Nina becoming sick flashed through her mind and her heart clenched in her chest. She turned to the soup and carefully took it from the table. Stirring the contents, she was surprised to see small pieces of meat.

*I'm lucky to get such a meal.* She drank from the bowl slowly, ensuring she wouldn't get out of breath. *I need to get better soon. For my sake, but also for Nina's!* The fact that Nina was now doing her chores worried her.

~*~

Annoyed, Meya opened her eyes to the loud chatter of Brit. She saw her room-mates enter, but a spike of fear went through her core when the door closed and Nina wasn't there. Gail and Lea came over to her, their faces worried.

"How are you feeling?" Gail asked.

Meya swallowed and answered slowly, "Terrible."

Lea took her hand in her own and rubbed it reassuringly. "Juris told us during supper what had happened. Just be glad you didn't pass out in a more… inconvenient spot."

Meya frowned. *Passing out in the Lord's bathroom is not inconvenient?*

Lea noticed her confusion. "I meant like on the stairs."

162

"Oh..." She cringed at the thought of tumbling down the stone steps.

Lea smiled. "Don't think too much about what could have happened. Focus on getting well."

Meya nodded and forced a smile. *And here I was, thinking I should focus on remaining sick.*

Lea gave her hand one last squeeze before walking away and joining the sisters at the fire.

It took Meya some effort not to show the scowl that was eager to take over her smile. *They didn't even bother to look at me. I guess Winnie just—* Her thoughts were interrupted as she noticed Gail still standing by her side. She turned her attention to the brunette, the scars around her lips forever reminding her of what she had done for the woman.

Gail placed a hand on Meya's shoulder. "If there's anything I can do for you, just ask. Alright?"

The contempt she had felt faded. Seeing Gail being kind and sincere towards her, offering her aid, made her heart constrict in her chest and her lip quivered. *She cares.*

A worried look settled on Gail's face. "Hey, what's wrong?" She knelt next to the bed so that their eyes were level.

"You're kind... Thank you."

Gail smiled and carefully hugged Meya. "How can I not be? We're friends, aren't we?"

Meya nodded, her chest burning. The moment Gail released her, she grabbed her kerchief and coughed into it. She looked up at Gail, but she didn't seem as fazed as Juris had been. The chatter near the hearth had fallen silent though, and the sisters were staring at her.

The silence lasted for a few seconds before Brit broke it. "Is she to sleep in the same room as us? What if we get sick too?"

"Where would you have her sleep then?" Lea asked, crossing her arms and looking sternly at Brit.

Brit shrugged. "I don't know. Just somewhere not near us."

"Well, you're free to find another bed if you don't feel comfortable here," Gail added. "I know a few soldiers who wouldn't mind sharing their bed with a woman like yourself."

"Gail!" Lea exclaimed, but her eyes betrayed her true feelings.

"What?"

Lea shook her head and turned away. Brit's face was bright red, but she kept her lips closed, clearly not in the mood to start arguing.

Gail faced Meya again, a sly smirk pulling her lips up.

Meya couldn't help but smile back. *Yes, we're friends.* Thinking of friends, she asked, "Where's Nina?"

Gail's expression turned neutral and she licked her lips. "She told me she would be here later." She bent down so she could whisper, "Lord Deminas requested her presence."

The colour drained a bit from Meya's cheeks. *He... what?*

"She'll be fine, don't worry." Gail squeezed her shoulder. "Want me to tell a story?"

It took Meya a few seconds to process what Gail had said. She nodded. *Yes, a story... I'd like something to distract me.*

~\*~

"Meya. Hey..."

Meya's eyes opened slowly as someone gently shook her arm. It was morning and everyone had left not too long ago for breakfast. To her surprise, Nina was the one who woke her. Immediately her pulse quickened and she tried to sit up straight, but Nina stopped her.

"I'm sorry. Please, don't get up."

"Where have... you been?" Meya panted heavily, anger and relief fighting for dominance. "You've been gone... all night!" Her lungs burned, but she managed to suppress the need to cough.

"I know! I'm so sorry! But please, calm down. I don't want you to get another coughing fit."

Reluctant, Meya obliged. *All I know is the Lord calls for your presence and you stay away all night! How can I be calm?* She took a deep breath. "What... happened?" Nina sat down on the bed, and it was only then that Meya noticed she was clad in just a towel. Blood rushed to her cheeks as she envisioned what had happened. "Did he...?"

All the stress was becoming too much and her body could no longer be controlled. She coughed violently, her entire form quivering as her lungs expelled lumps of yellow slime.

Nina handed her the kerchief from the bedside table, her expression grave. "I'm so sorry. Please, let me explain, alright? Try not to speak either. I see how hard it is for you."

Meya wiped herself clean and nodded, tears in her eyes from the physical exertion.

Nina sighed. " I really have no idea where to start."

Meya reached for her cup and Nina handed it to her instead.

164

"I wasn't completely honest with you yesterday... I didn't as much beg the Lord to let me visit you... I made a deal with him."

Meya's eyes widened and she lowered the cup. *Oh, please don't tell me he—*

"I was to come back after supper. I guess I expected something similar to what he had done to you... And I was partially right. He wanted me to massage him in the bath. But..." She averted her eyes, her cheeks darkening with shame.

"What did—"

"Don't speak, please! I feel bad enough already, I don't want you to cough." She sighed and loosened her towel. The light coming from the hearth wasn't much, and the sun had yet to rise, but it was enough to see the dark lines on her tawny skin. There was a single horizontal cut above each nipple. "I sort of let slip that I knew of him cutting you and drinking your blood..."

The colour had drained from Meya's face. She looked up at Nina and cupped her cheek. *I'm sorry he hurt you.*

Nina placed her hand on Meya's. "I didn't expect it to sting as much as it did. He didn't heal the cuts at first, but when I mentioned it..." She swallowed. "I don't think he liked me knowing that, but I assured him we had kept it a secret between us. Still..." She sighed. "I didn't want to have scars. I pleaded with him to heal the cuts like he had done yours."

Meya's eyes moved down to Nina's breasts. The lack of adequate light made it hard to see if the cuts had been healed or not.

Nina covered her face with her hands. "I'm sorry, Meya."

Confused, Meya placed the cup back on the table and grabbed Nina's arm with both hands. "What happened?" she asked softly and slowly, in order to avoid triggering another coughing attack.

"He healed the cuts... But I gave myself to him."

Meya didn't understand. "What?"

Nina pulled her into a hug. "I'm sorry, my dear. But... I allowed Lord Deminas to fornicate with me."

# Twenty One

Meya tensed up. "You... what?"

"I'm sorry." Nina held her tighter. "I just... It all happened so fast and at the time, it seemed like a good decision."

Meya gently pushed her away so she could look at her face, though Nina immediately averted her eyes. "Did he... force you?"

Nina shook her head. "No. I did it willingly—he even *asked* me to make sure. But..." She turned away, covering her face in shame. "I felt so dirty and used afterwards."

Meya bit her lip, unsure of what to say. She wanted to comfort Nina, but at the same time, she wanted to slap her across the face.

"After he had healed the cuts... He... He turned me around and..." Nina's words were slow, hesitant. "He... He took me from behind... Before he finished, he pulled out..." She ran her hands through her hair, a frustrated grunt leaving her throat. "It was all over my back!" She hid her face in her hands again. "He wiped it off using his towel, then passed me my own and told me to leave."

Hearing all this had turned Meya's face red with embarrassment. *I thought she had spent the night with him.* Memories of when she had done just that flashed through her mind. Though she had despised it, a part of her had found

166

solace in the act. *Maybe he does care about me?* Relief flooded over her, but it was swiftly followed by guilt.

*Why do you care about the Lord? You love Nina! And Lord Deminas just screwed* her*! Your lover allowed him to!* A spike of anger went through her insides, though it faded quickly.

*Nina has always been supportive of me. She was never jealous when the Lord did anything to me.* She swallowed and looked at Nina—she still had her face buried in her hands. *She said she had made a deal with him so she could come and visit* me*, to take care of me.* Tears stung her eyes. *I shouldn't be mean to her about this!*

She remembered how much the cuts on her breasts had hurt, and she felt even worse knowing Nina had gone through something similar. *But he healed my cuts and that stopped the pain. I can understand how Nina would have wanted the pain to stop too.*

A soft sob escaped from Nina as a quiver shook her hunched form. "You despise me, don't you?

Meya's heart ached as she realised she had been quiet all this time, contemplating what had happened. "N-no..." She wrapped her arms around Nina and pulled her close. "I'm sorry," she whispered.

Nina cuddled up to her, pressing her face into Meya's neck. "I'm sorry too, for making such a stupid decision." She sniffed. "That's why I didn't come back... I was too ashamed. First, I went to the baths, as I wanted to wash myself clean. But even then..." Her hold on Meya intensified for a moment. "I just couldn't bring myself to face everyone after such a thing. I feared they would notice and I didn't want to upset you in front of them. So... I spent the night in our secret place."

"But how do you... plan on explaining... your absence?" Meya had to fight the urge to cough.

Nina let go of Meya and shrugged. "I have spent nights away before in the past."

"But Gail knows... about the Lord."

The colour drained from Nina's face. "Oh, damn it! I totally forgot! I told her to tell you I was going to be late as I didn't want you to worry. And then things... Well..." She groaned in frustration. "Damn it!"

Meya placed her hand on Nina's shoulder, squeezing it slightly.

There was a knock on the door. Startled, a cough freed itself from Meya's throat, quickly followed by several more until her face was red.

"I...I'm so sorry," Gail said as she hurried inside with a tray of food in one hand and a jug in the other.

Nina rubbed Meya's back in an attempt to ease her discomfort. "Not your fault. Meya's just ill."

Gail placed the items on the bedside table. "I... eh... brought some breakfast. Juris asked me. He seemed rather uncomfortable being in Meya's presence." She rolled her eyes. "He seems to think she's contagious. If you ask me, if she *is*, then why is no one else sick? Especially you or Lord Deminas." She looked at Nina with her arms crossed and a brow raised.

Nina shrugged. "I don't know. I have no idea what ails her, let alone if it is something that can make others sick too." She took Meya's hand in her own and squeezed it. "Even if a physician were to tell me she is contagious, I would take care of her still."

Meya's face was still red from coughing, but the sweet words made her smile.

"So, Gail..." Nina licked her lips as she turned to face the brunette. "Tell me... How long were you outside the door, eavesdropping?"

Gail flushed as she stumbled over her own words. "I—What—I wasn't— What are you talking about?"

Nina sighed. "Come on Gail, I've known you long enough. Spill it."

With a grunt, Gail sat down on the bed next to Meya's. "From what I understand, you've invoked Winnie's wrath."

Nina's expression darkened with shame. "Great, just great. So you know, but does she?"

Gail looked Nina straight in the eye. "When they wondered about your whereabouts, I told them you had told me you had chores to do. Since you stayed away all night, I did notice both sisters being rather anxious this morning... But, you might still get away with it. Did anyone see you on your way over here?"

"Hell, no! I made sure to stay well out of sight looking like this!"

"Good. Then get dressed and act like nothing happened. If anyone asks, just tell them you needed some privacy—like you've done so many times in the past."

Nina considered this. "You do realise that you'd be covering for me then? Instead of telling the entire castle this juicy bit of gossip..."

Gail snorted. "Really? You think I'd dare spread any word about what happens in the Lord's private quarters after last time?" She moved her tongue over the scars surrounding her lips. "No thanks."

"Yeesh, and here I thought you were going to say you weren't going to tell nasty things about your friends."

Gail crossed her arms. "Now you're just being mean."

168

Nina giggled, stood up, and hugged Gail. "Come on, you know I am just teasing you."

"Better be careful, I can still change my mind and tell that jealous, little mute."

Nina held Gail at an arm's length, her expression serious. "You wouldn't!"

"No, I wouldn't... But you're not the only one that enjoys teasing."

Nina gave Gail a playful shove and they both laughed.

"Anyway, I had better get going now." Gail rose and straightened her robe. "I do expect some details from you in exchange for keeping my lips sealed, though!" She winked and left the room before Nina could protest.

Meya simply shook her head, her cheeks flushing red at the thought of what details Nina would have to tell. *I bet he's a beast in bed.*

~*~

"I'm worried about Meya... She's been sick for days now and that rattle in her breath sends shivers up my spine!" Gail hugged herself.

"She's a strong woman. She'll get better," Lea said, though her words lacked confidence.

"I'm happy no one else is sick." Brit ran her hand through her blonde locks. "I still remember how half the castle was ill years ago."

Nina frowned. "When was that?"

"A few years before you joined us here," Lea answered. "I remember it well, as I was one of the few who was not sick. It was a harsh winter, and servants and soldiers alike fell ill."

Brit smiled. "Yeah, you were lucky."

"You call me lucky for having to take care of you two and a lot of others? To watch so many of the people I came to know and love waste away?"

Both Brit and Winnie shifted in front of the hearth, their eyes cast down.

"It was a horrible winter. A lot of people died... Including dear Lady Tatyana." Lea sighed. "I hope to never experience such a thing again." She turned to look at Meya, who was seemingly asleep.

"I heard Lord Marius fell ill not long after his wife passed away?" Gail fidgeted with the hem of her robe.

Lea hesitated a bit before answering, "He did. However, he recovered rather quickly. As did all the generals."

Gail licked her lips as she contemplated continuing the subject. "Is it true that they got better after the arrival of that strange man?"

Lea frowned. "What *strange* man?"

"They call him Andreas. He was also here with the big battle in which Lord Marius perished."

"You mean *Commander* Andreas?" Nina interjected. "The soldiers still tell stories about that battle. They say he fought ferociously and with great technique. He advised Lord Marius in several battles."

Gail huffed. "Well, he didn't do a good enough job. Lord Marius died, and Lord Deminas nearly did, too, from what I've heard."

"From what *I* heard, Commander Andreas is the reason why Lord Deminas still lives. He went berserk after seeing his father decapitated, and Andreas supposedly saved him from a similar fate."

Gail crossed her arms. "Maybe so, but if this Commander is such a great man, where is he now?"

Nina shrugged. "No clue. He is abroad a lot, from what I understand. He comes perhaps once or twice every year and only stays when he's needed."

"Then why did he come here when there was no war, but half the castle was sick and dying? And why did Lord Marius suddenly recover upon his arrival, as well as all the generals who had fallen ill?" Gail's eyes shimmered with morbid enthusiasm.

"Gail, you need to drop this," Lea intervened. "You are going back into your old ways. I doubt the Lord will appreciate such talk."

"I can talk with all of you about this, can't I?" She looked at Nina, Winnie, and Brit before focusing on Lea again.

Lea shook her head. "You are insinuating dark things, Gail. If you continue, I fear for your safety."

Gail paled and stared at Lea. "What? Why?"

"Because... Someone else did so before you. When Lord Marius recovered, along with the generals, one of the servants spread rumours about witchcraft." Lea turned her gaze towards the fire. "He went missing not long after that, though we all knew what really happened." She faced Gail again. "So please, for your own safety: don't pursue these dangerous insinuations."

Gail swallowed and nodded slowly. "Alright."

"I never heard those rumours," Nina said softly, a slight quiver in her voice. "Is that why the mood in the castle turns so dark every time the Commander visits? I always thought it was because of the wars that people were so silent and afraid."

"It's probably a combination of everything," Lea answered. "Nasty rumours, impending war, people going missing... Those things are bound to affect people."

170

The colour drained from Nina's face. "People going missing... All the Lord's previous chambermaids and all the servants who were up and about late at night who disappeared... I think that all happened when the Commander was at the castle!"

Lea gave Nina an angry glare. "Don't you start this nonsense now, too! Rumours are bad and are not tolerated for a reason. It's all just coincidence. Now drop it before I need to worry about you getting your lips stitched too—or worse!"

Flustered, Nina turned around to look at Meya. Her heart skipped a beat when she noticed she had her eyes open. She jumped up and walked over. "Hey, you're awake. Do you need anything?" She reached for the cup on the bedside table, but Meya turned away.

Nina stared at her back for a few seconds before moving to the other side of the bed and kneeling. "Meya, you need to drink." She whispered to ensure the others wouldn't hear. "You're running a fever."

"I heard everything."

Nina bit her lip. "I know what you're thinking."

"I'm afraid."

There was a rattle in every breath Meya took and it made Nina worry even more about her. "And I'm afraid too—about your health. You're not drinking enough."

Meya closed her eyes. "Later."

"No, *now*." Nina rose and got the cup. "Come on."

Reluctantly, Meya opened her eyes. "Fine." With a grunt, she sat up a bit. She took the cup, emptied it, and sank back down. "Better?"

Nina brushed away the strands of hair plastered to Meya's forehead and cheeks. "You know I just want you to get better."

A brief smile appeared on Meya's face and she nodded. "Thank you."

"Go on, rest now."

Weary, Meya gladly closed her eyes.

A heavy sigh escaped Nina's lips as she returned to the others by the fire.

"Winnie thinks she's going to die," Brit said softly.

"Keep such negative thoughts to yourself, Winnie." Nina gave her an angry glare.

Winnie shrugged.

"I think she's right, though," Brit stated.

"Just shut it!"

Lea took Nina by her wrist and gestured for her to sit down. "No fighting, please. Meya's sick, but she's not deaf." She looked at the sisters. "Be nice."

"I didn't say it to be mean." Brit pouted. "It's just… She doesn't seem to be improving."

"Give her some time. She will," Gail said, crossing her arms. "If we all believe she will, she will."

Nina smiled. "Thanks, Gail."

~*~

The next evening, Nina stormed into their chambers, startling everyone inside. "Bad news!"

"What is it?" Lea asked.

Gail paled. "Don't tell me…"

"Tomorrow the men are packing. They will leave for war the day after."

Winnie shot up, tears in her eyes. She mumbled something incomprehensible and Brit had to sit her back down.

"If you are wondering: yes, Lord Deminas will be going to war too." Nina took a seat on one of the beds.

"How did you find out?" Gail asked.

"I was busy in the Lord's chambers when Juris came in. He is to announce the news to everyone during breakfast tomorrow."

Brit cleared her throat. "Where were you, though? Why didn't you tell us during supper?"

Nina glared at her. "Lord Deminas wanted to talk to me for a bit, so by the time I got down to the dining hall, you all had already left."

"Talk about what?"

"Brit, stop it," Lea stated.

"Indeed, that's none of your business," Nina added. She rose and went over to Meya, but she was fast asleep. "Should I wake her?"

Lea shook her head. "Better leave her. Her fever has increased and she was rambling when I got in."

Worry spread across Nina's face. "I hoped the rise would have passed by now… I noticed it after lunch. She was rambling then too. Did you wet the cloth over her forehead?"

"Yes. I ensured it was nice and cool. It might have helped her doze off so quickly."

Nina turned to Lea. "Thank you."

"No need to thank me. I want her to get better too."

They both looked at Meya. Her chest rose and fell at a faster pace than normal for someone asleep, the rattle in her breath clearly audible in the moment of silence.

~*~

Nina carefully opened the door to their quarters, hoping not to disturb Meya should she be sleeping. She peered inside: Meya was awake and looking at her. Nina closed the door and hurried over to her.

"Hey, how are you feeling?" She noticed her breakfast still lay on her bedside table, untouched.

"Cold. Hot. Sweaty. Tired. Heavy. My head's pounding and... my chest—"

"Hurts?" Nina interjected.

"Burns."

"Don't talk too much, alright? I don't want you exerting yourself."

"I don't care. I don't want to... be sick anymore!" She coughed violently and cursed. "I need to get... back to my chores. I don't want you... doing them."

Nina shifted uncomfortably. "You don't need to worry about chores. We're going to have it easy for a few weeks."

Meya frowned. "What do you mean?"

"The Golden Horde is planning to attack Tristanja, but Lord Deminas is going to strike first. They are leaving tomorrow, early in the morning."

The colour drained slightly from Meya's heated cheeks. "What? War?"

Nina nodded. "With most of the men gone, we won't have quite as many chores—"

"Lord Deminas is going... to war?" Meya erupted in violent coughing.

"Calm down! You're going to choke!" Nina patted Meya's back in an attempt to help relieve her.

"How can I be... calm after you told... me we're going—"

Nina pressed her hand against Meya's mouth. "Shush. I need you to calm down because I don't want you to pass out! Do you understand?"

Meya growled but nodded.

Nina placed the back of her hand against Meya's forehead. "Damn it, the fever refuses to pass!" She took the cloth and rinsed it in a bowl of water a few times. She folded it up and draped it over Meya's reddened skin.

"I'm sorry," Meya whispered.

"What?"

"I'm sorry."

173

"What for?" Nina frowned.

"You've been taking... care of me. You had to get... hurt in order to... do so. I'm sorry. I'm sorry you have... to do my chores. That... That..." She sniffed as tears started to well up in her eyes. "That you had to... have sex with—"

"Stop it," Nina hissed, her cheeks flaring up.

Meya's expression hardened. "You enjoyed it... didn't you?"

"What?" Nina couldn't believe what she was hearing.

Meya took the cloth from her forehead and tossed it at Nina. "You used me... didn't you? You wanted to get... close to the Lord!" She coughed again, the rattle in her breath growing louder.

"You're talking nonsense!"

"You *love* the Lord!"

Nina's jaw dropped and it took her a moment to react in a calm manner. "Meya, this isn't you. This is the fever talking. You know damn well that I love you and only you."

"Bollocks! You hate me and... despise me for being... close to the Lord!"

Nina rubbed her temples. "Meya, I think you are confusing me with Winnie. Winnie is the one who has a thing for the Lord, not me."

The anger slowly faded from Meya's face. She blinked a few times, confusion setting in. "How... Why..." Tears welled up again. "I'm sorry."

"It's alright. You're ill." Nina gently stroked Meya's greasy locks. "The fever is messing with your mind."

"I'm scared."

"I know, but—"

There was a knock on the door. Before any of them could answer, it opened to reveal Lord Deminas.

# Twenty Two

Nina gulped as her eyes enlarged and the colour drained from her face. "My Lord," she squeaked.

He entered, closing the door behind him. "Nina, return to your chores. I wish to sleep in a clean bed before going to battle."

Nina shot up and curtsied. "Of course, my Lord."

"Also, make sure to scrub the bath."

"Yes, my Lord." She was about to make her way out when she heard Meya speak.

"Does the Lord want... to have a good... fuck before he... goes to war too?"

Nina froze, unable to process what she had just heard. Meya's heavy, rattling breath was the only thing disturbing the silence. Slowly, she turned to look at the Lord.

His face was void of emotion, a single brow raised as he stared at Meya.

"Did you enjoy her? Did she manage to... satisfy your lust?" Meya's voice trembled with anger and sadness. "Why her? Was I not... good enough? Why—"

"She's raving, my Lord. Please, pay her no mind! It's the fever talking." Nina was panicking slightly.

"I'm not raving!" Meya screamed, triggering several violent coughs.

"Please, my Lord. Don't listen to what she says. Before you walked in, she actually confused me for Winnie. She's that ill."

"Winnie is—"

"That's enough," Lord Deminas stated. "Nina, go do your chores."

Nina . "Yes, my Lord." She gave Meya one last glance before hurrying out of the room.

Lord Deminas approached Meya and sat down on the bed next to hers.

"Are you here for... my blood? I don't think... it will taste... very good now." She panted, her lungs unable to provide sufficient oxygen. "You're better off... taking it from Nina."

"I will take whatever I desire, regardless of what you say." He leaned towards her. "Be it a good fuck or—" Lord Deminas was cut short as he had to grab Meya's hand as it lashed out for his face.

"Nina's mine!" She coughed loudly, nearly choking on the phlegm. With tears in her eyes, from both the physical and emotional exertion, she looked up to meet the Lord's.

Something burned behind the usually cool grey of his eyes, and despite the fever, Meya's blood chilled in her veins. Somewhere deep inside, her mind still worked, and that part was screaming, but the illness refused to hand over the reins.

"She's mine," she sobbed as tears rolled over her cheeks.

Lord Deminas' fingers disappeared into her red locks and grabbed them forcefully, pulling her head to the side so that he could whisper into her ear, "No, she's *mine*. Just as *you* are, and every other slave in this castle."

"I never agreed to... be sold like property!" More coughs, but the Lord kept his grip on her hair, causing her to tug at it herself with each spasm.

"Property is not asked for permission."

Meya raised her free hand to the lord's, which was still holding onto her hair.

"Don't." His tone was low and dark, and his grip on her right wrist tightened briefly.

Meya's left hand floated in mid-air for a moment, before she lowered it, her bottom lip trembling.

Lord Deminas let go of her wrist, but not of her hair. "Any further ambiguities regarding your position?

"N-no."

He tugged at her hair, causing her to wince. "You may be ill, but you have shown me more than enough disrespect than I am willing to accept. I asked if there are any further ambiguities regarding your position. Answer me properly."

176

"N-no, my...my Lord," Meya stammered, suppressing the need to cough while tears ran down her flushed cheeks.

He released her hair and straightened himself. "The consequences of your behaviour just now shall be dealt with when I return from battle."

Meya grimaced. "Then maybe it's better... if I do not... survive this illness... *my Lord*."

Lord Deminas narrowed his eyes. "You truly are testing my patience."

"Why me?" She turned her head to the hearth. "Winnie's been making rude... gestures this entire time... and you've not said... a thing to her!" She coughed again, grabbed her kerchief, and spat the yellow mucus into the already drenched fabric.

The lord lifted a brow as he looked around the empty room. "Winnie?"

Meya pointed at a spot between the hearth and the window. "There! She—" Another set of coughs wracked her body.

"It seems I have underestimated the severity of your illness." Any anger that had been on his face disappeared. "We are alone in this room."

Shocked, Meya turned to look at the lord. "B-but, she's right there..." She glanced at the fireplace again, only to emit a frightened squeal. With panic in her eyes, she clutched the blanket close to her.

"Who do you see now?"

Meya didn't speak, fear paralysing her.

Lord Deminas sat down next to her. He took her head in his hands and gently made her face him. "Look at me. We are alone in this room."

Meya's lip trembled as she closed her eyes and nodded. "I...I'm sorry, my Lord. I'll get better soon... and return to my... chores." Tears fell from her eyes as she opened them. "I'll be a good servant. I'll work hard. Please don't—" A sob interrupted her sentence. "Please don't replace me. Don't send me away."

The lord frowned. "Away?"

"I don't want to... leave the castle. It's safe here. Please, keep me safe." Her eyes pleaded with him as more tears rolled down her face.

Lord Deminas shook his head. "You're raving." He released her head. "I need you to calm down now, can you do that?"

Meya sniffed and swallowed. "Will you keep me safe?"

"We're going to battle tomorrow to keep *everyone* safe."

"No!" She latched onto his shirt. "What if you die?"

He gently peeled her fingers off of him. "You need to have faith in your Lord and his best men."

Meya opened her mouth to speak, but Lord Deminas placed a finger on her lips.

"Quiet now."

Reluctant, she obliged.

"I have a lot to do today still, so—"

"Then why did you—"

"Ill or not, your lack of respect is making me reconsider the reason for my visit." He stared at her, his displeasure visible in his cold eyes.

"Why did—"

"Silence!"

Meya cringed and tears rolled down her heated cheeks.

"You are too sick to speak to me respectfully, so just be quiet instead."

Afraid and ashamed, she nodded.

"Nina kept me informed about your health. As there doesn't seem to be any improvement, I decided to check on you myself."

She opened her mouth to speak but closed it again as the lord's glare hardened.

"Your condition is deteriorating. You are not near death, but as I am leaving in the early morning, I won't be around for when you will be. And from what I can see now, I expect that to happen in the coming days."

Meya trembled. "Death?"

"Yes. If your condition does not improve, you will die." There was a hint of regret in his grey eyes.

Meya shot forward again, meaning to clutch the lord's shirt, but he caught her hands in his own. "I don't want to," she sobbed, her already laboured breath worsened by her clogged nose.

"Which is why I am here."

She sniffed. "Why do you care... if I die?"

A subtle smile spread across his face and his eyes shimmered. "Good servants are hard to come by."

Sadness spread through her heart, as she had hoped for a different answer. "Why not let me... die and take Nina... as your chambermaid? You already—"

"Silence! Do not question my decisions." He released her hands. "Do you want to get better or not?"

Meya nodded, though she bit her lip in an attempt to quell the tears.

"Good." He turned slightly and took something from his belt.

A small yelp escaped from Meya's throat as she spotted the silver blade. She tried to move away from the lord, but he grabbed her by the shoulder with his free hand.

"No reason to be frightened. Relax." He looked at her intently.

Meya swallowed, though her eyes kept switching from the lord's face to the knife in his hand.

"I am not going to cut you."

This relieved her a bit, though she remained wary.

"I know this is going to sound strange and you won't want to do this, but I need you to trust me."

Meya remained quiet, adrenaline spreading through her veins as a cold sheet of fear covered her.

"You have witnessed the healing capacities of my blood for some time now. You will take my blood and it will make you better."

Her eyes widened in fright. "W-what? No!"

The lord's gaze became strict. "I am offering you a cure. I am willing to cut my own skin for you and let you drink my blood. Do you realise this?"

Meya shook her head wildly. "No! No witchcraft! No magic!" Panic overtaking her, she looked around, her instincts telling her to flee.

Lord Deminas placed the blade on the bedside table and took her head in his hands. He forced her to face him, ignoring her thrashing as she began to weaken. "Meya! Calm down."

But it was already too late. She started to cough, and within only a few coughs, her face had turned bright red and she was spewing up phlegm again.

The lord waited for her to recollect herself, observing her with a raised brow. When she was finally done heaving and wiping her mouth clean, he spoke again. "There is no witchcraft involved, or any other kind of magic. It would do you well to trust your Lord in this matter." His eyes hardened again. "And it would be wise to not tell others of this, as rumours about witchcraft are not taken lightly."

Her expression became timid and she nodded. "I...I'm sorry, my Lord."

"Now, the choice is yours. Do you want to accept my offer or not?"

Meya hesitated. Her eyes shifted from the lord to the drenched kerchief next to her, back to the lord. Her lower lip trembling, she swallowed and muttered, "I...I don't want to die."

"Then will you drink?"

Meya closed her eyes and nodded.

"Good." Lord Deminas took the knife from the table. "I don't want to waste any blood, so once I cut myself, you'll need to be ready to drink. Do you understand?"

"Y-yes, my Lord."

The suggestion of a smile tugged at his lips upon hearing her words. He pulled down the sleeve on his left arm and brought the knife to his skin. The silver bit into the delicate flesh and globules of dark blood appeared.

Meya cringed at the sight and turned away, but the lord quickly grabbed the back of her head. The haft of the blade pressed against her skull as he made her face him. Her eyes enlarged when she saw the dark blood flow from the cut and she opened her mouth to voice her horror, but the lord pressed his arm against it before a sound could pass her lips.

"Drink, before more gets onto the linens." His stern gaze locked with her terrified one.

The warm, metallic fluid pooled into her mouth, yet her body refused to swallow. Frozen in fear, she just let the quantity of blood increase.

Lord Deminas noticed and tugged slightly at her hair. "If you want to get better, drink!"

Tears rolled down her cheeks as she closed her eyes. She focused on swallowing, but it took several seconds before she finally managed to do so. The strange sensation of such a large amount of blood passing through her throat made her shiver. After the second swallow, she brought her hands up to grasp the lord's arm. The initial fear was waning, and her tongue started to move against the cut, causing a mischievous smile to appear on the lord's face.

"Now that's a good servant."

It didn't take long before there was no more blood flowing into her mouth. Cautious, she detached herself from the lord's arm. Her cheeks flushed, she looked at the cut: it had closed.

"You'll need more than that." He brought the silver down to his skin and made another incision below the first one.

Meya cringed but didn't look away this time. The lord moved the wound towards her, and Meya took his arm with both hands and placed her lips around the cut. The taste didn't bother her as much anymore, and she drank obediently. Still, within a mere minute, the flow of blood stopped and she released the lord's arm again.

Lord Deminas seemed to consider things for a moment. "Once more. I'd rather give you a bit too much than not enough."

Meya wanted to thank him, but the blood sticking to her tongue made her fumble for words. Before she could manage to speak, the blade had already created a fresh cut underneath the previous ones. The blood oozed out of the wound and she quickly pressed her mouth against his skin.

She was starting to feel a little queasy, but she kept drinking. Her tongue moved over his skin, lapping up every drop of blood that flowed from the wound. When the flow halted, she slowly pulled away. There was a trail that ran down the lord's arm, and she moved down to lick it up—though her bloodied tongue didn't make it much cleaner.

"That will do." Lord Deminas gently pulled his arm away from her. "I will clean up later." He pulled his sleeve back down, hiding the blood smeared skin from sight. The silver blade was also stained, but he licked it clean and wiped it off before putting it away.

Meya looked down at the linens and was ashamed to see several drops of blood had fallen onto them.

Lord Deminas noticed too. "Wipe off your mouth on that side, and I will flip them over for now. You can ask Nina to change them later."

She obliged. Upon seeing the dark smears, the nausea in the pit of her stomach increased. The fact that her tongue was still coated with blood didn't help much, either.

The lord took the sheets and pulled them off, causing Meya to shiver from the sudden cold, and she watched as he turned them over so the stains wouldn't be visible.

"Now remember, keep this between us." His eyes were stern. "Considering what Nina knows already, you may tell her, but if there are any rumours upon my return, there will be consequences."

Meya nodded. She was still swallowing profusely in an attempt to get rid of the metallic taste in her mouth.

"Then lie down now and rest."

"What... What happens now, my Lord?" Meya managed to utter.

Lord Deminas was silent for a moment. "You will probably be tired and sleep a lot for a day or two. You—"

There was a knock on the door. "My Lord? Are you still there?"

He contemplated the situation before answering, "Yes, enter."

Nina opened the door and peeked inside. "I'm sorry to disturb you, my Lord, but Commander Andreas has arrived and is waiting for you in your quarters. I informed him that you were busy, but he insisted."

"It's alright, I was about to leave." He rose and gave Meya one last glance before turning his attention to Nina. "I need you to change her sheets and ensure she drinks enough water." He moved towards the door. "Also, get her a bucket. She will most likely need it later."

Nina paled. "As you wish, my Lord." She bowed her head. "Will I still be able to finish my chores up in your quarters, or does my Lord wish not to be disturbed?"

"You can come up and finish your chores. Andreas and I won't be bothered by your presence." He left the room and Nina hurried over to Meya.

"Are you alright? What happened?"

Meya swallowed before answering, "I...I'm not sure." She licked her lips—the metallic taste seemed to linger there too. "Could you... give me some water?"

"Of course." Nina poured her a cup and handed it to her.

"Thanks." Meya drank the water greedily, glad to wash away the remnants of his blood from her tongue.

Nina scrutinised her. "Meya, what happened? Why does he want me to change the linens and bring you a bucket?"

Though she still felt nauseous, she doubted she would need a bucket for that. "I don't know about... the latter, but the sheets..." She gestured for Nina to come closer. "Keep this a secret?"

"Of course! What is it?"

Meya lifted the sheets so Nina could see the bloodstains.

Nina's eyes widened. "Don't tell me he came in here to drink your blood! You're ill! He could've asked me!"

Meya shook her head. "He didn't."

Confused, Nina tilted her head. "Then what happened?"

Meya bit her lip as she hesitated to tell her. "He... He gave me his."

"He... What?" Her face blanched. "Why? Did you perform some kind of magic—"

Meya waved her hands. "No. No magic. He told me... it has nothing... to do with magic. If there are any... rumours about magic... he will get upset."

"Then what?

"I...I don't know. He just said his... blood would cure me."

Shocked, Nina remained silent.

"Considering... it can mend wounds," Meya muttered hesitantly.

A deep sigh escaped Nina's throat as she ran her hands through her raven locks. "Well, let's hope it'll work on this then, too."

# Twenty Three

Meya gasped for breath as thick strands of saliva mixed with phlegm hung from her lips. She clutched the rim of the bucket that sat between her legs, knuckles white from the strain.

"That's it, I'm out of here," Brit said as her eyes shot from Meya to her sister. "You coming?"

Winnie rose without hesitation.

"What? Where are you going and why?" Lea stood in front of them, her hands on her sides as she scrutinised the two.

Brit pointed at Meya, who was gagging loudly. "That's why. I cannot sleep like this! I also do not wish to be anywhere near her when she chokes to death."

A slap resounded through the room. "Have you no heart?"

Brit didn't even bother to rub her cheek, she just glared at Lea. "I am no physician. What do you want me to do?"

"Show some support! I sat by *your* bedside when you and your sister were this ill!"

"You can't compare that! We weren't dying! Besides, we were in bed for a week. How long has—"

Meya's loud, retching coughs interrupted their argument. Lea and Gail eyed her grimly, while the sisters looked horrified and disgusted. The coughing turned to more gagging until she spat into the bucket, her raspy pants filling the room until Brit continued.

"How long has she been ill for? Hmm? You go ahead and try to convince yourself that she isn't dying, but I am no fool. The sound of her choking is going to give me nightmares!" She pushed Lea aside. "Now if you will excuse us."

"Where will you go?" Gail said, her voice trembling with restrained anger. She was sitting next to Meya, rubbing her back.

Brit huffed. "I'll sleep with the soldiers if I have to. I'm sure they wouldn't mind, considering they're going to war tomorrow."

Gail rolled her eyes. "Harlot," she hissed under her breath.

"Considering Nina's not here either, she might be doing the exact same thing." She held her chin up and left the room with Winnie following suit.

Gail rose to go after them, but Lea shook her head. The door closed and Gail sat back down. "Ruttish churl," she grumbled before turning her attention back to Meya, who coughed and spat out another mouthful of slime.

Lea sat down across from Gail. "Don't let them upset you."

Gail grunted. "They are the worst friends one can have."

"Not... friends," Meya rasped, more coughs following the words she spoke.

Gail rubbed her back. "I suppose you're right."

Lea sighed. "Talking of friends... Where's Nina?"

"I have no idea... I didn't see her at supper, either." She looked at Meya. "Do you know where she is?"

Meya shook her head.

"Maybe the Lord requested her presence? I mean, they *are* leaving for war tomorrow," Lea suggested.

"For what though? Do you really think he'd care if his desk is dusty or the bedroom floor muddy if he is to leave in the morning?"

Lea shrugged. "Who knows..."

Meya was unable to suppress another wave of coughing. Her head thumping from the exertion, she thought about what had been said. *I think I know...*

~*~

Gail and Lea were drifting off to sleep, Meya's steady yet noisy breath suggesting she was already gone, when the door creaked open. Nina slipped inside as silently as she could, but Gail shot upright.

184

"Where have you been?" she hissed.

Lea stirred and rose too.

"Where do you think?" She turned to look at Meya. "How's she doing?"

"She's finally asleep. She threw up all evening. Winnie and Brit left because of it."

"Left? Where to?"

Gail shrugged. "Brit stated she'd sleep with the soldiers if she needed to, but she was very set not to spend another minute in this room."

Nina shook her head. "Stupid girls... It's dangerous out there."

"Why do you say that?" Lea asked.

Gail frowned. "Yes, why? You were out yourself."

"I was at the Lord's, and just trust me on this." She sighed. "Though I guess come tomorrow, it'll be fine."

Lea and Gail exchanged glances.

"Now, if you don't mind... I'm exhausted." She crawled into her bed.

"Goodnight," Lea said.

Gail sighed, disappointed at not hearing any details. "Goodnight."

~*~

Meya was woken by someone sitting next to her. Still drowsy, she opened her eyes reluctantly.

"Hey, sleepy," Nina said with a smile. "You slept straight through the bells earlier. How are you feeling? I heard you threw up a lot yesterday..."

"I thought I was going to die," Meya managed to say in one breath. She turned to look where the bucket stood on the floor, and Nina followed her gaze.

Nina's face was already quite pale, but any remaining colour drained away as she picked up the bucket and peered at the contents. "Did... Did you see what's in here?"

Now it was Meya's turn to blanch. "Is there blood?"

"I...I don't know..." She stood up and carried the bucket over to the window. "I think the light is playing tricks on me..." The sunlight illuminated the contents, but Nina remained silent as she stared down at whatever was in the bottom.

"Well? What is it?" Fear twisted Meya's insides and she had to suppress the desire to just get out of bed and look for herself.

"It's not blood... I think." Nina locked eyes with Meya. "I've seen people cough up yellow slime before... But this is blue."

Meya frowned. "Blue?"

She nodded and walked over to her. "Here, see for yourself."

Meya took the bucket and tilted it so the light from the window hit the contents as best it could. A cold chill covered her as she identified the mucus on the bottom, which appeared to be just as Nina had described. "But how?" She looked at Nina.

"Maybe it's the Lord's blood? What colour was his blood?"

Meya wanted to say red, but thinking back to it all, she wasn't too sure. "I thought it was red... But it was rather dark..."

"The stains on the sheets were black."

"I'm sure his blood wasn't black—or blue for that matter. I would've noticed that."

Nina sighed. "I do think it has to do with you drinking his weird blood, though... We can agree that his blood is weird, right?"

Meya nodded and another chill went up her spine. "I'm scared."

Nina took the bucket, placed it on the floor, and hugged Meya close. "I'll clean that up so no one else will have to know about it."

"Thanks." Meya swallowed the bile in the back of her throat. *Just what did I get myself into by agreeing to drink his blood?* Thinking of the lord, she broke out of the embrace. "Where were you last night? What happened?"*Please don't tell me he wanted some company before going off to war...*

Nina cast her eyes down. "Lord Deminas requested my presence during supper... But the Commander was there too. Turns out they are the same." She rolled her left sleeve up a bit and showed Meya her lower arm. There were two cuts several inches below her wrist. "I had to sit there and drip into this large jug... I was so afraid they were going to let me bleed dry! I...I..." She shook her head and swallowed. "I actually passed out. When I woke up, still alive and with the wounds closed, I was so relieved! Both the Lord and the Commander were nowhere to be seen, so I just hurried out of there."

Meya stared at her in silence for a while. "I'm so sorry." She embraced Nina, her hand running through her raven locks. "I hope that had nothing to do with him letting me drink his blood."

"I don't know... They are off to war now. Maybe they needed the blood for some weird pre-war ritual?" She sighed and shrugged. "I'm just glad to still be here. I really thought I was going to bleed to death."

Meya's hold on her tightened for a moment, but a knock on the door made her release her promptly. They both turned to watch Gail rush inside, face flushed.

"Alright Nina, you need to explain something to me," she hissed as she walked closer to them. "Yesterday, you told us it was dangerous to be out."

Meya frowned, not understanding what she was talking about.

"Did something happen?" Nina asked, her voice quivering slightly.

"People are still looking, but it seems Chemi is gone."

Slightly ashamed that she still didn't know everyone in the castle, Meya asked, "Who's Chemi?"

"She works in the kitchen," Nina said. "But what do you mean, she's gone?"

"Exactly what you'd think. She was out late yesterday and she never returned to her quarters. Juris was asking around just now, as she didn't show for her duties this morning. Now, you came back quite late yourself yesterday and you said it was dangerous to be walking around... Did you see her? Do you know what happened to her?" Gail's eyes pleaded for an answer, but Nina just shook her head.

"To be honest, I didn't see anyone on my way back. Sorry."

Gail grunted. "Then why did you say it was dangerous?"

Nina avoided Gail's prying gaze. "Commander Andreas was in the castle... And well... He scares me."

"Then those rumours were true." Gail wrapped her arms around herself. "Poor Chemi... I fear we won't see her again." She sighed. "How many people have disappeared now while that man is in the castle?"

Nina shrugged. "I don't want to know." She rose. "But come on, Gail. Let's give Meya some rest."

"I also heard some other rumours..." Gail turned her attention to Meya. "People say they saw the Lord visit you yesterday; did he?"

Figuring it was no use to lie, Meya nodded. "He did."

"Why?"

"Just wanted to know if I would still be alive upon his return..."

Gail snorted. "Caring for a sick servant like that... Let's hope Winnie doesn't find out because I'm certain she'll be livid."

"Yeah, yeah, yeah." Nina ushered Gail towards the door. "We know Winnie's jealous. Now come on, get out. I'll finish up my things here too and then Meya can get some more rest."

"Alright, I'm going." Gail was about to step outside when she turned to look at Meya. "Are you feeling better by the way? Your breathing's less... laboured."

Meya smiled. "Yes, I'm feeling a bit better, I suppose."

~*~

187

Meya was drifting between sleeping and waking when she heard the door creak open. Despite her fatigue, she noticed someone standing beside her—though they remained silent. Too weary to look if it was Nina or not, she kept her eyes closed.

Something soft touched her face, though it quickly became rough. It took Meya a moment to realise just what was going on. *That's a pillow! Someone is trying to smother me!*

She tried to push the pillow off, but whoever was doing it crawled on top of her and placed their entire weight onto it. It was becoming very hard to breathe and she started to thrash, but her assailant remained in place, pushing the pillow tightly against her face.

Still weak from being sick, Meya feared she wasn't going to win the struggle. Her lungs burned with their want of oxygen and her head pounded. *No... This isn't happening. Get off. Get off! GET OFF!*

Tapping into every remaining bit of energy in her body, she managed to pull her legs up and kick the attacker with all her might.

The air that flooded into her lungs caused her to cough violently, but that didn't stop her from throwing the pillow aside and looking at who was trying to kill her. Stunned, she watched Winnie crawl back to her feet, her face flushed and her eyes wide with panic and fear.

"Y-you," Meya managed to utter, rage dripping from the single word. "You just tried to kill me!"

Winnie's eyes shot from Meya to the door. Without giving it a second thought, she rushed out of the room, nearly tripping over her own feet.

"You half-faced, flaming harpy! You tried to kill me!" Meya yelled after her, not caring about the coughing fit that ensued.

She stared at the door for a few minutes, allowing her heart and breathing to calm down again—though she gritted her teeth in anger.

*She just tried to choke me! Did she think I was too sick to fight back?* A chill went up her spine. *I should* have *been too sick to fight back. It's amazing I was able to free myself, let alone kick her away like that!* A nervous giggle freed itself from her throat. *She must have flown across the room, considering where she'd landed...*

Meya swallowed and lay back down.

*Just what did Lord Deminas give me? What's in his blood that would make me cough up blue phlegm? And what could make someone like me, who's been ill for weeks, suddenly find the strength to kick a grown woman across the room?* She shivered. *Not magic... Not witchcraft... But what then?*

188

Unable to sleep—afraid Winnie would return to finish her off—Meya kept her eyes locked on the door, thinking about the lord and his strange blood.

~*~

Meya had been staring at the bed across from her for an unknown amount of time, awake but zoned out, when the door to the room opened, startling her. Seeing Nina walk in caused her to relax a bit.

"Hey, you up?"

"Sort of..."

Nina frowned. "What's wrong?"

Meya swallowed. "I woke up with a pillow pressed against my face..." Ashamed, she realised her voice was trembling with rage, fear, and disbelief. "Winnie tried to smother me."

Nina froze, her mouth agape. "Winnie, what?"

"She...she tried to kill me. Crawled on top of me and pressed the pillow down... I couldn't breathe! I don't know how, but I managed to kick her off me. She ran out of the room looking like I had tried to kill her instead!"

Nina walked over and sat down next to Meya. She pressed the back of her hand against her forehead. "You don't have a fever..."

Angry, Meya slapped Nina's hand away. "You think I imagined it?"

Nina cast her eyes down. "Well, you *were* delusional yesterday... And the thought of her doing that, plus you kicking her off is just..."

"I can barely believe it myself, but it happened." She crossed her arms. "Seriously, does she want me to die so badly she couldn't wait to see if I would succumb to whatever ails me? Why does she hate me so?"

"I don't know why she'd try to kill you, but I can imagine why she hates you."

Meya raised a brow.

"Oh, you know." She sighed. "She probably heard that the Lord visited you yesterday."

"I know that, but I'm his chambermaid... What does she expect?"

Nina shrugged. "I don't know what she expects, but I'm pretty sure she wants to be as close to him as you are... Both in daily tasks, and getting a visit when sick."

"I don't get why she can be so jealous that she'd try to kill me, though. It's not like I am trying to steal any attention away from her—hell, I don't even want the Lord to have any interest in me."*Though I have to admit, him wanting to save me from dying was rather nice... And him bothering to capture the slaver and—*

"You don't need to tell me, I know." Nina gave her hand a reassuring squeeze. "Just do realise... Winnie was only six years old when she came to the castle with her sister. As a little girl, she was allowed some freedoms and she used to play a lot with the Lord when he was but a boy. I guess she's just spoiled in that regard."

Now it was Meya's turn to gawk. "She was six? And they accepted her as a servant?"

Nina nodded. "For reasons unknown, they did. Lea told me as it was such a special case, and well... She sort of became like a surrogate mother to the both of them."

"What happened to their parents?"

"Well, it was their dad who had pleaded for Lord Marius to take them, as he didn't want to see them grow up in a bordello. Their mother died not long after giving birth to Winnie. From what Brit told me, their dad had some... issues—the kind that causes debt. She seems rather happy to have ended up here, despite everything that has happened with her sister."

It was silent for a bit. "You know... I don't really care about how Winnie's life must have been hard. We all have our tales of woe, but that doesn't give anyone an excuse to try and kill someone!"

Nina sighed. "I agree. So, what now? Do you want to tell Juris?"

Meya shook her head. "No, forget it. However..." She bit her lip. "Do you think it's possible for me to relocate? I don't want to be in the same room as her anymore."

"I don't think that's possible without explaining what happened to Juris."

"Then maybe... Can I sleep in our secret place? I truly don't want to find out if Winnie will try again."

Nina thought this over. "I suppose we can sleep there... Most of the soldiers are off to war so it'll be a lot easier to sneak in and out. But when they return, you will need to sleep here again—or talk it over with Juris so he can take measures."

Meya sighed. "I really don't want to do that. I fear it will cause her to hate me even more, not to mention how Brit might react when she finds out about her sister's actions."

"I disagree. I really do think you need to tell Juris. I mean, she *did* try to kill you! That's not just some bad gossip."

"Which is exactly why I'd rather not... I fear the punishment she might receive. As angry as I am, I don't want her to be tortured, or even killed."

Nina scoffed. "You're too nice. If you ask me, she needs to see the consequences of her actions. But fine, your choice." She rose. "I'll prepare the room and come and get you when I'm done."

Meya smiled. "Thanks, dear. You truly take good care of me."

# Twenty Four

"Wakey, wakey," Nina said as she walked into the room, a bowl in hand. She closed the door behind her and walked over to Meya with a kind smile. "I brought you some supper."

Groggy, Meya opened her eyes and stretched. "I didn't even know it was suppertime yet."

"You slept through the bells again?"

Meya nodded and sat up. "I suppose I did."

A worried expression replaced Nina's smile. "This morning, too… You're sleeping quite deeply."

"I feel better though." Meya took the bowl of soup from Nina.

"That I can believe. You're no longer so short of breath and the rattle's gone too." Nina's smile returned. "I suppose the Lord's magic worked."

Meya cringed. "Please, don't call it magic. I don't want to get into trouble."

Nina sat down on the bed. "Don't worry about it. It's not like I would ever discuss this in the presence of others."

Meya sighed and sipped the soup.

"Anyway… I told Lea and Gail we would be sleeping somewhere else for a while. They asked why and where of course, but I just said that you needed some privacy and I would care for you. Gail wanted to know more, but I managed to shut her up."

"You didn't mention what happened?"

Nina shook her head. "Though I really do think you should tell Juris. She tried to *kill* you!"

"I know, I know." Meya groaned and rested the bowl in her lap. "I just don't want her to be tortured or worse... How did she react when you told about me sleeping elsewhere?"

"Brit and Winnie were sitting somewhere else, so they don't know."

"I wonder if Winnie told her sister..."

Nina huffed. "I doubt it. Brit always gets upset when Winnie does anything against the rules. She'd flip if she found out."

"Surely just because she fears the punishment, her sister would have to suffer... She didn't seem to care much for me yesterday when she left the room."

Nina shrugged. "I wasn't there, but I'm certain she cares more about her sister than she does about anyone else in this castle—even Lea. Still, I doubt she would condone an attempt at your life."

Meya remained quiet for a bit, contemplating what had been said. "Oh, what does it matter." She brought the bowl back to her lips and drank.

"It matters to *me*." Nina's fingers stroked Meya's red locks. "You're precious to me and she tried to kill you. I would have told Juris myself if you hadn't expressed your desire for secrecy. Hell, I would have told the entire castle—even if it resulted in my own lips being stitched! As long as Winnie got punished, it would have been worth it."

Meya lowered the bowl and sighed. "I know you care for me—and I truly appreciate that—but I have seen enough pain and suffering. I don't want to see more, let alone cause more myself. Yes, Winnie was wrong, and I am angry with her, but..." She hesitated for a moment. "I have seen the Lord's vengeance... Winnie doesn't deserve that. I mean, she tried and she failed. She didn't cause me any lingering pain. It just feels wrong to have her suffer his wrath."

Nina scoffed. "No lingering pain, huh? Please, do tell me why we are in this room, then."

Blood rushed to Meya's cheeks. "When I'm better, I'll go back to our chamber. It's just that I don't want to be an easy target."

"Saying that means you are afraid of her trying again."

Meya wanted to object, but she didn't know what to say. Yielding, she just took another gulp from the soup.

"Just think about it, please. Attempted murder is a serious matter. You need to tell someone."

"I will think about it, but I cannot guarantee that I will change my mind."

Nina grimaced for a second. "Alright, fine." She sighed and lay down next to Meya. "I suppose I will just have to accept your decision. But!" She glared at her. "I will remind you every day."

Meya rolled her eyes but smiled. "I love you too."

Nina wrapped her arm around Meya's waist. "Finish your soup. I've missed you and I want to cuddle."

"I fear it will be just that though: cuddling. I still feel exhausted. If I close my eyes, I'll fall asleep in mere seconds."

"I don't mind. Holding you is satisfying enough for me." Nina nuzzled Meya's side.

Smiling, Meya finished her meal.

~*~

The wind howled outside the chamber, snowflakes blowing past the window. Meya stared at the mesmerising sight, worrying about Lord Deminas and his men. It was the second day she had spent in the lord's old chamber, and the exhaustion finally seemed to fade away.

Bored, she climbed out of the bed and walked over to the window to peer outside. The land was white, the sky grey. *I hope they're alright out there.*

The thought of war sent shivers up her spine and she turned away. A wave of grief washed over her as she thought about her father, though the memories were vague.

*Mother always said he went to war to protect us.* She sniffed back a sob and removed the tears that were forming with the back of her hand. *Come on, Meya. Don't cry.*

Deciding she needed to do something to take her mind off of things, she walked over to the cabinet on which Nina had left her some clean clothes. She got dressed and slipped out of the room.

She was halfway towards the lord's chambers when she changed her mind. *I could really, really use a bath.*

Being sick for so long had caused her to lose track of time and thus the day of the week. She entered the bathing area and was disappointed to find the water in the baths was rather dirty.

*Great...* She sighed and undressed. *Oh well, at least the water won't be too cold.*

Washing herself in the tepid and dirty water, Meya longed for the lord's bath. The moment she realised this desire, she mentally slapped herself.

194

*You're spoiled*, she chided.

Thinking of the warm baths she had shared with the lord, she realised the only times she bathed here anymore was when she had her monthly bleedings.

*Yes, I really am spoiled.*

She sighed heavily as she thought of the lavish biweekly meals she ate with the lord.

*But that doesn't really count... He cuts my hand and drinks my blood in exchange.*

Remembering Nina's words regarding that, she rose with a grunt and stepped out of the water.

*Not only is it a good trade-off, but he's the Lord and I'm a mere servant. He doesn't even need to offer me anything in return.* Her heart leapt. *Yet for some reason, he does. He even gave me his blood to ensure that I wouldn't die. And then there's the whole thing with him letting me sleep in his bed after I suffered in Gail's place.* She bit her lip. *And he killed the slaver after torturing him. So... Maybe he does care for me?*

She shook her head as she dried herself off.

*No, I'm just a servant and he just thinks I do my chores properly—he said that plenty of times. Besides, Nina took over for me while I was sick, and she had to massage him too while in the bath. She also got to share his meal in exchange for some blood.*

An annoyed grunt left her lips.

*I need to stop thinking that I am special! I'm just his damn chambermaid!*

It irritated her how this thought hurt. Angry with herself, she quickly got dressed and left the baths.

*You're acting like you love this man. Stop it! You love Nina! Why do you crave this man's affection?*

Her fingers combed through her still wet hair, momentarily tugging at it in frustration. Not paying much attention to where she was going, she nearly bumped into Kadeem.

"Meya," he stated in slight surprise. "You're feeling better?"

"Oh, hey Kadeem," Meya managed to utter. "I am, thanks."

"Good. People feared you were going to die. Are you working again today?"

"I...I was going to try."

"If possible, could you help us out in the soldiers' quarters? Nina's been so busy doing your chores that I could use some extra hands. Ghulam is... young and not very efficient."

195

She nodded. "I suppose I could try and help. I need to find Nina first though and discuss what needs to be done."

"Fair enough." He gave her a nod and walked away.

Meya stared at him before he disappeared around a corner. *Such a strange guy...* She sighed deeply and made her way to the lord's quarters.

Out of habit, she knocked on the door before realising Lord Deminas wasn't even in the castle.

"Who's there?" Nina called out in surprise.

Meya opened the door and stepped inside. "It's me."

Nina dropped the cloth she had been using to polish the lord's desk and rushed over to her. "Why are you here? You should be resting!"

Meya smiled. "I was feeling better, and after being in bed for weeks, I decided to take a bath. I want to do something else today other than stare at the walls and sleep."

Nina hugged her and planted a kiss on her forehead. "I'm glad you're feeling better, but I just find it so hard to believe that you've recovered so quickly... You were delirious and raving only a few days ago!"

A nervous giggle escaped Meya's throat. "I have a hard time believing it myself, too. But, let's not talk about that. I want to do things, make myself useful. I ran into Kadeem and he said he could use some help in the soldiers' quarters?"

Nina nodded. "He's busy with this kid, Ghulam, replacing the straw in the mattresses. But from what I understand, the poor boy is not really helping." She couldn't suppress the grin that tugged at her lips. "He's been making quite the mess hauling the straw, leaving trails all through the castle."

"Hauling straw? Look, I want to try and do some chores today, but I am not sure if I feel fit enough to go around the castle lugging bales."

"Don't worry—I can help out with that. It would be nice if you could help with opening the mattresses, emptying them, refilling them, and sewing them back up. Ghulam managed to prick himself on the needle so many times, Kadeem no longer wants him near one."

Meya laughed. "Poor kid. But sure, I should be able to manage that. What about the Lord's chambers, though?"

Nina shrugged. "Juris told me to polish the desk, but I'm almost done with that. I did the bedroom and bathroom yesterday. As the Lord's away, I don't think I need to do anything there for a while... Though Juris did say his mattress' filling needs washing, but we can do that tomorrow—I want to tell Lea first, as she will have to rinse out the wool."

Meya nodded. "Alright. So I suppose I will just be helping you and Kadeem while Lord Deminas is away?"

"For now. You should speak to Juris really as he's the head of housekeeping."

"Any idea where he is now? I can go and speak to him while you finish up here. Then we can help Kadeem together, afterwards."

"No clue really, he's always walking around. It's best if you just stay here, maybe dust the shelves a bit? I'm pretty sure the bells will chime soon; you can speak to Juris during lunch."

"Yes, ma'am." Meya smiled teasingly at Nina, who shoved her in jest.

"Go on then, get to work before I need to *discipline* you."

Meya giggled as she evaded a slap on the rear and rushed out of the room to get a clean rag from the closet down the hall.

# Part Three
## Spring, 1240 AD

*The vernal season arrives and seeds flourish.*
*Cherish life, for the summer rain may wash it all away.*

# Twenty Five

Meya was placing wood on the just kindled fire when Nina slipped into the room behind her. Startled, she exclaimed, "Can't you knock? For a moment I feared it was someone else!"

"Sorry." Nina locked the door and sat down next to Meya. "Juris was being annoying. He kept asking me where we've been sleeping for the last month." She sighed. "Someone snitched and I am certain it wasn't Gail or Lea."

"Are we in trouble?"

Nina shrugged. "He tried to follow me, but I used a secret passage near the dungeons. I'm amazed he didn't know about that one—or he just thought *I* didn't know and went to look for me elsewhere. At any rate, I lost him. We just need to be careful that he doesn't try to follow us next time."

"So… Does this mean you will stop asking me every night to tell Juris about Winnie?"

Nina smirked. "Of course not."

Meya gave her a playful shove and she fell back onto the hide they were sitting on, giggling loudly as Meya crawled on top of her and tickled her sides.

"Oh, shhh," Meya quickly shushed, stopping her attack.

Nina panted, a grin still plastered on her face. "There are barely any soldiers in the castle. You don't need to be so afraid."

"It only takes *one* soldier to get us in trouble though… And what if Juris is still walking around, trying to find you?"

Nina's smile faltered and she sighed. "You're right." She pulled Meya into a hug, nuzzling her neck. "It's just that I love it when you tickle me like that."

"Tsss, you just love me touching you."

Nina flicked her tongue against Meya's earlobe and she squirmed in response. "As if you don't." She cupped her breast and squeezed it slightly while grazing her teeth along the sensitive skin of her neck.

A moan slipped from Meya's lips and she rose slightly so that she could peer into Nina's eyes. "You cheat. You know my weak spots."

An impish smile spread across Nina's face. "Oh, do I now?" Her fingers traced Meya's sides ever so lightly, covering her in goosebumps.

"Damn you," Meya hissed between her lips as she closed her eyes in delight.

Nina took the opportunity to push Meya off and to the ground, immediately getting on top of her and pinning her arms down. Nina's lips traced her neck from the jawline down to the collarbone, her hot breath tickling Meya's skin.

"Stop," Meya panted, but she made no attempt to get away.

"Why? I know you're enjoying this." She kissed her way to Meya's mouth, who eagerly answered. Their tongues entwined and it didn't take long for Nina to release Meya's arms.

Now free, Meya pushed Nina off without breaking the kiss. She rolled on top of her and used one hand to massage her breast. Nina's fingers found the bow-tie of Meya's apron and pulled it loose, after which she rolled the robe up, forcing Meya out of the kiss as soon as her breasts were exposed.

Meya sat upright and pulled the garments over her head, throwing it to the side. Nina untied her own apron, but before she could discard of the clothes herself, Meya helped her out of it instead. Dressed only in linen underwear and stockings, the cold still in the room chilled their skin.

"Want to get closer to the fire or crawl underneath the covers?" Nina asked.

Meya grinned. "Bed's good." She stood up and got into the bed, but as soon as she did, she shivered. "Oh God, it's freezing!"

Nina joined her and pulled the covers over them. "Come here then." She pressed her body against Meya's trembling form. Her fingers moved through her red hair as she drew her close, their lips meeting again.

Lost in each other's embrace, the temperature steadily increased until Meya threw the blankets off.

"Am I too hot for you?" Nina asked with a roguish smile.

Meya's eyes shimmered with passion as she merely grinned and pulled Nina closer. Kissing her hungrily, Meya's hands roamed Nina's skin until they found fabric, and her fingers slipped underneath the linen and went further down, exchanging smooth skin for pubic hair.

Nina gasped as Meya's middle finger dipped inside her.

"You have no idea just how hot you are," Meya whispered into her ear while she moved her finger in and out of her warmth.

Nina moaned and arched her back, her nails leaving tracks on Meya's shoulders as she moved down and used her free hand to cup one breast, while taking the nipple of the other into her mouth. Her finger still moving rhythmically, she flicked her tongue against the sensitive flesh.

Nina bit her lower lip in an attempt to quell a loud moan. "Now who's cheating?" she panted.

Smirking, Meya gently plucked at the nipple with her teeth and Nina gasped and grabbed Meya's breasts in response, squeezing them in ecstasy.

"Ouch," Meya hissed.

"Sorry." Though Nina couldn't help but smile mischievously.

Meya pouted, half-playful, half-serious. "You need to be gentle with me, you know this."

"Oh, I'll be gentle with you…" She removed herself from Meya's hold and pushed her onto her back. She lowered herself between Meya's legs and pulled down her undergarments.

"What are you—" Meya gasped as Nina took her hood into her mouth and flicked her tongue against her clitoris. Waves of pleasure went through her body and she arched her back, a long moan escaping her lips.

"Gentle enough?" Nina asked before resuming her actions.

Meya gripped the sheets, but then moved her hands to Nina's head and entwined her fingers in her raven hair. A moan resembling the word 'yes' was all she could reply.

Grinning contently, Nina slid her fingers between Meya's lips and let one slip inside of her. She moved it in and out whilst continuing to lick her now swollen clitoris. Meya's moans and tight hold on her hair encouraged her to add a second finger.

Meya gasped and bit her lip. "I want you," she whimpered.

Nina rose, locking her gaze with Meya's. "You already have me." She smiled slyly as Meya tugged at her hair to get her face closer to hers. Nina moved up but kept her hand in place—and in motion.

Hungrily, Meya claimed Nina's mouth, one hand still in her hair while the other gripped her butt. As they kissed passionately, Meya's fingers peeled away

Nina's underwear. Fully exposed, she slipped her fingers between Nina's slick folds once more.

Nina moaned loudly, though most of it got silenced by Meya's mouth covering hers.

Their bodies writhed in passion, the world reduced to just that room, that bed, their forms. They were completely lost in the moment until Meya suddenly froze.

Confused, Nina stopped. "What's wrong?"

"Shhh, listen."

The sounds of multiple people walking through the hallways slipped into their world and shattered it. Male voices, their chatter mostly about a decent bed and meals, resounded through the door.

"Oh God, they've returned," Meya whispered.

"Do you think they heard us?" Nina rolled off her and pulled up the sheets.

"I don't think so... They would be knocking if they had, right?"

"I suppose..."

They listened in silence to the boots passing them by and fragments of conversation. When it finally calmed down, they both sighed in relief.

"I guess we need to be extra careful again in the morning when going out," Meya said softly.

"Actually, we need to go back to our own quarters."

Meya pouted. "But I'm used to having you close every night. I can't just go back to sleeping all alone."

Nina cupped Meya's cheek. "I don't like it either, but with the—" Nina fell silent and slowly turned her head towards the door.

Meya's heart skipped a beat as she followed Nina's frightened gaze.

"... didn't ask any of the servants to clean it up after your last stay, but as that was only one night, I assume it's still in good condition. I'll ensure it gets cleaned up tomorrow by Kadeem again."

"I'm just glad I can sleep in a normal bed."

The sound of keys sent adrenaline coursing through both Meya and Nina's veins. They exchanged glances but remained frozen in place aside from that. The door swung open, revealing Lord Deminas with another man by his side.

The lord held up an oil lamp, though the fire in the hearth already illuminated a large part of the room. He raised a brow but didn't speak.

The man next to him stepped inside. "My, my, my, what have we here?" With a sly smile, he ran a hand through his short, dark hair. "Deminas, don't tell me you arranged these two women just for me?"

Meya's breath caught in her throat and her pupils dilated in fear. Nina grabbed her hand and squeezed it.

"I would have arranged lots of other things if I had known we would be returning tonight." He gazed at the women. "You two will have to explain yourself later. Get up."

Paralysed, Meya remained where she was, though Nina quickly jumped out of the bed.

"Come on, Deminas," the other man said. "After such a battle, I could use some relief." A devious grin spread across his face.

The colour drained from Meya's cheeks. She locked eyes with the lord, silently pleading with him.

"Nina can stay—if she agrees."

Meya's heart dropped at hearing this. She slowly turned her head to look at her.

Nina stared intently at the man. The frightened look in her hazel eyes had morphed into a cold resolve with a twinkle of mischief. "If my presence pleases Commander Andreas, I'll stay," she said with a teasing smile.

The commander smirked. He wanted to take a step towards the bed, but Lord Deminas placed a hand on his shoulder. He whispered something in his ear and the commander's smile wavered for a moment. He nodded. "As you wish."

Lord Deminas turned to Meya. "Get dressed and come with me."

# Twenty Six

Heart pounding in her throat, Meya pulled on her robe with trembling hands. Her eyes kept shifting from the ground to the commander. He leaned against the wall, his gaze fixed on Nina, who still stood next to the bed, naked aside from the stockings draped around her ankles.

*We're in so much trouble... Oh, Nina, I hope you know what you're doing!* Meya swallowed and glanced at the commander one final time before turning around. Her fingers fumbled with tying the apron behind her back, increasing her anxiety.

She exchanged a worried look with Nina, who gave her a very faint smile, reassuring her.

Lord Deminas impatiently tapped his boot against the stone floor as Meya quickly stepped into her clogs and hurried over to him, her head low. *Please don't hurt me, please don't hurt me...*

The lord took out a keyring and removed a piece. He handed it to Commander Andreas with a stern look. "Don't forget what I told you."

A mischievous smile curled his lips upwards. "I won't."

Lord Deminas gave him a curt nod and turned his attention to Nina. "Tomorrow after breakfast, you will report to my chambers."

"Yes, my Lord," she answered meekly.

He spun around and left the room, not even bothering to tell Meya to follow him.

Eyes cast down, she followed suit after closing the door behind her. After taking just two steps, she heard the lock click behind her and her breath hitched. *Nina, please stay safe!*

Lord Deminas was waiting for Meya further down the hall. The moment she caught up, he started walking again.

The lord's silence caused Meya's heart to pound nervously. *This is bad, this is bad...* She fumbled with her apron. *How upset is he? What will he do? What is the Commander doing to Nina? What did the Lord say to him?*

Her head spun with uncertainty and dread. By the time they reached his chambers, Meya was on the verge of tears. Lord Deminas opened the door and motioned for Meya to enter first. Trembling, she hurried inside the cold, dark room. Beads of icy sweat rolled down her back and she bit her lip in an attempt to keep her composure. The door closed behind her and she jumped slightly, nearly puncturing her own flesh with her teeth.

*Damn it, Meya. Stay calm. Just focus on your breathing.*

Lord Deminas stepped in front of her, the light of the lamp chasing the shadows away. "Look at me," he stated in a neutral tone.

Reluctant, Meya cast her gaze up, connecting it with the lord's. His grey eyes pierced hers, though she couldn't determine if she was seeing anger in them or not.

"Normally, I'd start off by asking what you were doing there, but the smell in that room already answered that question."

Meya's eyes enlarged and her face burned up. *Oh dear God...*

The slightest hint of a smirk appeared on his face upon seeing her reaction, but it faded quickly. "So instead, tell me why you two decided to play around in *my* old chambers instead of somewhere else."

Meya's lips parted to answer, but she didn't know what to say. *Why* did *we pick his old room?*

Lord Deminas raised a brow. "Well?"

"It...it's just that w-we were sleeping there, m-my Lord."

"I wouldn't call that *sleeping*. Now answer me." His gaze grew stern.

With her cheeks still on fire, Meya fumbled for words. "I...I mean— Ever since y-you left— I...I didn't—"

His fingers grabbed her chin and he lowered himself so that their eyes were level. "Answer me."

Meya inhaled sharply and the words gushed out. "We've been sleeping in your old room ever since you left because I was too afraid to sleep in my own bed." There was a second of silence, her heart beating rapidly in her chest, before Meya quickly added, "M-my Lord."

He retracted his hand. "And what caused you to be so afraid you'd rather risk my wrath?"

Not wanting to lie, because she knew it would only get her in more trouble, she whispered, "Winnie tried to kill me."

Disbelief and anger flashed in his eyes. He rose and walked over to his seat. There, he placed the lamp on the table and sat down, motioning for Meya to come to his side.

Blood drained from her face as she stood next to him. *I'm going to regret this.*

"Explain yourself."

Hesitantly, she told him the entire story. When she was finished, she felt both good and bad. Good, for she was finally able to tell someone aside from Nina, and bad because she feared what was going to happen to Winnie.

"I will have to deal with Winnie later. For now, I still want to know why of all places you two decided my old chambers were a good place to sleep in."

His piercing gaze made Meya want to look away, but she resisted. "Nina has been going there a lot, for a long time," she said softly. "We both thought it was a mostly abandoned room, my Lord."

"Do you realise the similarities between finding you there and finding Jaimy in my current chambers?"

Meya's pupils dilated and her heart skipped a beat. She fell to her knees, her hands flat on the floor, head touching the stones. "I'm so sorry, my Lord! Please forgive me! I didn't—"

"Silence!"

Tears streamed down her cheeks as she feared for her life. *Will he throw me off the balcony? Or will he mutilate my—* She cringed at the mere thought. The sudden memory of the lord telling the commander something before they left caused her blood to run cold. *What if he told him to hurt Nina?*

His cupped her chin again and gently lifted her face up. "Despite the similarities, I do hope you are able to see the differences, too."

Utterly confused by his apparent lack of anger, Meya's tears stopped flowing.

"Still, there will be consequences for your actions." A mischievous smirk flashed across his face. "Not only for trespassing, but also for your attempt to hit me before I left."

Meya paled as she remembered what had happened during her raging fever. "I…I'm so sorry for that, m-my Lord! I wasn't thinking, p-please!" She wanted to bow her head again, but he was still holding her chin.

He moved his face closer to hers until his lips brushed against her ear. "I know you were sick." His breath caused the hairs in her neck to stand up. "It's the only reason why I went easy on you then."

*Easy on me?* She swallowed. "B-but… You helped me."

He backed away so that their eyes could meet again. "That I did."

She wetted her lips, hesitating for a moment to ask the question burning on her tongue. "B-but why, my Lord?"

A coy smile pulled his lips up. "Because a dead servant can't be disciplined."

*Is he serious?* She gazed into his grey eyes. *Or is he playing again? But why?* She gathered all her courage and dared ask, "Is… Is that the only reason you keep me around, my Lord?" Her voice cracked halfway and she had to restrain her tears.

"I have several reasons."

*You know what? Just ask him. You're already in trouble as it is. Just try and get some clarity for once, to help stop those thoughts that keep you awake every now and then.* She took a deep, quaking breath. "M-my lord… Why?"

He raised a brow. "Why *what*?"

She swallowed, anxiety causing bile to rise in the back of her throat. "Why… Why have you done everything you have done for me? Why did you torture and kill the slaver? Why have you allowed me to sleep in your bed? Why do you allow me to join in your meal every time you drain some of my blood? Why do you bother healing the cuts?" The questions rolled off her tongue faster and faster. "Why did you visit me when I was so sick? Why do you look at me with all that lust, yet never force me to do anything? Why did you bed Nina?" Her voice finally broke. "Why not *me*?" Her vision blurred slightly from the tears and she closed her eyes, causing them to roll over her heated skin.

"Those are a lot of whys…"

Her eyes shot open when his thumb wiped away a tear from her cheek.

"I told you before: forcing oneself on a woman is barbaric and I loathe it." His eyes were hard. "As much as I own each and every slave in this castle, I will never obtain any pleasure from bedding anyone against their will."

Meya's face burned with shame and she looked away. *Great, now I've insulted him too.*

"Look at me." His voice was firm, but it lacked anger. The moment Meya's gaze connected with his again, he continued. "I see no reason why I need to explain any of my actions to you, so consider yourself lucky to have gained at least one answer."

"Th-thank you, my Lord. I'm sorry, my Lord." She wanted to look away again, feeling as if he was peering straight into her soul. *Why do I feel like that one answer has only made me more confused?*

He finally released her chin and rose from his seat. "Stand up." He handed her the lantern. "Get a fire going in the bedroom."

"Y-yes, my Lord." She hurried away, glad to be free from his prying gaze. *Oh God, what did I get myself into?*

She sat down in front of the hearth and piled some twigs in a conical formation, placing the tinder in the centre, then she opened the lamp and ignited a piece of bark. With this, she set fire to the tinder. Focused on her task, she didn't notice Lord Deminas entering the room behind her. The moment the kindling was burning, she carefully placed several logs into the flames. Pleased with the growing fire, she finally turned around and almost immediately turned her attention back to the hearth.

Lord Deminas was busy taking his heavy armour off—his leather leggings the only remaining piece.

*Damn it, Meya! He just returned from battle and he wants a nice, hot room and a clean bed to sleep in, of course he's going to get undressed. Besides, it's not like you haven't seen him naked before.* Still, she couldn't stop her heart rate from increasing. In her periphery, she watched his now nude form walk over to the bathroom and disappear into the darkness.

She turned back to the fire. *So... What now?* She placed a few more logs in the hearth and stared at the dancing flames, their heat pleasantly caressing her skin. *What does he intend to do next? Will he just go to sleep and deal with Nina and me in—* The sound of a bed creaking caused Meya to look up.

Lord Deminas lay on his stomach on top of the sheets and turned his head so that he could look at Meya. "Strip and come over here."

Meya's eyes enlarged and her heart skipped a beat. *But he just said...* She mentally shook her head. *Relax, just do as he says.* With trembling fingers, she started to undress.

A chuckle echoed through the room. "You haven't changed one bit."

Meya's ears burned from the remark. *As if I could ever grow used to this. Especially now, knowing you still intend on disciplining me.* A shiver went up her spine. *What if he may not gain pleasure from it, but decides to do it anyway just to punish me?* She swallowed and suppressed the rising fear in her gut.

Naked, Meya walked over to the lord and stood still next to the bed. His gaze went over every inch of her body. "Ah, how I've missed seeing your perfect form."

Meya bit her lip, unsure of how to respond. *Did he... Did he just compliment me?*

"Turn around, slowly."

Meya complied, still taken aback by the lord's earlier comment. *Is this good or bad?* Her heart pounded rapidly in her chest.

"Yes, a sight for sore eyes." He spoke softly as if saying it more to himself than to her. "There's a bottle of oil in the bottom drawer." He gestured towards the cabinet. "Get it and do your magic."

Confused, Meya went to get the item. Having found it, she held the small flask up. *What is it?* She returned to the lord, who had his hands folded underneath his chin. *What does he want me to do?* Her gaze went over his naked form, unable to ignore his well-toned muscles and firm buttocks. She mentally shook her head to snap out of it. "Wha—" She swallowed and tried again. "What does my Lord want me to do?"

"You once told me that you would be able to massage me better with some oil. That flask you're holding was a gift I once received; I've been saving it."

Uncomfortable due to her lack of clothing, Meya got onto the bed and knelt next to the lord. *He just returned from battle; he's been away for a good month. If there's ever a good reason for a good massage, this would be it.* She started to warm up her hands and loosen her joints when Lord Deminas suddenly huffed.

"Your scent is intoxicating. For your own good, I advise you to sit on top of me and to start quickly."

Embarrassed beyond words, she changed position, though she didn't feel any less ashamed. *Great, he smelled the sex in the room and now he smells it on me! Oh God, this is horrible.* Her eyes went down to look at her current pose. As if being above the lord's backside wasn't bad enough, she had one leg on either side of him, making her afraid to actually sit down. *What if I touch him? Oh God, I'm probably still slick! What if I get it on him?* Not wanting to find out, she refused to sit and instead remained in the awkward pose.

With a bright red face, she opened the flask and was surprised by a soft, woody smell. *Great, this should mask my scent—hopefully.* She poured some oil into her left hand and fumbled a little with closing the bottle again. After placing it out of the way, she warmed the oil between her hands.

"Where does my Lord want me to start?"

"You know where." There was a hint of amusement in his voice.

*I could have guessed.* She bent forward, brushed away the black hair that covered his neck and shoulders, and started. *Damn, he's tense.* She frowned. *I've never noticed any tension in his muscles before… Must be from the battle.*

By the time she was busy with his upper back, her legs had grown tired. Focused fully on her task, she sat down without giving it much thought.

Lord Deminas smirked. "I was wondering when you were finally going to sit."

Meya's hands stopped moving for a moment, before quickly resuming their task. *He's playing again, don't let it get to you.* She swallowed and gathered her courage. "Does my weight bother you, my Lord?"

"On the contrary, I think I'll prefer all future massages to be like this."

*Does he want them done naked too?* She sighed. *But of course he will.*

"Lower."

Meya had to relocate a bit to gain full access to his lower back. *If he wants the massages done like this, does that mean he will no longer bathe with me?* There was a sting of sadness at the prospect of no longer being able to enjoy the hot water. Annoyed, she shook her head. *You're spoiled, Meya!* Still, she couldn't help but feel bad at the thought of the bathing ritual—to which she had unwillingly grown accustomed to—come to an end.

"Is there a problem?"

*Damn, how did he notice that?* Her hands continued rubbing his back. "N-no, my Lord."

"Meya," he said threateningly.

She cringed. *He can't even see my face and he still knows when I lie! Should I just pretend I didn't?*

"Tell me the truth."

She bit her lip. *Damn him!* Her hands faltered for a moment. "I…I was just thinking, my Lord… About what you said regarding future massages…"

"And what would be the problem with them?"

Her hands fell still as her mind worked hard on forming a proper answer.

Growing impatient, Lord Deminas rose slightly and started to turn around. "Speak."

Startled, Meya quickly got off and sat down next to him, her eyes avoiding his. "N-no problem, m-my Lord." Her cheeks were blazing as she realised how his leg had grazed her crotch. *Oh God, did that just happen? Did I really—*

His fingers lifted her chin so their eyes met. "Spill it."

"I…I…" She swallowed, a cold sweat coating her skin. "I was just wondering if… if…" Her breath hitched as the lord came closer to her face, his

gaze burning into hers. "If that meant I'd no longer be joining you in bathing...
My Lord."

His lips curved into a smile once more, a mischievous glint in his eyes. "Is
it the hot water you'd be missing, or me?"

Meya's pupils dilated and she opened her mouth to counter, but the words
got stuck in her throat.

"It seems you're in need of a bath right now, though..." He finally released
her from his penetrating gaze, only to lower it to his leg and then to her crotch.

The fact that she had smeared some of her slickness onto his leg was one
thing, that he had noticed it was another. At a loss for words, her mouth just
stood agape, sheer terror and shame in her eyes.

His gaze met hers again. "I love it when you're all flushed like that..." He
moved forward, though Meya tried to keep the same distance, causing her to
fall onto the bed. Caging her between his arms and legs, he bent down to
whisper in her ear, "But I'm sure you're aware by now of what I like."

His hot breath tickled her skin, but the moment his tongue flicked against
her earlobe, a surprised gasp escaped her throat. Meya's thoughts derailed and
her body froze, stuck between fight, flight, and surrendering.

Lord Deminas trailed his lips along her neckline, down to her collarbone.
"You have no idea how badly I want you..."

Meya's breath hitched. While the lord kept trailing his lips along her skin,
going from the left to the right shoulder, Meya managed to free her voice from
the paralysis—though it was but a mere whisper. "B-but I'm your slave... I'm
already yours." She swallowed the lump in her throat. "What's stopping you?"

"You know what." He slowly licked her neck, causing her to tremble. "I
want you to want me too." His teeth grazed her skin and she squirmed. He
lowered himself, pressing his lips hungrily against hers.

Stunned by his erection pressing against her loins, she didn't answer his
kiss, and he pulled back after a few seconds.

He looked down into her frightened eyes, a hint of dejection in his gaze.
"What is it that you fear?"

Unable to answer, she faced away. *You know what...*

Leaning on his elbows, he cupped her cheek and made her look at him
again, though her eyes refused to make contact with his. "Look at me," he said
gently. "I will not force myself on you. If you do not want this, you are allowed
to say so."

Baffled by his words, tears welled up. She wrapped her arms around his
chest and pulled him into a hug, surprising him. "I...I'm sorry," she managed to
croak. "I'm just confused..."

"I can't tell it any more clearly."

She shook her head. "Not just that," she whispered. "But... But my heart belongs to Nina."

He rose slightly so that he could look into her eyes. "If you don't want me, say so."

Her lip trembled and she released him from her embrace. *But that's exactly the problem: I do want you.* She closed her eyes and faced away, unable to voice herself. *It's so wrong—I love Nina! Yet all the things he's done... Why do I have similar feelings for him? It's not right!* Her heart constricted in her chest and she swallowed back a sob. *Not to mention I hate how I tense up when he's so close. Do I fear him or do I fear the fact that he's a man?*

He caressed her cheek. "I'm not asking you to choose between Nina and me."

She turned to face him again. *And Nina never asked me to do so either.* She bit her lip. *Nina had sex with him... Wouldn't it be fair if I did, too?* Her cheeks heated up at the mere thought, though a cold chill followed the moment memories of the slaver resurfaced.

"I can tell you're in turmoil, but I can't read minds. Speak to me."

Meya swallowed and gazed into his grey eyes. *He cares. He won't admit it, but he does.* This thought gave her an idea. *I should ask him. If he can tell me how he feels, I'll tell him too and try to face my fears.* She wetted her lips and took a deep, quaking breath. "M-my Lord... Do you... Do you care about me? I...I mean..."*Am I special?* She wanted to say those three words, but her lips refused.

Lord Deminas lowered himself again so that he could whisper into her ear, "If my actions thus far still haven't made my intentions clear, let me tell you this..." His hand went up, fingers entangling in her hair. He gripped her red locks firmly and pulled her head aside, baring her neck. His teeth grazed the sensitive skin, causing goosebumps to rise. "I may own your body, but it's your soul that I want."

Meya's heart skipped a beat and she forgot how to breathe.

His lips trailed her neck. "So yes, I care about you."

She embraced him again, and with her heart pounding rapidly in her throat, she spoke with a slight tremble, "Then... Then I do want you, b-but..."

He released her hair and rose slightly so that he could look at her, his silence ushering her to continue.

"I'm afraid..."

"Of what?"

She swallowed, unsure of how to tell him. "The slaver—" Her voice broke and she looked away, tears in her eyes.

"Shhh…" He made her face him again. "Do I really need to tell you again? I'm not—"

Meya pressed her lips against his, completely taking him by surprise. *I know I'm a fool for thinking that, I'm sorry.* With her eyes closed, she relished the kiss. Her hands roamed his oily skin, pulling him close again. *I can do this. No more fear. I want this. I've wanted this for so long now.*

Lord Deminas' lips moved hungrily against her, his tongue seeking entrance and gaining it almost instantly. He leaned on his left elbow, freeing his right hand to roam her body. Meya moaned as he grabbed her breast and lightly pinched her already erect nipple. Her hands lowered and clutched his firm buttocks. Panting, she freed herself from his lips. "I want you."

There was a shimmer in his eyes. "Are you sure?"

She bit her lip and nodded. Lord Deminas repositioned himself between her legs and despite her intent, adrenaline still flooded her system. She focused on relaxing, on surrendering herself to him. *No more fear… You can do this.*

His fingers brushed through her pubic hair only to go further down. He smirked upon feeling the already present slickness. "Is any of this my doing, or is it all Nina's?"

Meya flushed red, but she managed to smile slightly. His finger slipped inside and she bit her lip in a futile attempt to stifle a moan. As waves of pleasure rolled through her body, she quickly forgot about her fears and yielded to the lust. His thumb found her clitoris and started to rub it, causing her to arch her back, her breasts pressing against his chest. He slipped in a second finger and silenced her reaction by pressing his mouth onto hers, their tongues meeting and encircling each other.

When Meya ended their kiss to gasp for air, Lord Deminas moved back and pulled his fingers out. He looked Meya straight in her eyes as he brought his hand up to his mouth and licked them clean, the sight causing her to look away in utter embarrassment. He took his erection and pressed it against her slick opening, regaining her attention. "I'll ask you one last time…"

Meya grunted, squeezed his butt, and tilted her hips, pressing herself against his tip. Taking the hint, he started to penetrate her. She gasped and arched her back. "C-careful," she groaned.

"Does it hurt?"

"A little. Just, go slow." She bit her lip and closed her eyes as her body adjusted to his girth and he gradually pushed further in. When he was fully inside, he cupped her cheek. She looked at him and was surprised to see worry in his eyes. Her heart leaped at seeing him like this and she grabbed his head and pulled him into another passionate kiss.

Carefully, he started to move. Meya's moaning and writhing underneath him, her hips thrusting to meet him, made it clear that she was enjoying it. He increased his pace and a low growl escaped his throat as Meya's hands alternated between grasping his buttocks, trying to gain a grip on his oily back, and entangling her fingers in his black hair.

The lord increased the strength of each thrust, causing Meya to draw red lines on his back with her nails. Most of her moans were now silent gasps as she was utterly lost in ecstasy.

"Look... at... me," Lord Deminas panted.

Meya's eyes fluttered open and locked with his. He gripped her hair firmly and she, in turn, gripped his with one hand while her other grasped his butt. They both panted heavily, a single moan escaping Meya's throat every few thrusts. Lord Deminas went faster and Meya arched her back.

She gasped and broke eye-contact as she felt him twitch inside, a wave of pleasure careening through her.

With a grunt, Lord Deminas relaxed on top of her and nuzzled her neck, his fingers still playing with her hair.

Meya's breathing slowed down and the fog of lust cleared in her mind. Her eyes grew big upon realising what had just happened. "M-my Lord... Did... Did you just finish... inside of me?"

A pleased grunt was all the reply she got.

"But... what if I become pregnant?" A wave of fear went through her insides.

"Trust me, you don't need to worry about that," he said and playfully nibbled her earlobe. "However, you should go to the latrine if you don't want to sleep on a wet spot."

She realised he was barely inside of her anymore and she followed his advice. She quickly rushed into the bathroom to clean herself up—which proved to be quite difficult in the darkness. Upon her return, she noticed the neatly folded kerchief that had been on the pillows was gone and Lord Deminas was lying underneath the sheets.

He looked at her and threw back the blankets, indicating where he wanted her to be.

Tired and still a bit unsteady on her feet, she crawled into bed with him. He pulled her close, her head on his chest. Relishing his warmth and scent, Meya closed her eyes contently and drifted off to sleep.

# Twenty Seven

Chiming bells woke Meya, though she continued to enjoy the warmth of the bed she was in and refused to open her eyes just yet. She snuggled up to the warm body next to her, her hand roaming the chest. Confused, she didn't find a soft breast, but firm muscles. The fog of sleep that clouded her mind rapidly faded away and her eyes shot open, but the few glowing remnants in the hearth failed to chase away the darkness in the room.

*Oh dear God, it wasn't a dream!* Shame and pride both fought for dominance in her head. Then she recalled the events that had led to it all. *Nina! What happened to her?* She swallowed. *What will happen to the both of us? That is, if the Lord still plans to punish us...* She pondered the possibility of him no longer intending that due to what had happened the night before. *Oh, who am I kidding... He's a sadist, of course he's going to punish us. But then again, he said he cared...* She screamed inside, as confused as ever by his intentions.

Lord Deminas stirred and pulled her closer, his erection pressing against her thigh. Her breath hitched, but the shot of adrenaline she expected didn't come.

"Good morning, my pet," he whispered into her ear, sending a shiver up her spine.

"G-good morning, my Lord," Meya squeaked.

His hand cupped her breast while he nuzzled her neck. "Want to go again?" He licked her skin and lightly pinched her nipple.

Meya squirmed. *Oh God, yes—I mean no!* She mentally tugged at her hair. *I don't know what I want! Well, alright, I do: I want to know what will ha—* She gasped as his fingers found her clitoris and stimulated it, sending waves of pleasure through her body. A moan freed itself from her mouth and she arched her back.

"Well?" He nibbled her earlobe and pressed his groin against her leg.

"I…I just need to use the latrine first," Meya managed to utter.

"Well, hurry up then." He released her after a final flick of his tongue against her neck.

She stumbled out of bed and entered the bathroom, the twilight of the impending sunrise making it easier to navigate. *Am I really going to have sex with him again?* Her heart leaped and she blushed at the prospect. *Well, why not? At best, it'll work to our advantage, and at worst...* She tried to think of a negative outcome but found none.

After relieving herself, she made her way back, heart pounding. *Oh God, this feels so wrong.* To her surprise, the lord had lit the candles in the room and was sitting on the edge of the bed. In the warm glow of the flames, she could clearly see the eagerness in his eyes. After a moment of doubt, she walked up to him, her gaze everywhere but directly on him. He placed one hand on her hip and the other on her cheek, his warm touch causing her to close her eyes and tilt her head into his palm. He rose and brushed his lips against hers. "Look at me." Her eyes opened slowly. "Do you still want this?"

Her heart fluttered in her chest and she nodded. He kissed her, but the moment Meya opened her mouth to allow his tongue entrance, he nibbled her lip instead. He pulled away to look at her mischievously before pushing her onto the bed, causing her to gasp in surprise.

He pulled her hips to the edge of the bed. "I'll make this quick so we can both get some breakfast." He placed his hands next to Meya's sides and lowered himself. "Don't forget: I'm dealing with you and Nina first thing after that." Using his teeth, he gently pulled on her left nipple before flicking his tongue against it.

Meya squirmed. *Why did he have to remind me of that? I don't want to think of—* She gasped as he pressed his tip against her opening. He moved it up and down a few times, his pre-cum mixing with her slickness, before penetrating her slowly. She moaned as her body adjusted much faster to him than it had the night before, and before he was even fully in, she pulled him closer using her legs.

Enticed by her actions, he gripped her hips and ravished her.

Meya arched her back and closed her eyes as she gripped the sheets, a long, loud moan freeing itself from her throat. Lost in ecstasy, she surrendered completely to the waves of pleasure roaring through her body.

Lord Deminas finally slowed a bit, only to pry her legs from his sides and to place them against his chest. Meya's eyes grew wide, not knowing what to expect next. He hugged her legs close and vehemently pounded into her.

"Oh, God!" She writhed, but she had nowhere to go. Her moans turned into silent gasps for air as the lord increased his pace and her eyes rolled back in her skull. The pleasure built up to a climax and she pulled the sheets towards her. "My... Lord!" She screamed and arched her back as the world shattered.

With Meya trembling and squirming wildly, it didn't take long for Lord Deminas to finish. He pulled her legs close and pushed in deeply, a satisfied grunt rolling from the depths of his throat. His ejaculation triggered another loud moan from her that ended in a mute scream, her body jerking on the jumbled-up sheets.

Lord Deminas pulled out of her and released her legs, lowering them to the ground. He remained standing for a moment, gazing at her panting and sweaty form contently, before disappearing into the bathroom.

Meya stared at the ceiling and noticed her legs had been asleep. Her breathing slowed down and the tingling feeling in her legs subsided. *Oh. My. God. That was amazing.* She thought of all the times that she had had sex before with a man—including last night—and concluded that this had been the best she'd ever had. *Nina's good too, but that's different.* She smiled. *I'm one lucky girl.*

She rose and groaned, her body sore. *Oh, damn.* She looked at the mess between her legs. *I guess I'll need to change the linens today.* Wobbly, she made her way into the bathroom. Barely able to walk in a straight line, she sniggered to herself.

"What's so funny?" Lord Deminas asked, a smirk on his face.

She walked up to him and placed her hands on his chest. "Me." Her eyes begged him for a kiss and he indulged her, their tongues entwining briefly before he pulled away.

"Enough now." His expression grew stern. "Get dressed and go eat. I expect both you and Nina here afterwards."

The latter felt like a splash of cold water in the face and Meya gave him a courtly nod. "Yes, my Lord."

~*~

217

With a plate of food in hand, Meya scanned the room. Most of the servants had already finished and left to start their duties, ensuring most of the tables were empty. Not seeing Nina anywhere—or any of her room-mates—she sat down at an empty table.

*Maybe she has already eaten?* She tried to keep her hopes up, but she couldn't help but be afraid that the commander might have done something to her. Anxiety replacing her appetite, she stirred her meal while lost in thought. A hand suddenly touching her shoulder caused her to jerk, a splash of porridge landing on the table.

"Oh, I'm so sorry." Nina sat down next to her, her face flustered.

"Don't worry." Using her finger, she cleaned up the spilled food before turning her attention back to Nina. "You have no idea how happy I am to see you." Resisting the urge to kiss her, she just gave her knee a reassuring squeeze.

Nina avoided her gaze and restlessly moved the spoon through her own breakfast, her raven locks obscuring most of her face.

"Are you alright?" Meya attempted to move Nina's hair behind her ear, but she pushed her hand away. Still, she caught a glimpse of the red marks staining her tawny skin. "What did he do to you?" she hissed, trying not to attract any attention from the still present servants in the room.

"Not here, later. Promise." She gave Meya a smile. "Don't worry, I'm fine."

Despite not fully believing her, Meya decided to let it go. *Later...*

They ate in silence, though they both only finished half their meal.

~*~

"So... Want to tell me what happened now?" Meya eyed Nina, who nervously fidgeted with her apron. They both stood in the lord's chambers, awaiting his return.

"I guess this would be the best time, considering I doubt we'll be getting any privacy for a while." She sighed and pulled her hair back, revealing several dark marks on her neck.

Meya frowned. "What the..." She ran a finger over the bruised skin. "Does it hurt?"

"No, not at all." She bit her lip. "How bad is it? I haven't seen them myself."

"Just big bruises really. Did he try to strangle you?"

Nina flushed red. "Sort of... But not quite."

Meya tilted her head. "What do you mean?"

218

"Well... I don't think I need to tell you we fornicated."

Now it was Meya's turn to blush. "I guessed that you would have."

"With how he was looking at us, I figured it would work to our benefit." She lowered her voice. "I hoped it might reduce whatever punishment we're going to receive."

Meya took a deep breath. "Well, you weren't alone in thinking that."

Nina's eyes widened. "No!" She gave Meya a playful shove. "Don't tell me that after all these months, you finally yielded and gave yourself to Lord Deminas last night?"

Meya avoided Nina's gaze, her cheeks burning. "And this morning..."

Nina covered her mouth in an attempt to stifle her laughter. "Damn. Well, now I don't feel so bad for doing the same thing." She embraced Meya tightly. "And I'm proud of you for overcoming your fear." Smiling, she pulled out of the hug but kept her hands on Meya's shoulders. "Did you enjoy it?"

Meya opened her mouth to protest, but after a few seconds, when words still hadn't found their way out, Nina took the opportunity to kiss her.

"It's alright—I don't mind." She grinned mischievously.

Flustered, Meya defensively folded her arms across her chest. "Why don't you just tell me what happened to you?"

Nina's playfulness immediately waned. Eyes cast down, she fidgeted with her apron. "Last night, while he was on top..." She sighed deeply. "It was all good, but then he suddenly wrapped his fingers around my neck..."

Meya took Nina's hands in her own and rubbed them reassuringly.

"I panicked when he started to squeeze, but as soon as I tried to hit him, he grabbed my wrists... He said he wasn't going to kill me because Lord Deminas had told him not to."

"So why did he try to choke you?"

"That's the thing... He told me to just surrender and not fight him. It was the scariest thing I ever did."

Meya frowned. "I...I don't understand."

"I just let him have his way. And every time my vision started to dim, he'd release me again. He made it some sort of sick game." She swallowed. "I'm ashamed to admit it, but... when I realised he wasn't actually going to kill me, I..." She bit her lip.

"You what?"

"I suppose I enjoyed it."

Flabbergasted, Meya's jaw dropped and she released Nina's hands. "But, how?"

Nina smiled sheepishly as she ran her fingers through her hair. "Because it was amazing sex." Her expression turned grim and she looked Meya straight in the eyes. "I'm not saying that what we have isn't good, it's just—"

"This was different?"

Flushed, she nodded. "Yeah, I guess that's the best way to describe it."

"So… What happened this morning? Did he do it again?"

Nina shook her head. "He had me sleep on the floor, in front of the fire. This morning, before the bells, I woke to him tugging at my hips. He…" She took a deep breath. "Damn, this is so embarrassing…"

"It's alright, you can tell me."

She smiled. "I know. You've had your share of embarrassing moments with the Lord too and you still told me." Nina sighed. "He positioned me on my hands and knees and… slapped my arse—hard."

Meya raised her brows. "He *what*?"

"I'm not saying it again. I'm surprised you didn't hear me scream, I yelped so loud. He kept smacking me and said he wouldn't stop until I remained silent. And I tried, really, but you know what he did?"

Biting her lip, Meya just shook her head.

"He made sure every slap was harder than the previous one! Or at least, it felt like that. By the time I managed not to make a sound, my buttocks were on fire. And if you think Lord Deminas is cruel, let me tell you this: Andreas then took me from behind, so he slammed against my sore ass every time!" She pouted. "I'm not sure if you noticed at breakfast, but it hurts to sit down."

Despite it all, Meya had a hard time suppressing the smirk that tugged at her lips.

Nina noticed and narrowed her eyes. "You think this is funny?"

"Maybe." She quickly tried to slap her rear, but Nina jerked away.

"Oh, no you don't!"

They both giggled as they jumped around the room, trying to land a hand on each other's behind.

"You two seem to be having quite a lot of fun."

The laughter immediately died down as they turned around to see Lord Deminas standing in the doorway. They hastily straightened their robes, curtsied, and managed to utter a greeting.

"It seems I wasn't the only one who was a little late for breakfast this morning." His gaze lingered on Nina, who quickly turned red. "I spoke with Andreas concerning the punishment for the both of you, and also regarding the circumstances that lead to your misbehaviour." There was a hint of amusement in his eyes. "We've come up with two options…" Letting the tension build, he walked over to his chair and sat down.

The women exchanged worried glances before turning to face him. He motioned for them to come closer and they quickly obeyed.

"Nina, you can choose between spending the nights in my old chamber, together with the Commander, for as long as he will be staying here, or you can take a trip with him down to the dungeons."

The colour drained from Nina's face. "M-My Lord!"

"What will it be?" He placed his elbows on the desk, intertwined his fingers and rested his chin on them.

Nina took a second before she asked, "Will he… hurt me if I go for the first option, my Lord?"

A small grin appeared on his face. "He has agreed to not cause you any long-lasting harm should you decide to do that. Though, that cannot be said for option two."

Nina bowed her head. "Then please allow me to go for the first, my Lord."

"Very well." He turned his attention to Meya, her face ashen. "Basically, the same applies to you; only you will be residing in *my* chambers should you decide to go for option one."

Meya swallowed. *I'm not sure how that is really a punishment; I enjoyed last night and this morning's events.* Her gut was telling her there was going to be more to it than Lord Deminas was letting on. *Whatever he's planning, it can't be worse than a trip to the dungeons! I'm already glad I'm not splayed on the rocky cliffs.* Bowing her head, she said, "I'd prefer your chambers over the dungeons, my Lord."

A single chuckle left his lips. "We expected you would both decide on the first option. Very well." He rose. "I've got some meetings to attend. You can both resume your chores for the rest of the day. It seems there's plenty to clean." A mischievous grin played on his lips as he looked at Nina, and then at Meya. "I'll see you after supper." He made his way to the door.

Meya fidgeted nervously with a lock of hair as she chewed her lip. *I can't believe we've just willingly reduced ourselves to harlots.*

"Oh, one more thing." He turned around. "Considering you took the easy punishment, we will have a special task for the two of you sometime later this week." He smiled wolfishly. "I know Andreas is already looking forward to it—and so am I." With that said, he left the room.

The moment the door closed, they both exhaled loudly in relief.

"That went a lot better than I expected," Nina said as she combed her fingers through her hair.

Meya glared at her. "Are you serious? Do you not realise what we just agreed to?"

She huffed. "I know I'm probably going to have it a lot rougher than you. If the Commander is going to repeat what he did last night and this morning, my neck is going to be black and blue by the end of the week, just like my poor rear! Hell, come tomorrow I'll probably have to eat standing up."

Meya bit her lip. *Considering what Lord Deminas did, she's probably right.* She took Nina's hands in her own. "You could have taken option two."

Nina's eyes enlarged. "Are you kidding me? Did you not hear what Lord Deminas said? I would have had to go to the dungeons *with the Commander*! Considering what the Lord did to Gail—and how I fear the Commander even more—option two was simply not an option! I'd rather have him beat my ass, which hopefully won't be so bad next time as I am going to seal my damn lips, over whatever torture that man can think up down in those dungeons. You might not have seen all the tools they keep down there for interrogation and punishment purposes, but I have. So no. Nope. Not going to happen."

Glancing down at the floor, Meya scolded herself for even considering the dungeons a possibility. "It doesn't bother you, though? That you're basically going to be his concubine?"

Nina shrugged. "If I'm completely honest, I wouldn't mind it at all if it was just fornication." She sighed. "I guess I need to confess something to you... The group of thieves I was with before coming here... Most of the women used seduction to get what they wanted. Being as young as I was, I didn't of course, but I did learn a thing or two from just observing."

Meya just stared at Nina, trying to comprehend what she was saying.

"As I grew older here, I wasn't afraid of using the same tricks. There's a reason why I was able to sometimes reside in the Lord's old chamber unnoticed. I got caught a few times at first, but being a woman can make a lot of problems go away." Her cheeks heated up. "That's why I didn't hesitate yesterday. And considering how we just avoided the dungeons..." She chuckled. "It worked."

*Well, that explains why she's always been so easy-going in regard to all the sexual things the Lord makes me do.* Meya considered what Nina had said, then shrugged. "I don't know what to say."

"How about..." She placed her hands on Meya's hips. "Thank you, Nina, for not getting us sent to the dungeons." She smiled cheekily. "And a kiss?"

Meya grinned. "Thank you, Nina, for gallantly getting your ass whooped and—"

"Oh!" Nina exclaimed and gave her a playful shove.

They both laughed for a moment, before Meya continued in a more serious tone, "You're right, though. I would have never been brave—or smart—enough to have tried using seduction to my benefit. If I had been alone in that room, I would now be tied up in the dungeons." She cringed. "So yes, thank you for saving our behinds." The smile crept back on her face. "Well, mine, anyways."

Nina ignored her last remark. "It's not so much about being brave or smart. Seduction doesn't work unless you're actually *willing* to do the things you plan to do. I'm proud that you were able to have sex with Lord Deminas to be honest, considering what you've been through."

Meya blushed. "I guess I've been wanting it for some time now. I was just afraid… But he was surprisingly… caring."

Nina huffed. "He'd better have been. If he had forced himself on you, I would have plotted to assassinate him." She grinned. "It would have been a worthy suicide."

Smiling, Meya gave Nina a short but passionate kiss. "We should stop talking and get to work though, before the Lord changes his mind regarding our punishments."

"You're right." She sighed. "Just one more thing… What do you think he meant with that special task?"

Meya thought for a moment. "I truly have no clue… But I doubt it's anything good if both he and the Commander are so looking forward to it." She shuddered as she recalled what had happened to Nina before the men had left for battle.

"I guess we will just have to find out. At any rate, it shouldn't involve the dungeons, so I consider that good." Nina walked towards the door. "See you at lunch, my dear." She blew her a kiss before leaving.

Meya stared at the door for a few seconds before taking a deep breath and getting to work.

# Twenty Eight

Meya stared at the alluring, hot bath. *I wish I could just slip in already.* She sighed and looked around the room—Lord Deminas was nowhere to be seen. Growing tired of waiting, she went into the bedroom and tended to the fire.

Minutes passed by as Meya prodded the wood in the hearth. *I wonder what Nina's doing right now...* She smirked at the thought of Commander Andreas slapping her butt, but quickly scolded herself over it. *It hurts the way he hits.* Still, her grin remained faintly as she imagined a rosy glow covering her lover's rear. A door closing behind her interrupted her thoughts.

Lord Deminas scrutinised her, a playful smile on his face. "Waiting for me?"

"Y-yes, my Lord." She rose and straightened her robes, though she immediately regretted it. *What now?* She fidgeted with her apron as she watched the lord walk into the bathroom. She was still hesitating on following him right away or not when she heard him calling her.

"You coming, or are you enjoying waiting too much?"

Blushing, she quickly hurried after him. Seeing that he was already busy undressing only caused more blood to rush to her cheeks. The way he looked at her told her enough and she started to untie her apron. *You'd think after all these months—let alone last night and this morning—I would get used to this.* She took off her robe. *But no, I still feel embarrassed just being naked in his presence.* She breathed in deeply through her nose and exhaled, mentally chastising herself.

Lord Deminas' sudden presence in front of her startled her. He placed one hand on her bare shoulder and cupped her chin with the other, their gazes locking. "I find it peculiar how little recent events seem to have affected you."

She bit her lip. *But they have!* She wanted to do something to show him, but the thought of initiating anything caused her body to petrify.

He moved closer, his lips brushing against her ear. "But I'm certain that will change over time."

Her knees grew weak from the sensation of his hot breath against her skin. His tongue flicked against her earlobe and a small squeak accompanied the moan escaping her lips.

Grinning craftily, he moved away and stepped into the warm water. "Now get in here and do your thing."

Meya took a deep breath, trying to regain her composure. "Yes, my Lord." She slipped into the bath and immediately relished the warmth. *Oh God, how I've missed this!*

Lord Deminas turned his back towards her and Meya got to work.

*I really don't care anymore. So what if I'm spoiled? I've had enough bad stuff in my life—I deserve nice things too!* She massaged his shoulders and noticed the tension she had felt yesterday was as good as gone. *I wonder what caused that to go away so soon... Was it the massage or the sex?*

Memories of earlier events caused her cheeks to heat up. *I wouldn't mind doing that again.* She licked her lips as her hands roamed his muscular back. *I'm surprised there aren't any marks; I could have sworn I scratched him plenty last night.*

The thought of leaving red streaks on his skin aroused her and she had to fight the urge to teasingly pull her nails over his back. *How would he react if I were to do that?* She bit her lip. *How would he react if I were to kiss his neck? Or nibble his earlobe?*

She kept massaging him, but the desire to do something else only continued to grow.

*What if I scraped my teeth over* his *skin for a change? Whisper in his ear... Pinch his nipple...* The latter caused a furtive grin to tug at her lips. *Oh, that would be so much fun... Would he get mad? Or would he enjoy it?*

"Meya…"

Shocked, she froze.

"Are you aroused?"

*How does he know these things?* She sighed. *Oh well. Considering he's onto me...* She yielded to her desires and slid her hands over his shoulders and down his muscular chest. With her lips close to his ear, she purred, "Yes, *my Lord...*" Unable to resist, she took his nipples between her fingers and squeezed slightly.

There was a low growl. In the split second before the lord rose out of the water, Meya regretted her actions. As he turned around to face her, she cowered against the edge of the bath. He glared down at her, water droplets cascading down his toned body, the scar on his left bicep glistening. His eyes were full of wild lust and he grabbed her by the throat, lifting her to her feet.

Even though her body was still hot from the arousal, adrenaline now flooded through her veins and she feared for her life. *This was a bad idea! Bad idea, bad idea, bad idea!*

"So, my little pet wants to play..." He moved his face next to hers and growled, "As you wish."

The bestial sound sent shivers through Meya's body, but somewhere deep inside, it also excited her.

He stepped out of the bath, his hand still around her throat. His grip intensified slightly, but he wasn't restricting her airflow. "Get out."

Too scared to do anything but obey, she carefully placed one foot on the stones, and then the other. As soon as she touched the floor, Lord Deminas moved his arm, forcing her to tiptoe along. He made his way out of the room, keeping Meya in front of him, his fingers still wrapped around her throat.

Meya's gaze darted from his eyes to her surroundings and just before he stopped moving, she realised they were standing in front of the bed. He released her neck, only to push her shoulders, causing her to land on the mattress. She gasped and scurried away from him, but he climbed on top of her before she could get far.

He pinned her wrists next to her head and lowered himself, a growl rumbling from the depths of his throat. "Still feel like playing?"

*No... Yes...* Meya was unable to speak, her heart pounding in her throat. She could feel his erection pressing against her skin, causing more internal conflict to arise.

Lord Deminas grazed his teeth over her neck and she squirmed, a whimper slipping from her lips. He repositioned himself between her legs and released one of her arms. Despite the freedom, she remained still, waiting for what would happen next.

"I asked you a question," he murmured.

Despite his animalistic demeanour, he still wanted to be certain she wanted him—this realisation caused the fear to dwindle and her own desire to take over. Instead of vocalising an answer, she bit her lip seductively as she kept her gaze locked on his.

Another low growl rumbled up from his throat at seeing her like that. Using his free hand to guide himself, he penetrated her—her prior arousal allowing for easy entry. She closed her eyes and bucked her hips, unable to suppress the moan bubbling up from deep inside. The sound of her enjoyment prompted him to roughly pound into her. He lowered his face to her neck and grabbed her by the hair with his free hand, his arm pinning hers down in the process. He tugged her head to the side, exposing the sensitive flesh, and bit down—though not hard enough to break the skin.

Meya writhed and moaned as pleasure and pain fought for dominance over her senses. When he finally released her neck, it was just to sink his teeth into a new spot. "M-my Lord!" She arched her back in ecstasy.

There was a low snarl before he relocated his mouth to hers, kissing her fervently. His thrusts increased in force and her muffled moans grew louder.

Unable to get enough air, she tried to free her lips from his, but his fingers still held her hair tightly, preventing her from turning away. Finally, he allowed her to breathe, but only because he went to ravage her neck again. Meya thrashed underneath him, the pleasure building up to a climax. Her hips bucked to meet him with every thrust, her body aching for release.

Lord Deminas placed his hands on the mattress and raised himself. He glared down at her, the fire in his eyes causing her breath to hitch.

Her hands now free, she clung to him as he fiercely moved in and out of her. Unable to control herself, she pulled her nails over the lord's back. A sly smirk tugged at her lips the moment she realised what she was doing, though it quickly faltered upon hearing the rumbling growl coming from his throat.

He went for her neck again, grabbing her hair with his other hand and pulling her head aside. She screamed in both pain and pleasure as he bit down into her flesh. Her eyes rolled up and she arched her back as she climaxed, a loud moan freeing itself from her lips.

Still writhing and twitching underneath him, Lord Deminas gave a final thrust, his release accompanied by a long, satisfied grunt. He relaxed on top of her for a moment as his breathing returned to a normal rhythm.

*Dear sweet God... Bad idea or not—it was gooood.* Meya smiled to herself, basking in the aftermath.

"Next time you want to play..." He nibbled her earlobe. "Just tell me."

Embarrassed, she stammered, "A-as you wish, my Lord."

227

He rose and slipped out of her. "Now get yourself cleaned before coming back to bed." The smile on his lips and the shimmer in his eyes betrayed his enjoyment.

"Yes, my Lord." Meya bit her lip in an attempt to hide her own smile as she hurried to the bathroom. *I fear Nina is indeed having it a lot tougher than I am.* She rubbed her sore neck and winced. *Or not...*

~*~

"My God, Meya!" Nina hissed as she watched Meya take a seat next to her. She quickly rummaged her hand through Meya's hair so that it would cover her neck.

"What are you doing?"

"Show some decency!" Her gaze darted around the room, but most of the people had already finished their breakfast—Nina's plate was almost empty too. "Just hope no one saw those bruises!"

Meya's cheeks flushed red—she had totally forgotten about the marks left by last night's events.

In a hushed voice, Nina asked, "Don't tell me he tried the choking game on you too?"

She shook her head. "No, he ehm… He did something else."*God, this is so embarrassing.* She looked around the table, but the older woman sitting at the far end didn't seem to be able to hear them.

Nina looked at her with raised brows. "Like what?"

*How do I even explain what he did?* Not knowing how to proceed, nor wanting to discuss it over breakfast, she just waved it away. "Don't worry, alright? Things just got a little… rough."

Nina huffed but didn't say anything as she finished her meal.

Meya eyed Nina's neck as she started on her own piece of bread, but the bruises didn't seem to be any worse. "What happened to you last night?" She grinned slightly. "Can you still sit?"

Nina elbowed her in the side, causing Meya to laugh. "It's not funny!" She glared at her and Meya quickly turned serious.

"Nina, what happened?"

"Nothing happened."

Meya raised a brow. "Considering how you're acting, I find that hard to believe."

Nina sighed. "I'm speaking the truth. After taking a quick bath, I went to his quarters. There was a fire in the hearth, so I expected him to be around…

But he just didn't show. I eventually fell asleep and when I woke up this morning, I was still alone."

Frowning, Meya took a bite of her food. "So you got lucky? No sleeping on the floor and no sore—" Nina's glare made her fall silent.

"I woke this morning, still alone. You're telling me I got lucky... But I think someone else didn't."

Meya paled and whispered, "Are you saying someone went missing?"

"I don't know, but I wouldn't be surprised."

Meya stared at the lump of bread, her appetite receding. *Winnie!* She jerked up and looked around the room, but there were barely any people left. "Have you seen Winnie?"

Nina nodded. "Yeah, she was here. Walked right by without even looking at me. Brit ignored me too." She huffed. "Gail sat down with me, though." She rolled her eyes. "It took her about five seconds before she saw the marks on my neck and started asking questions. Luckily, she had the decency not to press the matter when I told her to shut it."

"Do you think the sisters know what's going on?" Her cheeks heated up at the prospect of people knowing.

"I doubt it. They've been ignoring us ever since we moved to the Lord's old chamber."

"But they never were *that* cold."

Nina sighed. "Well, Brit might actually have an idea where we have been hanging out. And considering how Commander Andreas had some belongings brought up to the room by someone working at the stables... Odds are they know."

Meya lowered her bread. "What if they spread rumours? I...I don't want people to know what's going on!"

"You're better off covering your neck than worrying about those two spreading gossip. Brit seems to be the only one who really understands Winnie—and she's smart enough to keep her tongue." She smiled roguishly and stuffed the last bite of bread into her mouth. "Gail also knows better, so even if Brit tells her or Lea, we're still good." She placed a hand on Meya's knee. "So relax."

Meya took a deep breath. "You're right." She returned to her breakfast.

"I'm going to have to leave you to it... I've already been here long enough." Nina looked around. Certain that no one would see, she placed a quick kiss on Meya's cheek. "Love you, my dear."

Flushed, Meya turned around to watch Nina quickly make her way out of the dining hall. *Damn it, Nina!* She scanned the room, but the few remaining servants were facing away from her. *What if someone saw?* She sighed and turned her attention back to her food. She could still feel her lips on her skin and she longed for more. *I'm spoiled in multiple ways, it seems.*

She noticed the kitchen staff coming out to have their breakfast.

*Damn, it's already that late?* She started to wolf her food down faster, but then she spotted Abi and waved at her.

The girl saw her but didn't wave back. Instead, she looked away, her expression troubled.

Meya grimaced. *She better not have been hearing any new rumours about me.* She quickly finished her meal and got to work.

~*~

Later that day, Meya returned to the dining hall, and carrying her lunch, she looked around the crowded room for somewhere to sit. She spotted Nina and Gail at a table at the far end and she hurried over to join them. They were talking in hushed voices and were startled by Meya's sudden presence. "Everything alright?"

"Meya!" Nina turned towards her. "I was right!"

"About what?" A chill went up her spine. "Did someone disappear?"

Gail and Nina nodded. "Abi came to me this morning to get her robe fixed, and she was all red-eyed." Gail's expression was grave. "She was in love with this boy named Novak. He was supposed to meet her last night, but he never showed up. She looked for him during breakfast, but alas…"

Meya's eyes widened and her heart ached for the girl. *Would the Commander have taken him?*

"I told her to ask Juris, and so she did. I spoke to her when I went to get my meal…" She shook her head. "Juris knew nothing about his whereabouts and told her he was going to look for him and ask around, but we all know he's not going to be found."

Meya turned to Nina. "Have you checked the dungeons?"

Nina paled. "You think he's in there?"

"You could try. I mean, it's just you and Kadeem who go there. Any chance that place needs some cleaning done?"

Nina bit her lip as she considered this. "I suppose I could have a look. But what do I do if he's there? Or worse…" She lowered her voice to a whisper so both Gail and Meya had to move closer to hear her. "What if the Commander is down there?"

"Just tell him you're there for routine cleaning and get the hell out," Gail suggested.

Nina and Meya stared at her.

"What? You don't think that would work?"

They exchanged glances and Meya gave a doubtful shrug. "I suppose it might."

Nina fidgeted with a lock of her hair. "I'll give it a try." She narrowed her eyes at Meya. "But if I'm not here with supper, you better come save my ass."

Meya had to suppress a grin at the possibly literal meaning of the latter. "I promise."

"If he'll let me, I'll plead with Lord Deminas to suffer in your place," Gail said as she looked at Nina.

Nina smiled. "Be careful there; don't say things you don't intend to do."

"What? I'm serious." She pouted. "I would."

People who had joined their table were starting to look at the three women as they continued to speak in hushed voices.

"I think we should drop this for now and just finish our meals," Nina suggested.

Meya and Gail agreed, and they switched to lighter topics.

~*~

Time seemed to move slowly that afternoon, and Meya tried to make her tasks a bit more fun to help pass it faster. Careful to not spill anything, she heaved a heavy bucket onto the balustrade and peered down the mountainside, searching for Jaimy's corpse. She had made it her goal to try and eventually wash the bones out of sight, but as of yet, she wasn't very successful in moving them much. She aimed and splashed the water onto the remains. A few of the ribs got carried a bit further down the rocks, but that was about it. Meya sighed and pouted. *Oh well, I'll get her out of my sight eventually.* She turned around and, startled, dropped the bucket.

Lord Deminas smirked as he observed her.

"M-my Lord!" She hastily picked up the bucket.

He walked over to her and peered down the mountainside. "What have you been up to?"

Meya bit her lip, unsure of how to explain herself.

"Answer me." He narrowed his eyes, his patience clearly running thin.

"I...I just wanted to try and see if..." She swallowed before blurting out, "If I could wash her remains out of sight, m-my Lord."

231

The dark smile returned. "And why do you want to do that? Does seeing those bones bother you?"

Meya lowered her gaze as she gripped the bucket more firmly.

"Look. At. Me."

Her eyes immediately shot back up to connect with his. "I…I don't really know, my Lord… I just started doing it and…" She trailed off, not sure how to continue.

"Does seeing the bones bother you?"

She shook her head. "No. Not really, my Lord." The glint that appeared in his eyes made her shiver.

"Good." He walked back inside and Meya followed. "After supper, you're to go down to the dungeons and wait for me there."

Meya's eyes widened. *For what? Did I do—* Her heart constricted in her chest. *The special task?*

"I already ran into Nina when I went down earlier, so no need to inform her." A slight grin appeared on his face upon seeing Meya blanch. "Have I been understood?"

She quickly nodded and curtsied. "Y-yes, my Lord. As you wish."

"Good." He turned and exited the room without saying anything else.

Petrified, Meya stared at the door. *Did he catch Nina snooping around? Are we in even more trouble now?* She groaned and paced around the room. *Just what is this special task going to be that we need to go to the dungeons?* She stopped and took a few deep breaths. "Just… stay calm…" She sighed heavily. *Whatever is going to happen, you can get through it.*

# Twenty Nine

Meya quickly hurried down to the dining hall, anxious to speak to Nina—if she was even there. The bells had rung not too long ago, thus it was still relatively empty. Not seeing Nina anywhere, Meya sat down at a table in the corner. She eyed all the servants who slowly poured in and it didn't take long before she spotted Gail and she raised her hand to beckon her.

Gail sat down opposite her. "Hey, heard anything from Nina yet?"

Meya shook her head. "No… But I fear Lord Deminas caught her near the dungeons."

Gail paled. "Did he tell you that?"

"Sort of… I'm not sure really. I just hope she's not in any trouble."

Gail pointed at Meya's neck. "I've been meaning to ask you… Nina had marks too, what happened?"

Meya flushed and made sure her hair covered the bruises. "I…I'd rather not speak about it. We're both fine though, don't worry." She smiled.

Gail cocked her head and raised a brow. "You sure? Yours look rather—"

"Ugh, Gail, I told you to shut it," Nina said as she sat down next to Meya.

"Nina!" Meya wrapped her arms around her and kissed her on the cheek.

Gail coughed loudly, causing Meya to release Nina at once, her cheeks bright red.

"Are you alright? Lord Deminas—"

233

"I encountered him just as I was about to go down to the dungeons. I told him I wanted to clean the place, but he just dangled his keys and told me it was off-limits." She lowered her voice as other servants joined at their table. "He had this look in his eyes though… I wouldn't be surprised if Novak is indeed in there."

Meya bit her lip. *I guess we'll find out soon.* Not wanting Gail to know about their required presence at the dungeons after supper, Meya turned to her food instead.

Gail sighed. "Poor guy. I wonder what they're doing to him…"

"They? I think it's just the Commander," Nina whispered.

"Why do you think that?"

Nina blushed slightly. "Just a hunch. Besides, people have only gone missing while he's been in the castle."

Gail opened her mouth to speak but closed it when Lea sat down next to her.

"Hey girls." She smiled at Meya and Nina. "How have you two been? I seriously miss having you in the sleeping quarters."

Nina and Meya both adjusted their hair to make sure their bruises wouldn't be visible. Not wanting to involve Lea in the entire ordeal—knowing what she'd think of their apparent gossip—they just made small talk while they finished their meals.

~*~

Meya followed Nina towards the dungeons. Adrenaline coursed through her veins and the hairs on the back of her neck stood on end. *Last time I was here…* She shook the images of the slaver from her mind. *He wouldn't ask us to do anything to Novak… Would he?* A chill went up her spine and she hugged herself.

They halted in front of the doors, the torch on the wall causing their shadows to dance. "Do you think he's already inside?" Nina asked.

"I don't know… He told me to wait for him."

"We could knock to be sure?" Nina turned to the door.

"Let's just wait, please." Meya felt very uncomfortable and stalling whatever was waiting for them behind that door seemed like a good thing.

"Alright." Nina sighed and leaned against the wall. "What do you think will happen?"

Meya bit her lip and remained silent.

"Do you think he will torture us?"

Meya cringed as she imagined Nina in the same position as the slaver. "Wouldn't that be unfair? I mean, we chose option one for a reason! If they were just going to punish us here no matter which option we picked…"

Nina twirled a lock of hair around her finger. "Maybe it's a difference of time? Like, if we picked option two, we would have been in the dungeons for a while, but now only one night?" She sighed. "I don't know… I just can't think of any other reason we'd be here."

*I can…*

They waited in silence for a long time. Finally, a noise came from the other side and they both shot up. The lock turned and the door creaked open, revealing the commander. A grin stretched across his face, his grey eyes shimmering maliciously in the torchlight. "As expected." He held the door open for them. "Come."

Nina walked in, but Meya hesitated. "B-but Lord Deminas told me to wait for him…"

The commander just smiled and gestured for her to enter.

Not wanting to upset him, Meya hurried inside. The cells were all empty, but the light in the interrogation room up ahead caused her blood to run cold. *That's where Lord Deminas had the slaver… Is Novak hanging there now?*

Commander Andreas locked the door and walked past the women to the dreaded chamber. They followed him, their faces pale as they stepped into the illuminated room, the smell of blood and gore thick in the air. *Oh God…* Meya scanned the room. *This stench… What—* She jumped slightly upon seeing the lord sitting in a chair in the right corner. He smiled deviously as he rose to meet them.

The women curtsied. "My Lord."

Meya still had her eyes set upon the lord when she heard Nina gasp. Fearing the worst, she spun around.

Commander Andreas stood near a table, a sadistic smirk on his face. There were several torture tools on the dark wood, some of them clearly covered with fresh blood. The commander gave them a sideward glance as he moved his fingers over the many objects. Metal pins, clamps, knives, saws… He finally picked up one of the blades, examining it closely, though his gaze slowly shifted to observe their reaction.

Nina whimpered softly while Meya just stood gazing at the stained metal, petrified. *Please don't let him use that on us!*

"Aren't you two just adorable, frightened little rabbits," the commander teased.

Meya slowly turned to look at the lord. His foreboding grin caused her to tremble and she instantly forgot everything that had happened during the past few days. All she saw was a dangerous man. A sadist.

Commander Andreas walked away from the table and out of their sight. The fact that he still held the blade caused both women to spin around to see where he was going.

A short shriek slipped from Nina's lips while Meya clasped her hands in front of her mouth to prevent the same. They stared, wide-eyed, at the table that stood against the wall, right next to the door—they had missed it entirely upon entering the room. Upon it lay several slabs of meat and an apparently skinned thigh. The surface of the table was drenched in blood, as was the floor in front of it.

*Oh, dear, sweet God.* The world spun a little and Meya felt queasy. *Don't tell me that once belonged to—* Meya stiffened as Lord Deminas placed his hands on her shoulders.

"You two are in luck; Andreas already did all the hard work."

The commander smirked as he brought the dirty blade to his lips and licked it, a sinister glint in his eyes.

Nina whimpered again and grabbed Meya's hand, squeezing it tightly.

"Andreas and I had a lot of fun discussing possible tasks for the two of you." He released Meya and walked over to the commander. He observed the women, relishing the pure terror in their eyes. "Nina."

Her grip on Meya's hand became tighter at the sound of her name.

"Any idea what it is we want you to do?" The lord's eyes shimmered with excitement.

"N-no, my Lord," she stammered.

He turned his gaze to Meya, but she was still staring at the fleshy remnants of what had once been a person. "Meya." Her eyes shifted to meet his. "What about you?"

"Is..." She swallowed. "Was that Novak, m-my Lord?"

He smiled devilishly. "Does it matter?"

Meya hesitated. "I...I don't know... my Lord." Her gaze turned back to the meat, acid rising in the back of her throat.

"Well, if it bothers you so much to think of this pile of flesh as once having been a human being—"

Nina whimpered, but the interruption didn't seem to bother him.

"Then just think of it as having belonged to an animal—it's not that far from the truth."

Meya's gaze shifted to the Lord again and a shiver went up her spine at seeing his expression. *His eyes had held that same look when he showed me the slaver...*

"But enough playing around." Lord Deminas took a moment to observe the women before he continued, "How good are your cooking skills?"

Nina's grip intensified to the point that Meya could feel her bones shift. *What did he just ask?*

"Well?" His gaze was on Nina.

"I sometimes helped prepare meals before I came here. Though in regard to animals, it was mostly fowl and rabbits, my Lord," she managed to say in a hoarse whisper.

He looked at Meya. "What about you? Did your family's inn serve any good food?"

"I...I like to think we did, m-my Lord."

"So what's your experience in the kitchen?"

"I helped out with most meals, my Lord."

His smile broadened. "Good. Meya, you will be in charge of preparing the best meal you can with the meat provided. You are allowed to take all the extra ingredients you need from the storeroom. Once done, bring it up to my quarters. Nina, you will assist Meya and help tidy up the kitchen. Is the task at hand clear?"

"Yes, my Lord," the women answered simultaneously.

"Good."

Commander Andreas placed the blade he had been holding back on the table and left the room, his sinister gaze lingering on the two as he went.

Lord Deminas started to make his way to the door when he halted. "Oh, and Nina, you can clean this place up tomorrow."

"As you wish, my Lord."

"Now don't let us wait too long." He left the room without looking back. The door creaked in the distance and again as it closed.

It was silent for a while as the two just stared at the pile of meat.

"Does the fact that they drink human blood and also eat human flesh mean they *are* demons after all?" Meya whispered.

"I honestly don't know anymore, but it's frightening." Nina finally released Meya's hand and hugged herself. "I've been down here so many times. I've gotten rid of plenty of corpses that had been mutilated and tortured. But this..." She shook her head. "Actually eating the flesh of another person? I... I have no words for that."

Meya placed her hand on her shoulder and gave it a little squeeze. "Let's just get to work, before... Before the next meal becomes one of us." She shivered at the mere thought.

Nina nodded. "You're right."

They approached the table.

"Well, at least we know what happens to those who go missing now." Meya's stomach turned at the mere thought of how many people the commander might have killed and eaten.

"Not to mention your predecessors..." Nina poked one of the slabs but quickly retracted her hand. "I can't even... To think it belonged to someone I knew..." She turned around, taking a few deep breaths.

"It's alright." Meya placed the slabs of meat on her one hand and grabbed the thigh with the other. "I got this." She looked at the flesh. *Just pretend it's not human.*

"I seriously hope we don't run into anyone while carrying all of this," Nina said. "How would we explain ourselves?"

Meya paled. "I don't even want to think about that. I just hope he asked everyone in the kitchen to leave early." She shuddered at the thought of running into Abi whilst possibly carrying the flesh of her lover.

"Considering how he's managed to keep all this secret for so long, I assume he did."

Cautiously, they made their way out of the dungeon and towards the kitchen.

"I'm worried about you, though..." Nina said as they walked through the castle. "Lord Deminas clearly also drank the blood of your predecessors... And they eventually disappeared. Did they become supper? Does that mean you risk the same fate?"

Meya closed her eyes as she shuddered. "I...I want to believe, that if we were destined to be killed and eaten... that they would have done so already. Instead, they are making us do this. They didn't kill either of us—they took another servant." She swallowed. "Don't forget: while I was sick, you got to be his chambermaid for a while."

"I don't get it, though... I mean, it seems the Lord likes you in a way— why else would he bother to heal you when you were sick? Unless he just wanted to eat you later..."

Meya shivered.

"But I don't get why he doesn't kill me..."

"Maybe he just values you? It's just you and Kadeem who he trusts to clean the dungeons."

"So? He always has only *one* chambermaid and that hasn't stopped him from making them disappear."

Meya bit her lip. *She's got a point there.*

After Nina confirmed that the kitchen was deserted, they slipped inside. Nina lit the various oil lamps while Meya placed the meat on the counter and went to start a cooking fire.

"Let's just try not to think too much about it, alright?" Meya added some wood to the growing flames. "It's not like we can do anything about it if Lord Deminas decides to kill us." The thought alone felt like a stab to the heart.

"I suppose you're right." Nina sighed. "It's not as if we can escape. And even if we did, where would we go?"

Meya stood up and walked over to Nina. She placed her wrists on her shoulders, careful not to dirty her robe with her hands, and gave her a hopeful smile. "You always told me to just do my best. To be a good servant. So let's do just that."

Nina returned the smile before kissing Meya. "Alright then, let's get cooking. Maybe after this here is turned into a stew or something, it won't bother me so much."

Meya turned her head to glance at the meat. *Somehow, I doubt it'll make much difference.*

~*~

It took a lot longer than expected, but Meya was rather pleased with herself: the meat pie was starting to get a golden tint and the stew was nearly done. They were busy cleaning up the kitchen when the commander suddenly stepped inside, startling them.

He sniffed the air. "Smells good." He grinned. "How long till it's served? It's been a while and we're quite hungry."

Meya fumbled a little for words. "The stew's almost ready, but the pie needs a bit more time."

He seemed to consider what was said. "Very well. Nina, bring me a bottle of wine and some cups."

"Yes, sir." She wiped her hands off and hurried to the storeroom.

He walked over to the stew that simmered over the fire, stirred it, and pulled the ladle up to smell it.

Meya watched him anxiously. *What if he doesn't like it?*

He carefully sipped the hot brew. "Have you tasted this yourself?" He lowered the ladle and turned to Meya.

The glint in his eyes caused her heart to constrict in her chest. "N-no, sir." The last word tasted foul in her mouth.

He smirked. "You should."

*Is this good, or bad?* He approached her and Meya froze, unsure of what to do.

His fingers sifted through her red locks. "You know, in some cultures, hair like yours is regarded as a sign of royalty."

Meya's heart pounded in her throat. *What's that supposed to mean?*

"Then again, in these regions, you're more likely to be deemed a witch because of it."

Disgraced, blood rushed to her face. *The audacity!*

Commander Andreas smiled amusedly. "Though I'm quite certain about what Deminas thinks your fiery locks represent."

Her cheeks were ablaze, but her initial anger had been replaced with curiosity. The door creaked behind them and Meya turned to see Nina holding a flask of wine.

The commander gave Meya one last devilish smirk before making his way out. "Nina, come with me."

She quickly grabbed two cups and followed him. "What about the food, sir?"

"Meya, will you be able to finish things here alone and take supper up?"

She thought for a moment. "Yes, sir." A shiver went up her spine. *I really hate that word.*

He held the door open for Nina. "Good."

Meya watched them leave. All alone, she couldn't help but wonder what the commander had meant. *Was he trying to say having red hair is a good or a bad thing?* She turned her attention to the stew and stirred it. His remark regarding it bothered her.

*"Have you tasted this yourself?"*

She bit her lip. *As wrong as it is... I should. What if it's not good?* The mere thought of serving the lord something bad made her anxious. *It smells good enough, though.* Disregarding the origins of the main ingredient, she brought the ladle up, blew the contents a few times, and carefully sipped.

Unable to decide if it really was good, she took a bigger sample. Swirling it around in her mouth, she thoroughly assessed the taste.

*Hmm... An extra garlic clove and a little more wine should perfect this.* Pleased, she swallowed the stew without thinking and went back to work.

# Thirty

Carrying a very heavy tray, Meya made her way to the lord's chambers. Once there, she placed it on the ground and knocked.

"Enter," Lord Deminas answered from the other side, so she opened the door and went in.

"Ah, supper," the lord said with a devious smile.

Meya's eyes shifted to the commander seated beside him. *Where's Nina?*

She rested the tray on the corner of the desk and arranged the dishes. "I hope it will be to your liking, my Lord." Removing the cover from the first plate, she revealed the steaming stew.

Lord Deminas took a deep breath through his nose and grinned at the commander. "You were right—it *does* smell delicious."

Commander Andreas grabbed the large carafe that stood on the table and refilled their cups. "Did you taste it?" He turned his attention to Meya.

Her eyes enlarged and her cheeks flushed.

The commander laughed and elbowed the smiling lord. "I told you she would."

Lord Deminas remained silent, but the satisfied look in his eyes said enough.

*Oh God, this is embarrassing.* Meya finished setting the table, placing bowls and cutlery in front of the two men and the second dish next to the first.

"Tell me, Meya..." Lord Deminas scooped some of the stew into his bowl. "Did you like it?" He passed the bowl to the commander and filled the other one.

Meya opened her mouth to speak, but her lips refused to form words.

Lord Deminas looked up at her. "Well?"

"I...I did my best, my Lord." She cast her eyes down, her cheeks ablaze. "I think it tastes good."

"I can tell you improved it after I left," the commander said after having a bite.

*Does that mean it's good? Or is it just less bad?*

Lord Deminas brought the spoon up to his mouth and Meya bit her lip in anticipation.

*What will he say? Will he like it?* She fidgeted with her apron, her gaze focused on the lord's face. *What happens if he doesn't like it?*

"Well, this is something different," he said after swallowing.

Meya clutched her apron. *Please just tell me already if I did good or not!*

Lord Deminas looked up at Meya, his expression agonisingly neutral, and motioned for her to come closer. He scooped up some stew and held out the spoon. "I want you to taste this."

Meya paled and beads of cold sweat rolled down her back. *Damn it, this can't be good! I bet he wants me to taste just how bad it is!* Anxious, she closed her lips around the spoon and the lord slowly pulled it away, a sly smirk emerging on his face.

She carefully chewed the stew. The various fruits and vegetables mixed well with the sweet meat, while the herbs and wine provided a finishing touch.

"What do you think?" Lord Deminas' eyes gleamed mischievously.

"I...I don't know what to say, my Lord."

"How does it taste?"

"I think it tastes good, my Lord," she said with slight hesitation.

Lord Deminas shook his head. "I disagree." He turned to Commander Andreas. "What do you think?"

The commander grinned. "I think we got ourselves a little witch who knows how to cook her fellow man into a divine meal."

Meya flushed red and opened her mouth to protest the first remark when the second sank in. *Divine?*

Lord Deminas chuckled. "Yes, I agree." He gazed at Meya. "You did well, but now I can't help but wonder what else you've made us." He lifted the cover from the other dish to reveal the golden-brown meat pie.

"That looks promising," the commander said, licking his lips.

"I…I haven't tasted that, though," Meya whispered.

Lord Deminas smiled in amusement. "Are you afraid it won't taste good?" He leaned forward. "Or do you just wish to taste this yourself too?"

Her cheeks burned up even more. *He's making it sound like I enjoy eating human flesh!* Still, the earlier resentment she had had towards the meat had vanished.

He cut the pie and pinned a piece onto his fork. "I'll let you have the honour of tasting it first." His eyes glimmered with delight.

Meya wanted to protest—she felt like she *should* protest—but the pie looked so good and the smell alone made her mouth water. That one spoonful of stew didn't help either, as it had left her stomach wanting more. Even though they got decent meals as servants, anything extra to eat was more than welcome.

She opened her mouth. *Oh God, what am I doing?* She closed her lips and the fork retreated, leaving the sweet meat pie to linger on her tongue. *Oh God, why does this taste so good? This is wrong. This is so very wrong.* She closed her eyes as she swallowed, savouring the flavour.

The commander laughed. "She loves it!"

Meya's eyes shot open and she took a step back, embarrassed.

"No need to be ashamed," Lord Deminas said, clearly enjoying the situation. "Tell me what you're thinking."

After a moment of silence, Meya spoke softly, "It's delicious, my Lord… But it's wrong."

"And why is it wrong?" He took a bite from the stew without lifting his prying gaze off her.

"I…I made this using human flesh. Someone *died* for it." She cast her eyes down. "Eating another person is just wrong, my Lord."

"Well, I'm not sure if that someone is dead just yet…" Commander Andreas grinned as he looked at the lord. "What do you think?"

"Well, it's a long drop down that hole. Even if someone is able to survive that, there's no way out."

Meya blanched. *They cut Novak up and dumped him down a hole while he was still alive?* Her stomach turned.

The men laughed and continued their meals. Lord Deminas tasted the pie and nodded approvingly. "This is excellent."

The commander also took a bite. "I'm glad we agreed on this task—as much as I enjoy rare meat, this is a delicious variation."

A shiver ran up Meya's spine. *Demons… They must be demons after all!*

Lord Deminas looked at Meya as he spoke, "I'll be sure to ask her to cook again during your next visit." His pleased expression caused her breath to catch.

*Another visit, another missing servant.* She shuddered at the prospect. With a shock, she realised she still didn't know where Nina was. "M-my Lord..."

"Yes?"

"May I ask... Where's Nina?" She clutched her apron, anxious to hear the answer.

"On my bed," he stated casually.

"She had some wine, we took some blood, she fainted," the commander added, grinning wickedly.

Meya's pulse quickened. *Is she alright?* She swallowed and gathered her courage. "My Lord... May I see her?"

He seemed to consider this for a moment as he chewed his food. "Yes, you may. If she is able to walk, take her back to my old chamber." He drank from his cup, a nonchalant smile gracing his lips as he placed it back down. "You may stay there for the night."

Meya curtsied, her entire body trembling with anxiety. "Th-thank you, my Lord."

After receiving a curt nod, Meya had to restrain herself from running to the bedroom. To her surprise, the hearth was burning, ensuring there was a pleasant warmth in the room. Nina was lying on the bed, asleep. Despite her tawny complexion, it was still clearly visible that the young woman was quite pale.

Meya sat down next to her and caressed her cheek. Relief washed over her as she watched Nina slowly open her eyes. "Hey dear," she said softly.

Nina groaned and tried to sit up, but she slumped back onto the bed. "Everything's spinning..."

Despite knowing the answer, Meya still asked, "What happened?"

Nina just held up her left wrist—the cut was closed but still visible.

*Human blood, human flesh...* Meya shuddered. *They're evil.* She swallowed and to her utmost shame, she realised the taste of the meat pie still lingered in her mouth—and she desired more. *I guess that makes me evil too.* Memories of the night her family's inn burned down flashed through her mind. *Though I suppose I already was, considering I killed a man...*

Nina sat up again, slowly this time. "I need a drink." She looked around the room. "Where's the Lord?"

"He's having dinner with the Commander. I have permission to take you downstairs. Do you think you're able to walk?"

244

"I'll be fine. I just need some water and preferably some food, but I'll be fine." She smiled weakly.

Meya helped her stand and they made their way to the door. She knocked and entered upon the lord's approval. She was unable to stop herself from shuddering upon seeing the men enjoying their food and drink. The women curtsied and left the room, but the smell of food lingered in their nostrils.

Without realising it, Meya licked her lips.

~*~

Gail nearly slammed her breakfast onto the table as she sat down opposite Meya and Nina. "Please, tell me you've seen Winnie!"

They both frowned. "What are you talking about?" Nina asked.

Gail's gaze darted around the room. "She's missing."

Meya paled. *We were alone all night in the Lord's old chamber.*

Nina shook her head. "No, that can't be right. I saw her yesterday."

"When?"

She thought about it. "At breakfast."

Gail ran her hand through her hair, distressed. "That's the thing… As far as we can gather, she was last seen at lunch. Brit was hysterical last night. We tried to stop her from going out to look for her, but she pushed Lea away and just stormed out."

"Is Brit alright? Did she return?" Nina inquired, eyes big with worry.

Gail nodded. "Yes, but she cried herself to sleep. She's running around the castle now, looking for Winnie."

Nina and Meya exchanged glances but remained silent.

"If you two know anything, tell me!"

Nina shook her head. "It's nothing. I just don't believe she got taken. I mean, Novak disappeared the day before. And every time someone went missing, they went missing at night, wandering the castle… It just doesn't seem like that is what happened to her."

"I hope you're right." Gail sighed. "Maybe she just spent the night with one of the soldiers again." She shook her head. "But she would have told her sister if she did."

Meya considered this but still felt anxious. *What did Lord Deminas and the Commander do after we left them? The Commander never returned to his chamber… Did he go for a second victim so soon? But why? If he eats them… They both just had their meals, and they drank Nina's blood! What would they want another person for?*

245

Her blood cooled in her veins as she realised something. She pushed her half-finished breakfast towards Nina and stood up.

Nina frowned. "Where are you going?"

"You can have it. I…I forgot something." She rushed out of the dining hall, ignoring Gail who was calling after her.

*"I will have to deal with Winnie later."*

Meya shuddered as she recalled the lord's words. *He captured, tortured, and killed the slaver for what he did to me. He sealed Gail's lips for spreading lies about me. What would he do to Winnie who tried to kill me?* Despite her dread, a warm feeling spread throughout her body. *Why does he do these things? Does he do them because he cares about me?*

~*~

Anxious, Meya knocked on the door of the lord's chambers. She bit her lip as she waited for a reply, but none came. After knocking twice more, she entered. Frustrated that there was no one inside, she paced around for a while.

*He's probably still having breakfast.* She sighed. *I just need to be patient. He will be back and I'll ask him right away.* The various ways of how she could start the conversation went through her mind.

After several minutes, she groaned and shook her head.

*Enough of this!*

She took a deep breath and went into the bedroom to start on her chores. She had hoped being busy would help keep her mind off Winnie's whereabouts, but instead, the mute was all she could think of.

*Stubborn, little Winnie; jealous, little Winnie…*

Memories of the young woman ran through her mind. The constant look of envy in her eyes whenever she returned from the lord's chambers at night. The way she had pulled her towel away, exposing her and the still healing cuts on her breasts. The clearly growing contempt over the months that had followed, finally culminating in an attempt on her life.

Disdain caused her jaw to tighten. *She was so jealous of how close I was getting to the Lord, she would kill me over it! The foul harpy even tried to make it look like I would have died from my condition!*

Fuming, she sat down on the bed and stared at the barricaded door.

*Still, the churlish wench failed.* The memory of her panicked look and how fast she had fled the room caused her to smirk.

She took a few deep breaths and her rage subsided.

246

*Yes, Winnie deserves to be punished for what she did… But death?* She thought of what Gail had said earlier and immediately felt bad for Brit. *Her sister is all she's got.*

She rose and continued making the bed.

*I should try and speak to the Lord when I can. If Winnie is still alive, maybe I can keep it that way.*

~*~

Lea, Gail, Nina, and Meya ate their lunches in silence. They were nearly done when Brit walked over, her eyes red and puffy, and Juris was right behind her. She stood behind Meya, though she kept her eyes on the floor.

"Meya," Juris started. "I need to ask you something."

Meya looked up, tension rising in the pit of her stomach. "What is it?"

"I spoke to Lord Deminas earlier about the recent disappearance of both Novak, and now Winnie." His gaze shifted to the other women at the table. "He was unable to tell me anything regarding Novak, but he did have something to say about Winnie." He focused on Meya. "I don't know how to ask this nicely, so please bear with me. Several weeks ago, you and Nina suddenly started sleeping somewhere else. I've tried asking the both of you about this, multiple times."

He placed his hand on Nina's shoulder the moment she tried to rise and shook his head.

"But I never received a satisfying explanation. Lord Deminas informed me this morning that Winnie had tried to kill someone during his absence. At first, I thought this was absurd, but…" He sighed. "It would explain a lot."

"Is it true?" Brit asked, her voice quivering.

Meya's cheeks burned. "I…I didn't want to—"

"When?"

Meya noticed more and more people were looking at them. "When I was sick…" She lowered her voice in an attempt to stop others from overhearing. "She came into the room and… tried to smother me with a pillow."

Brit's eyes enlarged as tears spilled out. "You're lying."

Nina shook her head. "No, she's not. I saw her not long after it happened. I insisted she should tell Juris, but she refused—she didn't want to get Winnie into trouble. She didn't want to upset you."

Brit covered her face. "Foolish, foolish Winnie," she sobbed.

Meya turned to Juris. "What did Lord Deminas say about Winnie? Where is she?"

He averted his eyes. "He only said that she got punished accordingly."

*Punished accordingly?* Meya looked at Nina. *She would have told us if she'd seen Winnie down in the dungeons... So where is she?*

"It's not fair," Brit mumbled between sniffles. "She loves him. She always has. He cut out her tongue, but she still wants his love." She glared at Meya, her bloodshot eyes filled with anger. "You got what she couldn't get and she hates you for it."

Meya gasped and Nina protectively wrapped her arm around her. "Don't you go trying to place any blame on her! Your sister is responsible for her own actions. She tried to kill Meya when she was sick and weak! Winnie's jealousy is no excuse for attempted murder—especially not when Meya did nothing wrong!"

Brit took a step towards Nina, but Juris blocked her. "Stop it." He glared at Brit and then at Nina. "Both of you."

Brit huffed and stormed away.

The entire dining hall seemed to have been listening, the sudden silence deafening.

Meya hid her face in her hands. *Great, just great... Now everybody knows.*

Juris gave Meya's shoulder a reassuring squeeze. "I can understand why you wanted to keep this a secret, but you really shouldn't have. There's no blame on you. Not on why she tried to kill you, nor the punishment she has now received."

"I...I just didn't want any trouble. I didn't want Brit to be upset. I didn't want Winnie to—" Her voice broke. "What do you think Lord Deminas has done to her?"

Juris hesitated to answer, so Gail decided to speak instead. "I fear he might have killed her."

# Thirty One

Disgruntled, Meya made her way to the lord's chambers for the night. Lunch had already been bad, but supper had been even worse. *Everyone knows what happened.* She groaned as she still felt their curious gazes on her back.

With gossiping being a bad thing, only a few people had dared to ask her if it was true—to which she didn't even get a chance to reply due to Nina telling them off. The only person Nina didn't scare away had been Abi.

Meya closed her eyes for a moment as her heart ached for the poor girl. *Unlike the others, she just wanted to check if we knew anything about Novak...* But all they could do was repeat Juris' words and tell her that the dungeons were empty. *To top it all off, Lord Deminas and his men were celebrating something down in the main room.* Brit's hollow gaze flashed through her mind and a shiver ran up her spine. *I hope she doesn't think it has anything to do with her sister. Still, anything festive on this day would probably make her feel worse. She thinks—no, we all think—Winnie's dead.*

She sighed and halted in front of the lord's chambers. She knocked multiple times, but only silence greeted her.

*He's probably still downstairs.*

She stepped inside and checked the other rooms. The hearth was already lit in the bedroom, and steamy water fogged up the air in the bathroom.

Impatient, she paced around. *I wish I could just slip into that bath... When will he return? Will he even come to his chambers tonight?* She thought of the commander and how he hadn't shown up the previous night.

With a heavy sigh, she moved her fingers through the warm water.

*Such a waste to let this grow cold without use.*

For a brief moment, she contemplated bathing alone, but she quickly scolded herself.

*Are you crazy? He'd be livid!*

Still, her mind alternated between Lord Dcminas lifting her up by her throat and throwing her off the balcony, and him smiling at her slyly as she seductively motioned for him to join her.

She grunted and left the bathroom, blushing. *I am* crazy. *Very much so.* She sat down in front of the hearth and stared into the flames. *I wonder if Nina is alone too...*

~*~

It didn't take long before the door opened and Lord Deminas entered— albeit a bit wobbly. His eyes filled with a joyous spark upon seeing Meya. "Such a good little pet, waiting for me by the fire." There was a very slight slur to his words.

Meya frowned. *Is... Is he drunk? How much did he drink?* She rose up and curtsied. *This might be a good time to ask him about Winnie.*

Lord Deminas walked over to his wardrobe and started to undress. "Or are you waiting for something else?"

Meya's cheeks heated up as her mind immediately went to the steamy bath. "I...I was waiting for you, my Lord." Her heart rate increased. *It's not really a lie.*

Dressed in only his undergarments, he walked up to her, lips curled in a grin. "Is that so?"

Meya nodded. "Y-yes, my Lord."

His face was mere inches away from hers, his breath laced with alcohol. "Why?"

Meya's brows furrowed and slowly she replied, "Because you asked me to come here every night until the commander leaves."

"The Commander will leave in a few days from now. Are you going to miss staying in my quarters?"

The question took her by surprise and she fumbled for words, causing the lord to chuckle.

250

"Not to worry," he whispered into her ear. "If you enjoy it here, I'll take pleasure in your company."

Meya's cheeks were ablaze. In an attempt to change the subject, she asked, "My Lord, was the celebration downstairs because of the Commander leaving?"

Lord Deminas moved back and smiled. "Not directly. But how about you answer my question and I'll answer yours."

*Still sharp, but clearly drunk!* The lord's less intimidating demeanour made her grow bold. "Would I be allowed to ask more questions then, my Lord?"

He narrowed his eyes as he considered this, the smirk on his lips growing. "How about we make it a game? I ask you something and you must answer, and in turn, you may ask me something."

Meya licked her lips as she considered his proposal. *I'm certain he's going to ask a lot of difficult and embarrassing questions, but I could use this to my advantage. Besides, if he wants to know anything, he's going to ask it anyway—now or later.*

Lord Deminas walked over to the cabinet. He opened the lower drawer and took out the bottle of massage oil. "You can use this in the meantime." He threw her the bottle and Meya yelped as she caught it.

*Damn him! What if I'd dropped it?*

Chuckling because of her reaction, Lord Deminas undressed fully and lay down on the bed. "Get naked and massage my back. And you'd better make it quick, before I change my mind and want you to do my chest instead."

Realising that that would result in more than just a massage, Meya quickly complied. *He may be drunk, but he's as sexual as ever.* She sat down on his upper legs, her face burning as she tried not to think about riding the lord. *Would he even allow me to do that?* She mentally shook her head as she tried to suppress her arousal. *Focus, Meya!* She took the bottle of oil, poured some into her palm, and started on his back.

"So, for the first question, I shall repeat myself... Are you going to miss staying in my quarters? And no lies—I might not be able to see your face, but I will still know if you lie." He lowered his tone. "I'll have fun playing with my candles again if you do."

Meya's heart skipped a beat. *Alright, so lying is not an option.* She took a deep breath. "Yes, I will miss staying in your quarters, my Lord."

The lord emitted a pleased grunt. "Very well, your turn."

Slightly taken aback by the fact that he was actually serious about the game he had proposed, she stopped rubbing his back. *What do I wish to know the most? I have so many questions!* She wetted her lips. "How many questions will we do, my Lord?"

"Until I grow bored."

*I wonder how long that will take...*

"So, my turn again..." The amusement was clearly audible in his voice.

Meya stiffened. *Did he just...?*

"What is it that you will be missing?"

Trying to overcome the surge of emotions, her hands started to massage his back again, albeit slowly. *So, he's playing the game like that... I should have known.* Her mind went over all possible answers to the question at hand. "I suppose I will miss sleeping in your comfortable bed, my Lord."

"Is that all?"

Meya smirked. "My turn, my Lord." He shifted underneath her and this caused her pulse to quicken. *Shit, did I overdo it?*

"Well played."

Meya exhaled in relief. *Drunken Lord is a fun Lord. Alright...* She kneaded his skin as she thought about her question. *Do I start with personal questions or do I ask about Novak and Winnie? Maybe I should just start a bit light... Ensure he doesn't grow bored.* Deciding to play along with the game, she settled on her first actual question. "What was the celebration downstairs about, my Lord?"

He remained silent for a moment. "I received word of King Béla in regard to our request on becoming allies and standing together against the Golden Horde. We've been in negotiations for a while now, and today we received a positive reply and agreement to one another's terms."

"That's great news, my Lord!"

"Of all the things you could have asked me, why ask about the celebrations?"

"I'm afraid you might grow bored of the game if I were to start asking the big questions right away, my Lord."

He chuckled. "Fair enough. Now before you ask your question, move up to the shoulders please."

*Please? Did he just say please?* She shifted so that she could reach his shoulders properly, her cheeks flushing. After brushing away his long hair, she took some extra oil and started to work on his shoulders. *He truly is drunk.* She thought about what to ask next. "Why will the Commander be leaving in a few days?"

"It's part of the arrangement with King Béla. Andreas will go there with the official documents and ensure everything is settled. Now, answer me truthfully: are you afraid of the questions I might ask you?"

"I am, my Lord."

"Then why play?"

"My Lord, I will answer, but in turn I get to ask two questions as well." She grinned and took the lord's silence as his agreement. "I want to play because then I can ask you questions I would normally not get an answer to."

He chuckled again. "And this is why I like you."

Meya's cheeks reddened even more, and for a moment, she stopped massaging his shoulders. She gathered her courage and asked, "In what way do you like me, my Lord?"

"In ways lords aren't supposed to like servants."

Her heart constricted in her chest. She thought hard about how to phrase her next question. "If not as a servant," she hesitated, "as *what* do you like me?"

"Hmm..."

Insecurity tugged at her insides and she didn't even notice how her hold on the lord's shoulders intensified with every second he remained still.

"I've never given it this much thought. I will need to ponder this. Considering I didn't answer your question, I will allow you another one."

Meya screamed internally. *What's that supposed to mean?* She released the lord and immediately realised what she had been doing. *Oh, God...* She ran her fingers through her hair. *This is embarrassing.* She closed her eyes and took a few deep breaths. *What am I doing? Am I really trying to figure out if the Lord loves me? Is that it?* She tugged at her hair in an attempt to create some order in her mind. *Alright, different subject!* She exhaled slowly. "Why do you drink blood, my Lord?"

The silence that followed was deafening and Meya feared that she had overstepped a boundary.

"My...my Lord?"

"Continue your massage, please." His tone of voice was more serious now and less playful. "I should have anticipated that question, but it appears I had not. But, I shall answer." He paused for a moment. "I drink blood because I must. It keeps me sane."

*Because I must? It keeps me sane? What?* Meya furrowed her brows as she pondered his answer. *What does that mean?*

"Now, considering all you just asked, I've got a few nice ones for you." The playful tone in his voice was back. "What's your relationship with Nina?"

Meya's mouth opened, but it took a moment before sound dared to pass her lips. "I...I guess we're paramours, my Lord."

There was a pleased grunt. "I thought so."

Trying not to let his question derail her, Meya asked, "What happens if you— No, wait." She scolded herself. *Don't ask what happens if he doesn't drink blood—he just said it keeps him sane, so no blood would mean he'd go crazy. Don't waste your questions!* She bit her lip as she thought hard about what to ask. "*Why* does my Lord need to drink blood to keep sane?"

"You're asking good questions, my pet. I am no ordinary man. For what I am, human blood or flesh is needed. I don't know precisely *why*, only that I do."

"Then, considering you didn't really answer my question, do I get another, my Lord?"

He laughed. "Nice try, but no. I answered as far as I could. If I were to ask you something you would honestly not know the answer to, it would not warrant a new question."

*Fair enough.* Her mind tried to make sense of his answers. *Does that mean he has some illness that makes him require blood? But he specifically said human blood...*

"How do you feel about the fact that we have shared the bed together, especially considering you and Nina are paramours?"

Meya stiffened. *Oh dear God, did he really just ask that? Of all things, did he just ask that?*

"No need to stop your massage. Come on, continue and answer me," he toyed.

*He really knows what to ask! Fine, I'll get him right back at that!* She took a deep breath. "If you want to know, my Lord, I enjoyed fornicating with you. The fact that Nina and I are paramours does not alter this as she is fully aware of our... interactions—and not to forget, you had the pleasure of fornicating with her too. Which brings me to my next question: *why* did you decide to fornicate with her?"

Lord Deminas tensed up—Meya felt his muscles become rigid underneath her fingertips. "If you're going to play this game like that, I might have to end it."

"You said you were going to play until you were bored, my Lord." Meya was pleased with herself for remembering that. "It doesn't sound like you're bored."

"Using my own answers against me—you're getting quite bold." His voice betrayed his amusement. "Very well, I shall continue to play."

"Then try to relax, my Lord. Your shoulders are all tense." Meya couldn't help but smirk at having succeeded in cornering him yet again, only now to such an extent that he actually seemed uncomfortable. *As long as this doesn't come back to haunt me later...*

"I decided to have sex with Nina because she offered and I could use the stress relief."

Meya froze. *That's it? That's his answer?*

"My turn. Were you jealous Nina got to bed me before you did?"

A silent gasp slipped from her lips. *Is he truly drunk? Can he really be this sharp when drunk?* She closed her eyes and tried to relax. "Yes, I suppose I was jealous." The way he relaxed a little at hearing her answer only made her more agitated. "Why was my Lord stressed? Surely it wasn't related to the battle at hand."

He huffed. "Be careful, you're starting to make me regret having agreed to this game."

"It was your idea, my Lord." Meya felt like she had the upper hand again.

"That it was… Fine. Indeed, the stress was not related to having to go to battle, but rather with you being sick."

Her insides twisted upon hearing this. *He was worried about* me? *More so than about a battle?*

"Tell me, do you feel obligated to have sex with me?"

Meya cringed. *How do I put this?* She bit her lip and thought for a moment. "I…I am obligated to follow your orders, my Lord. If you were to command me to have sex with you, I would indeed feel like I had no choice but to obey." She noticed him tense up again. "However, you ensured me it was my choice and asked me if I really wanted it—you didn't command me. So if you wish to know if I felt obligated to fornicate with you when we did: no, I did not."

He relaxed. "I'm pleased to hear that."

"Why does—" She stopped and reconsidered what she was going to ask. *I need to change to those heavy subjects before he no longer wants to play.* "Why… did you kill Novak, my Lord?"

"I didn't."

Meya paled. *So he's still alive?*

"Why do you care about the young man's fate?"

"He's—" She wondered if she should tell him. *Would he be mad at Abi? Would he harm her?*

"He's what? Complete your answer—and no lies."

"One of the servants I know was his lover, my Lord. She's devastated and I feel sorry for her."

"Such a great and caring heart you have," he said with a mixture of amusement and sorrow.

"What happened to Novak, my Lord?"

"I have an arrangement with Andreas. If he happens to find any servants out and about after they're supposed to be in their quarters, he can do whatever he wants with them." He turned his head. "Neck, please."

Meya complied, though she was still trying to process the answer she had just received.

"Considering how caring you are, doesn't it bother you that you served us a meal made with human flesh?"

Meya took a deep breath and thought about how to honestly answer that question. "A part of me does, but another part of me doesn't, my Lord. I mean, eating another human being is wrong. But, the damage had already been done. Me cooking the meat would not change his fate."

Lord Deminas chuckled. "This game is a lot of fun."

*Why is he laughing?* The colour drained from Meya's face. "M-my Lord… Just what has happened to Winnie?"

"I thought you would never ask." He snickered. "I punished her for attempting to kill you. I cut off one of her legs, seared the wound shut, and dropped her into the pit where we leave all the corpses—though, she was not quite dead at the time."

The world seemed to slow down for Meya as she tried to comprehend what had been said. *He did what?*

"You had some of the stew and the meat pie yesterday… Tell me, how did Winnie taste?"

Meya's eyes enlarged as she sat rigidly on top of the lord. She noticed something move in her periphery and turned her head. The bedroom door stood slightly ajar. Her heart skipped a beat as she saw Brit standing next to the cabinet. Her eyes were filled with rage and tears stained her cheeks.

"I know you enjoyed it, but I want to hear you say it," Lord Deminas continued, clearly unaware of the intruder.

Meya's jaw dropped in order to speak, but her vocal cords refused to function. Her entire body felt like a block of stone as she locked her gaze with Brit's. The pure fury and sorrow that lay within her eyes paralysed Meya to the core.

Without saying a word, Brit shot towards the bed. The sound of her bare feet against the stones caused Lord Deminas to turn his head. Brit revealed a small knife as she lunged towards the two. Meya's instincts managed to take control and she scrambled off the lord's back and as far away from the deranged sister as the bed allowed. Lord Deminas started to rise, but before his chin was well off the mattress, Brit stuck the weapon between his shoulder blades.

Meya stumbled off the bed as she gawked at the scene, her heart pounding painfully in her chest.

Brit pulled the small knife out, only to sink it into his back again, and again.

Terror screeched through Meya's veins as she watched blood droplets fly through the air with every retreat of the blade. A part of her wanted to intervene, to stop her. Another part of her wanted to just run away before Brit decided to come after her next. These two conflicting desires resulted in her standing frozen to the ground, her eyes fixated on the knife going in and out of the lord's flesh.

*She's killing him...!*

# Thirty Two

As Brit pulled the blade out for the sixth time, Lord Deminas finally managed to rise and turn. With a ferocious scream, she aimed the blade at his face, but he grabbed her wrist. There was a sickening snap, followed by silence as the rage on Brit's face slowly drained away. The knife fell from her limp fingers and clattered to the stone floor.

Lord Deminas stood up, his expression beyond livid. He caught Brit's fist as she made a feeble attempt to punch him. A miserable wail escaped the blonde's lips as the lord crushed her hand.

Meya stared in horror at the two. Dark blood seeped from the multiple stab wounds in the lord's back, though it was but a mere trickle. Brit attempted to kick him, but he released her and shoved her to the floor before her knee could connect. Her head made a loud smack against the stone and her eyes rolled back into her skull.

Though her feet felt heavy, Meya took a few steps closer. The adrenaline in her system still made it appear as if time moved slower, each beat of her heart a loud drum in her own ears.

Lord Deminas sat down on Brit's legs, unbothered by his lack of clothing, and grabbed her tightly by the neck. The woman's eyes snapped open and she raised her hands in an attempt to stop him—but her right wrist was broken, as were the bones in her left hand. An agonising whimper slipped from her lips as she still tried to utilise her broken limbs, but it quickly faded as the lord increased the pressure on her neck.

"It seems stupidity runs in the family," he spat, dark droplets accompanying the words that left his lips.

Brit flailed underneath him, but to no avail. "It's your fault," she screamed. "My sis—"

Lord Deminas' grip on her throat tightened, preventing her from saying anything else. Brit's eyes enlarged as she gasped for air until a lurid gurgling sound replaced it.

Horrified, Meya watched Lord Deminas rise back to his feet while Brit writhed on the floor, clawing at her throat. The lord towered over Brit, glaring at her as she attempted to breathe. When her thrashings weakened, he lifted his foot and stomped upon her stomach. A haggard groan slipped from Brit as she doubled up, spasmed, and finally remained still.

*Is… Is she dead?*

Lord Deminas grabbed Brit's long, blonde hair and dragged her out of the bedroom.

Unable to stop herself, Meya moved closer to see where he was taking her. She knew just want he meant to do as she watched him open the balcony door, and he lifted the unmoving woman from the ground and threw her over the balustrade as if she weighed nothing.

He slammed the door behind him and paced back towards the bedroom. His chest heaved with each breath, a small trickle of blood running down the sides of his mouth and staining his goatee.

Terrified, Meya backed away. *How was he able to do that? How is he even alive?*

He walked right past her and went into the bathroom. "Get me some light in here," he grunted.

"Y-yes, my Lord." Meya quickly fetched one of the lit lanterns and rushed after him. As she lit the lamps in the room, the lord slipped into the bath. A little hesitant, she approached him, lantern still in hand.

There were six clear puncture wounds on his back—four on the right side of his spine and two on the left. As the light illuminated his skin, Meya paled.

The blood that seeped from the slashes wasn't red, but a deep, dark fuchsia. "Meya…"

A small yelp escaped from her lips at hearing her name.

"What happened just now, you are not to speak of it to anyone—not even Nina." He coughed, producing a dreadful, wet sound. "Do I make myself clear?" He turned to look at her, his grey eyes still filled with remnants of his earlier fury.

Frightened, Meya nodded. "Y-yes, my Lord."

He turned back around and splashed some water onto his face, washing the blood from his lips and chin. Another gurgling cough freed itself from his throat and he growled.

Meya winced. "A-are you alright, my Lord? Should I get—"

"I'll be fine."

She lowered her eyes, unsure of what to say or do. He coughed again, making her even more anxious. *How can he be fine? He got stabbed six times and he's coughing up blood!* She swallowed. *Purplish blood...*

It was silent for a bit, the lord's rough breathing and occasional coughs only interrupted by splashing water.

Unable to take it any longer, Meya looked up again. The bath water had turned a slight pink, but the wounds on the lord's back had stopped bleeding. Meya swallowed as she tried to comprehend what was going on.

"I can feel you staring."

Flustered, she averted her eyes. "I...I'm sorry, my Lord."

He sighed and turned to face her. "Come here."

She stepped forward, her heart rate increasing. Her gaze met with his and to her surprise, his anger had faded away.

He coughed again, coagulated, dark blood staining his hand. He looked at it for a moment before washing it off.

Tears prickled Meya's eyes. "You're not fine," she croaked. "How could you be?"

"I told you: I'm no ordinary man." He smirked. "I just need to get the blood out of my lungs."

"The not-red blood," Meya whispered and she shuddered.

"So you've noticed."

"Just... Just *what* are you, my Lord?" Her voice quivered as she finally uttered the question that had been burning inside of her for months.

Lord Deminas shook his head. "Tsk, tsk, tsk." He glared at her, his lips curling up.

The colour drained from Meya's face. *Did I go too far?*

"Brit may have rudely interrupted our little game, but I still recall you have yet to answer my question."

Meya's eyes widened. *Is he serious? Someone just tried to kill him and he's still able to think of the game we were playing?*

"How did Winnie taste?" He grinned, his eyes teeming with joy.

It took a bit before Meya remembered how to use her tongue. "I...I didn't know."

"That was the fun of it." His grin widened.

Meya's cheeks heated up and she regained her courage. "It was just meat. Beef, pork, fowl—I cooked using meat and it was delicious, my Lord."

"But it wasn't just some animal's flesh you cooked with—it was human."

Flustered, Meya looked away from his knowing gaze. "Please answer my question now, my Lord," she said softly. Guilt was sneaking up on her and eating away at the edges of her sanity.

"Very well." He coughed again, but this time he didn't clean his bloodied hands. "Do you see this?"

Meya peered at the lumps of coagulated blood—it was a dark purple colour, nearly black. She shivered at the sight of the unnatural blood.

"I am no demon, nor warlock. I was born a man, but I transcended. I am immortal. My blood is what makes me so."

Meya stared, her mind unable to comprehend what had been said.

"Does this frighten you?" He rinsed his hand.

After a few seconds of silence, Meya managed to nod. "Y-yes, but..." She swallowed. "I... just don't understand how this is possible."

"Something doesn't have to be understood to be possible. Some things just are."

"B-but, there's no such thing as real immortality. It only exists in myths and legends."

Lord Deminas' fingers clutched Meya's chin and made her look at him. He smiled coyly. "And yet here I am. Stabbed six times in the back and still very much alive."

Meya shivered as goosebumps spread across her skin. "But how? How does one go from being human to immortal?"

"By transcending." He released her and sank back into the water. "It all has to do with blood—special blood." He smirked. "*Divine* blood."

Chills ran up her spine. *But that still doesn't explain anything.*

"Speaking of which—get dressed. I want you to bring Andreas to me."

Meya mentally shook her head. "The Commander?"

"Yes. I need to discuss something with him. So go on." He motioned for her to get out of the room. "And no loitering. I expect you back here too."

"A-as you wish." She was about to turn around when she quickly added, "My Lord."

He smiled contently as he watched her hurry out of the room, only to cough up some more dark blood as soon as the door had closed.

~*~

Meya hurried through the halls with the lantern in hand. Her head was heavy and her body felt slightly numb.

*Just what has happened tonight?* Thinking back, it all seemed like a strange dream. *Did Brit really sneak into his chambers? Did she really try to kill him? Did he kill her?* Her head spun. *All those things he told me... Is he really immortal? Does such a thing even truly exist?* Blood rushed to her cheeks as she remembered the other things that had been said. *Did he really say that he liked me? That he was more worried about my health than going to war?* She rummaged through her hair with her free hand, frustrated. *Get it together, Meya! How can you be fawning over a man who's not even human? Who eats people and drinks blood? Not to mention you've already got Nina! You should—*

"Don't you know it's dangerous to roam the castle so late at night?"

Startled, Meya nearly dropped the lantern. She spun around and the light illuminated the commander's sinister grin. *I know the danger would be you.* She swallowed in order to keep the remark to herself.

He stepped out of the shadows and his grin faded to a frown. "What's going on?"

"Lord Deminas sent me to find you, sir."

He turned around and began to make his way to the lord's quarters, his pace fast. "What happened?"

Meya hesitated to answer. "Lord Deminas will explain."

The commander huffed. "The faint scent surrounding you is already explaining some things."

*Scent surrounding me?* Meya flushed red wondering what he meant. *Does he smell the massage oil? Please tell me it's the massage oil...*

They arrived at the lord's quarters and Commander Andreas went inside without knocking, causing Meya's heart to constrict in her chest. "What happened?" he bellowed.

Lord Deminas came walking out of the bedroom, a towel draped around his waist. "You're not going to—"

The commander snorted and laughed. "Turn around."

With her mouth slightly agape, Meya watched as Lord Deminas was unbothered by not only being interrupted but also by being told what to do. Without a word, he obeyed.

262

"Six times?" Commander Andreas laughed again. "What the hell were you doing?"

Meya anxiously fumbled with her dress, only now realising that she could be blamed.

"I was enjoying a massage and, suffice to say, I was rather distracted." Lord Deminas looked at Meya for a moment, before turning back to the commander.

*Oh, please, don't let this be pinned on me!* The blood drained from her face.

"Must have been very distracted for whoever did that to get *six* stabs in." He was clearly finding it more amusing than distressing. "Where is the would-be assassin anyway?"

Lord Deminas gestured towards the balcony. "It was the mute's sister attempting to get revenge. I lost my temper—crushed her throat and threw her out."

The commander crossed his arms as his face grew more serious. "Again? You're lucky you—" He turned his gaze to Meya. "How much did she see?"

Meya froze as both men stared at her.

"Considering the waves of fear coming off of her, I'm going to guess she saw it all."

Lord Deminas nodded. "Yes, she did."

"So I take it she knows?"

"I explained some things."

"You *explained*? Then she's a threat." The commander's eyes flickered with dark intent as he looked Meya up and down.

The ground seemed to fall away from beneath her. *Threat? Me?*

"No, she's good. I trust her."

Commander Andreas raised a brow as he turned his gaze towards the lord. "I knew you were drunk, but getting stabbed six times and confiding in a servant all in one night?"

Now it was Lord Deminas who laughed. "I don't regret the latter."

"So, why did you let her bring me here? I doubt you're so proud of getting stabbed in the back by a servant that you wanted to show me."

The lord's laughter faded. "Remind me in the morning to get you back for that remark."

Commander Andreas grinned. "Oh, you can get back at me all you want—I'm not going to forget this any time soon."

Confused, Meya observed the two men talking like old friends, hierarchy forgotten.

263

"I doubt you will. But, here's why I brought you here: I need you to refrain from taking any other servant during the remainder of your stay."

The commander's expression turned sour. "Why? We have our arrangements."

"I'm aware of that. But, Novak already disappeared, I had Winnie punished, and now I've got another missing servant—"

"Not missing. You killed her and threw the body out."

"There are already whispers in the castle. Another missing person is going to make things difficult in the future," Lord Deminas stressed.

The commander huffed. "You shouldn't have killed this one then. I would have had a great time with her if you'd kept her alive. I already had to cut my time short with the young man because of the mute." He glared at the Lord. "I take it you're not going to tell others about this then?"

Lord Deminas looked at Meya. "Brit disappeared. That's the story I want to be told, amongst servants and my men alike."

Commander Andreas turned around and opened the balcony doors, letting the cold spring air in. He gazed over the edge and came back inside, grinning. "You really need to work on your self-control."

"Why don't you show me your self-control as an example?" He smirked. "I'll let Meya here stab you six times in the back."

Meya's breath hitched. *What?*

"As if you'd risk me hurting your precious, little pet." The commander brushed past Meya as he walked over to the lord. He gazed at her, a sinister glint in his eyes.

Lord Deminas chuckled. "I think the girl has some potential."

"Oh, really? Tell me, what did she do when the knife entered your back for the first time? Or the second? What about the sixth time?"

Blood rushed to Meya's cheeks and she bit her lip in anger and shame. *It's not like I didn't want to help him! Just what was I supposed to do?*

"So she got scared." Lord Deminas shrugged. "I still think she has it in her. She already killed a man before—she can do it again."

Meya stared at him, eyes wide. "I…I had no choice." She balled her fists. *I'm no killer!*

The commander walked up to her, curiosity spreading over his face. "Now this is interesting."

Her gaze shifted from one to the other. "It… was self-defence!"

"I know," Lord Deminas said.

"I can understand why you've taken such a liking to her. Still, it would have been nice if she'd tried to save you." He snickered. "Oh, that would have

264

been legendary. A story to tell centuries from now: that one night, the terrifying Lord Deminas got drunk and attacked by one of his servants, only to be saved by his chambermaid." He laughed loudly and held his stomach.

Lord Deminas crossed his arms and glared at the commander with one brow raised. "Are you done?"

*These two…* Meya stared at them, utterly confused.

Commander Andreas took a few deep breaths, a single chuckle escaping his lips. "For now."

"Good. Then do we have an agreement?"

"Can you refresh my memory as to what you wanted me to agree to? I was too busy enjoying myself."

Lord Deminas sighed. "Consider yourself lucky for being my friend. I would never have such patience with anyone else—especially after tonight."

The commander sniggered again. "Do I really need to repeat myself regarding your self-control?"

The way Lord Deminas glared at him finally made him turn serious again.

"Alright, fine. Don't forget I drank just about as much as you did. Let me have my fun."

"The agreement is about your *fun*. No more disappearing servants during this visit."

"So I have to give up my fun because you slipped up?"

"You just spoke about self-control." Lord Deminas smirked. "I'm certain you can keep yourself entertained with Nina's company for the remainder of your stay—just remember: no harming her." He gave him a stern look.

"Because she's your pet's love, right?" The commander laughed. "Fine, consider this a favour. Just know the next time I visit, the first servant I catch out at night is going to suffer *exquisitely*."

Lord Deminas bowed his head. "Very well, then this is settled."

Meya's blood chilled in her veins. *What kind of arrangement is that? He just allows him to take whatever servant happens to be wandering the halls at night? He's fine with him torturing them?*

"Then I shall take my leave." Commander Andreas curtsied with a sly grin and made his way to the door. Before exiting, he turned around and smiled deviously. "I shall remember this, though."

Lord Deminas waved the remark away, unimpressed by his jesting. "Just keep it between us."

"But of course." And with that said, the commander left the room.

# Thirty Three

"M-my Lord," Meya started, gripping her dress firmly as she gathered courage, "why do you allow—"

He raised his hand to silence her. "It's not your turn for a question." He smirked.

Meya blushed. *He still wants to play that game?*

His eyes gleamed mischievously. "Tell me in all honesty: do you regret having killed that raider?"

The question made her heart constrict in her chest. Everything she had been taught wanted her to answer yes, simply because killing was bad. *I should have just knocked him out and ran.* She closed her eyes as memories of that dreadful night filled her mind.

The man pushing her down, his fingers entwined in her hair as he groped her breast. The small twigs underneath her snapping and prodding into her skin. His stinking breath as he panted in her face. The surge of adrenaline as her fingertips found the moss-covered rock. His grin as he started to loosen his trousers. The anger. The hate. The sensation of the rock colliding with his head. The satisfaction at seeing his eyes roll back into his skull. The second hit. The third. Being on top of him and reducing his face to a bloody pulp. And then, the victorious screams behind her of the other raiders, snapping her out of her rampage and causing her to run away from the burning inn, the gore-covered rock still clutched firmly in her hand.

"Meya," Lord Deminas said calmly but firmly.

Her eyes snapped open. "No. I would happily do it again." She felt relieved having said that.

The lord smiled devilishly before turning around and walking away. "Let's continue this in bed. My body is tired and I need to rest."

Face red, Meya watched him drop the towel to the ground and crawl underneath the covers. *I really need to stop being so damn embarrassed.* She undressed and joined him. A small squeal slipped from her throat as he pulled her close, his groin against her thigh.

"Now then... Your turn," he said, his breath tickling her ear.

It took Meya a bit to gather her thoughts. "Why... do you allow Andreas to take servants like that, my Lord?"

"It was part of an arrangement my father had with him, and something I agreed to uphold." His hand shifted to her breast and he simply held it, his thumb caressing her soft skin. "Considering your feelings towards the raider, if you had had the chance, would you have killed the slaver too?"

Meya stiffened as she fought to keep the dark memories at bay. "If..." She swallowed. "If I had had any weapon that night, and I would have been able to escape, I would have used it." Her jaw tightened. *If I would have been able to get away, I would have bitten his ear off.*

"Answer me this and you can ask me two questions in return. Why didn't you kill him when I gave you the chance in the dungeons?"

She was silent for a moment. "I... I don't know. I guess I was just overwhelmed. And... And I couldn't help but feel it would have been wrong. Killing him when he was no longer a threat. But—" Her voice broke.

Lord Deminas held her tightly, quickening her pulse.

Comforted, she took a deep breath and whispered, "He deserved what he got." She closed her eyes as tears escaped them. "My Lord... Why did you bother showing me what you did to him? Back then, you said—"

"I know what I said." He nuzzled her neck. "I wanted to test you, but I also wanted you to know that I made him suffer for what he had done."

Meya choked up. *But why?* Another tear slipped down her cheek. "Wha—" She swallowed. "What caused you to..." She hesitated to continue, afraid to voice the thing she so desperately wanted to be answered.

"Go on. I know what you want to ask. Ask it." His voice was as stern as ever, but with a certain warmth to it that gave her courage.

"Why take all that effort for me?" she asked softly. "A mere servant you had only just met."

He chuckled. "I can recognise a good, strong woman when I see one—even if she seems broken." He turned her over so that he could look into her eyes. His fingers caressed her cheek, wiping away the tears. "And I like a challenge."

Meya couldn't believe what she was hearing. *Is he serious?* Her skin grew hot and she bit the inside of her lip.

Lord Deminas smiled gently and moved closer so he could kiss her.

Meya surrendered, enjoying every second of the lord's embrace. The thoughts that had been buzzing in the back of her mind were no longer an issue. *He's a sadist. He drinks blood. He's a killer. He eats people. He's not quite human.*

The moment he pulled away, she longed for more, causing a sudden pang in her chest.

*He's not Nina.* The thought sent a wave of guilt through her mind. Torn, she averted her eyes. *Nina loves me and I love her. But, damn it... I think I love him too.*

"Look at me."

Meya's eyes immediately shot back up to meet his, even though his tone of voice had been soft.

"Does this bother you?"

"I..." Meya shook her head. "I just find it hard to believe that a Lord would care like that for a servant."

His eyes gleamed. "I suppose you've become more than just a servant."

Meya's mouth dropped slightly. "M-my Lord!" She swallowed as her mind tried to comprehend what he had said. "Do... Do you..." The words stuck to the back of her throat. Finally, they freed themselves in a mere whisper, "Do you love me?"

He seemed to consider this for a moment. "I desire to keep you safe." His fingers sifted through her red locks. "To see your spirit returned." He leaned towards her, his lips brushing against her ear. "I want to be the one to tame you, but without breaking you. I wish for you to entrust your soul to me."

Meya lay frozen against him, her blood rushing so loudly through her veins she could barely hear him speak.

"So yes, I think I love you."

Unable to restrain herself, she wrapped her arms around him, tears slipping from her eyes. *What do I do?* Her heart was torn. *I don't want to choose between him and Nina! Am I even worthy of him?*

Lord Deminas stiffened for a moment, causing Meya to loosen her grip. With a shock, she realised she had been hugging him—and he had multiple stab wounds in his back. She quickly released him and turned away, hiding her face in her hands.

"I...I'm so sorry!" She gritted her teeth as more guilt built up inside. *No. No, I'm not worthy.*

He gently tugged at her wrists until she revealed herself again. "What are you apologising for? I can handle a bit of pain."

Her lip trembled as she saw his playful smile. "B-but..." She sniffed. "The commander was right. I...I just stood there..."

Lord Deminas caressed her cheek. "I'm your Lord. I don't expect you to protect me—I am the one who should protect *you*." He pulled her close. "But, enough playing around. I need to rest."

Relieved, Meya closed her eyes and tried to relax into his warm embrace. *He's not mad at all!* Her thoughts returned to Nina. "M-my Lord... May I ask one last thing?"

"You may ask, but I might not answer."

"What... What about Nina?" Her heart pounded in her chest as she awaited his reply.

"What about her?" A single, soft chuckle left his lips. "Are you afraid I will forbid you from being with her? From loving her?"

Meya's cheeks heated up. *Is that so strange?*

"I already told you what it is I desire; I don't see how Nina could affect that in a negative way." He sighed deeply. "Now, be silent and sleep."

His answer only removed part of the guilt she felt, but it was enough to soothe her mind for now.

~*~

Meya quickly sat down in a quiet corner of the dining hall. She was once again late—thanks to Lord Deminas—and most people had already finished their breakfast. She had noticed Gail, Lea, and Nina sitting on the other side of the room, but she was not in the mood to face them just yet.

*Brit never returned last night. If they were to ask me, I'd need to lie.* She took a bite from her apple slice. *I don't want to lie to them.*

Lost in thought, she jerked up when someone touched her shoulder.

"It's just me," Nina said softly as she sat down next to her. "You're not avoiding us, are you?"

Meya glanced around, but Lea and Gail had left. She sighed. "A little."

Nina's expression turned grim. "So, I take it the Commander's absence last night and Brit's disappearance are connected?"

"I... I'm not allowed to say anything." Meya averted her eyes.

"Alright." Nina sighed. "Still, I hoped it wasn't the case. The Commander didn't stay away all night, like when Novak went missing."

Meya wanted to correct Nina's assumption, but she managed to keep her mouth shut. *Just let her think that; it's what Lord Deminas wants people to think.* Still, she felt as if she was lying to her and that hurt.

Nina placed her hand on Meya's knee. "Hey, it's alright. If you've been told not to say anything: don't. I understand."

Meya hugged her close. "Thank you." She bit her lip as she felt torn once more. She reluctantly released her. "There is something we do need to talk about, though."

"What is it?"

"Could we talk somewhere more private?" Meya glanced at the remaining servants.

"Sure. Just finish your meal and come down to the dungeons. I'll wait for you there." She smiled, planted a quick kiss on her cheek and hurried away.

*What? The dungeons? Why the dungeons?* Although tense, she continued eating her breakfast. *If she thinks she can sneak a peek for a sign of Brit...* She shook her head and sighed. *I wish I could just tell her.*

~\*~

Meya made her way down to the dungeons and nearly bumped into Nina when she rounded the corner.

"There you are! Come, quickly." Nina motioned for Meya to follow her, lantern in hand.

"Why are we even here? I don't know about you, but if I get spotted here..."

Nina just grinned before she slipped behind a corner. The moment Meya rounded it, she only saw an empty hallway. Confused, she looked around. The lamps on the wall provided meagre light, but enough to spot a person—if there had been anyone there.

"Nina?"

A soft giggle sounded behind her and she spun around. There was a light in a crevice between two support pillars and Meya hurried towards it. What normally was just a dark wall was now a small passage. Nina stood further down, holding the narrow, smooth door open.

"What is this?" Meya asked as she crept inside.

"Welcome to one of the castle's many hidden passages." Nina closed the door before turning to Meya, beaming. "This is one of the lesser known ones."

"Where does it lead? Also... Won't we be in great trouble if we're found here?"

"The guards only seem to check them at night." She started to walk. "Come."

They followed the cavernous path up a flight of narrow stairs, after which they came to a fork.

"That way leads all the way up to the soldiers' quarters, and that one leads to a locked door, but there's no key-hole, so I have no idea where it goes." She started to walk again, but Meya placed her hand on her shoulder.

"I...I need to talk."

Nina flushed and quickly placed her lantern on the ground. "Sorry. I got so excited showing you around that I forgot why I took you here." She looked Meya straight in the eyes. "What is it?"

Meya's stomach twisted inside of her and she looked away. *How am I going to talk about this? Where do I start?*

Nina's expression shifted to worry. "Is it about Brit?"

Meya shook her head. "No. I...I really am not allowed to talk about that." She took a deep breath. "A lot of things happened last night and..." She bit her lip, unsure of how to continue.

"It's fine." Nina took her hand in hers and gently rubbed it. "You can tell me anything, you know that."

Meya looked up. "I love you."

Nina smiled. "I love you too." She gave her hand a slight squeeze. "But I doubt that's why we're here." She took a step closer and placed her arms around Meya. "Or do you miss me?"

Meya swallowed the lump in her throat as Nina nuzzled her neck. "I do miss you. But... the problem is..." She gripped her tightly, afraid that what she was going to say next would cause her to slip away from her. "Lord Deminas confessed his love for me yesterday." The words spilled from her mouth faster than she had expected.

Nina stiffened. "Are you serious? I noticed the Commander was quite drunk yesterday... Was Lord Deminas drunk too?"

A nervous giggle escaped Meya. "Yes, he was."

"Well, they say a drunkard's tongue is an honest one."

Meya released Nina so she could look at her. "But... doesn't it bother you?"

Nina smiled teasingly. "You love him too, don't you?"

Meya's eyes widened and blood rushed to her face.

"You're so cute!" Nina exclaimed and she hugged her. "To think Lord Deminas would fall for a servant! I thought he was just playing around. I'm actually relieved that he loves you. It explains a lot." She moved back a bit and held Meya's cheek. "I'm happy for you—and no worries: your secret is safe with me."

"B-but... I love *you*," Meya whispered as tears prickled her eyes.

Nina's smile faltered. "Did... Did he tell you to choose between me and him? To not love me anymore?"

Meya shook her head. "No, but—"

"I'm not going to ask you to, either," Nina said quickly.

Confused, Meya frowned a little. "You're... truly not bothered by this?"

Nina's smile returned. "Should I be? You say you love me and I love you. So, what's the problem? If you also love the Lord, I can't force you to stop loving him—why would I? I'm just glad to hear he doesn't want you to stop loving me either." She held her close. "If your heart is big enough for two, I'm just happy to be one of them."

A sob freed itself from Meya's throat. "I just feel like I'm either betraying you or him."

Nina's fingers lovingly combed through Meya's locks. "Why? I know your feelings towards him and I am not denying you them. What about him? Does he know about us?"

Meya nodded. "Yes."

"Did he clearly state if it was a problem or not?"

"He... He said it was no problem."

Nina held her at arm's length, smiled, and planted a firm kiss on her forehead. "Then what's wrong?"

Weeping, Meya crashed into her embrace. Once she had calmed down a bit, she managed to utter, "My life... It's been so painful and now... with the Lord and the blood and everything else..." She sniffed and gripped Nina's robe. "I'm afraid to finally be happy."

Nina gently freed herself from her hold and wiped away Meya's tears. "You should never be afraid of that. If you spend your life in fear, you'll never truly be living—just surviving." An old pain flashed behind her dark eyes. "We might be servants, but that doesn't mean we can't be happy. Look at Gail! She used to be miserable, but ever since you managed to get through to her..." She beamed. "You changed her. She found herself in telling stories instead of gossiping and getting into trouble."

Meya was silent for a bit as realisation sunk in.

"I know something strange is up with the Lord, but I just hope you can be happy regardless." Nina took Meya's hand in her own and traced her fingers over the side of her palm—the place where he'd always cut her. "And know that I'm here for you. If you ever get sick or are just weak or tired—be sure to tell him I'll happily substitute for you."

Meya gave her a sly smile. "You just want to eat his food."

Nina gasped and gave her a playful shove. They laughed and hugged. "I love you."

"I love you, too," Meya said, the guilt she had felt earlier now gone.

~*~

Meya was humming a tune as she cleaned the floor, oblivious to Lord Deminas walking in behind her. It wasn't until his shadow appeared over her work area that she stopped, startled. "My Lord," she said, looking up at him. The way his eyes shimmered sent chills down her spine.

He gestured for her to rise. "Come with me for a moment. I have something to discuss."

Confused, she placed the cleaning rag on the edge of the bucket and followed the lord to his desk. *Why does he sound so serious? What's going on?* Meya stood before the now seated lord, nervously wiping her damp hands dry on her apron.

The corners of his mouth began to slowly creep up, and he motioned for her to come closer. "Sit." He tapped on the wood of his desk.

Flustered, Meya did as she was told. "Is… there a problem, my Lord?"

He smiled now and shook his head, his eyes glinting with something mischievous. He ran a finger along her cheek, causing her to tremble. "There's no problem…" The moment he came close to her mouth, she parted her lips slightly, but he removed his hand and merely smirked at the look of yearning on her face. "…*my pet.*"

Meya's cheeks ran hot but she remained silent. *What game is he playing this time?*

The lord straightened himself, his impish smile refusing to leave as he kept his gaze locked on Meya. "As you know, Commander Andreas will be leaving tomorrow. Considering… recent events, I want to do something *special* tonight."

The blood drained from Meya's face. *Does he want me to cook again? But I thought he wouldn't have another servant killed during the Commander's stay!*

Lord Deminas chuckled. "Rest assured, this is not related to the special task I had you and Nina do previously." He leaned forward, his gaze fixed on her, scrutinising. "However, it will take place in the dungeons." The brief moment of fright in Meya's eyes caused him to smirk, and he caressed her cheek. "You'll have to trust me when I tell you that this won't be a punishment of any kind." He released her and reclined, assessing her reaction.

Meya's thoughts were jumbled. Frowning, she managed to ask, "So, there will be no... cooking involved, my Lord?"

He simply shook his head. "No." The devilish delight that sparkled in his eyes made Meya skittish. "It's a lot more fun without telling you all the details beforehand. But, I will tell you this: it would just be the Commander and myself. I'm inviting you and Nina to attend, and you're both allowed to decline. If you do decide to join us, know that you are free to leave whenever you want. You won't even need to ask for permission."

More confused than anxious now, Meya tried to process what he had said. "My Lord, you say we're... *invited*? And are free to decline?"

He nodded with a sly smile. "You heard me correctly. If you and Nina do decide to join us, you're allowed to leave whenever you please. You may stay and observe or even... participate. There will be no obligations. Well, except for one thing." He leaned forward again, his smile broadening. "You're not to speak to anyone about what happens."

Meya suppressed a grimace. *That's the rule for just about every interaction we have.* She wetted her lips as she scrutinised the lord, his eyes filled with eager expectation. *No cooking or punishment of any kind... A genuine open invitation to join, but to do what? Observe or participate... What if there's a prisoner?* She shuddered at the thought of being offered human flesh or wine laced with blood—or getting to watch how the commander had his *fun.*

Lord Deminas chuckled. "You'll have to trust me on this." His fingers cupped her chin and his expression turned serious. "Though I do hope you'll decide to at least come and see what I've got planned, I can't stress enough that you are allowed to leave if you do not wish to stay. I don't want you—or Nina for that matter—to feel obligated to do *anything.* Do you understand?"

Meya nodded. "Y-yes, my Lord."

He leaned in, but stopped just before his lips would touch hers. Blushing, Meya kissed him, yet she couldn't help but wonder what she was going to find in the dungeons that night.

# Thirty Four

"It was very unnerving," Nina said in a hushed voice as she and Meya made their way through the castle. "The Commander was downright *giddy*." She held the lantern a little higher, but the passage down to the dungeon was deserted. Still, she waited to continue until the door of their destination came into view. She took Meya's wrist to get her to halt, and whispered, "Ever since Brit disappeared, he has been a bit..." She seemed unsure of the word she was searching for. "Grumpy? Unhappy? I couldn't really put my finger on it, and he wouldn't tell me either. But today, his entire demeanour was more like when he had just returned from battle."

Meya drew a sharp breath. *I know why he was upset after Brit—he was no longer allowed to hurt any of the servants. But if he is in such a good mood now...* She shuddered. "Did you hear about any prisoners having arrived, perhaps?"

Nina shook her head. "All the cells are empty. I'm certain of that." She turned to look at the iron door. "But what makes get him so happy if it's not someone to torture?"

Fidgeting with her apron, Meya whispered, "Lord Deminas did say there were no others here tonight, but what if there's simply nobody else *alive*? What if the Commander already flayed and prepared meals out of them?" Her nostrils flared, as if they might have been able to pick up the scent of roasted meat, had there been any in the air.

"Well, only one way to find out... We're allowed to leave at any time if we want, so it can't hurt to have a peek, right?" Nina turned back to Meya.

She gave her a sour smile. "I have to admit: I *am* very curious."

The blood suddenly drained from Nina's face. "What if *we're* the ones supposed to be getting tortured?"

Meya frowned. "Then why would the Lord stress that we were invited and can leave when we want, instead of just ordering us to come down here? Besides..." She placed her hands on Nina's hips. "He wouldn't get rid of us after all that's happened."

Nina smirked. "Not after confessing his love for you, you mean." She moved to kiss Meya but instead merely flicked her tongue against her upper lip before dashing away, sniggering.

"Hey!" Meya rushed after her, intending to slap her lover's bottom, but came to a halt in front of the dungeon door as it opened.

The two women composed themselves as the commander came into view. He scrutinised them with a devilish smile. "Indeed, Deminas would not want to get rid of his little pet."

*He heard!* Meya's face heated up. "C-Commander," she muttered as she curtsied, avoiding his prying gaze by looking down.

"Please excuse us, Commander," Nina said, bowing her head.

He merely stepped aside and held the door open, the smile still on his face. "Well, come on in then, or has your curiosity died at the doorstep?"

Flushed, the two women exchanged a look before going in, the commander closing the door behind them and locking it, though he left the key in its hole.

"As agreed, you may leave whenever you want." He nodded at the door. "But if you're truly as curious as I hope you are... I doubt you'd want to miss this." His eyes gleamed with sinister delight before he turned towards the interrogation chamber.

Meya and Nina took a deep breath at the same time, noticed, and chuckled nervously as they followed him. Nearing the closed door, their laughter faded, anxiety once more taking hold of them.

*What if Lord Deminas has arranged for some sort of private feast and invited us?* Without realising it, Meya sniffed the air. *Perhaps he stressed that we were allowed to decline things because he doesn't want us to feel forced to eat or drink anything? And maybe he doesn't want to take any of our—*

Meya bumped into Nina, who was looking straight ahead, her eyes wide and cheeks flushed. After an automatic apology, she followed Nina's gaze and her breath hitched.

In the centre of the room, wrists chained to the ceiling, stood Lord Deminas, clothed only in leather leggings. Commander Andreas walked up to him then turned to take in the women's reactions.

"Well, Deminas, it seems you were right." The commander chuckled. "Their expressions are indeed quite amusing."

Lord Deminas' gaze went from Nina to Meya; his eyes shimmered and he didn't bother trying to hide his sly smile.

Mouth agape in astonishment, Meya turned to Nina, but she was still gawking at the chained-up lord. Meya looked back at Lord Deminas, utterly perplexed at the sight of him like that, but he kept silent, still smiling.

The commander moved around the lord, trailing his fingers from one arm down to his shoulders, across his neck, and up his other arm. "These two have no idea what's about to happen, have they?" he said, amused.

Lord Deminas smirked, a muted chuckle barely audible through his closed lips.

Meya turned back to Nina again, grabbed her wrist, but remained frozen in place. Nina finally managed to look away, and the commander laughed.

"Meya," she murmured, her face reddening. "What…"

"I…I…" Meya's gaze shifted to the men, and she noticed the commander taking something from a table against the wall. Heart racing, she kept looking from Nina to the commander, who was approaching the lord with a small blade. A short yelp freed itself from her throat and her hold on Nina's wrist tightened.

"Meya," Nina said, placing her free hand on her shoulder. She glanced at the commander just as he stood next to the lord again, the blade's tip resting against his own lips as he smiled sinisterly at the two. Nina swallowed and placed some pressure on Meya's shoulder. "Come…"

Torn between wanting to stay and wanting to rush out, Meya allowed Nina to decide for her. It took some effort to tear her gaze away, but once she did, she let Nina usher her back into the main room of the dungeons. They rounded the corner and rested against the stone wall. From inside the interrogation chamber, the commander could be heard speaking, but it was too soft to make out the words.

"Is… Is he really…" Meya started, but she needed to take a deep breath and sigh before continuing, "Is he really going to let himself be tortured?"

Nina was still blushing. "I… I don't think so." She leaned over to whisper into Meya's ear, "You didn't notice?"

"What, the blade?"

Nina shook her head. "No. I mean... Ugh." She lowered her voice further. "I feel so perverted now, but... Didn't you see... the bulge in..." She didn't finish her sentence.

Now Meya flushed red. "What?"

"And the look on his face... Whatever they've got planned, I'm quite certain the Lord intends to enjoy it. At least, he seems to be enjoying the prospect of what is to come by the looks of it already." Nina leaned forward, attempting to glance inside and sneak a peek, but the angle didn't allow for that.

"You're joking," Meya whispered, though she too sneaked a little closer to the door opening. "And he wants us to watch?"

"Or even participate... That's what he said, no?"

They both inched further forward to glimpse at what was happening inside, holding their breath to hear what might be said. They looked around the corner and spotted the still chained lord, who looked straight back at them, smirking. Caught peeking, they froze, and only then noticed the dark line on his chest. Commander Andreas was behind him, one hand resting on his shoulder.

"What are they doing?" Meya hissed, though she could wager a guess.

"Is that blood?" Nina whispered.

The lord's intense gaze was becoming too uncomfortable and Meya hid behind the wall again, Nina following suit. "I... I think the Commander is bleeding him," Meya whispered, "and drinking his blood."

"Lord Deminas seems to be enjoying it," Nina replied, keeping her voice low. "Inviting us to such a thing..." She shook her head, swallowing the rest of what she wanted to say.

"Hey, I know one thing for sure," Meya murmured, barely able to restrain herself from smirking. "With the Commander entertained like this, he won't be slapping your rear tonight." She pressed both hands against her mouth to silence her sniggers as Nina gasped and gave her a playful shove.

When the laughter faded, Nina's expression turned serious again. "But... What do we do now?" She kept her voice down, not wanting to be overheard. "Do you want to watch or would you rather leave?"

Meya's cheeks heated up. "Honestly, I don't know..." She wanted to peek around the corner again but stopped herself. "I have to admit," she whispered, "the Commander was right: I *am* very curious indeed." She fumbled with her apron.

"But...?" Nina asked.

"I... Well..." Meya groaned. "It feels so wrong to watch, don't you think?"

Nina shrugged. "I find it rather funny, considering they walked in on us when... You know..." She smiled impishly. "And now they are allowing us to see them... like this."

With a raised brow, Meya asked, "Like *what* though? Torturing one another?" She went to peek again.

"I have a feeling it won't be just torture," Nina murmured, appearing beside Meya to also have a look inside.

Lord Deminas was still where they had last seen him, though several dark lines were covering his chest now. The commander was behind him, whispering something into his ear, blade still in hand. Both men noticed the women looking and locked gazes with them, grinning.

Meya shot straight back behind the wall, Nina following a second later. "They're toying with us," Meya hissed.

Nina tilted her head. "Had you expected anything else?" Meya grumbled in reply and Nina took her face in her hands. "How about we toy with them instead, hmm?" She raised her brows and smiled slyly. "I doubt we'd get the chance to play with a chained-up Lord again any time soon."

Blushing feverously, Meya needed a moment before she could reply, "How?"

"Oh, I have some ideas... If you agree, of course."

"But... Aren't you afraid he'll just get back at us later? Or what if things get out of hand and they—" Meya was cut off by a kiss.

"Shh, he did say we could leave whenever we want and that we wouldn't be forced to do anything. We can trust him on that, can't we?" When Meya nodded, Nina continued, "So... If things get too weird, we'll just leave. Alright?"

Although still hesitant, Meya nodded. "But how far do you want to go? Do you think you could cut him?"

Nina snorted. "Maybe. I could redo the markings he gave you all those months ago..." She traced her fingers across Meya's bosom. "Though by the looks of it, Commander Andreas already has that part covered."

Now it was Meya's turn to smile wickedly. "That gave me an idea..." She gestured for Nina to come closer and she whispered, "There are a lot of candles in there... How about I drip some wax on him?"

Nina giggled. "That sounds a lot more fun than cutting him, for sure!" She pressed her hands to her mouth, realising she had said that a bit too loud. "We might want to ask the Commander if we're actually allowed to do such a thing... Lord Deminas may have said we could participate, but I don't want to overstep and get in trouble."

Meya nodded. "Would you ask him?" She clutched her apron. "I still find him rather intimidating and, well... Considering you... You know." She gave Nina a wry smile.

"Oi." Nina tickled her sides until a laugh slipped from Meya's throat, and then she hugged her close and whispered, "Just one condition: if we go back in there, you let me know when things get too much and you want to leave, alright?"

"Alright." Meya wanted to kiss her, but Nina evaded, smirking.

"Come on then." She took her by the hand and led her back inside.

They both froze for a moment upon entering the room. The commander had his mouth pressed against the lord's chest, a small trickle of blood slowly making its way down, while the lord had his eyes closed, lips slightly parted in what appeared to be enjoyment.

With a shock, Meya wondered if Nina had ever actually seen the true colour of his blood. *He has healed her wounds, and she saw the dark stains on the sheets after he gave me some of his blood... But he was always careful when healing my wounds so as to not let me see much, or it was just too gloomy to make out the colour...* Despite the several oil lamps and candles burning in the dungeon, and the low fire in the hearth also emitting a pleasant glow, his blood seemed to be a dark shade of red instead of purple.

Commander Andreas licked up the escaped drops, leaving an already closed cut behind, and turned towards the women with a smirk. "Curiosity finally won?"

Awkwardly, Meya fumbled with her apron while Nina walked over to the corner of the room. She gestured for him to come with her, and with an intrigued look, he obliged. They spoke in whispers and Meya looked away, glancing at the lord. He smiled slyly and with a small tilt of his head, beckoned her to come over.

Still plucking at the fabric of her apron, she approached Lord Deminas. "My Lord," she started, keeping her voice down, "why are you doing this?"

His smile broadened and he chuckled. He leaned forward as much as the chains would allow and stated, "Because it's fun." He moved back, his intense gaze locked on Meya. "Why are you still here?"

Flustered, Meya didn't know what to say.

Lord Deminas leaned forward again and whispered, "Do you enjoy seeing me chained up?"

*Maybe?* She remained silent and looked away.

"Meya," he growled, causing her to immediately look back at him. "Answer me."

*Even in chains, he remains intimidating.* She swallowed. "I…I don't know, my Lord. It feels weird." A sudden presence behind her made Meya jump.

"Does it feel weird," the commander whispered into her ear, "to see your Lord like this? Does he still hold power over you, even when restrained?"

Meya stood frozen, unsure of what to say.

"Don't worry," Commander Andreas continued, "you're allowed to take control now." He moved to speak into her other ear. "Go ahead. Have fun. Command him, if you dare." He stepped back. "There won't be any repercussions if that's what you fear. It wouldn't be fun if there were." He chuckled. "Just don't try to kill him."

Meya's eyes enlarged and she glanced at Nina, but as she was oblivious to what Brit had attempted, the remark lacked further connotations. Nina smiled reassuringly and nodded at the lord. Meya's gaze returned to him but settled on his chest. To avoid looking at his face, she focused on the four cuts with streaks of blood staining his skin. She ran her fingers along the closed wounds; the majority of the spilled blood had been licked up by the commander, the remnants darkening as they dried.

With a mischievous tone, Lord Deminas asked, "Do you wish to cut me too?"

Meya shook her head. Slowly, with her fingers still roaming his chest, she replied, "No… There's no fun in that." She stopped herself from addressing him, and a sly smile tugged at her lips when he didn't remark on it. "Do you enjoy getting cut…?" She finally looked up to meet his gaze, and her heart jumped.

His expression was one of exhilaration. He leaned forward, his nose almost touching hers. "How about you answer my question first."

Adrenaline coursed through Meya's veins and she took a deep breath, licked her lips, and moved her face beside the lord's. "If I understand correctly," she whispered into his ear, "I'm the one in control now. So, you'll answer *my* question." Feeling bold, she dragged her nails across his chest, though she made sure to avoid the closed cuts.

Lord Deminas growled, then chuckled. "Make me."

Meya's face heated up. *What? But...* She took a step back and turned to look around.

Nina was giggling into her hand as she stepped closer. "Want some help?" she whispered.

Both Lord Deminas and Commander Andreas were now chuckling, but while the commander moved to lean against the wall, observing everyone, the lord wasn't going anywhere.

Meya eyed Nina. She wanted to ask her what to do but didn't want the men to overhear and laugh more. Nina smiled impishly and tilted her head a little, brows raised. *Oh, what the hell*, Meya thought, and gave her a small nod.

Without another word, Nina slipped behind the lord, trailing her fingers along his toned chest, his sides, and across his back. "Does the Lord enjoy being at the mercy of his servants?" she purred, looking over him at Meya, a wicked smile on her lips.

Although still anxious, Meya felt emboldened by Nina's daring. The moment the lord growled, she doubted their actions, but the rattling of the chains combined with the desire in Lord Deminas' eyes renewed her courage. She moved forward again, gently caressing his hot skin, and whispered, "Or just the mercy of your pet?"

Another deep growl and the women suppressed their giggles as they now continued to move around their master.

"Lost your tongue?" Nina asked, her lips close to his ear and a devious smirk on her face. "Answer us..."

Meya pressed her body against his, her nails moving up and down his sides, as she whispered into his other ear, "Yes, tell your *pet* what it is that you enjoy." She felt both silly and empowered, yet her heart was pounding loudly in her chest, afraid that what they were doing was going to come back to haunt them.

Lord Deminas gave a pleased groan, then said with a low voice, "You'll have to do better than that." He tilted his hips, ensuring his groin pressed against Meya.

Her breath caught for a moment as she felt his erection through the leather, but then she took a step back with a devilish smile. "I'd ask you to strip..." Her smile broadened as she noticed the slight change in his eyes. "But you'd be unable to comply." She moved in again, looked at Nina, and whispered, "Perhaps we need to assist you?"

Meya slipped her hands down his sides, over his hips, down his legs, then moved them to the insides of his thighs, and she had to suppress a giggle when the lord shuddered. Nina then ran her nails down his back, causing him to grunt and stretch.

"Well?" Meya asked. "Do you require our assistance..." She moved a hand just along his bulge, then pressed her groin against his leg and purred into his ear, "My Lord?"

Commander Andreas chuckled behind them and Lord Deminas finally answered, albeit with a husky growl, "Yes."

Meya slipped her fingers between his skin and the top of his leggings, her hands sliding from the front all the way to the back, slowly lowering it. His breathing was becoming heavier, and as she stripped him, a small voice in the back of her mind wondered what she was doing. *Am I really going to pull down his leggings and drawers, fully exposing him to not just myself, but also to Nina and the Commander?* Her cheeks burned as she thought back to all the times that he had made *her* strip. *Yes. Yes, I am.* She made eye contact with the lord as she dipped her right hand inside his drawers, pressed his erection against him, and used her other hand to drag the garments down. With some help from Nina, they lay draped around his ankles in no time.

Lord Deminas gave a yearning grunt when Meya retreated her hand, something wet lingering on her palm, but she moved away, smiling deviously. Nina tapped against his calves until he lifted his feet one at a time, allowing her to fully remove his clothes. With the garments discarded, Meya joined Nina behind him. She wanted to ask what they should do now, insecurity settling in. There was enough light in the chamber to illuminate his back and the multiple faint lines of where Brit had stabbed him.

*In another week, even those might be gone,* Meya thought and a shiver went up her spine.

Nina seemed oblivious to the markings, running her nails along his skin, only avoiding the few—already closed—cuts made by the commander earlier. She locked eyes with Meya, her eyes shimmering with playful delight. One hand still going across the lord's back, she used the other to pull Meya close and plant a passionate kiss on her lips.

Flustered, Meya needed a moment before she replied in kind, her head swimming. *Oh God, what are we doing?* She allowed Nina to press her against the lord, the heat of his skin radiating through her clothes and causing her mind to further derail. Their lips kept moving against each other, as did their tongues, and Meya's held Nina close. Nina's hands slipped from Meya's sides to the lord's and they both felt him shudder as he emitted a quiet snarl.

Nina pulled away from her lover's lips and chuckled at the same time as the commander did behind them. Amusement dripping from her voice, she murmured, "I think a certain Lord wishes he could turn around."

Meya pursed her lips to hold back a laugh. Head still swimming, her hands released Nina and moved to the lord's hips. He trembled as her fingers moved further to his front, following the lines down to his groin, but ensuring to not touch his penis. She closed her eyes, trying to imagine the look on his face. Upon feeling Nina's hands move between her and the lord's back, she opened them again. Nina's sly smile caused her blood to heat up further. Meya wanted to steal another kiss, but Nina moved her head beside hers.

As softly as she could, she whispered, "Want to take things further?"

Lightheaded and aroused, Meya nodded, though she was unsure of how they would proceed. She opened her mouth to speak but was unable to find words.

Nina stepped back, smirking. Meya immediately missed the pressure of her body and its warmth. Nina took her hand and pulled her along, moving before the lord. His eyes were filled with lust, his breathing heavy. Flustered, Meya noticed his erection twitch before Nina pressed her against him, trapping her between them.

"Perhaps like this," Nina purred as she nuzzled Meya's neck, "the Lord would be more pleased."

Lord Deminas gave a breathless groan, the chains rattling, while Nina trailed kisses along Meya's sensitive skin. Meya closed her eyes and leaned into the lord, something warm and hard pressing against her back. A quivering sigh escaped her lips and she moved against him, her body trembling slightly, while she slid one hand across Nina's back and the other along the lord's hip.

*Oh, God,* Meya thought, her mind foggy with ecstasy. *Are we really doing this? And with the commander looking?* She wanted to turn and see what he was up to, but Nina continued to kiss her neck while both her hands had now cupped her breasts, massaging them. A soft moan slipped her lips and she ground against the lord, causing him to growl in turn. *Why is this so much fun?* She lowered her hands and gave the lord's rear a good squeeze. Another growl and he bucked his hips.

Nina moved back a little to observe her lover and the lord, her impish smile widening. She then whispered into Meya's ear, "You want to tease him some more on your own for a bit? I need to use the latrine…"

Meya's breath stuttered for a moment, but then she nodded. *I think I can do that…*

Nina gave her a final kiss before turning and hurrying out of the room, and Meya took a deep breath as she faced the lord. Her heart-rate quickened at seeing his eager expression and the anticipation in his eyes. The chains rattled when he leaned towards her as far as the restraints would allow, and this sparked a new wave of daring in Meya. She took his chin, her fingers twiddling with his goatee, and murmured, "Is the Lord enjoying himself?"

His gaze bored into hers, but he merely growled in reply.

Meya moved her free hand down his chest, his abdomen, and along his pubic hair. Her hand brushed against his erection, and he drew a sharp breath, but his gaze remained unwavering. With a devious smile, Meya continued to caress him, feeling the heat radiate from his penis as she made it her goal to move alongside it without touching. "Well?" she purred, continuing to move her fingers through his pubic hair.

He grabbed his chains and lifted himself, wrapping his legs around Meya to pull her close. She yelped in surprise, her body now flush against his. "Very," he snarled, and tried to kiss her.

It took Meya a moment to remember that she was in charge. She allowed him to brush his lips against hers, but with a wicked smile, she pulled back and freed herself from his hold. The chains clinked as he released them, his eyes filled with lust and desire as he watched Meya back away.

The commander sniggered as he finally moved away from the wall. "Perhaps we should shackle his feet too?"

Meya's smile broadened and she nodded. She wrapped her arms around herself, only now noticing the chill in the chamber as she stood all alone. The fire in the corner burned low, and she went to add some extra wood while the commander tended to the lord's new restraints.

# Thirty Five

Kneeling, Meya stacked several new logs onto the pile of cinders and watched as the flames spread. The warmth of the fire was pleasant against her skin, but she couldn't help but desire the sensation of the lord's body heat instead. Blushing, she turned to see what the men were up to, but was startled by Nina draping her arms around her shoulders.

"Are you preparing to jab him with a hot poker?" she jested.

Meya huffed, shaking her head with a smile. "No." She kept her voice to a murmur and nodded towards the men. "Lord Deminas figured he could still use his legs and the Commander is now chaining them up, too."

"Oh," Nina said, her eyes twinkling with mischief. She moved to whisper in her ear, "Are you still enjoying yourself?"

Meya's blush intensified and she nodded. "Are you?" she whispered back.

With a smirk, Nina released her and stretched, then stuck out her tongue and winked. She reached out her hand and pulled Meya to her feet. Her voice barely audible, she hissed, "I'd like to take things all the way, but how about you?"

Heat radiated from Meya's face as she fumbled for words. "I... I suppose with you, and with the Lord... But..." She swallowed. "Not with the Commander."

Nina smiled and kissed her forehead. "Remember, you're allowed to say no. That's what Lord Deminas said, too. So, whatever happens, we'll have fun, but nothing between you and the Commander then." She hugged her close. "And if at any time you can't make that clear, I'll do it for you. Good?"

Meya closed her eyes and cherished the warmth of Nina's embrace, nodding. "I love you," she whispered.

"And I love you," Nina replied, releasing her. She took a moment to scrutinise her before taking her hand and saying with a naughty smile, "So, how about we get back to *tormenting* the Lord?" They turned to look at the men and froze.

The commander had finished fastening the restraints around the lord's ankles, but he had once more taken the blade and appeared to be drinking from a new wound he had made on the lord's chest. The weapon was still in his hand, resting against Lord Deminas' shoulder.

Nina nudged Meya and dragged her towards them. She let go of her hand and moved behind Lord Deminas. "It would appear that the Lord doesn't only enjoy being at the mercy of his servants, but also at that of his Commander..." Nina's gaze locked with Commander Andreas' and she gave him a sly smile.

The lord growled and the chains rattled, but the corners of his lips were slightly raised in amusement. Commander Andreas gave the now closed cut a final lick, leaving only slightly tainted skin behind, and returned Nina's smile with a smirk of his own. He went to put the blade away on the table and said, "There's a lot more that I could do to him than just this."

With a devious look on her face, Nina moved her nails across the lord's back, causing him to arch it. "Oh?" She turned to look at Meya, who still stood to their side, watching. "Should we ask him to show us what else he could do?" Nina scraped her nails over the lord's hips and towards his abdomen, a groan escaping his mouth as he closed his eyes.

The rush of what they were doing returned to Meya, her blood heating up fast. Seeing Lord Deminas fully restrained now, completely at their mercy, she felt even bolder than before. She stepped towards him and stroked a single finger across the length of his erection. His eyes snapped open, a hungry look in them, and a rumbling growl rolled from the depths of his throat.

"I don't know," Meya mused. "Does the Lord desire pain..." She gazed into his eyes, not wanting to miss a moment of his reaction. "Or pleasure?" With a cheeky grin, she took his shaft into her hand and slowly started to move it up and down.

Lord Deminas' eyes lit up and he yanked on his chains, trying to get closer to Meya, but she moved back enough to keep their distance the same—her face remaining tantalisingly close to his, just out of reach.

"Well?" Meya asked whilst continuing to stroke him. She almost giggled as she thought of something. Trying to keep a straight face, she purred, "Are you aroused?"

To her surprise, Lord Deminas chuckled at this, and her hand stopped. "If you wanted to ask me that," he said, amusement dripping from his voice, "you should've done so *before* grabbing me."

Meya felt like the floor had fallen away beneath her. She remained still, flabbergasted.

Lord Deminas laughed again. "You're such a cute pet." He tilted his head slightly, his smile now warm. "I'll give you points for trying."

Embarrassed, Meya didn't know what to say, or even what to do. Nina appeared behind her and gently removed Meya's hand from the lord's erection.

"Let me," Nina said with a wink before turning to Lord Deminas. "Perhaps your *pet* was a bit too nice." She pressed her body against the lord's, standing on her toes to be able to whisper into his ear, "Maybe you'll answer when *I* ask..." Her fingers wrapped themselves around his balls, causing him to draw a sharp breath as she applied just enough pressure to not hurt—yet. "Does the Lord desire pain or pleasure?"

The chains rattled slightly, and he grunted but gave no answer, so Nina increased her hold, little by little, until the lord finally murmured, "Pleasure."

Nina slackened her hold. "Now was that so hard?" When he didn't reply right away, she tightened her grip again.

"No," he grunted, his lips curling into a devilish smile, "but it's certainly a lot of fun."

Nina gave a final squeeze before releasing her hold on him. "Well," she purred into his ear, "glad to know our dear Lord is enjoying himself." Her body still against his, she turned her head to look at Meya and saw that she was still standing where she had left her.

Meya stared at the two, mouth slightly agape, breathing heavily. Her face was ablaze, heart pounding loudly in her chest. She was trying to decide what was turning her on more: the lord being under Nina's control, or Nina being in control of the lord. *Both,* she concluded and suckled her lower lip. *It's definitely both.*

Pleased at seeing her lover like that, Nina turned back to the lord. "Perhaps the Commander should have some more fun too..." She moved away from him so she could exchange a glance with Commander Andreas—he simply grinned back. Nina looked at Meya again. "What do you think?"

*I'd like to scratch a certain itch, that's what I think.* Meya mentally shook her head. After taking a moment to figure out how to phrase it, she said, "I think it's only fair. However..." She swallowed, not quite sure how much they could control the commander. "I'd like for there to be no more blood."

Nina frowned, but behind her, the commander laughed—and Lord Deminas soon followed.

The lord locked his eyes on Meya. "Such a sweet pet. Are you worried?"

Meya had been blushing from pure arousal, but now it was mostly from embarrassment—again.

"Don't worry," the commander said. "I'm not going to do anything he doesn't want."

Lord Deminas laughed again, his gaze still on Meya. "You think just because I'm chained up, I'm not in control?"

"Perhaps..." The commander moved behind the lord, trailing his fingers across his arm. "I should just show your servants all that you desire."

Lips curled in a sly smirk and a single brow raised, Lord Deminas leaned back as far as the chains would allow. "Do you think they'd want to know?"

Petrified, Meya's eyes widened, the implications of their words leaving her both intrigued and beyond curious, the fire inside her growing. Nina, in contrast, graciously moved in on the lord, her hands roaming his chest as their gazes connected.

"If we didn't want to know, we would have left by now," she purred. "And should anything happen that's not to our liking..." She stood on her toes and flicked her tongue against his earlobe, causing him to grunt. "...we'll simply leave you to the Commander's mercy and retreat to our own chambers for some fun."

The lord growled and then chuckled. "You don't have your own chambers."

Unlike Meya, Nina was not that easily fazed. "We currently share chambers with you and the Commander, so that's two unoccupied beds we can use." She moved a little to the side, pressing her pelvis against his thigh and slowly grinding up and down. "Or would the Lord prefer to watch his servants?"

A low growl was followed by the chains clinking once more. Lord Deminas reached for Nina as far as he could, lips raised in a smirk. "Consider yourself lucky I'm restrained."

Nina moved her face closer to his and placed one hand on his shoulder while she used the other to cup his balls. She took a moment to relish the tremor that went through him before whispering, "And why's that?" She squeezed slightly before releasing and stroking two fingers along his length. "Would you order us to give you a show, hmm?"

He gave a pleased grunt. "I might do that still if you continue to entice me like this."

Nina turned to Meya, beckoning her to come closer. "Does that mean our Lord indeed enjoys watching his servants?"

Blushing feverously, Meya stood before Nina and Lord Deminas, unsure of what her lover was planning. Her breath caught when Nina released the lord and tenderly wrapped her arms around her.

Nina nuzzled her neck and after kissing the sensitive flesh, making Meya quiver, she looked up at the lord, smiled, and said, "Or is it just *us* you wish to watch?" Not waiting for a reply, she turned to Meya and whispered into her ear, "Go ahead—you tease him now."

Meya trembled from the sensation of Nina's breath against her skin. *I want to, but where to start?* Her gaze went to the commander, who stood behind the lord, silently observing them with a dark smile. *And what has he got planned? Better yet, what had* they *got planned? If we hadn't come down here, what would they have been doing right now?* Her blood heated up and she licked her lips.

"It's alright. You can do this," Nina murmured as her hand slid down and grasped Meya's rear. "Remember that we're in control now. Don't let him intimidate you." She gave a good squeeze before letting go of Meya, then gently pushed the small of her back to make her step forward.

Lord Deminas tugged at his chains, giving them a good rattle. "No need to be afraid—I won't be able to grab you now."

"But *we* can grab *him*," Nina murmured from behind.

A wicked, little smile spread across Meya's face. She moved closer to the lord until her face almost touched his. "Would you *want* us to grab you?" She brushed her fingers across his skin as gently as she could manage, starting at his hips and moving slowly up his chest. "Because if that is what the Lord desires, I'm not sure if we should do that just yet."

His eyes burned with lust and a growl rumbled in his throat.

Meya turned to look at Commander Andreas, her wicked smile turning into a grin. "Perhaps the Commander would like to show us servants exactly what it is that our dear Lord so desires." She took a step back, straight into Nina's embrace, and heard her restrained giggles of excitement.

Lord Deminas' expression was a mixture of pride and excitement. "Well played, my pet."

Commander Andreas chuckled as he stepped forward and held the lord firmly against him. "It seems the women will get a show before we do." He released him, and upon walking away, gave a loud smack against his rear.

While the lord gave only a mere grunt, Nina jumped with a small yelp. Meya turned to look at her, eyes wide, then stifled a laugh.

"What?" Nina said, flustered.

"Don't worry, Nina," the commander said while he undressed, "if you desire to get some slaps, all you need to do is ask."

Face red, Nina instantly replied, "No, thank you." She placed her hands on her hips and glared at him as his garments fell to the ground, her composure returning as swiftly as it had gone. "You go right ahead and play with Demi instead." She smirked, her gaze moving to Lord Deminas and daring him to remark on what she had just called him. However, he was unfazed, his eyes locked on Meya. Nina pursed her lips and raised a brow, but her lover's attention wasn't even on the lord—it was on the commander.

Cheeks burning, Meya watched him strip. He was leaner than Lord Deminas, but still muscular. The complete lack of scars on his olive skin made her furrow her brow and tilt her head. *Does he really have none, or is the light in here simply not good enough?*

"Enjoying the view?" Nina whispered, causing Meya to immediately avert her gaze.

She wanted to protest but couldn't find the words.

"It's alright," Nina purred, placing her hands on Meya's hips and pushing her against the wall opposite the lord. "You're allowed to look." She trailed several kisses down her neck. "You're allowed to enjoy."

Meya whimpered, unsure of how to react to Nina's advances with Lord Deminas looking at her with such an intense gaze. Despite Nina continuing to kiss her, her hands firmly on her hips, the commander's movement caught her attention. He was walking towards a table in the corner, and she could see that his back was pristine—not a single scar. *No major ones, at least,* she thought. *Perhaps up-close, small ones might be visible?* She gasped when Nina grabbed her breast whilst simultaneously scraping her teeth along her neck.

"May I undress you?" she whispered before continuing her kisses.

The temperature in the room had increased significantly now that the fire was burning properly, though her arousal also helped a lot in ensuring she was no longer feeling cold. *Oh, why not? If we're going to have fun, might as well have* good *fun.* Her gaze followed the commander as he walked back to the lord, a small bottle in one hand while he held his erection in the other. Her eyes widened as she watched his hand move up and down without shame. She opened her mouth to speak, though no words came out.

Nina turned to look, saw the commander, then returned to Meya with a sly grin. "You asked..." She whispered in her ear, "If you want to leave, just say so." She moved back to observe her reaction.

Meya shook her head. *Oh, hell, no. This I want to see.* She licked her lips, the sound of blood rushing through her veins loud in her ears. *Say it. Come on, say it.* She drew a deep breath before muttering, "You may undress me."

Nina's eyes lit up, a cheeky smile on her face. "As you wish..."

Gaze locked on the men, Meya simply allowed Nina to remove her clothes piece by piece. Meanwhile, the commander stood behind the lord and grabbed his long hair, pulling his head back. Meya's breath hitched and she bit the inside of her lip. He whispered something inaudible into his ear and the lord's lips curled up. Upon his release, Lord Deminas instantly looked at Meya, his smirk widening upon seeing how she was already half naked.

Meya barely noticed how Nina trailed kisses all along her skin as she removed every item of clothing—yet her body shivered all the same. Instead, her full attention was on how Commander Andreas had opened the flask and was using the contents somewhere out of sight. It wasn't until Nina flicked her tongue against a stiff nipple that she managed to switch her gaze to her lover.

Nina's face was alight with exhilaration. "Enjoying the show?" Without waiting for an answer, she rose to passionately kiss her. Her still clothed body pressed firmly against Meya's, who trembled from the cold, stone wall, her head swimming with raging lust. Nina released her lips and instead trailed kisses down her neck, collarbone, chest...

Eyes closed, Meya moaned softly as Nina massaged her breasts, but her sudden stop made Meya open them in confusion. Her already flushed cheeks heated up more when she caught the sound of rhythmic grunts. Nina smiled impishly before turning to look at the men, and Meya followed her gaze.

Her breath caught in her throat at the sight of Lord Deminas, still bound, being taken from behind by Commander Andreas. Every thrust was accompanied by a rattle of the chains and a grunt. The moment the lord realised the women were watching, the corners of his lips curved up and he opened his mouth. Breathing heavily, he glared at them, the commander's pace unchanged.

Meya's gaze remained locked on the scene, but Nina turned her attention back towards her. Suppressing a snigger, she lowered herself to her knees and surprised Meya by pressing her thighs apart. Just as she looked down to see what Nina was up to, she gasped—Nina's agile tongue slid between her labia and flicked against her clitoris. Encouraged by her reaction, she firmly gripped her legs and continued to ravage her.

Meya stifled a moan, threw her head back, and entangled her fingers in her lover's raven locks. When she looked straight ahead again, her eyes met the lord's, and she smiled sheepishly.

Commander Andreas slowed down, hands still on the lord's hips, and chuckled as he observed the two. "We all get a show then?"

Nina ignored the remark, but Meya, flustered, averted her gaze, her knees growing weak while her panting only intensified. A loud gasp made her curiosity bigger than her embarrassment, and her eyes reconnected with the lord's. *He's loving this...* She gasped herself as Nina slid a finger inside of her, and Lord Deminas chuckled silently.

Nina moved it in and out a few times, then rose with a sly smirk. Standing to Meya's side—ensuring the men could see what she was about to do too—she held her hand up, her finger coated with her lover's slickness, and licked it clean in the most enticing way she could manage, her eyes shimmering with mischief as she did so.

Meya breathed heavily, and lamenting the loss of pleasure, she grabbed Nina by her robes and pulled her close, claiming her lips. She could taste herself and this only made her blood heat up further. She wanted to rip Nina's clothes off, but Nina pulled away and placed her hands on Meya's wrists.

With a devious smile, Nina shook her head and led her towards the men. "This will be more fun," she whispered.

*But I want you right now,* Meya thought, desperate for her touch. Nina spun her around and, with a gasp, Meya's back collided with the lord's hot body.

"Hello there, my pet," Lord Deminas murmured right next to her ear.

Meya shuddered as his breath tickled her skin. Every thrust from the commander made the lord's groin press against her backside and she whimpered. She was lightheaded purely from arousal, and she feared she might faint if it continued for much longer. She didn't even notice when Nina sank to her knees until she felt her tongue stimulate her again. With a moan, she pressed herself against the lord, her head beside his, as waves of pleasure careened through her body. Her hands sifted through Nina's hair, gripping and releasing.

Lord Deminas gave a long groan, and the commander slowed to a halt. "Getting close?" he inquired with a teasing smile, and then he gave a single, slow thrust. The lord merely groaned again in response.

293

Nina also halted, taking a step back and removing her clothes. Meya observed her, panting heavily, fearing she'd fall to the floor if she were to move away from the lord's support against her back. When the last piece of cloth fell to the floor, Nina gracefully stepped forward and planted a passionate kiss on Meya's eager mouth.

"I want to try something," she whispered to her, trailing kisses down her neck. "May I?"

Meya felt like she was floating and didn't quite register her question, yet she nodded.

Gently, Nina took her by the shoulders and moved her aside. The lord's front now accessible to her, Nina gave him a fierce look of anticipation before lowering herself. Commander Andreas, still unmoving, sniggered. Meya watched and sucked her lower lip as Nina took him fully into her mouth. He gasped and closed his eyes, and a moment later, the commander started to slowly move again. The lord shuddered and the chains rattled.

Meya couldn't restrain herself anymore—her body craved release. Standing next to Nina, she pressed her groin against the lord's leg, grinding in rhythm with the commander's thrusts. A firm hand slipped onto her hip, and it took her a moment to realise it was Commander Andreas'. Intoxicated with lust, she didn't mind the foreign touch—it only enticed her more. She moved further to the side, grabbed his wrist, and guided his hand down to her rear, which he willingly grabbed.

"No... spanking...," she panted as she locked her gaze with his, and he replied with a good squeeze and a devilish smile.

Soft moans rolled from her lips and she turned her head, resting it against the lord. She looked down at Nina, her heart quickening at seeing how she was pleasuring the lord with her mouth and herself with her hands—one was massaging her right breast while the other was between her legs.

Lord Deminas gave another long groan and the commander slowed, but the lord grunted, "Don't... stop." Complying, Commander Andreas picked up the pace, his grip on Meya's rear intensifying. The lord's grunts became deeper, morphing into low moans, until he began to shudder and gasp for breath. The commander continued for a little while longer, lord Deminas quaking in his chains as his mouth stood open in a silent scream of ecstasy, his eyes closed.

Meya continued to grind against his leg, painfully close to release, and she turned to look at Nina again. She no longer had her mouth around the lord's penis; instead, she was gazing up at him, her lips curled in a gleeful smirk. The hand between her legs had stopped moving, her body shuddering a few times as she removed it.

Realising what had transpired, Meya brought her own hand towards her crotch to help her over the edge. It took only a few flicks of her fingers and with a loud moan that she was unable to stifle, she clung to the lord, her body shaking from the orgasm.

Not a second later, Commander Andreas was the one to finish with a loud gasp, ensuring Lord Deminas jingled the chains once more as his body shook in response, a low growl audible from behind closed lips.

Panting, Meya slid to the floor. *I would have never dared guess that this is what Lord Deminas desired.* She sniggered when her gaze connected with Nina's. *But I'll agree that it was great fun.*

~*~

The day after the commander had left, the tension in the castle had noticeably eased. Meya snuggled into Nina's embrace as they lay on the lord's old bed. "Do you think Lea and Gail would be mad at us?"

"For what? For still sleeping elsewhere?"

Meya nodded. "I mean, Winnie and Brit are both gone."

"Winnie trying to kill you might have caused us to move out, Lord Deminas finding us then resulted in… Well, everything else." She chuckled. "But he gave us permission to sleep here. I'm not giving up this wool-filled mattress for my old straw one."

The thought caused Meya to blush. *I didn't even stop to think about that.*

With a cheeky smile, Nina stated, "If you ask me, I still think Lord Deminas allowed us to sleep here just so no one would notice if he makes you spend the night in his quarters."

"Don't forget: he's making you sleep here too." Meya smirked. "And you know the Commander will eventually come back again."

Nina stiffened. "One week with him was bad enough! I don't think my poor arse can suffer through that again." She rubbed her rear for emphasis.

"Oh, shush." Meya tickled her sides, causing Nina to yelp and giggle. "You already admitted you enjoy fornicating with him."

"Oh, the sex is great." She yelped again as Meya tickled her some more. "But the other things…" She shook her head. "And not just the slapping. At least when the Lord drained some blood, he was moderate. The Commander let me bleed until I passed out! That was so scary." She shivered and Meya pulled her close.

"Let's just hope the Commander won't be taking any blood the next time he comes around."

"Let's hope he'll just take it from whoever is unfortunate enough to bump into him when they roam the halls at night," Nina said. "And let's hope it won't be someone like Novak, but rather someone who did something to deserve such a fate."

Meya bit her lip and remained silent. *Like Winnie, or Brit?*

# Part Four
## Summer, 1240 AD

*Time knows no mercy and the wheel stops for no one.*
*Life and death, entwined in an eternal dance.*
*Break the cycle and transcend.*

# Thirty Six

"… and the princess followed the faun into the forest. They arrived at a large castle and she was once more reunited with her loving parents." Gail smiled. "The end."

The large group of servants that were seated around her clapped.

"That was a lovely tale," Nina said as she rose.

"I agree." Ghulam, a teenaged lad with short, black curls, looked at the sky. "But I think we need to hurry back inside."

Lea nodded. "Yes. It's late enough." She urged everyone to get up.

Meya looked at Nina and sighed. "But it's so lovely out." She gave Lea a pleading look. "Give us just a little bit. We'll be right behind you."

Lea hesitated. "Just… don't take too long, alright? It's late."

The group went inside and Nina cuddled up to Meya. The warm summer wind caressed their skin as they watched the lowering sun; half of it was already below the treeline.

"I love story time in the courtyard," Meya said softly as she closed her eyes.

"I love just sitting with you in the sun," Nina purred. She nuzzled Meya's neck, lining it with kisses.

Meya giggled and was about to kiss her back when she spotted a guard in her periphery. She quickly straightened herself, her face red.

Nina turned and froze the moment she saw the man. He gave a slight nod towards the castle, indicating they needed to head inside. Embarrassed, they quickly got up and left without saying a word.

~*~

Meya's eyes shot open. The room was dark—there was no fire in the hearth on account of it being summer, and the sun was still hiding somewhere below the horizon. Her heart hammered in her chest and a cold sweat coated her skin. She sat up straight and looked around.

Nina lay beside her, fast asleep.

*Something's wrong.*

She placed her hand on her lover's arm; relief washed over her when she felt that it was warm—alive.

Still, the sinking feeling in her gut didn't wane. She carefully climbed out of bed so as to not wake Nina. The cold stones underneath her feet comforted her, assuring her that she was awake. She walked over to the window and stared outside. The sky was clear and littered with stars.

She took a few deep breaths and closed her eyes. *You probably just had a nightmare you don't remember.*

A cold chill went up her spine and she tensed.

*No...* She swallowed. *It was no nightmare. Just like it was no nightmare then.*

She spun around, her gaze fixing on Nina's peaceful, sleeping form.

*The nightmare has yet to happen.*

Quickly, she got dressed and slipped on her shoes. She didn't bother with her apron, but she did remove the room's key from it.

*This feeling was right twice before.* She shuddered. *I don't know what will happen, but if it's anything like the previous times, it'll be bad and it'll happen soon!*

She hesitated on whether she should wake Nina or not. She leaned in and gave her a soft kiss on the forehead. Nina stirred but remained fast asleep.

Taking it as a hint, she silently left the room and locked it behind her. The halls were only sparsely lit, but she knew her way well enough. The feeling in the pit of her stomach intensified and she sped up. After two hallways, she was running. She hurried up the stairs and sprinted to the lord's chambers.

*This is bad, this is bad, this is bad!*

She was unable to shake the feeling of impending doom, and the adrenaline coursing through her veins only seemed to amplify it. Panting, she came to a halt in front of the lord's door. Without hesitation, she banged on it.

*He's going to be angry.* The thought passed through her mind, but it lacked weight.

After but mere seconds, she banged on the wood again, the sound echoing through the night's dead silence. Patience running thin, she opened the door. She rushed inside, but after just two steps, she halted on the spot, as cold metal was suddenly pressed against her throat.

Lord Deminas was on the other end of the sword, his eyes filled with rage, lips thin. The moment he realised it was Meya, his expression softened and he lowered the weapon. He grabbed her by the arm, pulled her inside, and closed the door.

"Explain yourself," he said as he took the large wooden bar and placed it into the metal holders on the door-frame.

*Why is he awake?* She eyed him in the light of the flickering lanterns on the wall. *Why is he dressed? He always sleeps naked, but now he's wearing leather leggings.*

Not waiting for her answer, he moved back into the bedroom. "Speak. I don't have time for games."

She hurried after him. "I...I don't know where to begin, my Lord." Her eyes widened as she saw him pull on his armour. "You feel it too?"

He glanced at her, his brows furrowed. "Why are you here?"

Meya gripped her skirt, embarrassed. "I woke with a bad feeling... It was too strong to ignore, my Lord. I've had it happen twice before and—"

The haunting, low sound of a battle horn echoed through the castle, followed by multiple bells tolling.

Meya's eyes widened as her blood chilled in her veins. *No... This isn't happening.*

Lord Deminas growled and quickly pulled on his chain-mail chest piece. "I'm too late—they're already inside."

"Th-they?" Meya wrapped her arms around herself. *But the castle is safe! It should be safe!* Tears prickled her eyes as waves of fear went through her in tune with the sound of the bells.

"The Golden Horde." He fastened the straps of his armour.

"But... didn't you defeat them two months ago?"

"We annihilated the army they sent to claim Tristanja. Slaughtered them while they were asleep." He rose and faced her. "That was but one army of many. We sought allegiances to ensure we could fight off the rest of them, but it seems they've come to get revenge earlier than I anticipated."

Meya bit her lip as beads of cold sweat rolled down her back. *Oh, God...*

Lord Deminas walked over to the bed and pushed the massive thing a metre aside. Meya watched in confusion until the lord pressed on the far corner of the newly exposed wall, opening a hidden door. Right behind it was another, locked with an iron bar. He removed it and exposed a dark, cavernous hole.

He turned around and rushed out of the room. Meya looked after him and noticed that he went to grab one of the lanterns off the wall, but then he hesitated. He hurried over to his desk, grabbed something out of the drawer and returned to the bedroom, before pressing something cold into Meya's hand.

"I want you to stay here. The doors are all bolted shut. Considering what I expect is going on right now, this is the safest place to be. However, should the enemy manage to break through, go into the passage, close and lock both doors. With any luck, they'll never find you there. But if they do..." He released her hand. "Protect yourself."

Meya looked at what she had been given: the silver knife Lord Deminas always used to bleed her. Another chill went up her spine and she clutched the weapon tightly. "Thank y—" Her words were cut off by the lord pressing his lips against hers.

For a few seconds, time stopped. The bells in the distance faded as his fingers caressed her cheek. She leaned into his touch and the world was no larger than just them. She savoured his warmth, his taste, but then he pulled away and reality came crashing back.

"Stay safe." With those two words, he turned around, grabbed his sword, and disappeared into the dark tunnel.

Meya watched the light of the lantern dissipate the further the lord went, until the passage was once more nothing but a black hole.

Meya stared into the darkness, her mind numb. The sudden silence around her caused her to jerk awake. The bells had stopped. Her heart constricted in her chest as she contemplated the meaning of it. Feet heavy, she made her way out of the bedroom. She approached the balcony and gasped.

Multiple torches illuminated the forest down below, the flickering, orange light giving the impression that it was on fire.

The weight of the world caused her to stumble back. *How many of them are there? How many have made their way inside? How long have they—*

Loud noises resounded behind her and she slowly turned her head to the door. Multiple male voices spoke in a language she was unfamiliar with and they banged on the wood. Eyes wide, she watched the heavy door tremble, but it didn't budge.

*I have to get out of here! Such an army*— Her insides twisted. *Nina!*

Her pulse thumped in her ears as she considered her options. The enemy blocked the hallway. She looked towards the bedroom where the hidden passage was. She took one of the lanterns and hurried down the unknown path, the silver blade firmly in her hand.

It didn't take long before she came to a fork in the road. Both sides had a door with a bolt, but only the left had been opened. *Lord Deminas must have gone that way.* She unlocked the right one, figuring she wouldn't want to go wherever the lord had gone—fearing there would be a battle there.

The second fork looked familiar and she realised it was the hidden path Nina had shown her a while ago.

*That means that way leads to the dungeons.* She turned to the other one. *And this one leads to the soldiers' quarters.*

She as good as sprinted through the musty tunnel, desperate to get to Nina. Her heart pounded painfully in her chest, her head whirling from the tension and adrenaline. She finally reached the end and she placed the lantern on the ground. She removed the ornate sheath from the silver blade and pocketed it. With the weapon firmly in hand, she slowly opened the small door.

She peered into the gloom from between two support beams and scanned the room for friend and foe alike. Not wanting to draw anyone's attention, she left the lantern and her shoes in the passage before sneaking out, the dark wooden panel closing silently behind her.

She pressed her free hand to her mouth as she spotted the bodies around her. There were dead soldiers everywhere; some on the floor, some still in their beds. The stones were slippery with their blood, nearly causing Meya to slide as she hurried towards the hallway.

*They never stood a chance!*

Tears prickled her eyes, but she managed to keep them at bay. She focused on her surroundings, her ears straining to catch every little sound. There was screaming in the distance and something akin to swords clashing, but it was too far away to be certain.

Meya reached the hallway and to her relief it was empty. She peered around the corner. Her heart almost stopped when she spotted a body on the ground, the armour unfamiliar. She clutched the silver blade as she moved past it. *That's at least one down.*

The lord's old chamber came in sight and Meya increased her pace. Her gaze kept shifting from the hallway in front of her to where the door was, her heart beating in her throat. She expected an enemy soldier to appear at any moment, but the darkness remained empty.

Her free hand travelled to her pocket to get the key, but her fingers froze as her ears caught the sound of heavy panting. She sneaked closer, her bare feet not making a sound. Her breath caught as she saw that the room was open, the door kicked in.

Time slowed down. A man dressed in leather scale armour sat on the bed, his back turned to her. His body moved rhythmically and in tune to his heavy breathing. Legs stuck out from beside him.

*Nina.*

Meya's blood boiled and her knuckles turned white from how hard she gripped the silver blade. She moved towards the man, silent as a ghost, holding her breath. Her mind was devoid of thought—it was running on pure wrath. She scanned the target.

His armour covered his entire torso and legs. However, his helmet lay on the ground next to the bed.

Every grunt he made increased her rage. She gritted her teeth and moved swiftly. Her left hand grabbed his long, black hair, whilst her other brought the blade to his neck. The silver split his skin, blood gushing out.

The man turned around and slammed his arm against Meya's head, causing her to fall to the ground. She hit the stones hard and the world spun. Though blurred, she saw him pull his sword. She rolled to the side as the iron came down, but it still sliced into her flesh.

She gasped, though more from shock than from pain. She crawled away from the soldier, afraid that he would strike again. There was a heavy thump beside her and she turned to look. The man had collapsed. Blood pooled around his head, expanding at a steady pace.

Adrenaline was still master of her body, enabling her to ignore the pain of the gash in her side. The silver blade still clutched firmly in her hand, she raised herself onto the bed.

"Nina…" She moved her bloodied fingers through her lover's raven locks. The lantern out in the hall provided sparse light, but it was enough to see her tear-stained cheeks and the dark markings around her neck.

"Nina…" Her voice trembled as she shook her, first gently but then harder. "Nina!"

Her eyes shot open as she drew a rattling breath. She turned onto her side and coughed violently.

"Oh, thank God!" Tears streamed down Meya's cheeks as she hugged Nina. "I thought you were dead."

"Pretty... sure... I came... close," Nina panted as she rubbed her throat. She pushed Meya off and climbed out of bed. On unsteady legs, she walked over to the exsanguinating corpse of her assailant and spat on him. "He's lucky... to be dead... already." She huffed and turned around, wrapping her arms around her naked and shivering form as she searched for her clothes.

"They've invaded the castle. We should get out of here—fast," Meya said. She rose but immediately fell back onto the bed. She placed a hand on her side and only then remembered that she had been stabbed. The realisation caused her mind to process the injury and the pain increased with every beat of her heart.

Nina had failed to notice Meya was hurt as she was too busy tending to herself. The moment she was dressed and feeling slightly less vulnerable, she looked at Meya. Shocked by all the blood, she hurried towards her. "You're hurt! Why didn't you tell me?"

Meya grimaced. "I'm not the one who nearly died." She had her hand pressed against the wound, but blood still flowed over her fingers.

"If you keep bleeding like that, you might be the one who does." Nina grabbed the silver blade off the floor and used it to cut the sheets.

"Why is it that you're always the one tending to me?"

Nina shrugged and pressed a bundle of cloth against Meya's side and bound it tightly to keep it in place. "Because you need it?"

"After what just happened to you, I—" Meya started, but Nina shushed her.

"No, don't. Let's not talk about that. Later, maybe, but not now. I'm alive, that's what matters. You, on the other hand..." She scrutinised the makeshift bandage and how it was already turning red.

Meya wanted to disagree but distant footsteps caused them both to freeze. When the sound of boots came closer, they exchanged glances. Nina gave the silver blade back to Meya and picked up the dead soldier's sword for herself. They moved away from the bed and took positions next to the door, their backs firmly against the cold, stone wall.

Both women were fuelled by adrenaline, yet they managed to keep their breathing as silent as possible as they listened to the nearing footsteps.

It didn't take long before a shadow obstructed the light coming from the hallway. A broad figure stepped into the room, gaze fixed on the corpse. Before he could spot them, Nina attacked him. The metal entered below his armpit—a weak spot in the man's armour—and he stumbled back, taken by surprise.

Nina pulled the weapon back and the man slumped to the ground. With an angry grunt, Nina knelt on top of him and used the sword's pommel to bash his

304

face in. The sound of crushing bones was quickly accompanied with the wet, slopping sound of the resulting gore as she kept unleashing her anger.

Meya watched her, but with the threat now gone, her body made it very clear to her that she was wounded and still losing blood—a lot of it. She pocketed the silver knife and slunk to the ground, tired.

Nina noticed and immediately stopped. "Meya!" She dropped the sword and hurried over to her. "I'm so sorry. Shit, we need to go. Come, can you stand?" She helped Meya up. "Where's Lord Deminas?"

"I...I don't know." The world spun slightly for Meya and she closed her eyes for a bit. "Tunnels. We need to get to the tunnels."

With help from Nina, they made their way to the passage as quickly as possible. Meya's side burned and blood kept seeping from the wound despite the pressure she kept on it.

"Hold on, dear, we're almost there."

Panting, they arrived at the hidden passage. Nina pushed against the panel and helped Meya inside. Unable to keep her balance, she stumbled, but Nina managed to keep her from fully falling to the ground.

Her chest ached, her side throbbed, and dizziness made it hard to focus. She swallowed back a sob. The stinging in her side worsened and she realised just how drenched the linen was.

"Come, we need to move away from here. The further we are, the better. I take it Lord Deminas used the tunnels to escape?"

Meya nodded, then shrugged. "I... don't know. Maybe. He left... through them."

Nina took the lantern off the ground and helped Meya into her shoes. "We'll find him then. Come, stand up. You can do it."

With some effort, she rose and clung to Nina for support. Gritting her teeth, she followed Nina through the passage as they ventured back to the lord's chambers.

Every step was a feat, her breathing laboured, her vision clouded. She was unsure how they had done it, but they finally found themselves at the base of the stairs. Disoriented, Meya looked up the winding path. Blood dripped between her fingers, her strength leaking away along with it. Exhaustion claimed her and she collapsed.

"Meya!" Nina knelt beside her. "Don't you dare give up now," she whispered.

"I'm... sorry," was all she could reply. Darkness surrounded her and she closed her weary eyes. The throbbing pain seemed to dull as the fatigue increased.

"It's going to be alright." Nina's voice trembled with sadness as she placed pressure on the wound to slow the bleeding. "Lord Deminas will find us and he'll know what to do." She sniffed. "Just hang on."

*I'm sorry.* It was becoming harder for her to remain awake.

"Stay with me," Nina whispered, but what she said next faded away as Meya slipped into unconsciousness.

*"... stay safe."* Lord Deminas' words resounded in Meya's head.

*Forgive me.*

"I told you to stay safe."

A warm hand wiped the strands of hair out of Meya's face, bringing her back to reality. She opened her eyes with a lot of effort. Lord Deminas was crouched beside her, his lantern on one of the steps illuminating his blood-splattered face.

Meya managed a crooked grin. "I... saved Nina."

The lord scrutinised her, his eyes filled with sorrow. "And you're dying."

"Please, can't you help her?" Nina pleaded.

"Let me see." Lord Deminas placed his hand on Nina's to signal that she could let go of the wound. He untied and removed the drenched pieces of linen. Blood streamed out of the wound and he quickly pressed the cloth back against her flesh. He nodded at Nina, who took the hint and placed pressure on the gash once more.

Meya winced and tears rolled down her cheeks. "I'm sorry." Her voice lowered to a whisper. "Please, I don't want to die." She choked back a sob.

"You won't. Do you still have the silver blade I gave you?"

Not waiting for Meya to reply, Nina answered instead, "Yes; it's in her pocket."

Lord Deminas searched her clothes and retrieved the bloodstained, silver blade. "This will take a lot more blood."

*I don't care.* She whimpered as the vertigo worsened. *I just don't want to die!* She focused on Nina. "Know... my heart... is yours."

Nina sniffed and placed a gentle kiss on her forehead. "I love you."

"I love you." Meya swallowed and gazed up at the Lord. "Please... My soul... It's yours."

Lord Deminas exchanged a glance with Nina before locking eyes with Meya and stating, "I accept your soul."

He slashed his lower arm and brought it to Meya's lips. She closed her eyes as the metallic fluid flooded into her mouth. *Please, let this heal me.* She swallowed lazily, as even that took a lot of energy.

306

It didn't take long before the blood stopped flowing and the lord removed his arm.

*But, I don't feel any better.* Meya didn't want to show her disappointment so instead, she smiled weakly. *Thanks for trying, though. You cut your own flesh for me yet again.* She wanted to tell him, but she was too tired to speak.

Lord Deminas removed the drenched sheet once more, blood immediately streaming out. He lifted her robe, exposing the deep gash.

Nina let out an anguished sob at the sight—their flight for safety had worsened it.

Meya realised she could no longer feel her arms or legs. She knew death was imminent, but she wasn't afraid. Nina was holding her hand, her presence comforting her. A sense of calm came over Meya and she had trouble keeping her eyes open. She gazed at Nina. *At least I saved you. I wish I had been there sooner, but at least you're still alive.* She smiled weakly. *You're alive and that makes me happy. I'm certain the Lord will take good care of you.*

She closed her eyes and—with a lot of effort—sluggishly opened them again. She looked at the lord, who cut his arm once more. This time, however, he lowered his arm to her abdomen. The purplish blood dripped onto her skin and into the gaping wound where it mixed with her own crimson blood. The tendrils of darkness tugged at her mind and resistance was becoming a struggle she no longer had the energy for.

*He's not giving up. He cut himself again to try and save me.* Content, with the two people she held dear next to her, she slowly closed her eyes again as they were too heavy to keep open. She focused her last remaining strength and managed to whisper, "I love… you… both."

Finally, she surrendered and allowed the darkness to devour her.

# Thirty Seven

Meya slowly opened her eyes. Disorientated, she realised she was sitting on a galloping horse. There was a firm arm around her waist, keeping her snug against an armoured body.

"You're awake?"

She turned her head and was glad to see Lord Deminas. "What happened?" She looked around. Relieved, she saw Nina riding next to them. "Where are we?" The forest they were in was bathed in a faint light—the sun was just coming up.

"Tristanja has fallen. I managed to capture two of their horses and we're riding west now, towards Hungary."

Sorrow washed over Meya as she remembered everything that had happened. *The entire castle... Everyone I knew... Gone.* She realised her side no longer hurt as much, though she still felt very faint and weak. She inspected her torn robe. To her surprise, strips of linen were wrapped around her waist. She frowned at the lack of fresh blood, though her dress was caked with it.

Lord Deminas noticed. "You're fine." He pulled her closer to him.

"Your blood... It worked?"

"Yes, your wound closed. But, it's different from previous times." His fingers caressed the top of her hand. "You were dying, but my blood saved you.

It changed you. You're like me now. Transcended. Immortal. However, there is a price."

*My soul...* Meya swallowed. "Must I now drink blood, too?"

"Yes, and eat human flesh. If you don't, you will slowly lose your sanity."

Meya lowered her eyes. *That's a heavy price to pay for staying alive.* The armoured horses they rode upon continued to run along the path, the rhythmic sound of their hooves a strange comfort. She turned to look at Nina, who had her gaze fixed on the road. *It's a price I'm willing to pay if it means I can stay with her.* She laced her fingers with the lord's. *And with him.* "Thank you for saving me."

He placed his head next to hers and whispered into her ear, "Thank you for entrusting your soul to me."

Meya's heart leapt. She peered over at Nina again, but she was still staring ahead of her. "Nina?"

"Let her be," the lord whispered. "She needs time to process everything that has happened. Like you, she's been through a lot."

Meya swallowed and lowered her head. *I wish I could hold her right now.*

"It's going to be a long journey and we must make haste to ensure the enemy won't catch up with us. We will gather some supplies at the nearest village, but we can't stay the night." He gave her fingers a gentle squeeze. "You will need to sleep, to help heal faster, but you must do so while we're riding."

"But what about Nina?"

Lord Deminas hesitated before answering, "Hopefully, she'll manage. Once we're safe we'll have time to properly mourn and deal with everything."

Meya rested her head against his chest.

"We will also need to get you some fresh blood—and soon."

Her thoughts went over all the bothersome men she had encountered during her travels. *Men like them, men like the slaver, men like the one who hurt Nina.* She drew a sharp breath through her nose. "Just give me a knife and leave me alone in town." She stared ahead. "I'll be fine."

Lord Deminas moved his hand to her cheek and turned her face to his so that their lips could meet. He ended the kiss and smiled at her. "I'm proud of you."

A sly smirk appeared on her face. "You made me this way."

He shook his head. "You were always this strong. You might have forgotten, but I saw the fire in your soul the moment I first looked into your eyes. It was nearly doused then, so I decided to put you to the test in the hopes that you would rekindle that flame." His thumb caressed her lips. "And you have. The only thing I made you is immortal."

Meya closed her eyes. "Thank you."

Lord Deminas straightened and focused on the path the horse was taking. "You can show me your gratitude by living. By showing me just how strong you are." The forest became less dense, slowly thinning out until they rode upon a grassy plain.

Meya opened her eyes, her spirit burning with fervour. "I will." She glanced at Nina. *And I'll ensure she will rise above it all, too.*

# Epilogue

Lord Deminas was strapping several bags with supplies to his horse when Meya returned from the cottage. "Any luck?" he asked.

"I managed to find some good dried meats and fruits, but a lot was spoiled." She sighed then smiled. "But I found some skins, which I filled with water from the well. No luck in regard to money—it seems the bandits who got here before us already claimed all that, except for a few coins that I found in a jar."

The lord took the bag from her and attached it to the rest. "At this point, we need to take whatever we can. We will get more supplies in town."

Meya looked down and fumbled with the dress she had scavenged from the ransacked house. "What about me? How long before…"

"We've got about a day, I'd reckon. But if we can't find anyone, I will just give you some of my blood. It won't be as effective, but it should help keep you sane for a little while longer."

"What about Nina's blood?"

"That would work a lot better, but I'd rather not. She needs her strength now more than ever. If there's truly no other way, then yes. But I'd rather avoid weakening her." He finished up and walked over to Meya. He cupped her chin and made her look at him. "Don't worry, I'll take care of you—the both of you."

Their lips met and Meya closed her eyes as she enjoyed the moment. The lord broke the kiss after a few seconds and smiled, but it soon vanished.

"We shouldn't loiter. How much longer does Nina need?"

"I'll go check on her, my Lord." Meya turned and rushed back into the cottage. She made her way to the back and knocked on the wall to announce her presence. "Nina…?"

After a few seconds, she replied, "Yes?"

"How much longer do you think you'll need? Lord Deminas wants to leave."

It was silent for a moment, except for the sound of water droplets. "I… I'll finish up right away and get dressed."

"Anything I can help with?"

"No," Nina replied hurriedly. "I'll be out in a few."

Meya's heart went out to her. *I know what she's going through.* With a sigh, she walked back to the front of the house. Instead of going out, she waited there for her. *That way, she at least doesn't have to walk out alone and feel ashamed.*

She sat down on the edge of the dining table. Her side no longer hurt, but her hand still went to the wound regardless. She had washed off all the dried blood and redone the bandages before putting on the clean dress she had taken from the musty wardrobe.

*The new bandages weren't even really needed,* she thought as she gently stroked her side. *Wounds that stop bleeding that fast... I suppose I'm indeed no longer human.* She sighed and hugged herself. *The cut was still visible. I wonder how long it'll take before that is gone too. Will it even leave a scar?*

She looked up from her reverie when footsteps came her way.

"Alright, let's get going," Nina said with a smile, yet she avoided direct eye-contact with Meya.

"Wait." Meya got off the table and walked over to Nina. "I know how you must feel." She took Nina's hands in her own. "I'm here if you need me. You're not alone."

Nina's smile faded and she looked away. "I know. It's just… I need time. I can't do this right now." She pulled back her hands. "I'm sorry."

Though it hurt, Meya understood. "Survival first."

Nina nodded. "Yes. Let's get going."

They walked outside. Lord Deminas merely gave a curt nod and waited to help Meya mount the horse—ensuring she wouldn't reopen her wound. When they were all mounted, he led the way, quickly increasing the horses' pace.

Meya wanted to look over at Nina, but she was riding behind them. *Be strong now. If Nina can do it, so can you. Survival first.* She bit her lip and forced the sadness down. *The Golden Horde is still around and might be right behind us. We'll have time to deal with all that's happened once we're safe.*

*Just like last time?* a little voice in the back of her mind asked.

*Yes. Just like last time.* She gritted her teeth. *I did it before, so I know I can do it again.*

She sniffed and sat up straight, suppressing her emotions. Unknowingly, her hand went down and rested on the healing wound. Lord Deminas moved his hand on top of hers and gave it a gentle squeeze.

Meya closed her eyes and rested her head against him. *With any luck, it won't take a year this time before we can breathe again.* She let out a shaky sigh. *For Nina's sake, I hope it won't take a year.*

The sun was still up when they reached a small village. They stopped in front of the local tavern and the lord helped Meya off their steed. "Why don't you go inside and see if there's anyone you... fancy." Lord Deminas' eyes shimmered. "We'll take care of the horses and join you soon enough."

Meya nodded as she straightened her dress. "Yes, my Lord."

"Wait." He motioned for her to come back to him. "Better to not call me that here, alright?"

Meya looked him up and down. "But won't your armour give you away?"

"It's no different from that of my generals. Besides, I doubt these peasants will be able to tell one warrior's outfit from the next in rank. So, no Lord and no name, am I clear?"

"Yes, sir," Meya replied with a small grin.

Pleased, Lord Deminas turned to Nina to help her with the horses.

Meya made her way to the tavern and stepped into the gloom. There were only a few people inside and she sat down at the bar while she observed her surroundings. One table had a few men laughing together; their clothing made her think they were farmers. Another table had a young couple sharing a meal and another had a single man staring solemnly into his cup.

"Hello love, can I get you anything?" the barmaid asked Meya.

She quickly searched for the few coins she had found and placed them on the counter. "Will this be enough for a cider?"

The barmaid passed one coin back to her. "Yes, it will." She took the remaining coins and went to get her order.

Meya turned to look at the people again. *The couple won't do—and getting just one guy away from that group would attract too much attention. But, the loner...*

The barmaid placed a large cup of cider in front of Meya. "Here you go, love."

"Thank you." Meya took it and greedily drank half before she spotted a woman entering.

The newcomer sauntered towards the loner and Meya cursed inside. The woman clung around the man, putting her arm around him, but he quickly shrugged her off. The group was making too much noise for her to be able to hear what he was saying, but his expression made it very clear that he was not fond of the woman's affection. *A former lover, maybe?*

"Oh, come on," the woman said loud enough for Meya to hear. "My dear, I know you're interested. All men are."

The man gave her a shove when she tried to get her hips closer to him. "My heart very much belongs to another. Go away."

"Your beloved doesn't need to know." She moved behind him and stroked her hands down his neck and chest.

This further aggravated the man and he grabbed her firmly by the wrists and threw her off. "Be gone, harlot!"

"Come on. You can clearly use some company. Are you sure you—"

"Annalisa!" the barmaid hollered and the woman flinched. "The man says he is not interested. Leave him alone or I'll be forced to kick you out onto the streets again." She waved her finger at her. "No pestering the customers."

"Yes, ma'am," she replied sourly, clearly unhappy. She walked away from the man and sat down at the bar instead.

Meya finished her cider and just as she sat the cup down, Lord Deminas entered—but without Nina. *I guess she stayed with the horses and the supplies.* Her heart constricted in her chest. *She probably wants some time alone.*

The lord walked over to her, but before he was even close to the bar, Annalisa had already risen, her eyes on a new prey. He sat down next to Meya and the well-endowed brunette took the chair on his other side.

"Why hello there, warrior." Her eyes gleamed as she moved a finger over his armoured chest.

Lord Deminas raised an eyebrow at her but remained silent.

Meya had to suppress the urge to stand up and push her right off the stool, but then she got an idea.

"If you're here looking to relax, my services are available for the night and I can assure you, I will be more than able to satisfy you."

Lord Deminas turned his gaze to Meya. "I'm certain I won't be in need of—"

"Oh, but my—nas," Meya quickly caught herself, turning his title into a name, "are you sure? It might prove to be... fun." She gave him a mischievous smile.

He caught onto her intentions. "Very well." He turned back to the harlot. "It seems my servant doesn't mind a little sharing."

Annalisa grinned. "Neither do I." She stood up and circled the lord. "So, when would you want to go? Just name your time."

Lord Deminas rose and so did Meya. "How about now? Do you have a room?"

Pleasantly surprised by his eagerness, she took his hand and led them out of the tavern. "I most certainly do."

314

~*~

Lord Deminas and Meya entered a small room that was located next to the tavern; the shabby building might have been used as its repository in the past. Annalisa locked the door and placed the key on the small table right beside it. "So..." She stepped closer to them. "Let's talk price first."

Lord Deminas placed a finger on her lips and pushed her towards the bed. "No need to worry about that now. Let's have some fun first, shall we?"

Annalisa giggled as she let herself fall onto the bed.

"Meya, why don't you help her undress?" the lord stated while he started to loosen his chest armour.

Though reluctant, as she was not interested in the harlot at all, she started to sensually caress and undress the woman. *Just consider it acting—she'll be dead soon anyway.* She swallowed, a sudden hesitation of what she needed to do washing over her.

"Hmm," Annalisa moaned as Meya's hands slipped over her exposed breasts.

*Oh, please,* Meya thought as she rolled her eyes. *How far do I need to take this charade?*

Lord Deminas grinned as he joined the two on the bed—he had stripped down to just his leather leggings.

Annalisa immediately climbed on top of him, pushing him down. "Oh, I love myself some warrior men." She tugged at the edge of his leggings and bent down to lick his stomach up to his chest, causing the lord to grunt in excitement.

Meya took a deep breath, a slight pang of jealousy gnawing at her insides. Still, she played along and positioned herself behind Annalisa. She cupped the woman's breasts and continued to gently massage them and play with her nipples. The weight of the silver blade in her skirt's front pocket seemed to increase more and more, her fingers twitching to grab it and just be done with the horrid task at hand. *How should I kill her? Slit her neck and drink from the cut?* The thought made her a bit queasy.

Annalisa was now rubbing her groin over the bulge in the lord's leggings while her hands roamed over his muscular chest. "So, tell me, warrior... What would you have me do?"

Meya felt apprehensive about what might happen next. *Does she really need to die so that I can live? She might have been pestering that guy earlier, but does she really deserve death over that? This is, after all, just a job for her.*

*A way to make a living. Who knows what hell she's been through to end up like this.*

Lord Deminas rose up to kiss the woman, one hand gripping her hair and the other her breast—even though Meya's hand was already there. Meya let go of the harlot and reached for the blade.

*I should—*

A sickening crack interrupted her thoughts and Annalisa slumped sideways onto the mattress and half onto the floor.

Confused, Meya stared at the dead body that lay splayed between her and the lord. She looked up at him, trying to understand what had just happened. "You... snapped her neck?"

"Yes." He took the harlot's legs and shoved the rest of the woman off the bed and onto the floor, a look of disgust spread across his face.

"But... But I thought you wanted me to—"

"Kill the first person you're to consume? Yes, I do—but you're not having this one." Lord Deminas stood up and started to go through the stuff in the small room.

"But... why? I thought you said I only have—"

"I'm not letting you consume someone who is ill," he stated while he dug through piles of clothes.

Meya paled. "What?"

Lord Deminas turned around. "When she got close to me, I could smell it on her breath. There's a demon in her chest. It wasn't strong, so she probably didn't even know she was sick yet herself. Still, I'm not risking it."

"D-demon?"

"That's what we call it here—phthisis."

Meya finally understood, though most people she knew referred to the disease as consumption—and nobody had ever mentioned demons before. "But aren't we... immortal? Can we even get sick?"

"I won't get sick, but I don't know about you. In your current state, still weak, still needing to recover from changing..." He shook his head. "You *are* still changing. So, no, I'm not risking it. We'll find someone else."

Meya lowered her gaze, unsure of what to say.

"Come," Lord Deminas said. "Help me look through her stuff. Money, clothes, food, anything we can use. Nina's waiting and we should be on our way as soon as possible again. The Horde won't be far behind."

Meya nodded, the reality of the fact that they were escaping a powerful enemy coming back to her.

As they rummaged through the harlot's possessions, they didn't notice a key turning in the lock. The moment the door creaked open, they both jerked up. A scrawny boy stared at them, no older than twelve.

"Who are you? Where's my sis—" His gaze fell upon the corpse and almost instantly his eyes rolled back and he fainted.

Lord Deminas rushed over and closed the door. He picked the boy up by his dirty shirt and smelled his face like a predator would his prey. He turned to Meya with a grin. "His sister might not have taken good care of him in regard to keeping him well-fed, but he's healthy."

Meya took a step back. "He's just a kid!"

Lord Deminas' grin faltered and his face hardened. "When the Golden Horde comes here, do you think they will let him live just because of his age?"

Meya flushed and averted her eyes.

"Look at me and answer."

She quickly locked her eyes with those of the lord again. "No, they probably won't."

"Even if this kid somehow manages to escape, do you think he'd survive long in the forest?"

She looked at the malnourished human hanging from the lord's grasp before returning her gaze back to him. The truth pained her. "N-no, my Lord."

"Then if you truly wish to live, you will take this boy. Give him a swift death, because the other villagers won't get that privilege once the Horde arrives." He tossed the kid towards Meya, who caught his thin frame in her arms.

She laid him on the bed and grabbed the silver blade. *I do wish to live.*

*But so does the boy,* a voice whispered back to her.

She thought back to the raid on the castle and how the enemy had slaughtered the lord's men. The sound of swords she had heard in the distance, the screams. She sighed and stared at the blade. *Well, I actually have a chance at living.* She shifted her gaze to the kid. *If I don't kill you, I might need to take blood from Nina—and I'd rather not. Sorry, but Lord Deminas is right. Your life will end soon anyway, but at least this way, you will help us.*

Clinging to that thought, she cut the side of the boy's throat and immediately planted her lips on the red stream that gushed out.

~ To Be Continued ~

317

# The Battle
## Spring, 1232 AD

The first light of dawn crept over the fields, the sun itself still hidden behind the forested mountains. The tall grass, which was normally covered with dew at this hour, was now splattered with blood. Armoured men trod around one another, their weapons and shields clashing. The sounds of fierce battle roars combined with screams of agony had replaced the usual birdsong.

The warriors of Tristanja had been outnumbered three to one at the start, but the odds were beginning to level out. The barbarians may have had more men, but their skill, weapons, and armour were clearly inferior. Wounded, dying, and dead men littered the battleground, the majority belonging to the enemy who had been foolish enough to challenge Lord Marius' reign.

The lord himself went through his opponents like a raging whirlwind. His sword sliced and stabbed at every weak spot he noticed was left exposed. Using his shield, he blocked incoming attacks and knocked several enemies off their feet. One of the generals that stood by his side would finish the fallen before they could rise again, while another parried incoming counters from those that tried to rescue their brethren.

A bit further down the field, Deminas was mimicking his father's movements. Commander Andreas covered him, though he was killing almost twice as many as the lord's son.

The total number of men standing declined rapidly, the ground turning crimson. A large group of barbarians started to make their way towards the lord. Several of them fell, but they too claimed their share of victims.

Lord Marius and his two generals noticed the group coming. The final eight that reached them tried to overpower them, but three fell before they took one of the generals down. The Lord kicked one off as he blocked another, his remaining general piercing number three after he shield-bashed number four. Number five circled around them, waiting for an opening.

The lord's sword sliced through the second's throat, after which he quickly spun around, parried number five, and sunk his sword into number one, who had fallen to the ground.

At the same time, the general was still fighting number four—and lost. The man fell to his knees after the enemy pulled back his blade to charge at the lord.

Lord Marius caught the attack just in time, but their swords intertwined. Number five seized the opportunity and stabbed his blade through the Lord's exposed armpit.

Roaring, Lord Marius knocked number four away. His sword flashed through the air, disappearing just below the enemy's chin, a fine red mist erupting before he slid off and slumped to the ground.

Number five twisted the blade before he pulled it out, taking a step back from the wounded lord.

Lord Marius spun to attack the man that had managed to make him bleed, but he lost his balance. Just as he stumbled over, he noticed number one had grabbed his ankle. Despite his mortal wound, the man had managed to remain alive long enough to aid his comrade.

Number five didn't hesitate upon seeing the lord distracted and off-balance. He raised his blade and swung.

Deminas looked up the moment he had heard his father roar. The battle had been almost over; only two dozen hardy enemies remained, all scattered in small groups across the field. His eyes widened as he realised what was happening and he bounded towards him, Commander Andreas not far behind.

Number five's blade cleaved the air, connected with the lord's neck, and went straight through it. Deminas screamed in anger and disbelief as he watched his father's decapitation. Rage clouding his judgement, he blindly charged at the man. Focused purely on number five, he failed to see the remaining enemies flocking towards him. The warriors of Tristanja thinned their numbers as they went, but two managed to evade the defenders.

As Deminas reached his father's killer, his blade aimed at a weak spot between chest and neck, he didn't notice the two new enemies flanking him. With a bestial roar, he pierced the man and knocked him to the ground. He remained on top of him, twisted his sword, and watched the life leave his eyes.

"Your left!" Commander Andreas screamed as he barely blocked the attack that came from Deminas' right.

Deminas wanted to rise, but the assailant was quicker: his blade slipped under his chest armour, piercing his side. His eyes widened in surprise as he the cool metal sank into his flesh. Still, he managed to react by turning the sword in his hand and slamming the cross-guard into the enemy's face.

The barbarian's skull shattered and he slumped to the ground, leaving his sword embedded in Deminas' flesh.

Commander Andreas turned around after he managed to eliminate the other attacker. "Never let your guard down!" he hissed as he knelt beside him.

"My father… is dead," Deminas panted.

The battlefield now devoid of enemies caused every warrior of Tristanja to flock towards the fallen lord and his gravely wounded son.

"As grim as that may be, you should never let rage fuel your actions," Commander Andreas continued to berate the young man. He inspected the wound and gritted his teeth. "You're going to bleed out if I remove the sword."

Deminas eyed the nearing warriors. "Tell them... to leave us. Tell them... to go back... to the camp."

The commander raised his head. "Everyone go back to the camp. We will mourn and celebrate later."

The men responded in unison with "yes, sir," and they all turned away without question.

"Pull... it out," Deminas hissed.

"You'll die," the commander stated.

"No." Deminas nudged at his father's corpse, the blood covering the stump of his neck so dark that it was nearly black. "I know. He told me."

Commander Andreas grinned. "Then you also know of the agreement I had with him?"

Deminas nodded.

"Very well." Commander Andreas pulled out the sword, causing Deminas to stifle a scream.

Blood streamed out of the wound and Deminas placed his hand on it in an attempt to slow the flow. "If I survive..." He glared into the commander's grey eyes. "I'll be Lord. And any agreements... my father had... I will uphold."

Commander Andreas removed the glove of his left hand and the leather arm-guard, then unsheathed the silver blade. "In that case, consider this your blood oath."

The silver bit into the commander's lower arm, the blood that streamed out quickly turning from scarlet to a deep, dark fuchsia. He moved his arm over Deminas' wound, letting the strangely coloured droplets drip onto the opened flesh. When the flow of purplish blood abated, he cut himself again, deeper this time.

Deminas opened his mouth and the commander placed his sliced arm against his lips. As he drank, his hand slid off his wound. Slowly, his eyes closed, unconsciousness claiming him.

~*~

When Deminas came to, the sun had climbed further into the sky, though it was still morning. He looked at his side: the wound was dressed.

321

Commander Andreas walked over to him, grinning. "I take it you had a good nap?"

Grunting, Deminas sat up. He was light-headed, but aside from that, he felt fine. The commander offered his hand and Deminas took it, allowing himself to be pulled to his feet. "Where... is my father?"

The commander nodded towards an improvised stretcher on which the late lord lay. The neck had been cleaned of the dark blood, the head placed right above it. His hands were draped around the hilt of his sword and his shield rested over his legs.

Deminas' eyes filled with a mixture of pride and sorrow. "Thank you," he stated solemnly.

"Do you think you can help me carry him back to the camp?"

"It's my duty as his son and the new Lord of Tristanja," Deminas answered.

They walked over and grabbed either side of the stretcher, made from pikes and leather taken from armour. As they crossed the field and entered the forest, the commander said, "There are several things you must know regarding your new... life."

"If this is about needing to feed on human flesh or blood, I am aware."

"Did Lord Marius tell you about the reason why, too?"

"No, for I did not question that. I asked him about his recovery, as he had been near death, and why his eyes had changed. Rumours in the castle spoke of black magic, but knowing they were false, I wanted to know the truth."

Commander Andreas chuckled as he shook his head. "People always think of witchcraft."

"Enlighten me, then, on the reason for needing to consume humans."

"It's simple really: if you don't, you'll go insane. And when you do, you will kill friend and foe alike in a bestial rampage."

"That sounds like a valid reason." Deminas tightened his grip on the stretcher. "When am I supposed to start this in order to keep my sanity?"

Commander Andreas grinned. "Soon. Your body is currently recovering from nearly dying. Transcending from mortal to immortal. This means you will need to feed within the next day, three tops. Though you will probably be anxious and paranoid by that time, so best to do so quickly. We can return to the field later and can cook up some of the fallen's flesh while it's still fresh, and before other predators get to it."

A sinister smile tugged at Deminas' lips. "That won't be a problem. I have plans for those bodies, anyway. I'll have the men prepare for that after we've settled the formalities. I won't leave until every last one of those barbarians is spread across my border. Those harbouring the same ideas should realise how foolish they are and turn right back around."

His still brown eyes burned with determination.

"As the new Lord of Tristanja, I shall ensure every enemy fears us. Anyone daring to set a foot within our borders looking for a fight shall do so trembling."

# Afterword

There are several things I'd like to clarify. While this story is fiction and I tried my best to ensure proper consent was given for the more important/sexual parts in this book, I also tried to keep the power-dynamic intact for a master-slave relationship in the time period this story takes place in. That said, I want to put extra emphasis on how important consent is—and that how Lord Deminas tried to 'help' Meya deal with her trauma is most likely *not* the best way for people to deal with it in reality. (Never force people to strip against their will, or force physical contact of any kind without their approval.)

Adding to that, I also want to stress to my dear readers who feel like engaging in some kinky activities after reading this book to do their research first. I'm very serious about this as there are certain activities being performed in this novel that can lead to injury when performed without proper research and self-education beforehand.

When it comes to wax-play, know, for example, which type of wax you are using as some will melt at a much higher temperature than others, and can leave burns when used.

Knife-play can be very exciting, but this too can lead to serious injury if you're not careful. A knife with a blunt edge might sound safe, but the false sense of security that it gives can be the cause of tearing skin (as opposed to cutting it) when pressed too hard. If the bottom (the person being played with) jerks or otherwise moves, cuts or even stab wounds might be the result. So please be aware of the risks and do proper research on how to proceed as safely as you can, also when deciding what type of blade you'll use—and make sure you know what to do if things *do* go wrong.

Actual blood-play is no different, and it should go without saying that one should be aware of the risk of transferring any blood-transmittable diseases. Those who are serious about engaging in this should consider getting themselves tested beforehand.

Basically, for anything kinky, I'd like to advise people to practise it 'safe, sane, and consensual.' Safe, as stated by the examples above, but also when it comes to STDs and contraceptives. Those who are Transcended might not need to worry about the latter, but us humans do when it involves at least one person with a functioning womb and one with viable sperm. (Unless someone wants to become pregnant, of course. In that case, disregard the contraceptives bit.)

Sane, as decisions need to be made with a clear mind and not under pressure or when intoxicated. I find it helps to ask yourself if you would regret doing something at a later point in time. If you're certain there won't be any regret: go for it.

Consensual, as already stated at the beginning, should go without question. However, I'd like to add that, especially for anything kinky, consent *can* be withdrawn at any time and that this must be respected. When engaged in role-play, or when any form of restraints are used, a safe word can come in handy. This can range from a random word (like 'pineapple' or 'umbrella') to using the 'traffic light' system. The latter uses RED to indicate an immediate termination is desired, while YELLOW/ORANGE is used to signal things are becoming uncomfortable and that RED might be called if things continue without change. If a top asks a bottom how they are doing, GREEN can be used to indicate all is well and they are fine. If a safe word is used and it is ignored, it's sexual assault—and this should not be taken lightly.

Don't be afraid to discuss your boundaries and what you are and aren't comfortable with your sexual partner(s)—and to all involved: respect those boundaries. *No* means *no*.

And last but not least: be sure to offer aftercare after an intense play session. For the bottom but sometimes also for the top. Again, do your research before engaging in anything kinky to ensure everyone involved enjoys the activities and remains safe—or as safe as possible—both physically and emotionally.

# Acknowledgements

I have so many people to thank that I'm certain I'll think of a dozen more to add the day after this is printed, and a dozen more a week later. Because of that, I'll try to keep it short on purpose.

To my husband, whose support enabled me to write. Without him, this book wouldn't exist.

To Kristyn, who is one of my biggest fans and who has been an amazing support throughout the majority of my writing career so far.

To Alina, who is always excited about my writing and has motivated me a lot with her drawings and art.

To Jesse, who made the gorgeous cover wrapped around this book.

To Ashu, who helped me by creating gorgeous social media graphics and I can't thank him enough for having been there for me.

To Sasha, to Marije, to Renee, to Elyse, to Christine, and to all my Wattpad readers who have supported me: thank you. Especially those of you who took the time to leave me a lot of comments. You made writing this book so much more fun ♥

And to Gurt Dog Press, who believed in me and this book. Thank you for being such amazing people.

# About the author

L. B. Shimaira is from the Netherlands, born in 1989, is married and has a daughter. She has a Bachelor of Applied Science degree and at the time of this publication (2020) works as a research technician and helps develop vaccines.

She considers herself a horror addict, having been into the genre since she was a little kid. As she often finds horror too predictable, she enjoys trying to make her own works full of surprises—and avoid the standard clichés.

The majority of her works are inspired by her own dreams and nightmares, giving them a vivid sense of realism. She struggled with depression as a teen, is a self-diagnosed autistic, and received therapy for PTSD in 2019. When she states she needs to write in order to stay sane, she means it.

She currently identifies as pan grey-asexual and recently discovered she is idemromantic. She uses she/her pronouns but is perfectly fine with they/them too. Thinking about her own gender too much can give her quite the headache—especially since feelings fluctuate—so she prefers to state her sex is female while her gender is simply queer. Polyamory tends to sneak into her works, even if just a notion, and LGBTQ+ characters are always present in her novels.

You can connect with her via various ways through www.shimaira.com.

A Gurt Dog Press
Publication 2020

CPSIA information can be obtained
at www.ICGtesting.com
Printed in the USA
BVHW081134181120
593625BV00011B/1036